BEAR CREEK
MASSACRE

Ft. West
SIERRA DIABLO
SIERR
Gila River
Bear C.
GILA APACHE RESERVATION
16
17 Ft. Bayard
SILVER CITY 18
19
BURRO Mts
20 Hot Spring
Minbres
IX XIX XVIII XVII XVI XV XIV XIII XII XI X IX VIII
21 G R A N T
Ft.

CHAPTER 1

Mary woke up to a sound in the night. As she lifted her long matted hair from the pillow, she turned her head to the sound outside of the mountain cabin. The sound seemed to come from the barn about one hundred feet away. It sounded like her two horses whinnying.

Mary pushed off the covers and her feet touched the cold floor. The wood creaked as she put on a robe and walked to the fireplace in the living room, near the front door of the cabin. The fire was a mass of charred wood, and near the bottom was a faint red glow that made shadows of furniture on the walls.

Wood was piled three feet high near the front door. She tossed two chopped pieces of wood into the dying fire. The smell of burning wood entered her nose as she warmed her hands near the fire.

She then peeked into her child's bedroom, where the door was ajar. Jesse, the boy, lay with his cheek against the pillow and his eyes shut. There was a slight smile on his face.

Mary turned her head at a groaning sound outside, and then heard the dog named Rusty bark inside the barn, where he slept and where the horses whinnied in their stalls. From that distance the sounds coming from the barn were almost a whisper. The silence that night and the shape of the wide valley caused any noise to become pronounced, especially sounds of howling wolves and yipping coyotes that walked north to Bear Creek or far west to Gila River, where the Gila Apache Reservation was found.

She walked to the wooden cupboard, grabbed a stool and reached for the Sharps rifle above the cupboard. She gripped it tight, her knuckles white, and walked into her bedroom. After putting on her boots, she waited at the front door.

There was a small window at the front of the cabin. Outside the New Mexico hills and mountains were covered with two feet of snow, a rare occurrence and something she was not expecting that winter.

Frost lined the edges of the window, and her breath fogged the glass. She could see nothing but darkness and falling snow, even after her eyes adjusted to the dark. Then she placed a small piece of wood in the fire and listened for howling wolves. She heard howling somewhere north, where Douglas fir and aspen trees stood motionless in the slow wind. The wolves were not likely to attack her, as they were mostly skittish animals. But the sound of howling close by still caused her to be cautious.

She grabbed a coal-oil lamp and lit it and carried it in her right hand, the rifle in the left. When she opened the front door of the cabin, she felt a hand on her back. She quickly turned around and fell back against the doorframe.

"Ma?"

She sighed, closed the front door and leaned the rifle against a wall. "Jesse, what are you doing?" Her heart thumped fast, but gradually slowed. A mass of cold air had entered after opening the door and it enveloped the room.

"Nothing."

"Jesse," she said, looking down at the boy that was half as tall as her. "What are you doing awake?"

"I heard a noise out at the barn," said Jesse. He pointed and rubbed his eyes that were barely opened. He wore his long johns and stood barefoot with his hair over his ears. The hair was messy and looked almost grey in a certain light, just like his father's hair, his father that had passed away from tuberculosis a little over two years ago.

She turned her head as the dog barked again. It was a loud and frightening bark.

"Old Rusty woke me up," he said.

"Go to bed," she said. "I'll see what's the matter. You go on to sleep."

"It's them wolves," said the boy. "Old Rusty can handle them."

The boy scratched his head and walked barefoot to his room. His head was just above the doorknob when he walked into his room and jumped back into the warmth of his bed.

The woman opened the front door and closed it fast to prevent the cold air from entering the cabin again. The coldness slowed her fingers and limbs. She went on. The barn was a minute or so away and was the only other building in the area for miles.

Old Rusty the dog slept in the barn with the two horses. He barked in a constant deep roar. Her boots crunched the snow; all else was silence. She turned back to the cabin, but all she could see was the snow falling in the night.

Not even stars were visible. The only light came from her lamp.

As the barking got louder, the woman's grip on the rifle grew firmer. The smell of horses was distinct and bitter. She opened the barn door, and with each inch it opened it made a creaking sound. The horses became quiet when she entered. The woman looked at their eyes and their eyes turned to the end stall, the one that was always empty. Their heads moved, as if in attempt to speak and tell her what was at the end stall.

It was a horse; a horse Mary had never seen was in the last stall.

"Rusty?" the woman said. "Rusty? You all right, boy?"

She put the rifle against a stall and closed the barn door to keep the warmth inside. The dog barked near the end stall, the third stall. On her right was a big room of hay stored for the winter. She grabbed and held her rifle again. Mary said, "Rusty? Come out of there."

She perspired and peaked into the last and final stall. The strange new horse blinked at her and at the dog. She could hear heavy breathing and the barking dog. Old Rusty stood on its four legs near the mass of black shadows. She edged forward and the light illuminated the brown boots and then up to the brown pants and grey button down shirt. Then the face of the stranger, a man, appeared.

"Help," the stranger said. The stranger's eyes barely opened. Only a thin white was visible. His hands held the leg that had a darkened black splotch over the top of his thigh and down to his knee. He wore a gun belt with a Colt, but there was no coat on him. His head lay against the yellowed hay. She dropped the light and pieces of glass scattered on the ground.

Mary stepped back and covered her mouth with her hand. The injured man didn't glance at the rifle in her left hand. Neither did he mind the St. Bernard barking at him.

"What—what happened?" she asked. Her eyes couldn't leave the sight of his wounded leg.

The man's eyes were closed, though she could not see that in the dark barn. The man's horse was silent and ignored the barking dog.

"You hear?" she said.

The dog barked and the woman touched Rusty's back to calm him.

"Quiet, Rusty. Quiet."

Rusty stopped barking, sat and watched the strange man in the barn. The other door of the barn was open, so Mary closed it tight to prevent the cold air from bothering the horses and Rusty.

Then she glanced down and saw the light from the lantern still bright. She held it up and walked a few feet towards the man. The dog was silent. All she could hear was the horses moving their heads and the man's deep breathing. His breathing was louder than the wind that tunneled through the valley where she and her son lived.

She used her boot to move his motionless boot so that it pointed to the ceiling, but when she did let go of it the boot fell back to its old position. His legs were apart, and the boots lopsided. When she walked a few more small steps she was standing close to his boots and holding the lantern above his face.

The woman covered her mouth. His hand's shook, though it was hard to see from where she stood at first. The man's brown Stetson hat had a curled brim; it lay near his horse and was covered in hay. And he wore a gun belt with a holstered six-shooter. He wore no coat and the top of his button down long sleeve shirt exposed his chest hair that was partially frosted from the snowstorm. His face was course like cowhide, and he had a beard that looked as sharp as the spikes from a prickly pear cactus. She picked up his cold hand and dropped it like a heavy stone, and then his eyes opened wide.

He grabbed her hand and pulled her

forward. "Help me." It was a faint whisper, yet it was not an order. It was a man asking to be saved.

The strange man glanced at her from the floor of hay. His chest rose and fell in deep convulsions.

Mary put down the lamp and moved his hands away from his wounded leg. There was a piece of torn linen wrapped around his leg. She saw the damage and frowned.

"Let's get you in the house," she said.

She set down the lamp and grabbed his arm. She tried to lift him, but his body was limp. It was like pulling a body from underneath the snow.

"Come on," she said. "If you don't lift yourself, you're going to die."

The stranger shook his head and tried to stay awake. When he pushed himself off the floor he held to the side of the stall. His arm was around her shoulders. He was surprised she held him up. When they were out of the stall, the woman looked back at the new horse and saw the clump of bloodstained hay. Then she picked up the lamp with her free hand.

Mary kicked the barn door with her boot. It swung open. The cold air attached to her skin, like wearing a shirt drenched in freezing water. The wounded man shivered. She closed the barn door and led the man back to the cabin that was invisible in the falling snow, using her tracks as the guide. Snow piled two feet above the barn roof. The man wobbled, his breathing erratic.

"That's it," she said, encouraging him.

He faced her. She was in her thirties and had dark, long hair. She helped him with effortlessness and without complaint.

The smoke from the cabin's stone chimney rose, and the light from the fire was visible in the frosted front window.

The front door opened.

"Jesse," said the woman. "Push the door wider."

The boy's mouth was open. He could not keep his eyes off the strange man.

"Jesse! Wake up. Push open that door."

The boy opened the door wider, but it was difficult with the snow in the way. Then he got out of the way and rubbed his eyes. His mother helped the stranger to the boy's bedroom. The stranger groaned as he went, but no words were spoken.

Jesse stood near the door to his bedroom.

"He'll need your bed," she said, turning back to Jesse. "He's hurt."

"What hurt him?"

"I don't know yet."

"Is he dying?"

The man, exhausted from the walk and lost blood, closed his eyes as his back lay on the bed. The cabin warmed his reddened hands and gaunt cheeks. His beard and eyebrows and hair were frosted. Each hair follicle appeared frozen near the end, like an aging man's goatee that turns white near the end. His face was gaunt and hungry. And his boots went a foot off the bed, yet the bed was made for an adult.

The woman was taking off the man's pants to see the damage in his leg. But as she did so the man touched her hand and said, "What's your name?" It was barely a whisper.

"I need to fix you up. You lost a lot of blood. Now, I've done this—"

"Name?" he said, his voice deeper and louder than the previous whispering. He felt her soft hand, though it was a strong hand, a working hand. He saw her face now, yet it was still blurry, like in a dream. Her hair was disordered and thick and it flowed down to her lower back. Her robe still had snow on the shoulders, and so did her thick hair. It was the eyes he was focused on, but after the eyes it was the name. Maybe the last name he would ever hear.

She put the lantern on the bed table.

"Mary. That boy over there is Jesse."

The stranger closed his eyes once more.

"What's yours?" she said.

He couldn't answer.

She turned and said, "Jesse, get my medicine bag. Do it fast. Hurry." Her voice was frantic but controlled.

The boy hurried to her bedroom and came back with the medicine bag. Mary pulled the stranger's pants down more and with it came the bandage. The gun belt stayed on his waist. Her eyes widened when she saw the bullet wound, but then she was comfortable at work. She had seen worse wounds when she was a nurse during the Civil War.

"Hold the lantern near me."

Jesse did as he was told. She used a tourniquet above the wound to prevent bleeding. The boy's gaze was to the stranger and the wild features of him. He looked as if he would blend in with the wolves that were running and howling outside on the mountains.

"How'd he get hurt?" said Jesse.

"I told you," she said. "All I know is he got shot. Don't know who shot him."

She found the bullet in his leg and picked out a tool to retrieve it.

The boy stared and noticed the Colt Peacemaker holstered near the stranger's waist. "Is he an outlaw?"

"I told you. I don't know what's going on here. He's got a horse out in the barn. Old Rusty was barking away at him. That was the noise."

"That's—that's a lot of blood," said Jesse.

"He's lost a lot of blood. No telling who shot him. Even if he lives, he'll be weak."

"Boy, is that a lot."

She glanced at Jesse and then at the man's leg.

"Are you going to faint? You need to tell me if you are. I don't want that lamp to drop and start a fire."

He stared at the lamp and noticed it was broken. "How'd this break?"

"I dropped it. No more questions. I have a tricky part here."

She checked for a pulse and then put her ear against his chest. He was not breathing. She used her hands and pushed against his chest to resuscitate him, then pulled up his body so that the back was against the wall. She lifted his hands as well and after a minute he breathed warm air and smelled the fir trees that the cabin was made of.

Mary used a towel to wrap above his leg to reduce the bleeding. Now his body was warm and the frozen parts of his beard and hair melted. His body perspired. The entire body glistened under the lamp. The stranger touched his chest to feel his own heart. When he did so, the chest hair was stained, and then he glanced down at his hand near his side.

The woman took out the bullet and dropped it on the wooden floor. Jesse stared down at it.

"I need more light, Jesse."

He held up the lamp. His arms shook from holding it for so long.

She grabbed a bottle and poured some of the liquid on the wound. The stranger yelled, but he spoke no words. He was breathing hard and fast. The woman used scissors to cut off a white material and then she used it to wrap around the wound.

The man stared at the boy with his dark eyes and then his eyelids felt heavy once more. He closed them. The woman checked his pulse. Then she covered the man with a blanket that went up to his chest.

"Will he live?" asked the boy.

Mary undid the tourniquet above the wound and let the blood flow and harden at the wound below the wound dressing. She picked up the cartridge and put it on the bed table. The cartridge had been shot at an angle so that it smashed into the bone and was flattened at the end. Jesse set the lamp on the table and stared at the crushed cartridge.

Mary shook her head. "We'll find out."

The man's mouth was shut tight. His breathing was slow and deep. His nostrils flared with each breath.

Mary checked the pockets of the man's pants.

"What are you doing?" said Jesse.

Mary took out the wallet and tried to find any identification of the man.

"You robbing him?"

Mary squinted at the boy, and the boy stared down at his bare feet.

"We need to know what happened. Whether he broke out of Silver City jail or was just shot by an outlaw, we need to find out."

The Colt was still around the man's waist, and so were the cartridges on the worn gun belt. Mary covered the man with the blanket and returned the wallet.

Mary sighed. "He's a U.S. Marshal. I see the badge there, but that's all."

"Can I see the badge?"

"No," she said. "Leave him alone."

She walked out of the bedroom and her son followed. Jesse's head turned, watching the sleeping man as he walked away from the bed. Mary stood and warmed her hands in front of the fire. Jesse sat down in a leather chair and wrapped his arms about his legs.

It was a long while before Mary warmed up. Old Rusty and the horses were silent, but the wolves howled somewhere up north and their howling echoed over the valleys and mountains.

"What will we do?" said Jesse.

Mary looked outside the front window of the cabin. The snow was carried almost diagonally by the wind. She could hear the wind against the cabin and the douglas fir that surrounded the cabin. The snow-heavy branches brushed against one another. The animals in the forests began to flee from the storm and hide in caves and trees and bushes.

If there were no snow, she would be able to see for miles. And she would be able to see the Rocky Mountains and the snow covering them and the black jagged rocks jutting out from them. And then she would see a downward slope leading to a trail made by animals that made their way to Bear Creek in the north. It was a trail made before man had even set foot in those lands. But she could not even see the little trail. All she saw was snow in the night.

"It's getting worse," she said.

"What is, Ma?"

"The storm. We'll have to wait until that

man gets strong. Then take him to Silver City. Doctor Newman will help him."

Jesse watched her from the chair. "When will he be strong?"

"I don't know. And we don't know how long this storm will be either. Once the storm is clear, we can head out to the city and ask the doctor to come here. If he won't, which I wouldn't blame him, we can borrow a wagon and move him there." She sighed. "But the hard ride there would be awful for him. It wouldn't be easy taking him there." She half-spoke to herself, but she was used to talking to herself in the last two years.

"Ma?"

She used her robe sleeve to wipe the foggy window clean of her breath.

"Ma?"

"Hmm?"

"Can I have some water?"

She went to the kitchen, which was only ten or so feet away, and then came back with the glass. He took it in both hands and drank. "You can sleep in my bed tonight," she said.

She glanced inside the open room where the marshal rested. She could see the medicine had put him into a deeper sleep and that he was exhausted from all the lost blood. There was something else to him that she could not describe. It was as if he was trying to say something, but was too tired to even open his eyes to tell her. His eyelids and fingers twitched constantly; she thought it was from the medicine.

She watched as Jesse put down the glass and walked barefoot on the cold floor. He jumped into her bed and fell asleep within a few minutes.

Mary listened to the tree branches moving outside. A great hurl of wind and snow blew the trees and rushed down the mountain. Her back felt hot, so she stepped away from the fire. Her back was to the boy's room now as she sat in the chair in front of the fire. With her eyes drawing heavy and the wind calming her just as her mother calmed her as a baby, she closed her eyes and slept.

Jesse opened his eyes in the night. He looked around, but everything was dark. His mother's bedroom door was open, and he could see the shadows the flames made against the walls. And he could hear the light crackling of the fire and feel the fire's warmth circulating the small cabin.

Jesse pushed off the covers and listened. Then he walked on the cold floor and swallowed as he saw his mother was not in her bed with him. She was in the chair near the fire with her legs curled up.

The boy walked to his own bedroom. The wounded man lay in his bed. There was only one thing stuck in the boy's mind. He walked closer to the man. It almost sounded like he was snoring. He pushed the covers off the man so that the Colt Peacemaker was visible. A faint glow from the fire illuminated part of the room.

Jesse reached for the Colt, but a hand grabbed his wrist. It felt strong and secure. He gasped.

"Jesse, what are you doing?" said Mary.

"Huh?"

"Get away from there. What do you think you're doing?"

"Nothing. I was—nothing."

"Well, you go on back to sleep," she said. "Leave him alone."

"Shouldn't we grab his gun?" said Jesse. "He could be a bad man."

"He's a marshal, remember?" She looked down at the man's face. "He's too weak to do anything anyway. Just look at him." Jesse stared. He waited for the man to wake up, but the man was in deep sleep.

Mary covered the weapon with the blanket. She felt the man's forehead, then his pulse.

"Is he cold?" said Jesse.

"A little."

She tucked her robe in tight, as if the man's coldness was infectious to her. Then she put her hand on Jesse's shoulder and led him outside the room.

"I don't want you near him again," she said. "We don't know much about him. He is just a stranger. Even though he's a marshal, he could be corrupt. Lord knows Silver City is a haven for corruption. He could be from there. We know he was shot, but we don't know by whom. Either way, he doesn't look good. Once the storm blows over, we'll handle it."

"When will that be?" he said.

"I don't know. Could be a few hours or a few days. We just have to wait. No telling when he'll regain his strength."

"But he could shoot us, Ma."

"He wouldn't shoot the woman who saved him," she said. She shook her head and looked into the roaring fire. "No, he wouldn't do that. He asked me to help him and it was not a demand. He doesn't look like a killer."

Jesse rubbed his eyes and walked back to his mother's bedroom, snuggling underneath the covers and falling to sleep once more. Mary was left to worry and wait for things to become clear. Outside the snow still fell in heavy clumps that piled high on the branches. The wind constantly beat against the cabin. She could see nothing outside the window but darkness.

Mary waited for the storm to pass. Her mind was filled with worries and thoughts, and she could not fall to sleep. After a few minutes she felt she had forgotten something. "What is it that I—oh, my. The rifle," she said. "I forgot the rifle in the barn."

She walked inside her bedroom and saw Jesse was asleep with his head under the covers. She then peered inside the room with the stranger and saw he was still asleep. She walked to the front door and brushed off remnants of snow from her pants.

The front cabin door was hard to open again. She had to hit her shoulder against the door to push the snow out of the way. Then she squeezed through the small opening.

Her breath showed in the air and the fingers moved slower in the cold that ran down her limbs and caused the hair on her forearms to rise straight like pine needles.

The lamp was in her left hand. She walked faster, as the snow was coming down hard and fast. The darkness and silence and the thoughts of the marshal getting shot and hiding in her barn frightened her. She stared down and saw her previous boot prints, then she looked up and saw a snarling wolf. Its teeth were visible once she held the lamp higher. It was the same teeth that broke bones in two, the same teeth that killed elk, moose and deer.

The woman was motionless for a while. She turned back and heard faint howling somewhere in the trees. The wolf snarled and kept his flashing eyes on the woman. He was larger than Old Rusty in the barn, and Rusty weighed more than one hundred pounds.

She was too far from the cabin, and the barn was behind the wolf that blocked her path.

She stared down at the lamp and held it in both hands. Then the wolf grew bolder and stepped forward once, twice, and now the woman held the lamp like a weapon. The wolf appeared far larger once close. Its white fur was almost invisible in the snow that piled on its wet fur. Only the giant teeth and the wolf's glowing eyes were clearly seen in the dark.

She looked back at the cabin and then at the wolf. "Rusty!"

Her voice seemed loud in the quiet night. The wolf walked closer. Her boots crunched the snow behind her, and the wolf's eyes glowed brighter in the darkness.

"Rusty! Wake up, Rusty!"

The wolf's breath in the air was puffing out

in fast bursts. Then Mary heard the dog bark and bark. The wolf turned its giant head at the barking.

Old Rusty smelled the wolf and barked. The doors to the barn bellowed.

"Help! Rusty."

The two front doors of the barn bellowed as Rusty ran and hit his body against it. The wolf snarled at the woman once more and then turned its head at the strong smell of the dog. The barn doors opened and Old Rusty sniffed the snow and saw Mary and the wolf. His heavy ears perked up slightly. He sprinted towards the wolf, and his paws pressed deep into the snow as he ran after the wolf in the dark.

Mary waited for the dog to return, but there was no sound. The wolf and dog were gone.

She walked inside the barn and found the rifle. "There it is," she said.

On the way out she touched the muzzle of both her horses and adjusted the blankets on their bodies. The stranger's horse was in the third stall, eating hay. She was about to go outside, but she went and grabbed a large blanket on a shelf and placed it on the stranger's horse. The barn was warm and it smelled of horses and dog and hay. After she covered the new horse she looked down and saw something hidden in the hay.

She picked up the marshal's hat that was left behind. She turned it around as she held the brim. Her left hand held the rifle and the right held the lamp, so she put the hat on her head and walked outside the barn.

She stopped and listened for the dog.

"Rusty! Rusty." Her voice echoed in the valley and carried over the trees.

Then she saw the glow of eyes and then the dog's tongue and big ears.

"There you are. Come here."

The dog walked up to her. She petted him and felt his heart that beat fast against his thick fur. Then she placed her fingers on his fur and tried to find scars or bites.

"Good boy. I guess you scared him off, huh? Go on inside the barn." She led him inside and closed the barn doors after making sure the horse and Rusty had enough water.

She made her way back. The entire way she listened for more wolves, even though the wolf that had crept up on her before made no sound when stalking her. On the way back she saw the tracks the wolf made going down the mountain.

She walked inside the cabin's front door that could barely open in the deep snow. She squeezed through, going inside sideways, and then closed the door and stamped her feet on the floor to get the snow off. Her cheeks were red. As she set the gun against the wall, she warmed herself near the fire. Then she heard the floor creaking.

"Jesse," she said. "Can't sleep?"

"No." The boy walked over and sat in the chair by the fire with his legs crisscross. "What's that?"

"What's what?" she said.

"That on your head."

She smiled a little. "Oh, it's the man's hat. My hands were full, so I put it on."

"I like it."

"You want to try it on?"

He nodded.

She placed it on his messy hair. The hat was so big it covered Jesse's eyes. He pushed the hat back. "It smells like sweat," he said, and put the hat on the floor.

"Don't do that. I'll give it to him."

Mary glanced inside the room, but it was too dark to see if the marshal was awake.

The boy noticed her eyes focused inside his bedroom.

"Are you giving him his hat now?" asked Jesse.

"Yes."

"What are you waiting for?"

She put the hat on the dinner table and sat in the chair. It seemed the night was longer than the day. She stared at an old wooden clock and saw it would be light in two hours. But she didn't feel tired. She didn't even think much of the wolf outside; that was part of living far from people, out in the wilderness.

A groaning sound rose from the silence. Mary turned to Jesse and the two looked at each other. The man in Jesse's room breathed heavier and said something, but neither the boy nor his mother heard what was said.

Mary stood up and took notice of the rifle. She grabbed the lamp and peered into Jesse's bedroom.

"The light," said the marshal from the bed.

"What's wrong?" said Mary. She walked into the bedroom. "What happened to you?" She edged forward until the light showed the man's leathery skin and the wrinkles near his eyes.

She waited for a response. The man opened his eyes and stared at the woman, and then he tried to see the rest of the room. His eyes closed in pain.

"Are you in pain again?" she said. "I can give you something—"

"Water," he said.

Mary set the lamp on the bed table and went to the kitchen and came back. She held the glass for him, as his hands shook. The water spilled on his beard and on the pillow. He drank it fully, as if it were his first glass of water after not drinking for days. He coughed after he was done.

"Now, what happened?" she said. "I need to know who shot you. Tell me what happened."

The marshal looked past the woman at Jesse peaking out from behind the doorframe. Then the man's eyes turned to Mary, and the eyes opened wide. A whisper carried out from his strained voice and the single word caused the woman's heart to pound. "Apaches."

<h1 style="text-align:center">CHAPTER 2</h1>

"THEY SHOULD HAVE TURNED AROUND," said Baishan, one of the Apaches watching the stagecoach burn near Bear Creek.

The flames were thick, and the fire crackled. The roaring fire and the wind were the only sounds. Howling wolves came and went, but none during the last hour.

The three Apaches wore thick animal fur of wolf and buffalo. They sat on horses as the snow fell and piled on their shoulders and legs and the horses' manes. They watched the stagecoach burn.

One of the big wooden wheels was flat on the snow, black and charred from the fire. Snow was piling on the wheel and on the fur the Apaches wore. Their deerskin pants were dark and worn. And the moccasins were brown and rose almost up to the knee.

Their Henry rifles were put away in rifle holsters on their horses. One of the men had a big buffalo fur coat that covered his head and torso from the snow; he appeared tall even when sitting on a horse. His name was Baishan, which meant knife. He was known to finish off wounded men he shot by using his knife. The other two men could not see Baishan's face under the big buffalo fur, only the breath in the cold air.

"That was a foolish thing," said Roman, who wore the wolf fur and shook his head at the burning stagecoach. His face glistened before the burning stagecoach. "A foolish thing."

Baishan turned his head slowly. "You don't understand, Roman. You are still learning. You don't see what will happen if we allow outsiders to push us away from our lands."

Roman watched the crackling fire that roared high in the sky.

They waited. There would be no one to come. They were far from the closest city, Silver City.

"No, Baishan," said Roman. "I already learned everything. Killing travelers is not something I still need to learn." Roman shook his head and looked away. The fire still roared in the falling snow. There was darkness everywhere, and no moon, as the moon was hidden under the veil of snow and blackness. The wind spread the fire and carried the black smoke higher. "This is not good," Roman said to himself.

Baishan turned, his face emotionless and rough and dark underneath the big buffalo fur wrapped about him. He had long dark hair, like the others. All three Apaches appeared stern and exhausted. "What do you think, Marco? Are you with me?"

Marco sat on the horse and wore the buffalo fur, but the fur was not as thick and wide as Baishan's. He nodded at the man. "I am with you. You know I am."

Baishan turned his eyes back to Roman.

Roman left them and rode his horse around the burning stagecoach near Bear Creek. The creek was frozen and piled with snow, but a few places on the creek had thin ice and holes where the ice had not yet formed. The boulders near the creek were white circles rounded with the snow. And the leaves of bushes were powdered with snow and frozen stiff. Roman led his horse to the stagecoach tracks and looked up to see where the deep lines in the snow originated.

"That boy," said Baishan to Marco, "is weak in heart. He believes in peace, but there is no peace without war. The two are the same. He sees little. He is coddled, like the others. Why do you think I left the reservation? The others refuse to fight."

"Roman can understand," said Marco. "I've known him my whole life. Give him time."

"Time is something we don't have." He motioned with his hand at the land. "Soon the land will be covered with Mexicans and white men. No room for Mescalero. No room for our family. They say 'go savage. You ugly thing.' But we are not leaving."

Marco moved his long hair from his eyes. "You think the white men will lie to us?"

Baishan smiled a little and chuckled. "They already have. First, they say 'here is your home. This area.' They point on the map. Then they say 'here is your new home. It is this area now.' They point on map. But the chief had to squint and kneel to see the area on the map. It was nothing. Our home was like a mountain, but now it is a little cave. And in their towns we are told we are savage and ugly. There is no home but the one we keep. And we must keep our home and tell the white men to stay away and never come near us."

Marco listened and nodded. "Yes, but we have the reservation. It is—"

"Nothing. It is nothing," interrupted Baishan, his voice rose but was as steady as a blade.

"We have promises that—"

"Have they fulfilled their promises?"

Marco looked down at the snow.

"They have not," said Baishan. "A promise from Apache is true, but a promise from a white man is a lie."

Roman got off his horse and walked around the burning stagecoach. The horses that led the coach ran off after Roman set them free. He picked up a hat partially buried in the snow. The beige hat had a feather stuck out of it. He dropped it, then placed his hand against a spruce-fir weighed down by the heavy snow. He breathed heavily and saw the woman's blue face in the snow, and then he looked away, as he could not view the woman much longer. He used his hands to cover the face with snow, and then he covered his face with his hands.

Roman used the tree as a shield against the snowstorm. The far side of the creek had animal tracks in the snow that led along the bottom of a bluff and trailed off to the forest. When he rode back to the other two men, he saw they were surveying the area.

"Roman. Come here," said Baishan.

Roman reluctantly dismounted and stood in front of Baishan. Baishan was a foot taller than Roman, and had high cheekbones and a thick neck.

"You look sad. What is it?" said Baishan.

"Nothing."

Baishan squinted behind Roman and noticed the stagecoach was almost burned completely. The fire was a fizzle and only the stagecoach seat was still on fire. The snow came down fast now and helped douse the fire.

"Did you find him?" said Baishan to Roman.

"The man on the horse?"

"Yes," he said. "I shot him, but he fell from his horse. You finished him, didn't you?"

Roman stared back at the stagecoach. "I couldn't find him."

Baishan walked past Roman, almost brushing shoulders with him. His face was wooden and focused on the land. The fir, pine and juniper trees were clustered together and made it hard to see anything. He watched the trees for movement, but he could only see the tree shadows that the dying fire made.

Baishan followed Roman's tracks by looking down at the snow, and when he had come upon the tree Roman used as cover he saw the beige feathered hat. Baishan crouched. He picked up the hat and held it with two fingers, as if it were delicate or diseased. Then he moved his hand against the snow and found the white woman, then the white man with her, and finally the Mexican stagecoach driver once he walked ten feet towards the charred wooden wheel. He grabbed the wallets and put them in a satchel. Then he grabbed each body by one of the limbs and piled them near the creek.

Roman shook his head. It was his first attack on people of any kind, but this was not the first for Baishan or Marco. He began to see the stories from Baishan in front of his eyes, the stories told with bravery and honor.

"Now they'll know not to enter our land," said Baishan. He stood next to the bodies.

"The man," said Marco, reminding Baishan.

Baishan nodded to Marco. "Let's see if he lives. I shot him near the creek. Over there."

They mounted their horses. Roman followed Marco and Baishan. They rode without hurry. When Baishan shot the white man on his horse, the white man fell off the horse and hit his head against a tree trunk and didn't move. Then Baishan and Marco shot the man and woman in the stagecoach, the driver and then burned the stagecoach. It happened within the last hour.

The snowstorm worsened during the long night and obscured the moonlight. The snow extinguished the stagecoach fire. The three Apache's rode away from the stagecoach. Their eyes adjusted to the darkness, but they could still not see far in the storm. They could barely even see Bear Creek, which was about thirty fee to their side.

"There," said Roman, pointing. "You shot him around there."

Baishan turned to Roman, surprised by his admission, and rode up to the area. There was a hill covered in large boulders and aspen trees.

Baishan crouched and pressed his hand deep into the snow. Then he did the same with his boots. He walked closer, carrying the Henry rifle in his left hand, and peered through the forest that was a column of tree trunks. He looked up and saw the branches piled with snow. He couldn't see the top of the trees. There was no sound except trees moving in the slow wind. The branches creaked. The wind carried the snow that was as fast as falling rain. His hand was cold from the snow, so he placed it underneath the thick buffalo fur.

He turned, watching the area in each

direction. His footsteps were not as silent in the deepening snow.

"Come out," said Baishan. His voice echoed across the creek and in the valley. The mountains on the opposite side of the creek lifted the voice high into the air.

Roman rode up to Marco and said, "Why don't we go back? There's nothing here."

"Quiet," said Marco. "He might be hiding. See over there? Those boulders. That's where I would be. Baishan will go over there next. He'll kill him. Watch."

"Why? I thought Baishan was a warrior, not a murderer." Roman looked away, saying to him, "All the stories were made up."

Marco frowned at Roman, as if he had said something strange.

Baishan pushed his shins and feet through the snow and made deep trenches as he walked within the forest of spruce-fir. There was no path in sight. The darkness hid everything. The moon and stars were still blotted out from the storm, and the storm thickened so that the Apaches couldn't see more than thirty feet away.

Baishan leaned down and searched for tracks. He touched the bark of a tree and peered up at the falling snow. Then he looked down and saw a faint track in the snow. He crouched and found another, then another. He stood upright and followed the tracks.

"Horse tracks," he whispered.

He followed the path to an area where large boulders clumped together on the side of a hill. Now his eyes casted down and then up toward where the tracks appeared to end, behind a large boulder. Baishan brought the Henry rifle up and held it with both hands, his finger on the trigger.

The Apache listened for panting, heard nothing and glanced down at the tracks. He slowly made his ascent to the boulder. When he had gotten closer he noticed the barrel of a rifle. The rifle leaned against the boulder. Baishan now walked faster and aimed the rifle. The rifle that was against the boulder fell against the snow and Baishan held his rifle steady at the sight.

The rifle was against the snow, but there was no man behind it. Baishan looked around the area and found no horse or white man. He held the rifle in one hand again. Then he crouched and picked up the white man's rifle. He turned to leave, but then spotted something peaking out from the snow.

Baishan set the rifles against the boulder, grabbed the thing in the snow and held it up. It was a bloodied discarded rag that was almost frozen stiff. Baishan followed the horse tracks back down the hill.

Marco walked behind him. "Have you found his body?" Then his eyes met the two rifles. "Where is his horse?"

Baishan halted and watched Marco beside him.

Marco saw the horse tracks and said, "He survived?"

"For now," said Baishan.

The two stared at one another and then slowly watched the tracks trail off up the snowy hill.

"Only a fool would leave his rifle," said Marco.

Baishan left Marco and walked beside the horse tracks that were far apart. "He galloped away," Baishan said to himself. Then he turned back to Marco and saw Roman staring down at the tracks. "He escaped," Baishan said to Roman.

"He won't make it far. You killed him already. Let's go home," said Roman.

Baishan walked up to Roman. Baishan stood tall and towered over the young Apache. "We will finish it." Then he walked back down the hill, his boots crushing the snow that was knee-high.

"Finish the massacre, you mean?" asked Roman.

Baishan's back faced Roman. Baishan stopped. The sound of Roman's voice echoed in the valley. It was the only sound. Baishan said, "The storm is getting stronger. He won't last long." Baishan put away the white man's rifle, mounted his horse and rearranged the buffalo fur to prevent snow from falling on the interior clothes. Then he brought the rag to his nose and smelled it and placed it in a satchel. The horse moved and stepped slowly up the hill.

Marco mounted and was close behind Baishan.

Roman mounted last and looked back towards where he and Marco came, from the Gila Apache Reservation in the west. Baishan lived in a small camp just south of the reservation with a group of Mescalero Apaches that fought with him. The two Apaches from the reservation met Baishan in the night. Roman assumed he would be spying on an enemy tribe or a cavalry that was getting too close.

It seemed the night was much longer and that the storm would never pass. Everywhere was darkness and snow, and in the entire night Roman saw each shade and shape of snow, from the needle snow to the octagon-shaped snow, and knew every sound of what a nighttime snowstorm brought.

Roman brushed off snow from his horse and whispered calming words to his horse. Then Roman moved the wolf fur off his body and brushed off the snow from the fur. Some of the snow had melted, but the fur shielded him from the freezing water. He wrapped his body once more with the fur.

Baishan and Marco disappeared in the snow. Only their tracks remained.

Roman, like Baishan, knew tracks of all the animals in the region. He knew black bear, bighorn sheep, cougar, deer, elk, pronghorn antelope and coyote tracks by sight and touch. He, like the other two Apaches, knew tracks of all kinds. But Roman hadn't killed a white man, and he had never hunted man before.

He followed the other men, staring down at the horse tracks as his guide. His horse pushed through the snow, lifting its legs and finding the path. After following the tracks for a while, Roman saw the other men had halted and lay motionless in the falling snow. He rode up a steep hill and passed a hillside of aspen.

Baishan and Marco appeared much larger on account of their thick fur coats. In the snow, from a distance, it almost looked like they were some undiscovered beasts. The two were on a steep hill that was treeless, barren of even bushes or rock or cactus.

"Why are we stopped?" asked Roman. His horse slowed until he was beside the other men.

For a while neither man answered. They scanned the hills and mountains and trees. An owl flew low and its wings flapped once and glided to the trees once more. To an Apache a hooting owl meant a bad omen.

Roman looked ahead of the horses. "There are no tracks," he said. "What happened to the tracks we followed?" He dismounted and walked in a circle around the horses.

"We think the snow has covered the tracks," said Marco. "But it's unlikely. The tracks stopped here."

Baishan puffed out the fog-like breath. The owl hooted somewhere. The barren land ahead of them was grey in the night. The horses moved their heads to get the snow off. And the cold caused their limbs to stiffen and their blood flow to slow.

"He tricked us," said Baishan. "He's smarter than I thought." The other men looked at Baishan. He turned to them, his face stern and contemplative. "His tracks trailed off somewhere behind us. We have to turn back."

Roman shook his head. "Back? Leave him.

He is dead. You shot him. You saw him fall. He is like an animal that is shot and runs off somewhere to die. He won't come back."

"I give the orders, Roman," said Baishan, his voice loud and deep. His face was dark beneath the big buffalo fur. "You are just a young man. If this was going to be difficult for you, I wouldn't have asked you to come. But you are Apache. And this is part of being one."

"This is not Apache," said Roman. "Does the chief know about this? Does he know you kill innocents?"

"Leave the fighting to us," said Marco. "You killed deer with me. You are a good shot. Why are you whining now?"

"I'm saying this is wrong. We shouldn't be here. Those people back there were innocent travelers. And that man who shot at us, the man who got away, he is probably dead. They died for nothing. This was not bravery."

Baishan listened and looked south. There was a faint view of a mountain beyond. The snowstorm was weakening. The falling curtain of snow thinned and the light from the moon tried to make its way to the land. Grey clouds became visible and the owl earlier flew to another tree and perched atop a long branch.

Marco rode back down the hill, leaving

Roman and Baishan alone. Roman stared down at his cold hands that he rubbed together.

"You're young," said Baishan. "I don't expect you to understand what we've done."

"Then why ask me to come along?"

"The rest of the tribe is tame. They believe that the reservation is safe and that letting the white men take our lands is the best decision. But when will they end? I have seen the forts. One is called Fort West. The other Fort Bayard. They control us this way. They keep us contained. Soon they'll attack when their numbers increase. It's war. We are in a war, especially with Mexicans. You know of the Mexican soldiers that came from Sonora, don't you?"

Roman shook his head.

"No? Then maybe you'll change your mind after I tell you. More than 400 Mexican soldiers came from Sonora and attacked our camp while most of us were in town trading for goods. There were over 400 women and children in the camp. The guards of the camp were killed. Many women died. My wife—Ela. She was one of the many killed. Tara, my little boy, was murdered. My mother was killed. Many died. Our supplies and weapons were stolen. It was a terrible massacre."

"I'm sorry," said Roman. "No one told me."

Baishan looked away. He didn't talk for a while. "No one speaks of it, but not many survived."

"Did you seek revenge?"

"Yes, when we came back to camp a woman who survived told us what happened. We followed where she said the Mexicans went and ambushed them at a creek."

Roman looked up and found the snowstorm lessening. The sky was still black, and the night had been long and quiet. Roman was silent. He remembered the stagecoach driver was Mexican, and then he understood the deep hatred from Baishan and why he shot the driver quickly.

Marco rode back up the hill to them. He said, "I found the tracks. They go south."

Baishan rode back down the hill, his face somber and his voice low as he passed Marco. "Show us."

CHAPTER 3

Mary paced near the foot of the bed, figuring out what to do. When she heard the wounded man mention Apaches had shot him, she couldn't think straight. The marshal mentioning Apaches caused her to grab the rifle and set it near a place where she could grab it quickly. Then she told Jesse, who was sitting in the chair near the fireplace, to go back to sleep.

Outside the snow came down in thick clumps. It was still night, though the morning would arrive soon. It would be a long journey to Silver City, and she had no means of transporting the marshal. She wasn't strong enough to carry him and the storm outside was terrible. She wouldn't be able to see anything.

The man was awake, but he was tired from

the blood loss. The night was much longer for the man, the man who was so far nameless, rough-looking, the type that had served in the war and was unafraid of death after experiencing brutal battles between the north and south.

"Ma'am?" he said. "Ma'am?"

"Yes?" She woke up from her worrying and stood near the bed. The lamp was on the table and showed the man's eyes that glowed amber in the light.

"Where am I?"

"You're in my son's bedroom. We're in a cabin. Now, I need to know about those Apaches you told me about. Where did they shoot you?"

The man licked his lips. His voice was strained as he spoke. "Out at Bear Creek. I was escorting a stagecoach going south to Silver City." His voice was dry. He looked at the empty glass. She went out, filled the glass with water and came back. He pushed his body up so that his head and upper back rested against the wall. He squeezed his eyes shut, as it hurt to move his leg. He drank and set the glass down, his hands shaking with each movement. "On the way south the weather got bad. The snow picked up. And we couldn't see much. It was rough terrain, too. So we decided to stay put and see if it would pass. It didn't. We made a fire and settled in, hoping the storm would move east. It got dark fast. I started a fire. The man and woman in the stagecoach decided to stay inside of the stagecoach. The driver was near me. He kept looking around west, where the Gila Apache Reservation was."

"And they attacked you?" she said.

"Hold on," said the man. "I'm a marshal. Part of my job is escorting people in territory that's known to be dangerous. I knew of the danger. I warned the people they shouldn't be going anywhere near there, even if they're passing around it. They needed to go more east, far east. But they wanted to get to Silver City in a hurry. I sure wished they had listened to me. Poor folks got murdered by Apaches."

"How many?" said Mary. "How many did you see?"

"I don't know. I couldn't see them. They were hidden well. I saw two hidden behind the trees. Could be more."

She was silent and let him go on. Her heart beat quickly. She thought they could be outside getting closer to the cabin with each minute. The man's calm and patient attitude made her feel a little at ease but not by much.

"I heard a shot," he said. "And I stood up and turned. The Mexican fell near the horses.

Then I grabbed my rifle and ran for cover behind a boulder. I couldn't see them. I didn't know who had shot or why. Then I heard another shot, near me. The snow was coming down pretty hard then. And I could barely see. Then I saw a man in a thick buffalo fur sneaking in the forests. I looked around. I found my horse and rode up the hill, thinking I could get him away from the folks hiding in the stagecoach. But then I heard another shot—felt it, too. I fell off my horse and I must have been knocked out for a while because when I woke up the stagecoach was on fire." The marshal drank the rest of the glass of water. "And that's when I looked down and saw the pool of blood, my heart thumping hard and my leg like a stone. I couldn't walk. I was useless against them. I thought I'd ride to Silver City or Fort Bayard out east of here. But I felt I was about to die."

"You almost did die," she said.

The man looked down at the blanket. He lifted it and saw the work Mary had done to help him. He smiled a little. "All thanks to you. Are you a doctor?"

"A nurse," she said.

"Were you a nurse in the war?"

"Yes."

"You did a fine job, ma'am. I should have

died. I almost wished I had died. I failed those people. I let them die."

"You were knocked unconscious and outnumbered. It was you against a bunch of Apaches. The odds were against you." She tried to comfort him, but he appeared sullen against his actions back at Bear Creek.

"I hit my head against something," he said, admitting what caused him to be out of action.

"Did they see you escape? Did they follow you?"

The marshal squinted his eyes and tried to remember. A few hours ago were a long time to him. A lot of things happened during the night.

"I don't know," he said. He combed back his long hair with his shaky hand. "I hope not."

"You hope not?" she said. "You hope not? I have a son here. Our home is here. I don't want Apaches coming to burn it like the stagecoach. Didn't you turn back and see?"

The marshal got caught up in Mary's anger and glanced down. "I'm sorry. It's a lot to take in." He saw the worried look on her face. "I turned back many times, but the storm got worse. I saw nothing but darkness and snow. And I doubt they would come after me in that storm."

"It's not that heavy," she said. "They could find us. They could find us and kill us all."

"Hold on. You're assuming a lot and—"

"No," she interrupted. "What I know is that Apaches came and killed innocent people that aren't even trespassing. And they surely could have killed you. And they could come and follow your tracks to here. I need to be more than worried. I need to know if they followed you or not."

"The storm is terrible," he said. "I saw you go out earlier. Can't see a thing. Apaches are warriors, but they won't come all the way out here. It's too crazy. They would wait for the storm to clear at least. Then—"

"So we have until the storm blows over?"

"I wasn't saying that, Mary," he said. He wished he hadn't said they would wait for the storm to clear. He forgot he was talking to a woman with a young son nearby and that his tracks were easy to follow.

The marshal saying Mary's name surprised her. The talk of Apaches caused her to sweat and feel that she was stuck in a hole during a flood. She turned away and closed her eyes. She had not asked for his name, but she felt names weren't important when Apaches might knock down the front door any minute. She felt she had to be armed and ready, just as her husband had taught her before he died of tuberculosis.

"Can you walk?" she said.

"I wouldn't think so."

"No," she admitted. "You wouldn't be able to. You just got shot and there is still a storm out there. We'll have to wait for it to pass."

"I feel like I'll fall asleep any minute."

She nodded. "You lost a lot of blood. You won't be able to stay awake. You need rest."

"I'm afraid I'm in no shape to even ride a horse," he said. "I've been shot before, in the war. It was during the Battle of the Wilderness. I couldn't ride a horse for a week. Lost so much blood I felt like I would pass out. The doctor that fixed me up said it takes a long time just to stay awake after losing that much blood."

Mary leaned her back against the wall near the bedroom door. There was no telling whether the Apaches would come for them. She thought she was too far from the reservation for them to visit her, but, then again, the Apaches had killed innocent people before. She read about massacres in the newspaper when she visited Silver City once or twice a month. It was common for massacres to happen between the cavalry and the Apaches. That's why the man on the bed had escorted the people down south. Sometimes Apaches would burn homes, kill cowboys and raid travelers. The cavalry was the obvious solution, and the cavalry would fight off Apaches and sometimes escort people from place to place. Fort Bayard's purpose was protecting settlers and travelers, and it was just east of Silver City. Fort West was north of the Gila Apache Reservation, and the soldiers there protected miners from Apache raids.

"And why did you escort that stagecoach?" asked Mary.

"It's my job as a marshal," he said. "And, well, I like to get paid. Should have been an easy job. But the folks who hired me wanted to go a different way. I won't go on about it."

"You don't sound angry about it."

"I'm not," he said. "Just depressed it ended up this way. I didn't want to see folks die."

She folded her arms. "What's your name?"

"Lane. Marshal Lane McCree."

"You escort people often, Mr. McCree?" Mary unfolded her arms and adjusted to the man. She felt safer, knowing he was a marshal. The thought of him being a lawman didn't really dawn on her until now. Some lawmen were corrupt, but Lane didn't appear to be, especially after how he looked after talking about what happened to those people back at Bear Creek.

"You can call me Lane," he said. "Everyone calls me that."

She nervously stepped to the doorframe. He seemed to watch her every move now. Lane McCree was more awake now than he was a few hours ago. And now that they knew more about one another, both felt comfortable with the others presence.

Mary still had reservations. The appearance of the wild beard, rough and weathered skin and the sweaty figure didn't quell her attitude towards Lane. Although she had been lonely living with her son in the cabin for a couple years, she was cautious about letting others get to know her. Her reserved nature showed in her slight frown that always seemed to be displayed on her face.

"I told you my story," said Lane. He coughed and drank the rest of the water. "I'd like to hear more about you."

Mary shook her head. "With Apaches on their way? I don't have time for talk. I have to know if we're safe or not."

Lane coughed. "I doubled back on my tracks. I got off my horse and made tracks in the snow. Awful looking tracks. But I thought they wouldn't see much in the storm, especially at night with no moon to light the way. That gave me some time. I think it will be a day, if they ever come. You can go on to sleep." He took off his gun belt and set it down on the blanket beside him. Then he took out the Colt and watched the barrel shine as the lamp lit the steel. "I lost my rifle when I got shot. But I have my gun. You go on to sleep. If they followed me here, it will be a while. In this storm, it'll take a day or two. In the morning I'll try to walk to my horse. I'll even crawl if I have to."

"Sleep?" she asked, raising her voice. "You're saying I can sleep after what you told me? I should sleep when they could bust through that door and kill us?"

Lane stared at her. She looked away, keeping her eyes on the snow through the windows. "Sleep or not, it's up to you. When the storm is clear, we can hightail it out of here, whether I pass out while riding or not. I don't want to stay here for long. And I don't want you and your son to stay here either. I really don't even know why you're all the way out here in the mountains. It was a miracle I found your barn."

"My late husband, James, liked it out here. I mean—well, this was his idea of a perfect home. Bear Creek isn't far. Silver City isn't too far either. About two hours or a little less, depending on weather. He liked to be alone, and so did I. We have never been bothered here, and we like it that way. Peace and quiet is good for the soul, as my ma used to say."

"Good for the soul, and good for getting attacked. You're in what used to be Apache territory."

"I thought they'd be gone by now. They're in a reservation, aren't they?"

Lane snickered. "It doesn't keep some of them from going off and killing Mexicans, settlers, travelers—you name it. It doesn't do much."

"Then what is it for?"

"Good question," he said. He closed his eyes in pain and touched his leg. He breathed heavily and felt exhausted once again. All the talk was tiring. And the cold was getting to him. He pulled up the blanket. Even though he was sweating, he was cold.

"Are you in pain?" she said. Her frown disappeared and now she was attentive and caring once more, without worry or discomfort for a short time. "You want medicine?"

"No," he said, shaking his head. "I'm just tired. It was a throbbing pain, but it's over." He turned his head and saw the cartridge on the bed table, the one that had pierced his leg. "That's a big one. I'm glad it didn't kill me." He glanced around the room and now took everything in. He saw the wooden dresser and then a carved wooden horse sitting atop it. Then he saw Mary's bright eyes illuminated by the lamp. He became fully aware he was alive because of Mary. At first, it was a vague awareness, as he couldn't think clearly. But now he was aware that he was so close to death, just as he was close to death during the war. He was used to life or death situations, and he didn't think much of them. His closeness to death only caused him to grow closer to the reality of death, to welcome it like his friends had welcomed it as he watched them die during the Battle of the Wilderness in 1864. "Thank you for saving me. I'm sorry I brought this on you. I know you think I'm bringing Apaches here, but we don't know it yet. If they come, you hand me that rifle there and I'll handle them."

"But you couldn't handle them back at Bear Creek. What makes you think you can now?"

"I'm not bleeding everywhere now. And we have cover here. You know the area. We can plan it out, just in case they come."

"You can barely stay awake," she said. She stared at him. His eyes were slightly open, and he was falling asleep. She raised her voice. "You hear me?"

Lane McCree was asleep, exhausted from the blood loss and the long ride in the storm.

Mary walked out of the room and into her bedroom. Jesse was asleep in her bed, his ashen hair just above the covers. Then she noticed the time after viewing the clock in the kitchen. It was four in the morning. The sun would rise over the hills and mountains soon—assuming the storm would blow away. As she stared out the front window, she saw the snow falling constantly. It seemed there was no end to the storm, as if it would stay there along with the darkness.

Mary sat in the chair in front of the fire and listened for any movement outside. Old Rusty the dog was asleep and so were the horses. All she heard was the crackling fire, her nervous breathing and the wind blowing against the branches of swaying spruce-fir trees that surrounded the cabin and covered part of the mountains. She tried to go to sleep, but couldn't. Her mind darted from one worry to the next. So she stayed near the warmth of the fire and waited for the long night to end.

THE THREE APACHES FOLLOWED THE tracks made by the white man.

Snow piled on their thick fur coats and on the horses that trudged slowly through the three feet of snow. The storm seemed to follow them as they rode south on the rough terrain. The wind made a screeching sound as it barreled through the little valleys and forests and carried snow diagonally.

"It's too dangerous, Baishan," yelled Roman. "Let's turn back! There's no point in going on. Turn back! The man is dead!"

Baishan ignored him. He got off his horse and walked in the snow, crossing his arms for warmth and glancing up at the snow that fell quickly. The snow fell on his face and dark hair as he looked up, then he squinted his eyes at the wall of snow.

Marco and Roman waited and shivered. Their faces felt numb from the cold.

Baishan crouched and looked around at the deep snow and aspen trees. Then he turned back and motioned to the other men. They followed Baishan off the white man's trail and found a refuge against the falling snow.

The refuge wasn't a cave, but a place below a rock cliff that protected them from the falling snow. It was the best they could do, as they could see nothing in the storm. The snow came from behind the cliff so that the snow flowed almost at the same steep angle as the mountainside.

The men dismounted and led the horses to the cave-like area. Then they were all relieved and breathed comfortably. In the darkness they touched the walls of the rock cliff and adjusted to their new surroundings.

Baishan collected wood and the other men did the same. Soon they had a fire. Then they sat around the fire on the cold rock. Smoke drifted up to the ceiling. And strange shadows of the Apaches, with their thick fur coats, flashed on the walls. The light from the fire was blinding after being in darkness for the entire night.

"What if the man is at a city or a fort?" asked Roman.

"Then we go back and get more men to attack," said Baishan.

"From where?"

"My camp has ten good men. Since I'm no longer allowed in the reservation, I've gathered some men to fight with me," said Baishan. "They are good men. They would fight."

Roman shook his head. "You would risk Apache lives for one man?"

"One man can kill many."

Roman fell silent for a while. Baishan had strong beliefs and stuck to them. He would never give up, even if fighting meant death.

Marco said to Roman, "You're not told everything at the reservation, because most people there want to be told comfortable lies. They don't want the truth."

Baishan nodded gravely. "Listen to Marco, Roman. He understands."

Marco continued: "What if a man got into your teepee and said 'this is my home now. Your home is over there.' So you build a new home because he has many weapons and men standing behind him. But then he takes your new home. And then you are pushed further. You can only be pushed so much. We have been pushed to the edge, so there's no way to go but attack."

"Yes, but attacking invaders is one thing," said Roman. "Killing innocent, unarmed women and men is wrong. They aren't fighters. They are travelers. What good comes of it?"

"Travelers in *our* land," said Baishan, speaking deeper. "What they bring is the cavalry and the cavalry brings war. It is like walking into someone's home and saying you move over there. And then the white man takes over and tells you to get out of your own home, your own sacred land that have been part of the Apaches for thousands of years."

Roman shook his head. "It's not the same to me. If we are peaceful, they'll show us peace."

Baishan said, "That assumes they are peaceful, but they just fought their own people. The north and south fought, the union and confederates. They say over one million of their people died." Baishan pointed to the falling snow outside. The storm was constant. "No, the white men are warriors like us. They even kill their own people. You've heard this. We all have."

Roman glanced down at his knee-high moccasins.

"There are no fair answers," said Baishan. "I admit this. I want the Apache to survive. I don't want us to be pushed out of our lands. What would our fathers and their fathers before them think? They would shake their heads, watching us submit to the invaders. We fight back, just as we did after the Mexican troops slaughtered our women and children at Janos."

Roman heard about Janos before, but he was only two years old when the events Baishan mentioned took place, in 1858. He only heard the word Janos once or twice, and even then it was when people whispered the word, scared of mentioning it. "Did you know Geronimo?"

"Yes. I've spoken to him. He's the greatest Apache warrior. Some say he knows magic."

Roman began to understand Baishan's attitude towards Mexicans and white men. He was young and he had learned a lot from his people. But hunting white men was new.

Roman misunderstood the massacres from Mexicans and the retaliation from the Apaches, as he thought they were related to land disputes. But now he knew it was personal, as the women and children being killed at Janos was not war but slaughter. And the countless other battles and massacres only fueled Baishan's rage towards Mexicans and white men.

"I still don't agree with killing those people back at Bear Creek," said Roman.

Marco sighed. "You didn't even kill them. Baishan and I did all the work."

"We could have spoken to them first," continued Roman. "Tell them to go back east. We have to defend our lands from Mexicans and white men. But the settlers and travelers aren't fighters. They're innocent."

Baishan nodded. "We'll leave this to rest, Roman. We'll speak about something else now. I have stated my reasoning." He threw a stick into the fire and watched the flames rise. "I have tried peace. It has never worked. Peace is temporary. War always results. It is difficult for someone as young as you to understand, but in time you'll see."

"All this," said Marco, gesturing towards the dark land outside, "is a land of war. It's not for settlers and travelers. They should know they are our enemy, that they are not friends. It's like a stagecoach riding in the center of two armies fighting. What they bring is more of their people, and the more people they bring the more enemies will come. We'd be overrun if we let them stay. Mexicans and white men kill our people. No one cares about our people, Roman. We have to show that we won't back down, that Apaches protect their lands from invaders. We won't be slaughtered like the white men do to the buffalo."

Baishan's face was stern and contemplative, his eyes fixed on the fire. Then he looked up. "You see? Marco is older, so he understands what we have been through. You, too, will realize this. I have told you of the slaughter, how the Mexicans slaughtered my family. The same happened to Geronimo. Apaches have a tragic past that has made us who we are today. The bad things have helped us see clearly and avoid what happened in the past. We are cautious. Once we came to a peace treaty with the Mexicans, but they got us drunk off Mescal and killed more than 20 of us. So, you see, there can be no peace. We have tried it. Peace doesn't work. Peace, for most people, is control. White men put forts around us to keep us contained. It's a forced peace. They know there are more of them than us. But even death is better than being caged up in a little area."

"To you," said Roman. "We still have land. We can help keep the Apaches alive by joining the white man."

Marco laughed and tumbled over on the rocky ground.

"What's so funny?" said Roman.

"I'm not sure you have been listening," said Baishan to Roman.

"I have listened."

"Then you would know my answer."

Marco gradually sat up and then glanced at the snow with the others. The snow drifted slowly, and now the black sky and the stars were visible in the north. The storm blew to the east. White clouds were stretched out in the distance, hovering over the mountains.

"It will be morning soon," said Baishan. "Then we'll go on."

Outside the pines and juniper were heavy with snow. The Apaches looked out at the stars over the white mountains. Clouds separated to show the moon. And now they could see once again.

The men took off their fur coats and brushed off the snow. Baishan inspected his Henry rifle. The fire was burning out, but there was no need for it anymore. They could see the land with the moon shining faintly over the forests, valleys and mountains.

Baishan walked out from the fire and stood and watched the land for any smoke drifting in the dark sky. The clouds hung low over the mountains, and it was hard to see when a cloud drifted in front of the moon. The land was unsettled, barren of settlers. He could not see any sign of people. And he had no idea whether the white man had fallen and was buried in the snow during the blizzard or not.

He could be a day ahead, thought Baishan. Or he is dead. If the man fell off his horse, the horse might have kept going through the snow. The man could have fallen off his horse and tumbled down a mountain.

Then Baishan walked back to the young Apaches. He broke off a branch from a tree and dropped it into the fire that was dying out. The flames rose.

Roman and Marco looked up and were surprised by him building up the fire. Even though he said they would leave in the morning, they assumed he would want to leave in a few minutes now that the storm was gone.

Baishan sat again and the others relaxed. "We'll eat," he said. "It might be a long ride from here. Either way, we have to make it back after we find him, and that might take a long time. It will be slow riding."

Roman said, "Why are you so focused on one man? He is probably dead."

"He trespassed and his people have slaughtered us," said Baishan, raising his voice. "I've told you this before. What else do you want me to say? Maybe you should stay in the reservation and work there. Maybe you aren't made for fighting."

"I can fight," said Roman.

"Then what would you fight for?" asked Baishan.

Roman looked at the fire and thought of an answer. "For freedom, justice and to protect our people."

Baishan held his hands on his knees and said, "That's what I fight for."

There was silence until an owl hooted somewhere and a wolf howled in the west. The hooting owl was a bad omen. The men heard the owl and were quiet for a while. It was a bad sign.

Some of the animals that hid from the storm were out walking in the forests. The snow was grey in the night. An eagle flew over the fir trees and landed on the crown of a tree. When he landed, some snow fell from the tree branches. The Apaches could see animal tracks in the snow that led up to the cliff they used as cover.

The men passed around deer liver and ate it along with black berries. Their fingers were stained from the food, so they wiped their fingers on the snow. Their teeth looked red from the liver.

"It's good you have questions," said Baishan to Roman. "I forget you are young and you try to understand the ways of the Apache. That's good. But one day white men or Mexicans might come and raid our camp, then you will know why I fight. Then you will know why I chase after this white man. Why does any man fight? He has a reason. Sometimes he is told what to do, so he does it. Other times he comes from a tragic past, of death. Then he has an even greater reason."

"Roman has no reason yet," said Marco, nodding at his young Apache friend. "He has to know more. You told him enough, of our women and children being slaughtered. But it's not enough for him to fight. He has doubts."

Baishan's face was casted in flickering shadows by the roaring fire. He could smell the fire burning and hear it cracking. The sparks jumped from flame to flame. And he could feel the warmth, a welcome after the long cold night.

Baishan contemplated Marco's words. "You are right. My reasons are strong because they are based on terrible experiences. Roman is just beginning his life. He has not seen war. And he does not believe we have good reason to kill the trespassers."

Roman watched them converse like a child watching its parents speak.

Marco said, "He'll see once we are pushed even further."

"I don't want to see that," said Baishan. He sat with his back rigid. "I don't want to see that happen to any Apache. We fight to prevent what happened in the past, when the Apache were slaughtered."

"So how will he understand?" asked Marco.

"He will have to lose everything as I have."

The men didn't sleep, but kept their eyes on the land and the stars shining bright just above the white mountains. When the sun was about to climb above the mountains the Apaches rose without speaking and mounted their horses.

Baishan rode at the front, Marco close behind and Roman far behind. Roman watched the men ahead. He saw them speaking and he thought it was about him.

An Apache not willing to fight is not to be trusted. And Roman knew this and realized that he wasn't in the same state of mind as Baishan and Marco. Roman understood Baishan's reasons to fight against Mexicans, but not his reasoning to fight unarmed men, women and children. Roman thought he knew his friend Marco, as he had known him since he was five years old, but now he wasn't sure he fully knew him. Marco seemed to side with

Baishan, following him like a duckling follows its mother.

Roman never knew much about Baishan. He was thought to be more legend than reality. Baishan was named an outsider. He lived with a small band outside the Gila Apache Reservation. Roman only heard rumors about Baishan and what he had done to cavalry and Mexican troops. Baishan knew Roman's father, Norroso, who had died during a battle against Mexican troops. Baishan thought of Roman as a forlorn nephew. But that was hard to see, as Baishan never showed much emotion.

The three Apaches rode on and kept to the trees. There was no road to speak of. The land was wild and untamed.

The horses' breath showed in the cold air as they made their way through the fresh snow. Roman rocked side-to-side on his horse. He fought against sleep. His eyes felt heavy and his arms weak. He wondered how his horse felt.

Roman saw Baishan and Marco stop up ahead. Baishan jumped off his horse and landed in the deep snow. He pushed his shins and knee-high moccasins against the snow and then found something against an aspen tree. He held up a fur coat made of buffalo, then smelled it. His face appeared disgusted, his nostrils widened. Then he brushed the snow off the buffalo coat and looked inside the coat. A hand came out from touching the interior and he stared down at the hand. Then he scraped his nails against the lining and saw the discolored snow and the fur that was dark. Baishan turned back to the men.

"The white man's coat," said Baishan to the others, his back turned to them. He held up the discarded buffalo fur coat that was found against the tree, almost buried in the snow.

Baishan looked at the red sun rising over the mountains and coloring the clouds in the east. His breath, like smoke, bellowed from his mouth and rose in the air. "He is near death."

CHAPTER 5

MARY WOKE UP TO THE SOUND OF BIRDS singing high up in the trees and on the top of the stone chimney outside. She looked around and found she was sitting in the chair ahead of the fireplace. The light from the window brightened the room. The fire was almost extinguished, so she stood up and put a log of wood into it.

She walked into her bedroom and saw Jesse wake up. The sunlight entered the front window of the house and shone in a little square on the wooden floor of the bedroom. The boy moved his hair from his face and said, "Ma?"

"Yes?"

Mary had on brown trousers from last night. She put on a white blouse, put her tall boots back on and put the robe away on her dresser. The robe was stained with blood. The cabin was warm, so she left her coat on her dresser and sat on the bed.

"That man still here?" asked Jesse. The boy's hair was messy as he lifted his head from the pillow.

"Of course," she said. Then she slowly realized what happened in the night. Her heart began to beat hard. She walked to the front window and looked outside.

Something was in the forest of pine and spruce-fir. It was hard to see from the shadows the trees made on the snow. It looked like it was night in the treed areas. The sun had come up just over the snowy mountains, and now the mountains were cast half in shadow and half in light.

"What's over there?" she said aloud.

She didn't even blink as she saw the figure move out from the shadows and appear in the light. The figure walked slowly and cautiously, raising its head and looking around when it saw movement in the sky or forests.

Her heart slowed. It was a deer, a buck, with its horns moving up and down as it fed on the earth below the deep snow.

Mary turned around and saw the rifle against the wall. She grabbed it and put it on the kitchen table, where she and her son ate all their meals.

Jesse walked out from his mother's bedroom in his white long johns. Then he peeked into his own bedroom. Marshal Lane McCree was asleep. Mary looked into the room with her son. She thought the marshal would be asleep, as he was badly wounded and barely survived the night.

Mary walked inside the bedroom and checked the man's pulse. She touched his neck and Lane opened his eyes as wide as a rabbit in the claws of a falcon. He grabbed her wrist. Mary tried to pull away, but the grip was strong.

"I'm checking your pulse," she said, assuring him.

Lane looked around the room, sweating and bewildered by his surroundings.

"You're in the cabin, remember?"

Lane looked at the boy standing at the bedroom door. He let go of Mary's hand. "I remember now. I remember." He pushed his body up to get his back against the wall. It took all his strength. His body glistened with sweat and his mouth tasted like metal. He saw the sunlight coming in from the living room and was glad for it. "No Apaches."

"No," she said. "But if you're ready to go I'd

like to leave. Immediately." Her voice was stressed. She was in no mood to wait for Apaches.

"Leave?" he said. The man pushed down the covers and looked down at his wounded leg. It was a pitiful sight. "See that? Look at that. How can I even walk?"

"You can try. I want you to try right now. Come on." Mary put her arm around Lane's back and helped him turn his body so that his feet were on the floor. He didn't complain. He squeezed his eyes shut. The wrinkles showed around his eyes. "Are you all right?" she asked.

"No, but I want to go as badly as you. I don't know if you got crutches, but—" Lane looked down at his shaking hands and his leg that was throbbing and discolored. When Mary helped him turn he felt a tremendous, sharp pain in his leg. And he felt as if his arms and even his good leg were not a part of him. He felt weak and fragile, and he doubted he could walk even one step or have strength in his arms to hold crutches. He remembered the night in one instant, the longest night of his life, and he remembered seeing the blood ride down against his horse's fur and then on his hands as he tried to stop the bleeding. Then he remembered his disorientation in the night and how he thought he would die alone as he always thought he would die.

"Mary," he said.

Mary was surprised by her name being called. She wasn't used to it. She was only used to being called Ma by Jesse or 'miss' when shopping in Silver City. "Yes?"

"I'm very weak. I might fall."

"I'll catch you."

"You're not that strong," he said.

"Don't doubt my strength, Mr. McCree. I've carried men double your size in the war. Now move it or I'll drag you away."

The man smiled, but he tried not to. "How would you lift me onto a horse?"

"Move it," she said.

Lane had one arm around Mary and the other pushed against the mattress. His arms shook and it felt like the arms were thin sticks about to break. He had lost a lot of strength in the night.

He pushed the bed and tried to rise, but he fell back, closing his eyes in pain. The leg now felt worse than when he woke up. It felt like it had opened up again.

He yelled out in pain.

Mary stood up straight and saw the man's leg again. She lit the lamp by the bed table and put her hands on the leg. She felt his pulse again. His heart beat as if he were running. He was covered in sweat.

She put her hands on her hips and looked at Jesse at the door.

"I'm hungry," said the boy.

"You'll have to wait," she said.

"Is he going to eat with us?"

"I don't know."

She scratched her forehead. Staying was not on her mind; neither was eating. She wanted to get the man on a horse, but she had no way to do so on her own. Even with a man around it would be hard to lift Lane onto the horse.

Lane lay with his head against the mattress. "I'm useless," he said. "I'm weaker than a baby."

"I told you. You lost a lot of blood. And you got shot. Won't be easy getting up after getting shot less than six hours ago." She sighed and turned away. She paced in front of the foot of the bed. She knew he wouldn't be able to walk, but the thought of Apaches at Bear Creek disturbed her. The cabin was far from everyone, so she thought no Apache would come all the way to her home and definitely not after the storm. But she wanted to be at Silver City and tell the sheriff about what happened at the creek.

Lane closed his eyes and breathed heavily.

"Did you stop when you rode here?" she asked.

"Huh?"

"Did you stop on your way here? I need to know."

"Did I stop," he said to himself. "I—let's see. I rode here and never stopped. No idea why I didn't stop for cover. I was in that storm and I had nowhere to go. We just kept going."

"We?"

"Jim and I," he said. "Jim's my horse."

"But you didn't stop? You never stopped, not even once?"

"No. No. I rode here all the way from Bear Creek."

Mary breathed once more. "You think the Apaches will follow you here?"

"I didn't look back once. Even if I did, I would have seen darkness and snow. It was night."

"You think they followed or not?" she asked, raising her voice a little.

Lane shook his head. "I don't know. You think an Apache will do one thing, but they surprise you. No telling if they did or not."

She covered the man with a blanket. "You can't walk. I knew it. Let's get you some food. You're probably starving to death."

The man moved one of his legs, but Mary helped him move the other back onto the bed. Then Lane lay flat against the bed, his lean body showing pain all over it.

Jesse said, "Ma, I'm hungry."

"I know," said Mary, her voice now more relaxed, but still strained with anxiety. "We'll all eat now." Nothing else we could do, she thought.

She went into the kitchen and opened cupboards for pans. Jesse stayed at the door to his bedroom and looked at the man. The man lay with his head against the pillow and stared right back.

"Come here," said Lane, motioning with his shaky hand.

The boy stood still.

"Come here. I want to show you something."

The boy walked forward in his long johns. When he was near the bed he sat down and saw the sheets stained maroon and he smelled sweat and medicine from the man's breath.

Lane moved his hand and took out his metal badge that was rusted and worn from long years under all types of weather. He lifted it in the air, trying to hold it still with his shaking hand. "Here," he said.

The boy held the badge in his small fingers and looked up at Lane. He handed it back.

"No, you keep it," said Lane. "You hold onto it for me, for now." The marshal scratched his spiky beard that was a few inches too long. "You wanted to hold my gun, huh?"

The boy nodded and grinned.

"Here. I saw you reach for it a while ago. You thought I didn't see you, huh?" Lane took off his gun belt that he had put on earlier. He kept taking it on and off, not knowing whether he should deal with the cartridges that pushed into his lower back or not. Taking off the belt felt strange after wearing it from morning to evening every day, sometimes for the entire night. He took out the Colt and emptied the cartridges and handed the unloaded gun to the boy. "It's heavy for you."

The boy grabbed it and placed it on his lap. He looked at both sides of the revolver and smiled as he pointed it at the wall. It was a big gun in the boy's small hands.

"Nice, huh?" said Lane.

"I like it," said Jesse. "Shoot any bandits with it?"

"Sure, when I have to. If they shoot at me."

The boy looked at it one last time and handed it back to Lane. He then put it back in the holster and left the gun belt on the bed.

Lane then felt his dry mouth with his tongue and reached for the empty glass of water. The boy noticed.

"I can get you water, mister."

"Lane," he said. "Call me Lane."

The boy went out and came back. Lane drank all the water in one long gulp.

"You're mighty thirsty," said Jesse.

Lane wiped his beard of water and looked at the boy with the greyish hair. "Sure am. Jesse, isn't it?"

The boy nodded.

"You bring me some more water and we can talk more. Show you how to shoot that Colt, too."

"All right." The boy ran out of the room and came back with the glass filled. Jesse kept his eyes on the sloshing water that almost went to the brim.

Lane drank it all once again, his head and back against the wall. The pillows kept him in position. He felt dizzy, like he was about to pass out, but he tried to stay awake. As he lay there the boy sat down on the bed.

The marshal could smell bacon and eggs, the smell rising from the kitchen and curving throughout the cabin to enter the bedroom, and he could hear the bacon sizzling in the kitchen and birds chirping outside.

Lane handled the revolver. He said, "Watch" to the boy. He pulled back the hammer with his thumb. Then he pulled the trigger, aiming the gun at the ceiling. There was a clicking sound from the revolver. "See that?" He gave the gun to Jesse. "You try. But never point the gun at anyone you don't want to shoot. Understand?"

Jesse nodded. He had to use both thumbs to cock back the hammer. Then he aimed at the floor and pulled the trigger using three fingers. There was another clicking sound. Jesse smiled when he heard it. "I did it!"

"Good," said Lane. "Now you can shoot. Maybe in four years your daddy will teach you to shoot with bullets."

"My daddy?" asked Jesse.

"Where is your daddy anyway?" Lane forgot about Mary mentioning it.

"Gone."

"Where's he gone?"

The boy looked down at the floor. "Heaven."

"Oh," said Lane. "I'm sorry. How'd he die?"

"He was sick. Ma said he's in Heaven."

Lane watched the boy look down at the revolver. Jesse gave the gun back and put his hands on his lap.

"I bet he is," said Lane. "I'm sure he is. When did he die?"

"Two years ago." The boy pointed to the bedroom window pointing south. He looked outside the frosted window. "He's buried in the back. Ma and I go and talk to him there, see if he's comfortable and all."

"That's kind of you," said Lane.

They could now smell the bacon and eggs more than ever. Jesse still looked at the marshal's badge like it was a new toy. Then he set it down on the dresser with his wooden horse.

"Dinner's ready," Mary called from the kitchen.

Jesse ran to the kitchen, his bare feet cold against the floor. But he didn't mind the cold. He sat in a chair at the table in the kitchen.

"Is he awake?" asked Mary.

"Yes, he let me hold his badge and he taught me how to shoot and I told him about daddy out back."

Mary stopped for a moment. The Apaches were on her mind but now it was her husband, James, that passed away. She scooped the eggs and bacon and biscuits onto plates and handed one plate to Jesse.

"What do you say?"

"Good morning," said Jesse.

"No, well, yes, but the other thing."

Jesse looked confused for a second. "Thank you?"

"Welcome," she said. She turned her attention to Lane McCree. "Is Lane still awake? Did he fall asleep again?"

"He's awake," said Jesse. He began eating. His feet dangled under the chair.

Mary walked into her bedroom and went to the mirror. She looked at herself for a moment. She was not used to guests, but now she felt the need to comb her hair more and to adjust her clothes a bit. She then went into the kitchen, grabbed a plate and a fork and went to Lane.

Lane had his eyes barely opened when she entered, trying to fight off sleep. With the sunlight brightening the cabin's interior, he finally had a clear view of Mary. She is probably in her thirties, he thought. She looks far different than the night before.

He watched her set the plate on the bed table.

"Thank you," he said. "It smelled good while you were cooking. Looks good, too."

"Welcome. I'll come back later." Mary went out and ate with her son.

Lane grabbed the plate and set it on his lap. He ate fast, his mouth now warm from the hot food, and then when he was done he set the plate on the table. He felt much better now, his energy returning some but not completely.

The forks clinked against the plates in the other room. It was a welcoming sound. Lane had not been around a family for a very long time and he loved being not alone for once. He then brought up the blanket, as his body shivered despite the warm meal.

Jesse walked into the bedroom without stopping. He wasn't shy anymore. He liked the man and thought of him as kind.

Lane watched the boy walk to the dresser and pick clothes to wear. The boy dragged the brown trousers on the floor and sat on the floor while putting them on. "Good food, huh?" said Lane.

Jesse nodded, then grabbed a blue flannel shirt and buttoned it up. Lane looked away as Jesse put on clothes. Then the marshal saw Jesse grab his wooden horse on his dresser and sit on the bed with his feet dangling off.

The marshal said, "Your buttons aren't right, Jesse."

Jesse looked down at his shirt. Some of the buttons were in the wrong holes and he wasn't aware of it.

"Come here on this side," said Lane. "Let's button it up right."

Jesse looked down at his shirt, his chin

dropped down, but he couldn't see the problem. He walked over and Lane unbuttoned and then buttoned the shirt in the right places.

Mary walked into the bedroom and saw Lane buttoning the boy's shirt. "Oh," she said.

"Morning," said Lane. "Just helping the boy button his shirt right."

"Well, that's kind of you," she said. "Say thanks to the man, Jesse."

"Thanks!"

When Lane was done Jesse walked to his wooden horse and put it on the table next to him.

"That your horse?" asked Lane.

"Yes. Pa made it for me."

"He was a good carpenter," said Lane. He picked up the wooden horse and looked over all the minor details. It felt smooth. The craftsmanship was excellent.

Mary folded her arms and said, "He built this cabin too. All the furniture. The barn."

"A lot for one man to do," he said.

She shrugged. "It's what he loved. He loved making things."

Mary stared at Jesse looking outside the window. She remembered Lane might have been followed. "Jesse, get away from the windows. Now."

"Why?" He turned to face her.

"Come here right now."

He did so. She walked to the window and peaked out, watching for movement among the fir trees that were weighed down from the snowstorm. The bright sun made the snow hard to look at. It was like staring at the sun itself. The sky was clear and blue. The dark clouds drifted east.

"Apaches might have followed him. Understand, Jesse? We might be attacked."

Lane frowned, his face stern. "She's right. You and your son can just go on and leave. Ride off to Silver City or Fort Bayard, whatever's closest. I don't need you dying for me. I'm nothing to die for."

"You hush," she said. "The Apache's might not even come here. They probably think you're dead. You're half-dead already. If they follow you here, I'll tell them you're dead."

"Tell them?" said Lane. He almost laughed. "Ma'am, they aren't going to like that. They would find the tracks leading here and shoot you without saying a word. These are Apaches that killed three people. They aren't the friendly type."

Mary paced near the bedroom door. Having the man stay here was not an option. She thought the Apaches would ransack the place and maybe even burn it down like the stagecoach at Bear Creek. She wanted to keep her home but not die for it. And she didn't want to leave the marshal to die, helpless on the bed. She was no coward; she knew that. But she was still afraid of her son being harmed, of losing him and of losing her own life. She bit her fingernail and thought it over. "Well, then what do we do?"

What do we do, he thought. What did I do in the war, when we knew the enemy was marching towards us? We waited or marched on.

"Well, you don't want to leave me here. So we'll have to wait until I can walk." He faced her now. "How long until I can walk?"

"I don't know," she said. "That depends on how fast you heal. It could be days or weeks. I can't tell. Even a doctor would say that."

He turned his attention to the boy who was staring at his wooden horse on the table. Lane grabbed it and handed it to the boy. "We'll stay," said Lane. "And wait to see if they find us. It was a long ride here. If they ride all the way here, then they must really want me dead."

THE THREE APACHES TRAVELED SINGLE FILE in the snow and rode in a beeline around pine and aspen. The traces of the snowstorm made their journey slow and difficult. The sun was a sliver of yellow that rose over the mountains, and with the sunlight the Apaches traveled faster.

The clouds in the east and south were grey and white. They couldn't see the storm in the east anymore. It was broken up somewhere in the east. And now the sun was clear except for a stray cloud here and there.

It was a hard ride. Not many, including Apaches, rode this deep into this land. It was rocky and treacherous. While riding at the edge of a steep mountain clear of snow, the horses stumbled over hard, slippery rock. Marco almost fell down the mountain with his horse. It would be an immediate plunge, with no way of jumping onto solid ground.

After leaving the steep area, they rode on snow again. The white man's tracks were faint after the great snowstorm, but it was still easier to see than during the night.

The men rested once more. Knowing the land was barren of people because of the rough terrain, they built a fire that blew smoke up in the clouds. Baishan was the first to gather wood for the fire. The others did the same. They sat and overlooked the mountains while the fire grew. Roman and Marco sat with their hands on their knees.

"He kept going," said Marco, speaking of the white man's survival.

"Farther than I thought he would," admitted Baishan.

Baishan pitied the white man. It would be a pity to kill a man who kissed death and lived, he thought. A man who fought the land and enemy and survived both is a brave warrior.

"He is probably dead," said Roman, implying that following the tracks was all for nothing. He knew the other Apaches were violent, and that they would not stop hunting the white man. Now Roman wished he were home, making spears and jewelry with his mother. That's what he loved doing in the quiet reservation. He smiled, excited by the thought of returning home. He wondered if he would be in trouble for leaving the reservation. He had never left unannounced until last night.

"True," said Baishan. "But we must find out. He is ahead of us because we got caught in the storm and had to wait for it to pass. He could be far ahead. Maybe we will meet him tonight."

"Meet him?" said Roman. "Don't you mean kill him?"

Marco said, "You will complain again? Didn't you hear what Baishan said?"

"It didn't make sense to me."

"You're a little mother's baby. You go back to her," said Marco, motioning to where they came. "Go!"

Roman jumped up and got his hands on Marco's neck. He squeezed the neck until Marco's face was red. And once he did so Baishan stood up and slapped the back of their heads. The two separated, closed their eyes and rubbed their heads.

"You are both children," said Baishan, towering over the two on the ground. He raised his voice and it was like a cougar's growl. "Little children. Spoiled! Neither of you understand."

"I do," said Marco.

"No," said Baishan. "You follow everything I say without thinking. You can't decide anything for yourself. It has to be decided for you. When will you grow up?"

Roman sat again and looked down at the fire and heard it crackling under Baishan's deep breathing. Then he saw Marco walk away to the trees, punching a tree branch as he went.

Baishan sat down again. He kept his eyes on Roman, even though the young Apache was looking down, avoiding his glance. Baishan began to breathe slower. He closed his eyes until he eased his anger.

"You are young," said Baishan. "I treat you like the men in my camp. They fight with me because their families were slaughtered. Some lost loved ones. Some lost everything. But you? You lost a father when you were very young. You have a mother and you work in the reservation. You don't know war. I forget this." Roman looked up again. "I'm treating you like a son because I have lost my own family by the Mexicans. I lost everything but you." He looked away. "I wanted you to fight so that what happened to me doesn't happen to you. We Apaches are alone. Everyone tries to take our land. We are fighting people that want to slaughter us. Who knows what will happen? We may lose everything. Our people might be slaughtered. But I wanted you to learn to fight. Our land is a battlefield. Marco has that right at least. I don't want you to die like your father and my wife and child."

"You fight soldiers then," said Roman. "Not innocent travelers."

Baishan shook his head. "I saw the Mexican stagecoach driver and I shot. It reminded me of the Mexicans who slaughtered us. It might not be our lands to white men, but it is still our land to me. We are forced into reservations, herded into them like cattle." He opened his mouth to speak more but stood up and walked away instead.

Marco came back from the trees and sat down. The two sat in silence near the warmth of the fire. Black birds flew over the trees, soaring with the wind that flowed up the mountains side and through the swaying branches of trees. Snow fell from the branches every so often.

It was quiet. Out from the silence was Baishan, who was only heard when he passed around food to eat. They ate, hungry from their journey in the night.

They left last night, yet it seemed to Roman that they had been gone for far too long; that the journey was not so much a journey but a torture. He wished he could not disappoint

Baishan, but he knew he already had. Roman knew he was not a brave warrior like him. Roman was not passive though. He fought his battles and won. Once a boy attempted to hurt him, but Roman fought back and won. But he didn't think of fighting as winning or losing.

Marco and Roman ate without fighting. Baishan watched the two of them like a cautious and stern parent. He was both, and also a good father. But those days of parenthood and of marriage were long ago. He was a warrior, and he would be a warrior until death, the same as his father and his father before him. A long line of warriors with dark skin, stern faces, dark eyes and fiercely loyal to their people.

"You two done fighting?" asked Baishan. It was almost a sigh, like a tired parent exhausted from fighting siblings.

Roman nodded and turned to Marco. Marco agreed.

"Good. We have enough enemies. If we're enemies with ourselves, then we'll never survive." Baishan stood up and watched for smoke rising above the mountains. It would be easy to see in a day of clear sky and sparse clouds. But there was no smoke visible. Maybe the man was dead or had gone to a town that Baishan didn't know existed. Either way he would not give up until he found the man, dead or alive. It didn't matter to Baishan.

Baishan's fingers were slow to move. The cold was worse than the previous day, but none of them complained. Baishan petted his horse and dropped his hand down to its legs, feeling its warmth pumping in its veins, warming its body.

"Let's go on," he said, mounting his horse.

Hidden in the thick forests, the Apaches traveled in the deep snow. Baishan stared down at the tracks in the snow trail. The tracks meandered, aimlessly going this way and that.

The tracks had no order to them. The white man was bewildered in the storm during the night. The tracks resembled an animal's; such as a rabbit hurrying away from a cougar.

Baishan slowed his horse and looked down at the river. It was a steep descent. His horse must have been nimble, thought Baishan.

The river was frozen and covered in snow. Baishan could see with his good eyes that the man crossed the frozen river and re-entered the thick forest. The trail was long. Looking down at the river, it would take a while to cross.

The descent was too steep, so they rode north through the trees. Baishan held up his hand. The others halted. They rode single file. It was quiet except for a bird or two.

They hadn't been out in the open yet, only at night near Bear Creek. Baishan watched the trees for any movement. He could see the trees move in one area, so he watched them. Nothing returned. Then he waited more.

A big horn sheep stepped cautiously out from the forest and looked around for predators. It could see none, so it walked to an icy waterfall. Its curved horns lowered as it drank water from the unfrozen area of the river, watchful of its surroundings.

Baishan continued without a word. They rode down a hill. The horses stepped around jagged rocks and a great felled tree.

Then Baishan jumped from his horse and surveyed the tracks. He followed them, stepping into each one. They were smaller tracks than his. But as he stepped forward he heard a cracking sound in the ice. He stepped quickly back until he could only hear the sound of the river rushing below the ice and snow. He moved his hand against the snow that covered the ice like a blanket. As he got closer he heard the water rushing fast. The melting snow had brought even more water to the river, and now the river was full and deep.

Baishan turned back to the others. Roman got off his horse. Any sound from them in the valley could be heard from far away, so they were careful to speak. Even though they thought no one lived in the area, they were still careful and silent.

"We must go around," whispered Roman.

Baishan turned away and looked at the other side. It was not far away, yet the river had cracked under his weight.

"It's too thin," said Roman.

"The white man crossed, so we will cross."

Roman watched as Baishan crouched on the river. He walked to the center and held his arms out. He heard nothing, so he walked back and led his horse on the river, following the tracks the white man had made.

When Baishan had made it halfway, the horse's front left leg fell through the ice and was stuck. Baishan's eyes widened at the sight. He foolishly tried to lift the horse with his strength, but the horse was too heavy. The other side of the river was twenty feet away. Baishan walked to the other side of his horse and tried to pick up the snow with his hands, yet there was too much snow to move to reach the ice.

The snow fell through the opening the horse made in the ice. It was like a funnel. The horse whinnied and tried to lift itself from the hole.

"Baishan," yelled Roman. "Leave him. He will die. Leave him!"

Baishan ignored the boy and his sudden outburst. He walked to the horse and looked at the others one last time. "I won't let him die like this."

Baishan broke the ice with his moccasins. He fell into the dark water, the icy river collapsing below him. The river carried him below the ice. He swallowed cold water that burned his throat and tried to see in the pitch-blackness below the ice. His muscles knotted. There were only a few inches of air above him and he was not able to reach it. The river forced him down, pulling down his drenched clothes that felt like weights.

Roman watched the horse fall into the river, yet it broke the ice with its weight and strength and came out the other side, twenty feet away.

"Baishan!" yelled Marco.

The two Apaches mounted their horses and rode along the river.

Baishan felt the top of the ice with his fingers. It felt jagged and his fingers began to bleed and feel numb as his body was pushed downriver, hands scraping against the ice. He tried to push from the bottom stones of the river, but he could feel nothing below him but water. He could see nothing. It was blacker than the previous night. Below the icy river everything echoed, including him as he sucked in air once as the opening above him widened.

Then Baishan fell in the dark void. He was in the air, his feet moving unconsciously as one does when falling from a great height. Then his entire body was below the water again. He realized it was a waterfall and that he had to find air again or he would soon drown.

He was pushed so deep into the water from the fast current that he was twenty feet below the surface. Everything was dark. He had no idea which way was up and which way was down. His head could be just above the stone riverbed for all he knew.

Then he heard shouts coming from somewhere. And he listened for them, faint and constant. He swam to the calls.

He hit his head against the ice and was dizzy for a few moments. Then he punched the ice hard, though the water and the cold slowed his movements. He heard the ice crack. He punched the ice once more and saw the jagged crack widen and burst open. Then his head burst through the ice and he looked around.

Roman ran to Baishan and kicked the ice around him. The ice cracked and fell below the ice sheet and was carried downstream. The current was fast, but not as fast as it was upstream.

Roman grabbed one hand and Marco grabbed the other. They pulled him, but had trouble. Baishan was very heavy, but they pulled and pulled until he was panting on the snow. He wheezed. The cold seemed to slow his heart to a slow and hard thump against his chest.

"Let's make a fire," said Roman to Marco.

They scurried around for sticks broken from trees and bushes. They tried not to pick ones that would cause a thick smoke, yet neither cared too much about that.

Baishan crawled, his limbs feeling numb.

Roman said, "Put your clothes on that tree. Let them dry."

Baishan couldn't think. He looked around cautiously and took off his fur coat. Roman grabbed it. The fire was made and a thin flame rose. Marco went away and grabbed more wood. When he came back Baishan was bare except for his deerskin pants. He sat and squeezed out the cold water from his pants and from his fur coat.

"I can dry your coat some," said Roman.

Baishan's teeth chattered. His muscular body was red from the cold, though it was barely visible on his dark skin. He touched his arms and his chest, rubbing each part in fast movements.

"Horse," whispered Baishan. "My horse."

Roman squinted at him. "He's fine. He made it to the other side. We'll find him later."

A thin smile appeared on Baishan's face. "He could make it, but not me." He almost laughed, but he was too cold to even do that.

"He broke all the ice away," said Roman. "And swam diagonally to the opposite side. I saw him. But he had trouble with the current."

Baishan looked back at the river. The waterfall was more than thirty feet tall. He could hear it roaring behind his back. Part of it was frozen white. Long icicles draped down it. The river widened at the bottom and then narrowed downstream.

"The white man's horse weakened the ice," said Baishan. He closed his eyes and opened them wide. It felt like the eyelids were freezing. His wide jaw slowed as he spoke. He touched the fire and then touched his face.

Baishan got closer to the fire. Marco stacked even more wood on the fire. Now the flames rose higher. Baishan lay down by the fire, almost a foot away. Roman had cleared a tree branch of snow and had placed Baishan's long sleeved tan shirt and fur coat on it to dry.

"I'll go find the horse," said Marco.

Baishan looked up and then back, checking his surroundings. "On the opposite side of the river?"

Roman laughed a little and so did Marco.

Marco said, "See that part of the river? No horse tracks over there."

Marco walked away, mounting his horse and riding to where the white man went. He rode up a hill to make it up the decline the river made down the mountain.

Roman watched Baishan sit up and lay on his other side by the fire. They both felt the fire on their faces and saw the smoke rise to the tree above them.

"Maybe it's a sign we should turn back," said Roman. As he said this, he contemplated whether it was a wise thing to say, even though their spirits were higher than before.

Baishan stared into the fire. His breathing was heavy and slow. "Could be," he said. "You are far from your reservation and I am far from my camp. These lands are home to no man. Only animals."

After Mary, Jesse and Lane finished eating, there wasn't much to do. The fire was full, flaming up in thin bursts. And there was a fog edging away over the hills and disappearing when the sun rose over the mountains.

Mary kept staring out of the windows, always searching the trees. She thought Rusty wouldn't bark, as Apaches walk quietly. But she went against her thought. Rusty had good ears. He was not that old. He chased off that wolf and, if he wanted to, he could kill a man.

She walked into the bedroom and sat down in a chair near the foot of the bed. Jesse sat at the foot of the bed while Lane McCree leaned his back against the wall and glanced outside the window at the snow piled on tree branches.

"Where are you from?" asked Mary.

"Out east," said Lane. "Tennessee."

"You fought there during the war?"

"We went all over," he said. "But the major battle I was in was the Battle of the Wilderness. After that I got sick, barely survived and was told my time in the army was done. Not many soldiers could say that. I was one of the lucky ones."

Mary sat in a wooden chair and nervously watched the rifle leaned against the wall. Jesse handed her the marshal's badge and she took it and looked at it, then gave it back.

"What brought you all the way over here?" she asked.

"Work. Same as everyone."

"You don't need to travel across the country for work. You could have found plenty work in the east."

He scratched his beard and felt the hair that poked him like rough bristles on a wire brush. He could still smell the bacon in the air and, for a while, his mind was off of the pain in his leg and the Apaches.

"Well," he said. "I just wanted to get away from the east. And I wanted to see the frontier. I heard there was plenty work in the west because it was still wild out here, with the Mexican and Apache war and not much law around for those living in the west. I thought I could do some good, so I was a deputy in Hot Springs just south of here. Word came to town that Silver City needed law, so I moved there and tried to do some good."

"It's a rough town," she said.

"You got that right. Rougher than I imagined."

"What did you do there?"

"Helped put away drunks, intimidated criminals by standing with the other lawmen with rifles, protected settlers and travelers heading west or around the region. I did a little bit of everything."

"Why were you up north? You said you were heading south to go to Silver City. Why were you up there?"

"I helped transport a fugitive halfway to Denver. Then I ran into those folks trying to head south." He shook his head. "I didn't even want to go south. I could tell there was a storm coming, but they insisted. I told myself I'd regret it if I didn't protect them and hear about their death in the papers. Sadly it turned out terribly."

"You couldn't have known that would happen. It's not your fault," she said.

"It doesn't make me feel better about it. They counted on me." He dropped his head, but then looked up towards Mary. He felt he looked into her eyes for too long, as she blushed and turned away.

Mary didn't know why she blushed or why she felt good with him around. She thought he was honest, kind and strong; all the qualities her last husband held.

"Ma," said Jesse. "Can I go feed Rusty?"

Her eyes widened. Jesse always fed the dog, but now she wasn't sure of it. "I think I better do it. It's too dangerous out there."

"Rusty can protect me," said the boy. "He's not a scaredy cat."

"Apaches aren't friendly," said Lane to the boy. "You don't want to see one, especially the ones I saw at Bear Creek."

Jesse pouted. "What about Rusty? He's hungry."

Mary stood up and bit her nail and then grabbed the rifle. "I'll go feed him."

Before she went out of the bedroom, Lane said, "Hold on. You know how to shoot, right?"

She almost laughed, staring around the cabin in the middle of the untouched wilderness. "Of course I do. Why wouldn't I?"

"Sure, you know how to kill animals, but what about men? Ever killed a man before?"

"You know I haven't," she said.

"No, I don't. I never assume. I can see you've killed deer. Saw those antlers on the wall near the fire. But killing a man is different than killing a deer. I don't want you to freeze up in case an Apache aims at you."

"I'll be fine," she said. "I'll be out and back in five minutes or less. If I see them, they'd be at the top of the mountain in the west. It's a big valley. I'd see them clearly." She faced Jesse and said, "Stay here. I'll be right back."

She looked outside at the snow and trees. The sun was bright. The snow reflected the light like a mirror and made it hard to stare at directly. She could see nothing but birds flying in the sky and the valley and mountains covered in white.

As she stepped outside, the cold covered her limbs quickly, bringing a sharp chill to her skin. She forgot her jacket, but her nerve kept her moving forward in the deep snow. Her tracks were still visible from the night, so she used them to walk to the barn. The snow was cold against her legs, even through the pants. When she got to the barn, Rusty walked out from his bed of hay and wagged his tail at her in greeting.

"Hi, Rusty," she said.

Rusty's tongue lolled. The horses were fed grain and the dog was fed meat. She sighed after she saw there were no Apaches around.

Rusty lapped water in his bowl and was happy with the food.

Rusty was usually let out to run around in the snow, and the horses were usually let out to run in the corral. But the snow was thick and it was one of the coldest days of the year.

Mary entered her cabin and stamped her boots on the rug. Bits of snow fell off. She hurried to the fire. Then she sat back down in Jesse's room. Lane watched her as she entered.

Mary squinted at him, studying his eyes and hands. His hands shook before, but now she couldn't see them, as they were under the blanket.

Lane was drowsy, but not as much as in the night, when he was barely alive. He stared right back, but then he glanced away.

"What happens if they come?" she said.

The marshal looked confused.

"I mean, what is the plan? Shouldn't we know what to do?"

"Sure. We'd fight back. That's the plan." He coughed and the veins in his neck bulged. He reached for the glass of water with his shaking hands.

Mary got up and handed him the glass of water. She tried to think about what to do.

Lane put the glass on the table and hid his hands. He felt weak, exhausted and surprisingly good as Mary touched his forehead.

"You're warm," she said, in an almost disappointing tone. "Very warm."

"What can I say? I was a dead man until I found you."

"Yes," she said. "But we still have to know one thing: can you fight?"

Lane wiped the sweat from his forehead. "Oh, I'll fight all right."

"You can barely hold the glass straight."

"I'll fight, all right?" He raised his voice, but Mary appeared disaffected. His breathing was deep as he pushed himself up until his head lay against the wooden wall.

"Hold the Colt then," she said. "Let me see your hand."

"I can fight," he said. The sudden outburst exhausted him. "Look. I've seen Apaches massacre entire villages. Men, women, children. Only out of hatred for white people. Maybe it's to show how brave they are. But I don't see bravery in that. No. I've come out here to protect travelers, settlers, to bring law. And I won't have Apaches kill folks that want to settle in little villages or head out west to California. We share the land out east. That can happen here." He felt his dry mouth with his tongue. "I'll fight. They killed those people down at Bear Creek without a word. These are not friendly Apaches. I've seen and met friendly ones in El Paso, and they were honest folk."

He went on: "There's no bravery in killing innocent folks. They weren't even in the reservation. They were going down to Silver City." He shook his head, remembering the vivid details. "It's a shame. You think it's a regular day, but then some tragic thing like that happens."

Mary's hands were folded neatly in her lap. "Well, then we'll have to be ready."

Lane nodded, but he didn't hear her, as he was half in a daze. "You can die any day. Right when you least expect it. Those folks at Bear Creek realized that too late."

She wanted to ask him again if he could hold up the revolver without shaking, but she resisted. Maybe she could fight alone against an unknown amount of Apaches. But there was no knowing if anyone would be able to find the cabin or if they would even care to follow the tracks.

The cabin was about half a day away from Bear Creek, depending on the weather. The land was dangerous to ride on, so she thought even Apaches wouldn't follow the marshal to her home. Maybe there was nothing to worry about, and that he would get well and she would send him away. Still, she worried, as she always worried when the food was slim or when the snow was bad or when the coyotes yipped and howled like fiends in the night.

"You look worried," he said.

"I am."

"Don't be. I won't let anything bad happen to you or your son. Nothing. I'm bed ridden, but I can still shoot. If need be, I'll crawl on my belly and shoot."

She forced a thin smile on her unparted lips. "Thank you. It's just a lot." She watched Jesse play checkers on a table with wooden pieces, scratching his chin and thinking things over. "We've gone to Bear Creek plenty of times, Jesse and I. Knowing there were Apaches there makes me want to always be on guard."

"Well, you chose isolation. You could live in a city."

"Yes, but I like to be alone."

"No, you don't," he said.

She frowned at him. "I just said I did."

"You aren't alone, ma'am. You have Jesse, your dog, horses. You aren't alone. If you didn't have a son or animals, then you'd be alone. Then you'd go crazy living out here. You'd want to see at least one person a day."

"I guess so," she admitted.

"I was like you," he said. "I used to have a wife. Well, I thought she was mine, until she cheated on me. I have had a bad run with women. So I went off alone, thinking they were all the same way—liars and cheats, you know." He looked up at her. "But now I think I found a good, honest woman, a rare beauty, if I may say so."

She was stern looking, still serious about the Bear Creek matter, but she gradually smiled. "Well, thank you, marshal."

"Lane," he corrected her kindly.

"Lane. I don't get many compliments."

"You wouldn't. Not all the way out here," he said.

"No. I guess I've been in this cabin for a while, waiting for something."

"Waiting for what?"

"Change," she said. "Or something. I'm not sure."

"Nothing'll change if you just wait. You have to do something to make change. That's what I figured before heading out west. All my life I wanted to get away. After my parents passed away I had no reason to stay. So I made the change."

"I'm sorry about your parents. It was hard to do, wasn't it? Moving out west."

"At first. But then you don't get afraid of change like you used to do. You just adapt to things better." He readjusted the blanket to touch his shoulders. "You can't change much all the way out there," said Lane. "Even a mile from town would be better than here. I can tell you want to see people, more than just visiting town once every month or so."

Mary folded her arms. "I haven't thought much about it. I've been busy all the time. Never having much to think about but farming, hunting, feeding the horses and Rusty and watching over Jesse."

"You don't need to do all those things alone."

Her pale face bloomed of a reddish color. She had not been talked that way since her husband died. "Oh, I—I guess not. But with Jesse growing up I can—"

"Not Jesse, but a husband. Someone who cares about you and helps you out. Someone who loves you for who you are."

Mary stared into Lane's eyes that were lighter in the sunlight coming through the windows. She could feel her heart swell and her palms sweat. The embarrassment she felt eased away and now she felt vulnerable, as if opening a door to herself and letting Lane inside. But then her stubborn nature returned and she closed that door as quickly as one would during a storm.

"I don't need anyone," she said.

He looked down at himself in shame and thought his bushy beard that looked more like a bird's nest than a part of his face was taking away from his usual handsome appearance. He was not one to have a smooth face. He appeared more animal than man, with the long hair curled behind his ears and the beard that was rough to touch. The cold caused a beard to be necessary; it would be silly to shave. He began to doubt himself, as all men do after a setback.

I'm a stranger to her, he thought. And I'm already thinking about her as someone I love.

He joked in his mind that he had been alone for so long that maybe any woman would excite him, but he shook his head from the thought. Mary was more than the women he had known.

Lane was reluctant to go on in conversation. He thought she had her reasons to refuse to open up. She had strong opinions, and he was not used to that. He was used to women who were slow to think and fast to cheat; he was never sure why he attracted those types of women. In his mind, he just met an angel, a good person with morals who stood up for what she believed in.

Mary played checkers with her son at a little table in Jesse's bedroom. Lane then picked up his Colt and loaded the revolver and hid it below the blanket. Mary noticed Lane do this and nodded slightly, as if approving the gesture.

Lane then moved his body, breathing heavily as he did so, and put his trousers on and then the gun belt. He was ready now. Come Apaches or the Devil, he'd be ready to fight, just as he had done so back in the Battle of the Wilderness. He had been close to death in the war and in the long previous night. And being close to death made him unafraid to die.

Jesse grew bored of the game and walked to the fire in the living room. His mother followed.

The sun was almost directly above the cabin when Lane fell asleep.

"Can't we put Rusty inside?" Jessed asked his mother.

"Well, I guess it won't hurt. I'll go get him. He can stay here for a while, but then he has to go back. He'll break things again if he stays inside for long. He's a big dog, not made for this little cabin."

Jesse smiled. "His tail breaks things. He can't help it."

Mary grabbed the rifle and put on a coat.

Then she pushed the door open against the three feet of snow. The door opened about two feet wide, but it was enough for her to squeeze through. She closed it quickly to keep the warm air inside, then she retraced her steps in the snow.

There was a cold wind against her face that made her close her mouth tight and hurry to the barn. The wind blew her hair as she went. Sometimes the long hair moved so that it covered her eyes. She regretted not bringing gloves, as her hands were stiff and cold.

When she opened the door Rusty came out of his stall of hay and wagged his tail. The horses' ears flittered happily. She checked the food for the animals and made sure they had water. She closed the door fast. It was surprisingly warm in the barn, but that was because it was air tight and partially insulated with stone that kept the cold wind from blowing into cracks in the barn.

Mary petted the horses and Rusty. Then she turned to Rusty. "Come on, Rusty. Back to the cabin."

The dog ran outside, his black nose covered in snow and his tail wagging. He had trouble running in the snow, sometimes falling into a deep patch of snow, but he couldn't care less.

Mary stood near the cabin and watched the

mountains in the west. They rose high above the clouds, much higher than the mountain the cabin rested on, and she could see something moving on one mountain. She squinted and saw what it was: a big horn sheep. The sheep walked slowly up a steep incline that had snow that tumbled off the mountain in a great heap.

The valley was quiet. One last breath shown in the air, then she walked inside, letting Rusty run into the cabin.

"Rusty!" said Jesse. The dog's tail wagged and the boy hugged the dog. "You're warm. Why are you so warm?"

Mary put the rifle on the kitchen table. "He's a warm dog," she said. "And the barn wasn't cold. James knew it might get this cold." She caught herself speaking about her husband, and she quickly turned her mind away from the thought. She said to Jesse, "Don't let that tail of his knock over anything."

"He won't," said Jesse. "He's a good boy."

Mary walked into the bedroom and saw Lane with his eyes opened. He stared out the bedroom window and had the blanket up to his shoulders. His breathing was calm, and he wasn't sweating anymore.

She touched his neck and felt his pulse. "Your pulse is fine. How are you feeling?"

"Better than before."

"Good. Maybe you'll be able to walk in a week or so."

"I'd like to try walking tonight," he said.

"Good."

Some anger was still in her voice. He realized his tracks to her cabin were like a blood trail, and that he was like a wounded animal that a hunter runs after. Gradually something dawned on Mary; they had to leave the cabin soon.

CHAPTER 8

Baishan sat by the fire and let the water dry from his drenched clothes. His moccasins were next to him on the snow and his buffalo coat hung on a tree branch. The wind chill made his trousers freeze and harden. After a while of sitting he walked back and forth, squeezing his muscles to force blood throughout his body.

The two men waited for Marco to fetch Baishan's horse that survived the freezing river. After Baishan fell into the river, Roman saw Baishan's horse make it to the far side and wait on the riverbank. It was a loyal horse, so it didn't run away. And they knew Marco would come back within the hour with the horse.

"Walking is helping," said Baishan, walking

around the fire. The smoke rose in the sky but was fanned out by the tree branches above.

Roman stood near the river and listened to the roaring sound of the waterfall and the river flowing underneath the ice. "I wish we could move this fire with us, carry it with us like a bag. It would warm us for the entire ride and make the cold bearable."

Baishan sat down near the fire with his legs crisscross. He frowned at the young Apache. "That's a strange thing to say. That's something a shaman would say."

"I like their ideas."

"Yes," said Baishan. "But those ideas are others ideas. What are your ideas?"

"My ideas?"

"There's a reason people call you Curious Fox. Your curiosity takes you in circles. Never finding an answer. Always question after question. Find your own answers. You rely on others too much."

"I just found an answer," said Roman. "I said we could move the fire. That's my answer to the cold. My idea."

"That can't be done, Roman."

"It can. I'm sure it can." Roman watched Baishan turn his face towards the waterfall and wait for his horse to come back.

Baishan was silent for a while. He walked

to his deerskin shirt and put it on. Then he grabbed his moccasins and buffalo fur and put them on as well. The clothes were cold and almost frozen in certain areas. But as he sat closer to the fire his clothes warmed up a little and some of the hardness went away.

"I'm saying you could have gone home already," said Baishan. "You have asked me questions about my reasons for fighting and I have told you them. Your questions have led to more questions." He warmed his palms by the fire and then the back of his hands. "You are like a man who disagrees with the leader yet follows him anyway."

"I follow no one," said Roman.

Baishan nodded. It was the right answer and he was as proud as a father is for a son's progress in learning how to use a bow or a tomahawk.

It was a good answer. When he was younger, Baishan used to think of Geronimo as someone to follow, but then he realized he would have to find another person to follow when Geronimo was gone. And then another after that person was gone. He found that relying on oneself was the best path. And to take wisdom from people, sometimes discarding ideas and sometimes taking on ideas.

Roman looked up at the sky, and even the

sky looked cold. A few clouds clung around the mountain peaks. And downstream the river slowed and was covered in a fog that slowly disappeared as the sun rose above their heads. Now the pine and spruce-fir trees made short shadows on the land..

Baishan closed his eyes and listened to the river flowing behind his back. His heart slowed. In the river, when he was trapped below the ice, he thought he would die. Everything was dark in the river, but he didn't think it was that bad. It was a quick panic, rushing down the water in complete darkness, but now he contemplated whether his ancestors wished him to go another way. He thought of the river experience as a warning, maybe the ancestors beckoning him to leave this life behind and join them in peace in the afterlife. He questioned if he still believed in such things, in the afterlife and in spiritual ideas.

"The river pushed us far," said Roman. "The tracks are up there."

Baishan opened his eyes. "A sign?"

"Could be."

Baishan frowned at the thought and looked up at the sky. Nature was sacred to Apaches, as their ancestors were part of the wind, mountains, trees, rocks and rivers. Nature guided Apaches and it would be foolish to ignore the signs.

"We have come this far," said Baishan. "We must be close. No wounded man could make it beyond the next mountain."

"He could have."

"I shot him. You saw the rags, the coat. He took off his coat. Only a man near death acts so foolish."

"The Creator will protect us," said Roman. "We should pray to him, see that our journey is safer."

Baishan didn't believe in the Creator, the Apache's god that created earth in four days. He believed in nothing except for death and life. He understood both life and death in his fifty years as a Mescalero Apache.

"You pray for us," said Baishan, encouraging the young Apache. He knew Roman believed in spiritual things.

Roman prayed to himself, thanking the Creator for everything and then asking for safe passage to the white man's land. He asked for a safe journey back home and that, if they died, they died honorably. He thanked the Creator once again and then felt much better and happier.

The sun was now above their heads. The shadows were short. And up near the waterfall they spotted Marco leading Baishan's horse with a rope. Baishan sighed with relief. His body was warm, yet parts of his clothes were still wet. He knew the clothes would still be wet after the day was done, but that was off his mind. The journey could continue now.

Baishan smiled at the sight of the horse that appeared healthy and unharmed.

Marco led the horse to Baishan and handed him the reins. The horse lowered its head and smelled Baishan's long and dark hair as Baishan closed his eyes and put his hands on the horse's neck.

"He's not hurt," said Marco. "I saw a scrape where the ice sliced him, but it wasn't bad."

"I think our journey to the white man is almost done," said Baishan, standing up now to greet the horse. He breathed deeply and watched the land now bright under the sun. "By the end of the day we'll be finished."

"Finished?" asked Roman.

"Finally," said Marco, still on his horse and eager to leave the land and go back to the reservation to his young wife.

"Put out the fire," said Baishan to Roman.

Roman used his moccasins to kick snow onto the little fire. Then he walked to his horse and mounted.

Spirits were high. The sky was light blue

and there were few clouds—a good day to ride a horse. It was still cold, but they accepted the cold like a brother and rode single file back up the steep hill and a quarter mile to the white man's horse tracks.

When we find the white man in a village, thought Roman, what will Baishan and Marco do? They might burn it down and kill all the people. But what would I do?

Roman followed Marco's horse and Marco followed Baishan's horse.

Baishan and his horse falling into the water had set them back greatly. The white man's tracks were up ahead, but the horses and the men were tired from the long night.

Roman looked back at their tracks in the snow. It's midday, he thought. Others might have seen the stagecoach and the bodies near the creek. We could be followed as well.

Roman, Curious Fox, turned his eyes from behind his horse. The fir trees obstructed his view of the frozen river. The partially frozen waterfall roared down the mountain and was almost deafening. If the Apaches spoke, no one would be able to hear what was said.

Long white icicles hung from the waterfall and off the edge of the cliff beside the waterfall. The sound of the waterfall was behind them. They followed the river back to the tracks.

Before they had found the tracks, Roman thought of what Baishan said, about how he should not follow anyone. He thought Baishan wanted Roman as a follower. Wasn't that the reason for asking him to come along? Was it all a test?

Roman couldn't find an answer to his questions. He had too many questions but no answers for his curiosity. He followed and thought that he should turn back and go home. But the reservation now knew he was gone. His heart beat quickly. His mother would be worried. She might think he was hurt or worse and send out a search party. He was not one to stray far from the reservation. No, she knew that Baishan always tried to get Roman to come 'hunt' with him. She would be worried, waiting at the reservation for her boy to come home.

It was settled then. Roman would follow the other two but only for a while. He would choose his own path after the day was done. Whatever happened he'd find peace and answers without Marco or Roman. He never had troubles when creating spears, tomahawks and jewelry. He only had troubles when he followed someone.

Baishan slowed his horse and the others did the same. He found the white man's tracks. They trailed up to a hill and went around pine trees. It was dark within the trees. Baishan looked inside the darkness, seeing if the white man was hiding for an attack. It would be unwise to go into the darkness, but the white man led them inside there. There was no choice.

Baishan signaled for the men to follow. The journey went on into the forest, yet it was slow going. The deep snow made for slow riding. And they didn't know what they would find on their way through the dark forest.

It was a wild region. There was no trail, man-made or animal-made, so the path they followed was alien to the land and to the men. The white man could have fallen from a cliff, as the Apaches knew the white man traveled in the nighttime snowstorm. They were more careful now.

The horse tracks led around a mountain. The wind was much stronger now that there were few trees around. The trees weakened the wind that blew up the sides of the mountains. They rode on the side of a treeless mountain, high up in the sky.

Roman turned his head. He was far from home, the farthest he had ever been. He looked down and touched his horse. He thought they would take an easier way back, and that thought made him look forward to the journey back home.

The wind was so strong that they had to pull their fur coats to shield them from the cold wind. They squinted and watched for rising smoke in the sky.

In a clear sky, smoke could be seen for miles, and they all watched the sky for it. Smoke meant people, and they knew none of their people would be in these lands, only the white man.

The Apaches stopped at the top of a hill.

"Why are we stopping?" asked Roman as he rode his horse to be by Baishan's side.

Baishan said, "Smoke."

Roman squinted his eyes to where Baishan was staring. They could see for miles at the top of the hill. But Roman could only see the tree-covered mountains and hills and the snow and blue sky. There were more clouds in the west and south, but he couldn't spot any smoke. The white clouds hovered near the mountain peaks.

Roman couldn't see any smoke on the horizon. He thought it was his eyes, and that Baishan had much better eyesight.

"Where?" said Roman.

Marco looked at the others and then at the sky. He, too, couldn't find the smoke.

"It's far," said Baishan.

"Is that where we're going?" said Roman.

"If the tracks lead there."

"Are your clothes still wet?" asked Marco.

"That doesn't matter." Baishan turned his head to the dark forest behind their backs. Their trail led out into an open field and then to the treeless hill. He searched the area and watched for movement.

Roman noticed this and said, "What are you looking for?"

"I feel like we are being watched," said Baishan.

"You feel that too?" Roman looked with him and saw a flock of birds flying over the trees and using the wind to propel them over the hills. "Someone might have seen the bodies. We could be followed."

Marco shook his head. "No one would ride all the way out here, Roman. Even if they did, we've been riding single file. No one knows there are three of us."

"He's right about not being followed," said Baishan. "No man lives in this region." He sighed and stared at the rising smoke. It would take the rest of the day to get there, and he wasn't looking forward to the long ride to it. The smoke could be from someone other than the man they were hunting, but he thought it would be the white man that was perhaps dying by a fire. It would be a sad death, he thought, to survive and soon after die. "Come," he said to the young Apaches. "The tracks lead down the mountain."

Roman heard Baishan sigh and lead the horse down the slope. Did he doubt his decision of following the white man, thought Roman.

But there was no turning back, as an Apache followed through with each goal. He would complete the massacre at Bear Creek by killing the wounded white man. Then he would go back to his camp and not speak of this day again.

They rode to a deep valley covered in pine trees that rose more than forty feet above them. It was darker and harder to see, but a few rays of sun made their way through.

Baishan noticed a dark figure lurking in the shadows of the forest. He held up his hand and the others stopped. He squinted and watched as the heavy sound of the figure grew louder and louder. It was a clumsy and large figure, not caring if it was heard or not. Now it was in sight.

It was a white man, a mountain man with a long beard, wearing a hat made from raccoon. The raccoon tail draped behind the white man's head. He had a stocky figure and wore a thick coat made of buffalo. His boots were heavy and made his presence known from a long ways away.

Baishan knew the white man could not run. There was no horse in sight as Baishan looked behind the white mountain man.

The white man watched the snow, breathing heavily. Then he looked up and saw the Apaches watching him.

The white man gasped. He held a rifle, but he saw he was outnumbered. Gripping the rifle tight, he yelled out to the three Apaches. "I'm not here to fight. I can turn around. I can turn around right now and you all never see me again."

Baishan didn't understand the white man's language, but he replied, "Why are you here?"

"I don't know what you're saying," said the white man. "These lands are free. No one owns them. I got nothing against you."

"You've come to kill us, like all the other white men? First, Mexicans. Now, white men." Baishan's face was emotionless, but now his lips turned downward as he looked over the mountain man. "This is the best they could send?"

"I'm—I'm going to go." The white man turned around, but kept half his face turned to see if they would follow. He began to make his way down the mountain.

Baishan grabbed a tomahawk and in one quick movement brought his arm back and threw the tomahawk. It sliced its way through the air and cut deep into its target: the tree.

The white man heard the sound of the tomahawk hitting the core of the tree. It was wedged deep inside the tree. The mountain man's eyes widened and then he shuffled his feet, using the trees as cover. He was no warrior.

Marco held his stomach and gave a high-pitched laugh. "His face was dumb. Baishan, you missed on purpose, right?"

Roman saw the white man hurry down the mountain, repeatedly turning his head to see if he would be followed. It happened within a heartbeat.

Baishan jumped off his horse, gripped the leather grip and pulled the tomahawk from the tree. The white man vanished, but Baishan kept his eyes on where the white man went. If the white man came from that direction, it means more of them would be found there.

When Baishan mounted his horse again, he looked at Roman to see his reaction. He could see nothing in his face. "See? I can show mercy."

"That was not mercy. That was a threat," said Roman. "And there was no reason for it. He was a hunter, not a warrior."

Baishan said, "I know he wasn't a warrior. He should be one. In these lands, he should be ready to die."

"He was scared," said Marco.

"So would I," said Roman, "if I saw men with rifles appear out of nowhere."

"He should have shot us," said Baishan. "That's what the white men do when they enter our land. They shoot at us when we are out hunting buffalo."

"That's how we have their rifles," laughed Marco.

They continued down the valley, following the trail that curved to the side. It was a meandering trail that went the opposite way the mountain man went.

Baishan looked up, but could not see the smoke anymore, as they were in a valley blindsided by two mountains. He couldn't see smoke, but he thought the white man was close. One white man meant more of his kind. There had to be a town nearby.

CHAPTER 9

Rusty the dog wandered the cabin and went in and out of rooms. His tail wagged as he walked, enjoying the attention. Jesse followed the dog around to keep the dog's tail from knocking over vases and bowls.

"We'll have to let him out soon," said Mary to Jesse. She watched the boy, who was just a head or two taller than the dog, laugh and hug Rusty. Then the dog licked the boy's face.

"Why?" asked Jesse.

"He'll have to pee."

"Oh."

"Come on," said Mary. "He can come back tonight." But then she thought it wouldn't be safe at night. Lane could've been followed. "The barn is warm. He'll be safe there."

Rusty walked into the room where Lane

was sitting at the edge of the bed. Lane watched the big dog walk into the room and then saw it raise its ears. The dog's tongue went back into the closed mouth.

"Rusty, isn't it?" asked Lane.

The dog was cautious. They never got visitors. Rusty walked up to Lane and smelled him and then felt the man's hand on his head and ears.

"Does Rusty bark often?" said Lane.

"Whenever there's a deer, raccoon or wolf, he'll bark," said Mary. "But the barn is far enough so that it's not too loud. The barking still wakes us up sometimes though."

Lane said, "That's good. He lets you know what's out there."

"He's a big dog," said Jesse.

"Sure is."

Lane stopped petting the dog, as the dog walked out of the room, its tail wagging high in the air. Mary followed the dog and led him outside. In the hurry she forgot the rifle.

Now that it was midday, the land was bright. Mary watched as the dog walked through the deep snow and back to the barn. Its black nose was dusted with snow.

Well, Rusty will let us know if someone is out here, she thought. The dog lifted its nose and Mary noticed this. "What is it boy?"

Rusty sniffed the air and picked up a scent. Then he brought his nose down and sneezed.

Mary sighed. She led the dog back to the warm barn. Then she checked on the horses. She would let them out when it was safe, and with Lane telling her about the Apaches she felt like she had to look over her shoulder every minute.

When will I stop worrying about the Apaches, she thought. They might come here in a month or even a year.

She closed the barn door and then went back into the cabin. Her cheeks were red, so she warmed herself near the fire. Then she heard Lane in the other room.

Lane pushed himself off the bed and stood and held on to the wall. He breathed heavily as Jesse watched. "I'm all right," he assured the boy. "I just want to get back. I have to tell people what happened. Those Apaches might be hurting more people."

"I can help you," said Jesse.

The man smiled. "I'm not sure you're strong enough."

"I was strong enough to use that revolver of yours. I can shoot."

"It's more than just pulling the trigger," said Lane.

"How?"

"Well," said the marshal, leaning his shoulder against the wall, letting his weight go mostly on the good leg. "You have to judge the person with the gun. Will he shoot you? What kind of person is he? What did he do? Are his hands fidgeting? Is he nervous? Is he hiding behind something? How do you reach him if he's hiding? You know, you have to know a lot. They usually aren't going to be out in the open if they care about their life. They could be taken by surprise, but most of the time people really fight for their life. Even people unafraid of death fight for their life. Saw an Apache get shot once and then keep running towards us and shooting wildly."

Mary walked into the room and sat down. She sighed with relief. The dog would bark if there were anyone or any animal outside, and she was relieved after knowing that.

"Need help walking?" she asked Lane.

Lane said, "No thanks. I can handle it." He stepped away from the wall and tumbled to the floor.

Mary helped move him so that he was sitting on the bed again.

"I told you I could handle it," said Lane.

"Of course." Mary put her hands on her hips. "Well, we can try tonight."

"We?"

"I don't want to stay here if there are Apaches that might be following your tracks. I can't handle the risk."

Lane shook his head. "I'm sorry. This all shouldn't have happened."

"You did what you had to," she said.

Lane pushed his body so that his head was against the wall near the head of the bed. He felt much better than he did in the night. His wounded leg was not as numb, but he still felt tired and hungry constantly. The hunger and exhaustion came in waves, forcing his eyes to droop down. He tried to stay awake. He felt responsible for this family, and he wanted to protect them. He didn't want anything bad to happen to them, but that response was not out of duty but morality.

Mary sat in a chair near the bedroom door and said, "What are Apaches like? I've seen a few before in Silver City, stern-looking men that didn't look at anyone, going about their business. I just can't picture them being violent."

Lane smirked. "Have you read the newspaper, ma'am?"

"Well, not often."

"Then you should know a little about the massacres by Apaches."

She frowned and let her hands drop to her lap. "Well, what's your opinion of Apaches?"

Lane scratched his big beard. "They're like anyone else."

"What do you mean?" she said.

"What happens to any group of people threatened by an outsider? They fight back. People die. If someone tells you that your house isn't yours anymore, you'd get angry. You'd fight for everything, especially if you put decades of work into your home. The Apaches have lived here for thousands of years. They're unpredictable like anyone. Some are good, some bad. I reckon people don't like that answer. Sure, some of them raid villages and scalp people, and those are the ones the law goes after. But it's like white people; some are good and some bad. There have been white people that have massacred entire towns. There is nothing complicated about it. We, like any lawman, go after the bad ones."

"You friends with any Indians?"

"Any Apaches?"

"Yes."

"A few. But they live in towns and villages filled with white people. They are not wild as you think. They are farmers, ranchers, cowboys."

"I think the only ones I've seen in town were the hunters."

"They're around too."

"Why do you think they left their tribe? Why'd they move in with white people."

He shrugged. "Didn't like how things were going."

"What do you mean?"

"White people keep pushing west, and the natives don't like that. They're moving into their land. Soon there will be a war. There have been raids in opposition, but it won't be long until a war breaks out. People will do anything to prevent being invaded. It's natural. Those three apaches I said I knew—they know what will happen. Might as well blend in, they thought."

"What would you do if you were an Apache?"

He shook his head. "Nothing good comes out of it, either way. There's no winning. There's just too many people moving west, and with them come the military. I don't know if they'll live. They can either die a hero or blend in with the enemy. I don't know what I would do. Dying wouldn't be all too bad. At least you fought for what you believed in."

"Well, you still didn't answer."

"I would fight. It's what I do. All I'm good at."

"All you're good at is killing?"

"Whatever you want to call it," he said.

"That's what it is. It's killing."

"All right," he said. "What else would you do if you found out a family been murdered on the road, and the little boy and wife taken? Family was heading to California, just passing through."

She was silent as she fiddled with the bottom her shirt.

"Of course," he said, "a few white men done the same, except we found the woman."

She got up and walked out of the room. There was nothing else to say. The marshal had spoken this way before and nothing good came from it.

It was the ugly truth, but he didn't want to lie about how things were. And he didn't want someone to feel comfortable when bad things were happening all around their home. It was either a comfortable lie or an uncomfortable truth, and Lane never wanted to lie.

She's upset still, he thought. It's the pain in my leg and the claustrophobia of being in this cabin in the middle of nowhere.

He waited for her to come back, and after a few minutes she went back inside and sighed.

"I'm cooking soon. Maybe later you'll be able to walk some."

"Maybe," he said, in an apologetic way.

Then she went out again. Lane heard her moving pots and pans in the kitchen. He could feel it warmer in the cabin. The midday sun shined brightly and began to melt the snow.

Jesse walked into Lane's bedroom. "Did you like Rusty?" he asked the man, jumping on the bed and then sitting with his legs crossed.

"Sure," said Lane. "He's a big dog."

"Ma said he fought off a wolf earlier."

"When was this?"

"When you were sleeping," said the boy. "She had to get the rifle. She had left it in the barn."

"Lots of wilderness out here," said Lane, looking outside the window at the bright snow and spruce-fir trees. "Ever think about moving to a city?"

"A city?"

"Maybe not Silver City, but somewhere safer. Maybe Kansas City or to El Paso. You'd meet boys and girls your age."

Jesse shrugged. "I don't know. Would they like me?"

"Sure they would."

"Do you like me?"

"Very much so," said Lane.

Jesse looked down at his little boots. "I guess so."

"Food's ready!" called Mary from the kitchen.

Jesse jumped up and ran out of the room. In a while Mary came with a plate of food and set it down on the bed table. She noticed Lane fell asleep again. He couldn't stay awake for long, yet he tried to stay awake. He didn't want to fail another group of people. He didn't want to fall asleep when Apaches rode outside, but he couldn't help himself.

Mary touched the man's chest and felt his heart. His pulse was all right. And he wasn't sweating as much as he did during the night. He smelled like a carcass, but that didn't surprise her.

Lane opened his eyes when she was leaning over him. "Mary?"

"Oh," she said. "Here's your food." She motioned to the plate and backed away. "How are you feeling?"

"Better."

"Good," said Mary. She already ate, so she sat in the chair by the wall and watched Lane and sometimes stared outside the window. With a trimmed beard, he would look distinguished, like a gentleman. But he looked sickly and gaunt. It was his eyes she was focused on but also how he treated her son. She listened to his talks about the cabin, its remoteness, of leaving and of wanting change. Now she thought of the man as someone closer. He was friendly, kind and strong. A trustworthy and intelligent lawman.

She kept thinking of him and she suddenly realized this man was similar to her husband buried out back. Both good men. But Lane was more talkative, and her ex-husband, James, was the reserved type who was a diligent and skilled carpenter. Lane was a lawman, and some of them were violent and lived violently. But, if Lane was like that, he didn't show it. He killed bad men, as he said so, but Mary thought that kind of life couldn't be too bad for the soul. After all, he only killed those that were violent and tried to kill him.

She smiled at thinking of him this way.

"What are you smiling about?" he asked.

"Nothing."

"Doesn't sound too funny."

She stood up and sat on the bed. Surprised by this, he straightened up.

"Heard you talk to Jesse about El Paso and Kansas City," she said.

Lane looked around for the boy. "Does he go to school?" he said, avoiding her question.

Mary grinned. "No school around here."

"It's important, don't you think?"

"James," she said. "Jesse's father. Wasn't educated in school. He was a carpenter, built all kinds of things. He didn't need school. Neither did I, but I went to school in Oklahoma when I was young."

"What about friends? A child needs friends."

"I'm his friend."

"Lady," said the marshal. "You're all cooped up here out in the middle of nowhere. Don't you get sick of being out here? Don't you want to get that change you talked about? You've been waiting for change, but I don't see it out here."

"Don't call me lady," she said quickly. "And don't talk down to me. None of this is important." She stood up and pointed out the window. "Could be a tribe of Apaches coming here and all you're talking about is school and friends and nonsense."

"I didn't mean to insult you," he said. "I just wanted to talk."

"Well, you're sure easy to talk to. You're beating around the bush. Why don't you just go ahead and say it?"

"Say what?" he said.

"Don't act like you don't know. You're getting at something."

He turned his face away and then back at her. "All right. I'll tell you. I don't like seeing folks in this dangerous an area. I don't like seeing you depressed and acting like something would sprout out of the ground and change your entire life. You're in a bad place, and I can see it. And I don't like how you're dragging the boy around with you. This attitude isn't doing much for you. You're holding onto this cabin because it's the last thing you have to remind you of your husband." He sighed. "It's a natural thing to do. You try to hold onto something that isn't coming back. Call it nostalgia. But you need to move away from here. Live a new life. Your husband is probably doing just fine in Heaven. He's just waiting on you to move on." He felt he shouldn't say it, but he did anyway. "And I think you're the prettiest woman I've ever seen. And I'd like to get to know you better."

It was all too much. Everything she tried to forget but couldn't was placed right in front of her eyes. She turned quickly, went to the living room and sat in the chair near the fireplace.

Lane slumped his shoulders and turned to the empty glass of water on the bed table. Won't be a refill for a while.

CHAPTER 10

ALL DURING THE DAY AND NIGHT BAISHAN thought of turning back. The white man should have been found in the snow. The blood trail was long. He saw the red rag and coat of blood.

He kept going, and the others followed. Sometimes Baishan turned back to see if Roman would go back home.

The young Apache persisted. Roman was as stubborn as his father. But he didn't have the hatred in him. He didn't hate the white man or the Mexicans as Baishan did. There was no hate in him, but he still followed.

Baishan followed the trail down the valley and then up a hill. After a few hours they stopped in a cluster of aspen. Baishan squinted and saw the grey smoke rise in the clear blue sky. The others saw, too. They weren't far. It would be dark when they reached the cabin.

"See the smoke?" Baishan asked the others.

"Yes," said Marco. "Finally."

"That might not be where the white man went," said Roman.

Baishan listened to the birds soaring in a V-shape above their heads. Then the horses shuffled in the snow, wary and cold. He smelled the horses that had a similar smell to him.

"Only a white man shows smoke for so many to see," said Baishan.

"But maybe not our white man," said Roman.

"Our white man," said Marco. "He calls him *our* white man. Might as well give him a name."

"He has one. I'm sure. Yes, why *not* give him a name?" said Roman, turning to Marco and staring in his eyes until Marco scoffed and faced the smoke again. "Wounded Fox. That's what I'll call him."

"Wounded Fox," said Baishan, in his mountainous voice. "He will be Dead Fox soon."

Baishan rode up the trail and Marco followed without turning back.

Roman stayed put for a while until the

other men waited for him to follow. Then he went on.

Maybe it was a fort, thought Roman, like the one north of our reservation. I have not been this far. I don't know what is out here. There could be many white men in these lands.

Roman listened to the wind blowing past him, picking up the horse's mane and letting the hair float in the air. It was snowing in the north and west, but it was a slow storm and none of the men could tell where it would head or if it would be as bad as the previous one. It would be unlikely. The last snowstorm was one of the worst. In all his long years Baishan had never seen a storm like that.

The men were hungry, but they didn't stop to eat. Baishan wanted the men to be hungry and angry. A meal makes man slow and tired. The hunger kept them going and caused them to focus on the task. It wouldn't take long to reach the white man anyway.

Roman watched the sky and saw the grey smoke growing bigger. He saw the smoke through the tall trees ahead of them. Then he saw Baishan turn back to him, his black eyes cold and distant like hawk's eyes.

"Roman," called Baishan. "Come."

Roman rode until his horse was at the side of Baishan's.

Baishan nodded at the smoke just over the mountain. "The tracks lead here."

"I see," said Roman.

"The white man's home," said Baishan, "is just over that mountain. He is wounded. An easy kill."

"Yes, I know. I'm sure you will be glad it's over."

"I want you to kill him."

Roman frowned and shook his head. "You shot him. You should finish him."

"I want you to," said Baishan. "Show me you are Apache. It's an easy thing to do, to kill a wounded animal. Think of him as a wounded animal. You hunt. You understand that sometimes the animal survives. You hunt the animal, put him out of his misery." He looked at the red sun falling from the sky. "Kill him."

Marco watched Roman, looking for a sign. Then Marco said, "I will do it. He is a—"

"No!" said Baishan. "Roman can kill the enemy."

"He is no Apache," said Marco.

Baishan quickly turned to Marco. "And you speak too much," he said to Marco.

"I can't kill him," said Roman. "I kill deer and buffalo. But not man." He felt like he was apologizing and he didn't know why he was speaking that way. "I can't kill him."

"No?" said Baishan. "What if the white man shoots me? What if I die? Will you shoot back? What if your friend is shot? Will you fight then?"

Roman thought about it. He was not a killer. He could kill an enemy, a true enemy, but he wasn't sure who was the enemy in this situation.

"I don't know," Roman finally said.

"You'd let us die," said Marco, raising his voice. "Traitor! We should kill you now!"

"Then kill him," Baishan said flatly to Marco. "Kill him, if you are brave enough. He is your friend, isn't he?"

"An enemy now," said Marco.

"Then kill him."

"I will!"

"Take out the rifle," said Baishan.

Marco breathed heavily. His nostrils widened, but his anger subsided after looking at Roman. Marco dropped his eyes to the snow and shook his head.

"It's a difficult thing to do," said Baishan to Roman, putting his hand on the young Apaches shoulder. "You remember what I said earlier?"

"About choosing my own path?"

"Yes."

"I do."

"Remember that," said Baishan.

"I will."

"Never forget," said Baishan. "No one can choose your path for you."

Baishan rode ahead. The tracks were faint and deep in the snow. When Baishan rode off, Marco faced Roman. Marco looked angry, but gradually his face appeared emotionless. Marco realized he never thought of Roman as a friend, just a tool to help further his life.

Roman pushed Marco out of his mind. He never liked Marco, as Marco always bothered him with things he wanted him to do. Now he knew the bad feeling he had around Marco was real and true. The bad feeling was trying to tell him something, but he never listened. Now he listened to his heart and he felt it was telling him to go back and that death would only come from going further.

But that feeling was erased as quickly as a passing thought. The task was almost done. He could always turn back if there were too many men to fight. Would he fight then? He would have to fight. No horse rode fast in the deep snow. There would be no escape.

So Roman followed Marco and Baishan, trailing behind them, his torso swaying on his exhausted horse. "It won't be long," he told his horse aloud. "We will make it back. And when we make it back home I will feed you and not take you out in the cold again. I'll keep you near the fire and treat you more like a brother. Aren't we brothers?" He thought he heard the horse say something, but it was just in his mind. "Yes? I think so too. We will be alone again. We are best alone. That's when we are happy."

The other Apaches were far ahead, but Roman didn't try to hurry. He wanted to be far from Marco, as he thought Marco would try to kill him. He threatened his life, and Roman didn't think that life was something unimportant. Marco could kill him any second, or he could wait and kill him another day.

No, thought Roman. He is scared. His talk is always big and never the truth. He always lies. I didn't even see him shoot any of the people back at the creek.

Still, Marco could state lies about Roman around the reservation and maybe cause everyone to go against Roman. He was one to do so.

I wouldn't care about that, thought Roman. I don't care what anyone thinks. I will choose my own path.

He caught himself already using Baishan's advice and smiled at his new words. He began to speak greatly of himself and of great things he will do, stating that he will marry someone beautiful and build many things and maybe become an important man who people listen to for advice. Yes, he began to see things clearly, that he was not just a follower as he used to be. He made his own choices. He would not follow Baishan after the day was done, and he would not be Marco's friend.

It took another hour to reach the smoke. The Apaches watched from the mountain and saw the cabin and barn and corral and the tracks leading down to the cabin. The smoke from the cabin's chimney rose into the sky that was now grey because the sun hid behind the clouds in the west.

"Let's get this over with," said Marco.

"No," said Baishan, holding his hand on the center of Marco's chest. "We wait until night."

"They won't see us even at this hour," said Marco. "There are no windows on the west side of the cabin."

Baishan shook his head and that was it.

Roman squinted at Baishan and wondered why he didn't want to kill the white man immediately. He could be alone. Maybe he was dying on the floor near the fire. It would be an easy kill.

An act of surprise was a safer bet. Baishan wasn't taking chances. The man survived the shot and the snowstorm. He was not a weak man, as Baishan originally thought.

There was no knowing what was down there. Part of the cabin was obscured by spruce-fir trees, and the shadow of the mountain the Apache's were on made the area around the cabin dark already.

The sun was still up. But it would be dark within an hour or so. Then they would plan their attack.

Baishan dismounted and led the horses away from the mountain's edge. He sat and tried to stay warm. His clothes were still drying from falling into the icy river. They would be dry on the way back to his camp, but he didn't think of the cold or the camp, only the white man inside the cabin.

Roman and Marco sat with Baishan. Their differences were set aside for now. And now they pulled up the fur coats to prevent the cold wind from blowing into their faces.

"I want to shoot him," said Marco.

Baishan nodded. "If you have the shot, take it."

"I will. I wanted to kill him since I saw you fall into the river. He caused us all this trouble. I wish we had found his body in the snow."

Roman ignored Marco and went off alone. He saw a chipmunk on the snow. It made noises and scurried away. Then Roman sat in the decompressed snow, with his back against a fir tree. He prayed again, asking the Creator to protect his life and to allow the white man, if he is worthy, to live.

Then he looked back from where he came. He was far from the others. Maybe they knew he was asking for two opposites at once. Maybe they saw what he was thinking and knew he was not a killer. But Roman didn't care anymore.

Roman and the others left almost one day ago. It was a long day and Roman wished it were over.

CHAPTER 11

Mary sat near the fire and thought about what Lane McCree said. He was honest about his opinions of her and her boy living out in wild lands. She could see that he was worried about her. No one had worried about her in a long time. It showed that he cared.

She turned her head back and saw through the opened door that Lane watched her. She walked over to Lane with her arms crossed.

"I guess I never liked thinking about it," she said.

"About what?"

"My husband's death. I couldn't think clearly after he died. It was like I died with him."

"It was like that when my parent's passed away," said Lane.

"Mine too," she said.

Lane looked outside at the darkening snow and the shadows the trees made on the snow. "Can you help me walk? I don't want to be in your way anymore. I feel like I'm ruining all the fun."

Mary smiled a little. She put her arm around him. Lane took two small steps and then held the wall with his right hand. His legs were wobbly. He tried putting a little weight on his wounded leg, but that only made it worse. He felt a sharp pain that shot throughout his body.

"Are you all right?" she asked.

"Fine." He squeezed his eyes shut. "Let me go. I'll try to stand by myself."

She stood ahead of him and watched as Lane moved his wounded leg a little on the creaking floor. He breathed heavily. The pain was there, but he tried to not think about the pain.

"Well, I walked a little."

"That's something," she said, encouraging him.

He moved a little more. Now the blood was flowing better. He could feel his wounded leg. Now he felt good and strong.

"You're doing good," she said. "Maybe try walking to the door and back."

He nodded and tried turning his wounded leg. His wounded leg shuffled on the floor, but he tried to lift it higher. It felt much heavier than the other leg, like it was double the size.

Then Lane moved a foot and then another until he was at the doorframe. His breathing slowed.

Mary said, "Good. You're making fast progress."

"Maybe we could leave today," he said.

Mary looked up at Lane. "Really? You think you could get on a horse?"

"My horse can get low while I get on him." He turned around and tried to walk back to the bed. He made it in a minute or so.

"You're healing faster than I thought," she said. "Does your leg hurt?"

"Like Hell."

"Oh, well, why didn't you say so?"

"I didn't want to worry you," he said. "You're the type to worry."

"How do you know?"

"I can just tell."

She moved her hair away from covering her face. "Could you leave today or not?"

"In an hour," he said. "My leg is throbbing." Lane brushed his long hair back with his hand. He looked outside at the darkening snow.

"How's your aim with that Sharps rifle over there?"

Mary looked back at her late husbands rifle. "Good."

"Good?" He sat on the bed and rested. The pain was strong now that he put pressure on the wounded leg. "Good. We might be followed when we leave soon. I just want to know that you can protect yourself. Now, I don't want to worry you. I just don't want you to miss. It's just like shooting a deer," he lied.

"I'm not stupid," she said. "I know there's more to it than that."

He chuckled. "Yes, I'm sorry. I'm used to attracting women who don't know a coyote from a wolf."

"You should know how I am by now. An hour ago you told me about all my issues, like you already knew all about me."

"I don't know you," he said. "I'd like to though."

She thought about it. She had suitors when she went to Silver City, but she always said she was with someone, even after her late husband's death. "Well," she said. "I think—"

Jesse ran into the room and jumped on the foot of the bed. "Hey, mister, have you seen a yo-yo before?"

"Uh, no," said Lane, peeking at Mary for a quick moment.

She smiled and sat down in the chair.

"I'll show you," said Jesse. "You hold it here and then let the string go down. See? You try."

Lane took the yo-yo and copied Jesse. Then he did the sleeper from over the bed. "I got the hang of it."

"You do it good," said Jesse.

"I had one back home. I can show you some more tricks later."

"We're about to go to the city," said Mary to Jesse.

"Why?"

"I told you," she said. "It's not safe. We might come back another time. But we have to go in an hour. You go on and pack your things. We'll be leaving soon."

Jesse didn't mind leaving the cabin. Staying inside during the heavy winter made him feel almost claustrophobic. He wanted to go, so he went over to his dresser and began packing things into a bag.

Lane and Mary looked outside the bedroom window at the waning sunlight that casted long shadows of trees. It would be dark soon.

Lane waited for Mary's response.

"We can talk about things once we're in Silver City," she said.

He agreed.

In an hour, Lane stood up and wobbled to the bedroom door again. It was slow and steady, but it was better than being bedridden. He wore his gun belt and his Stetson hat. The clothes smelled of sweat.

Mary gave Lane her late husband's coat. It was a coat made of leather. Her husband, James, had made it. It was too cold to be without a coat. It would take two hours or so to get to Silver City.

Lane made the walk to the front door. He looked around the cabin for the first time. It was a small cabin. He saw the fireplace and felt warm near the fire. Then Mary opened the door for him. Jesse walked out, lugging a bag with him.

"We'll be gone for a short while," she said to her son.

"When will we come back?" he asked.

"When it's safe."

Lane walked out, using the side of the cabin for support. He looked up and saw the grey sky and the clouds forming in the west. He looked down the mountain. He knew if he saw an Apache it would be because the Apache wanted to be seen. He looked anyway, trying to see movement in the trees. He couldn't see anything. He felt the cold against his cheeks. The wind blew his beard around and made him wish he were back inside the warm cabin.

"Where's my horse?" asked Lane.

Mary pointed to the west. "In the barn. I'll open it for you and bring it."

"Thank you."

She held a rifle in her hands. It was quiet when she walked in the snow to the barn. The area grew dark, especially in the motionless trees.

She opened up the barn doors and went inside. The horses turned their heads to stare at her. Rusty walked out of his stall of hay.

"I'll be back, Rusty. You stay here. The horses have food and water for the rest of tomorrow. Then we'll return." She led Lane's horse out of the barn and over to Lane.

Lane squinted at the mountains. It was too hard to see from far away, but he looked anyway. He was too careless before, even though he was caught by surprise. He still blamed himself for the massacre at Bear Creek. Now he looked at everything as if it were a foreign land.

"Here he is," said Mary.

"Ma?" said Jesse.

"Thank you, ma'am. Looks like we'll be all right."

"Ma?"

"What, Jesse?"

The boy pointed to the west. "There's a man over there."

Lane quickly turned; his right hand gripped his Colt. He saw an Apache that was three hundred feet away. He stood at the edge of a mountain in the west and stared down at them. Then the Apache turned and disappeared.

"What was that?" said Mary.

"Apaches," said Lane.

"Are you sure?"

"Get inside the cabin," said Lane. "They found me. They followed my tracks and found me. We can't outrun them in this snow. We have better chances inside."

She stood in shock.

"Hurry," yelled Lane.

She woke up from her stupor and led her son inside.

"Where are we going?" said Jesse.

"The Apaches are here," she said. "They followed Lane."

"We aren't leaving?"

"No," she said. "Go to the kitchen and stay

away from the windows. Kneel down here," she said, overturning the wooden kitchen table.

Mary gripped the rifle tight and waited for Lane. The door was still open.

Lane walked inside and closed the door shut. He looked through the front window and then through the window in Mary's bedroom window. Then through the last window in Jesse's room. It was too dark to see anything. The sun had set, and the half-moon partially hidden behind clouds was not bright enough to show anything.

Lane took out his Colt and held it in his right hand. Then he walked to the kitchen and saw the boy behind the table and Mary standing with both hands on the rifle.

"I'm sorry," he said to Mary. "I led them here."

Mary shook her head. "You did what you could. You were caught by surprise. Said so yourself."

"Did you only see one, Jesse?"

"Yes."

"All right. That's not bad. But there was more than one. I saw at least two back at the creek. There could be a dozen of them." He regretted saying that. "I'm sure there aren't."

"No," said Mary. "We'll handle them. I can shoot."

"Good. They'll probably try to sneak around. So I can watch from your bedroom window and see if they come that way. You watch from the front, but don't peak out. Stay hidden. You holler if you see anything, and I mean anything. Even if it's a deer or wolf. We'll make sure they shoot first. But it's obvious they followed my tracks and came a long ways here. I traveled all night without stopping while the storm was right on my tail. They must really want me dead."

"Do you have any enemies?" she asked.

"None that I know of. No Apaches at least. I put men in jail, but I don't call anyone an enemy. I'm cautious of people, but I don't call anyone an enemy."

"Well, I guess these are the bad Apaches, as you called them," said Mary.

"Bad Apaches," he said. "You can call them that. Apaches that kill unarmed travelers. Yes, they're bad all right. I can lean against the wall here. We can still talk to each other."

Mary nodded. She looked frightened, so he put a hand on her shoulder.

"You'll be all right," he said. "You were strong enough to save my life, so you're strong enough to do this."

"I'll be all right." But the words didn't ease her anxiety.

"You think that dog will bark?" he asked.

"If he hears them or smells them."

"Let's hope he does. I'm counting on him to. When he barks, we'll try to watch outside. They might try to smoke us out. If they throw fire, we head to the back windows. They'll expect us to come out front. Then we'll shoot whoever is out there."

"All right."

"Jesse," said Lane. "You stay hidden. My horse is just outside. If they capture or kill us, I want you to take my horse and ride quickly to town."

The boy nodded. "But what about ma?"

"You'd have to go if I get shot," said Mary.

"I'm not leaving you," said the boy.

"You have to," she said, crouching to look him in the eyes and brush some of his long hair back. "If you love me, you'll do this. All right?"

"I will," said Jesse sadly.

"Good. If there's too many of them," said Lane to Mary, "well, you just ride away with your boy. I can shoot as many as I can. I'm fast with the Colt."

"Won't they take our horses away?" asked Mary.

"They might. But we'll figure it out. There might only be one Apache. In that case, there's not much to think about."

Lane stopped talking and listened. There was no sound outside except the wind that blew from the west. The marshal began to sweat and feel another burst of pain in his leg. He tried to keep his mind off the pain. There was no time to think of pain.

Mary turned her attention to the front window. There was nothing but a dark blue on the snow and trees. She was happy it was not pitch black like it was during the last snowstorm.

Mary turned back to Lane. The marshal glanced outside one window and then another. He barely breathed as he listened. He knew he wouldn't be able to hear the Apaches. Even in the snow Apaches were as quiet as a fox hunting mice hidden in tunnels beneath the snow.

Then Rusty the dog barked.

Lane turned back to Mary. "Here they come," whispered Lane to Mary. "Get ready."

Lane turned to the sound. There were no windows on the west and east sides of the house, so they had to wait for them to get closer. Lane didn't like that, but there was no other way.

The marshal walked to a bedroom window and wobbled along the way. He held the revolver in his right hand and looked outside to see a flash of light coming from the west. He couldn't see the barn, but he knew what the fire meant.

"They're burning down the barn," he said to Mary.

"Oh, God," she said. She walked to the front window and peaked out. She covered her mouth with her hand. "The horses and Rusty. Oh no."

"The barn?" said Jesse. "But Rusty is in the barn! And the horses!" Jesse stood up and went to the window.

"Stay in the kitchen," said his mother. "It's too dangerous out there. Rusty probably got out. He's smart enough to."

It was too late. Jesse opened the front door and ran outside.

CHAPTER 12

ROMAN SLEPT WITH HIS HEAD AGAINST A tree trunk, far from the others. Baishan came over and shook Roman awake and the three of them set off down the mountain. Roman was in an almost dream-like state, his eyes barely open and his mind not fully awake and aware of what was about to happen.

They rode down the mountain under the cover of darkness and got off their horses just before reaching the barn. The horses were left in the forest. Then they walked in the snow.

The white man's tracks led to the barn. Baishan walked to the barn and placed his ear against the outer wall. He heard quiet breathing.

Baishan signaled to Marco to go to the right

of the barn. Roman followed neither; he stood and shivered in the snow. Baishan walked to the left of the barn. Marco watched the cabin for movement. He saw the smoke from the chimney and thought someone would come out after seeing his or her barn on fire.

Baishan took out the rest of the oil he had after using most of it on the stagecoach, and then he poured it over the outside walls of the small barn and let the oil drip slowly down the walls.

Roman then saw what was going to happen. The man, maybe asleep in the barn, unable to make it to his cabin, would finally die like the others. He tried to tell Baishan he didn't think it was right, but he knew there was no telling him anything. Baishan would do whatever he wanted to do.

Baishan took out a match and ignited the barn. He walked back, almost crouching as he went. The fire roared immediately and enveloped the walls. The flames jumped to the roof and grew to almost cover the entire barn.

Roman watched and felt his heart beat quickly under his palm. He saw Marco with a rifle, hiding behind a bush. Then he saw Baishan wait on the other side. There were two doors to the barn and each Apache waited for someone to come out. The doors were not yet on fire.

The wait felt like a long time.

No one spoke. No one could hear anything but the crackling fire and the flaming wood. Then the Apaches heard a noise near the cabin.

Baishan turned and aimed his rifle at the sight. A little boy ran in the snow towards the barn, his feet plunging down in the snow with each small step. The boy pushed himself off the snow and kept getting stuck in the deep snow.

"Baishan," yelled Roman.

Baishan lowered the rifle and turned back to Roman. Roman motioned for him to lower the rifle and to not shoot. It was an odd thing to do. No one commanded Baishan, yet he lowered his rifle and let the boy run.

The white man's son, thought Baishan. Like the others, he will try to kill me one day.

The boy seemed to not even see the Apache towering over him like a tree. The boy just kept running to the door and yelled, "Rusty!" He banged his fist against the door.

Then the front door of the cabin opened and Baishan turned to see a woman peeking out. She aimed the rifle at Baishan and shot.

Baishan ducked and hid behind the barn. She hit somewhere in the forest behind Baishan, missing his shoulder by a foot or less.

Then another shot went off, somewhere in the south.

Someone screamed; a scream that sounded like it could come from a man or woman.

The boy was just tall enough to open the barn doors. Rusty barked and whined, his big nose smelling the fire and feeling the heat around him. The horses whinnied.

"I almost got it," said the boy.

The door flung open. Rusty was about to run out, but then the boy noticed the dog was waiting for the boy to let the horses out. The horses banged their long legs against the stalls and tried to break the stall doors open. It was hard to breathe in the barn, as the black smoke filled the inside.

The boy was careful not to get in the horses' ways as he opened each door. The horses galloped out of the burning barn and in to the snow outside.

Another shot went off.

The boy ran outside and was grabbed by the arm.

"No!" yelled someone nearby.

Marco grabbed the boy and held the boy against his chest. It was easy to lift the boy. When Baishan saw the woman with the rifle, he smiled and shook his head.

Roman stood and tried to see the others. They heard the dog barking at Marco.

"Where is the white man?" Baishan asked the woman. He turned his attention to Marco, who held the boy close to his chest, his arm around the boy's belly.

"I don't know what you're saying," she said. "I just want my boy."

Rusty lunged at Marco's leg and bit the man's leg with his sharp teeth. The man yelled out in pain.

Just then another shot went off. Marco fell to the snow.

The boy escaped his grasp and ran to his mother. Baishan hurried to the woman and grabbed a hold of her, letting go of the rifle and putting his arm around her stomach. Then Baishan took out his knife. It was the knife he had killed dozens of white men with, and it was how he got his name. Now he watched as Jesse ran to hide behind Lane.

Lane wobbled out and aimed his Colt at Baishan. There was tremendous pain in Lane's leg, but all he thought about was the knife pressed against Mary's neck.

Rusty lunged for Baishan's leg, but Baishan kicked the dog in the head and the dog was limp on the ground, unconscious.

"I know you," said Lane McCree. "I saw you at Bear Creek! You're the one!"

Baishan turned and saw Marco was dead. His face was down in the snow.

"You must die," said Baishan to the white man. "It is the only way. If there are more, I will kill them too. I will kill every man and woman who enters my home."

Lane pointed the barrel at him and looked around for more Apaches. He saw no one else.

"You let her go. There's no reason to hurt her."

Mary struggled under his grasp. His strong forearms were like metal squeezing her body, suffocating her. She felt the knife against her neck and could feel it already cutting her skin with ease.

"All right." Lane put the gun on the snow, closing his eyes in pain as he did so. "See? Now, shoot me instead." He tried not to look at the rifle near Baishan's feet. It would be a quick move.

Baishan cut open Mary's neck and dropped her limp body to the snow. Then, in one quick movement, he picked up the rifle on the snow. But before he could aim another shot went off.

Lane had his hand on the revolver grip, but he hadn't shot yet. He only aimed at Baishan. He looked in every direction until he found a young Apache walk from behind the burning barn, holding the rifle he just shot. The young Apache held the rifle in one hand and stared at the woman holding her neck and Baishan's face in the snow. He shook his head. Then he saw Lane.

Roman was unafraid of the white man. He carried the rifle in his right hand to let the white man know he wasn't going to shoot.

Lane slowly let his finger slip away from the trigger and put the Colt back in its holster. Then he fell to the snow, his leg failing him. He pushed himself from the snow and then made his way to Mary.

In a quick movement Roman walked back to his horse and rode down the mountain. He chose a different path home. Lane didn't even watch the Apache go, as he was focused on Mary's bleeding neck.

Lane touched Mary's neck and looked behind him at Jesse. "Get my horse and one other one, Jesse. We're going to Silver City."

Jesse did as he was told. The horses were not too far.

Lane tore off a piece of his shirt and tied it around her neck to stop the bleeding. Mary coughed blood and tried to see through the tears.

"Jesse," she whispered.

"He's fine. He's getting the horses. You'll be fine, too. We're getting you to a doctor."

There was tremendous pain when he pushed himself up, using Baishan's rifle as a crutch. His leg still hurt. He lied when he said it felt better. Mary stood up and walked with him to the horses, holding her neck along the way.

"I can ride," she whispered.

"Are you sure?" he said. "You've bled a lot."

"Trust me. My horse is fast. You keep up with me." She told Jesse to get on the horse. Then they rode together. Lane followed them. It was a slow ride in the deep snow. The horses were excited from the fire and the shots, so they ran fast, taking enjoyment in galloping again.

Rusty watched near the cabin as they rode down the mountain. Lane didn't turn back to see the Apaches. But he thought the big Apache that cut Mary was dead. No one should have survived that shot, but then he realized he shouldn't have lived either.

Mary held Jesse tight. She felt her neck that was bleeding more from the rough riding, with the constant bouncing. It was difficult riding and she began to sweat even in the cold. But she knew she could make it. It was an hour or two to the city. She had to make it. She just had to not pass out, and that was getting harder to do the longer she fought sleep.

Lane rode behind Mary and watched her. He made sure she wasn't going to fall. It was a bad idea to let her ride alone. The wound was deep. It looked almost as bad as his leg wound.

How can she act like that when her neck is open? he thought.

They brushed against the snowy tree branches and made their way to a road and then headed east to Silver City. It was the middle of night and the moon illuminated the way. There was no sound but the constant breathing of the horses as they galloped to the city.

They reached the city. The wooden sidewalk and taverns and stores were a good sight to Lane McCree; it was home.

He knew Doctor Newman, the most popular doctor in town. He carried Mary with him and entered the unlocked doctor's office. Jesse ran with him. Mary was unconscious, with her head limp against Lane's shoulder.

Lane cradled her in his arms and set her down on a table as the doctor rubbed his eyes and lit a lamp to see the dying woman. Lane stepped back and watched the white-haired doctor with glasses work. The only real words from the doctor seemed to be "hmm" and "let's see here" and "hold the lantern higher."

Jesse couldn't see above the table his mother was on. He didn't see much, as it was too dark to see her wound back at the cabin.

The wound was sewn shut. Doctor Newman washed his hands in a bowl of water and dried them with a rag. He said, "What happened?"

"Apaches," said Lane. "One cut her open. They're all dead."

Newman shook his head and placed the rag on a table. "Savages. I thought they were stuck in reservations, but I guess you can't tame animals."

"Some are all right. It's the ones that cut Mary open I'm cautious about."

"Sure," said Newman. "But it's a big jump to go from teepees to cities. They can't seem to handle themselves."

"How's Mary?"

"Fine. She'll wake up. She didn't lose too much blood. You mind telling me how Apaches ended up around here? The Gila Reservation is pretty far from here."

"I was attacked at Bear Creek. I was protecting a stagecoach when Apaches attacked us. I got shot in my leg. I must have been knocked out, because I fell off my horse and woke up in the snow. Then I saw the stagecoach on fire. I fled and found Mary's cabin."

"Savages," said the doctor, shaking his head. "Want me to take a look at that leg?"

"If you don't mind."

"I'm already awake. Might as well."

Doctor Newman gave Lane crutches and medicine.

CHAPTER 13

MARY WOKE UP TO THE SOUND OF CHIRPING birds outside the doctor's office. She looked up and saw the glow of the lamp in the room.

Horses pulled stagecoaches filled with people, and wagons carried supplies on the dirt road that was muddied by the melting snow. Gun shops, clothing stores, inns and barbershops lined each side of the road. A wooden boardwalk was on each side. It was much warmer than the previous day, and the sky was cloudless.

Lane sat in a chair, asleep. His chin was dropped low to his upper chest. His crutches were against the wall.

Mary felt her sewn neck. She then got up, feeling fully rested, and looked outside an open door at the street busied with people. It was so bright outside that she thought it must have been midday. The sun shined bright and the snow was melting off the verandas and rooftops. Pools of water were along the road and the big wheels of wagons splashed the water as they went.

"Mary," said Lane. He opened his eyes wide. "Did you just get up?"

"Yes," she said. She felt her neck again. The wound didn't cut too deep for it to change her voice. She was glad for that and glad to be alive. "Where's Jesse?"

"Over there."

Jesse was asleep on a bed in the corner of the room. Mary walked over and ran her fingers through his ash-colored hair. Then the boy woke up and smiled.

"Hi," said Jesse.

"Are you hurt?" she asked.

"No, just tired."

"We'll be sleeping safely from now on."

"Where's Rusty?" said the boy.

Lane walked over to the boy and peaked at the stitches on Mary's neck. "He's back at the cabin," said Lane to the boy. "But I can go get him for you."

"You don't have to do that, Lane," said Mary. She smiled a little and looked down at her boots. "We can go back there together."

"I'd like that," he said.

"Are those Apaches dead?" she asked.

"I think so. I don't think more will come to the cabin. Still, I think you should—"

"I know, I know," said Mary. "It's just hard to do. I don't know where to go."

"Tell you what. I'll help you sell your home and move somewhere. Name a town and I'll escort you there. It's the least I can do. You saved my life. I want to return the favor, and—" He stopped and looked away.

"And what?"

"I like you Mary. I really like you. I want to get to know you more. That might take months or years, but I'd like to know you."

Mary brushed Jesse's hair and sat on the bed. "I feel the same way about you. You're a good man. I could see that when I first saw you in that barn." She looked out the front door and saw the melting snow on the verandas. "I don't know if I want to live here. But I don't know where to go either."

Lane said, "El Paso is a good town. It's not too far. We can put the cabin up for sale, load up a wagon and head out there tomorrow."

"You have a job here. What will you do?"

"I know a man there, a Texas Ranger that might have something. That's why I mentioned it. El Paso is growing fast. It needs people. I won't intrude on you either. I'll find a place for myself and see how things go." He sighed, took off his Stetson hat and brushed his hair back with his fingers. "I've been wanting to leave here for a while. I always wanted to go back to Texas."

"Well," she said. "I guess it's that time. I've been in that cabin for too long. I've wanted to be near people and move on. I guess this is a sign. So, yes, I'll go to El Paso."

She grabbed Lane's hand, which caught him off guard. He hadn't felt a woman's hand in a long time; it was an odd sensation.

They left the city after Lane told the law what happened near Bear Creek. He was then asked to tell a soldier what happened. The soldier would relay the news to Fort West, as it was closer and usually dealt with issues around the Gila Apache Reservation.

Later that day Mary put the cabin up for sale. No one seemed interested in the cabin, but she thought someone might buy it in the next year or so.

Lane trimmed his beard since it looked like Spanish moss. He looked younger and more handsome after bathing. Didn't smell like a dead animal either. He ate big meals that built his strength back to what it was before he was wounded at the creek.

Then they left for the cabin and, once there, packed their belongings. Mary and Jesse didn't own many things, which made moving easy. It was sad to see the cabin one last time. They wouldn't miss the seclusion though. They looked forward to a new city, where they hoped for a better and safer life.

The next day the horses and wagon were ready. Their belongings were tied down and secure. Lane had crutches to help him walk, and they were put in the back of the wagon.

The dog, Rusty, was alive and well. He had some scratches and a bruise on him, but that was all. And the bodies of the Apaches would be dealt with later that day by the sheriff and deputy of Silver City. The Apache horses were taken by the sheriff and his deputy as well. They found the wallets of the people killed in the stagecoach, which the sheriff said was "mighty convenient." Then they knew the whole story—that the man and woman were newly married and the stagecoach driver was a man from Mexico who helped travelers go from town to town.

After everything was settled, Mary decided it was finally time to leave the cabin behind and go to El Paso, Texas. It was a bit sad to say goodbye to the cabin, but she thought it was time to move on.

Lane rode his horse and Mary and Jesse rode on the seat of the wagon that was pulled by her two horses, one that was hers and one that was her late husbands, carrying their belongings in the back. It would be a bumpy and long ride. Before Mary went away, she visited her late husband's gravesite with Jesse. Jesse waved goodbye and Mary touched the top of the cold tombstone one last time.

Lane stood by his horse and waited for Jesse and Mary. When they got back, Jesse held up the silver badge Lane had given him. "This is yours," said the boy.

The marshal held it up and watched it shine under the bright sun. "I'll be needing this, huh?" Lane lifted the boy onto the wagon seat. Then Rusty the dog jumped onto the wagon seat.

Mary drove the wagon and looked back at the cabin as the snowy trees veiled her sight of her home. She turned and saw Lane looking forward at the trail they made when he had rode with her to Silver City in the night.

Lane still had pain in his leg, but it was minor; it came and went. He kept his mind off it. He looked forward to his new life. Maybe he could be with Mary; it was worth a shot. He knew he only had a limited time on earth, so he wanted to make the most of it.

COURAGE STANDS ALONE

CHAPTER 1

1899, SAN ANTONIO, TEXAS

JIM PETERSON FED HIS FIVE CATS SCRAPS OF meat as they rubbed their bodies against his jeans and left traces of their fur on the old man's pants.

Their tails swished in the hot Texas air as Peterson stood up and walked away from the shed. He walked towards his two-bedroom wooden house overlooking five hundred acres of land. Most of his land was untilled, as he didn't have the money to hire farmhands or the strength to do the work himself. In his old age, he did what he could.

Peterson owned two pigs, a house, a shed and not much else. He used to own a horse, but he sold it for money; he hadn't used a horse in recent years.

Peterson stopped below an oak tree and looked to the red sun rising above the earth and the clouds stained the same color.

The air was warm and windless. Big clouds covered the sky and moved from the Rocky Mountains in the west and left shadows over the crops and the green hills in the west.

There was not much to do. Jim Peterson sat in a rocking chair and waited. He didn't know what he waited for besides the crops growing— maybe to die and live with his wife that passed away a few years prior. It wasn't a bad thought to him. Death was accepted and immediate, and living took all his energy. He smiled at the thought, as he was prepared for whatever might come. He was ready. In his mind, his wife was waiting for him. All he worried about was who would feed his cats after he died.

Peterson watched the cats as they cleaned their fur and licked their paws on his front porch. One black cat with big yellow eyes and a long tail jumped onto his lap and he petted it with his wrinkled and calloused hands. The other cats came and went through his cornfield. He didn't mind when they went away. Stray cats were cautious cats, so Peterson didn't worry too much about them.

Peterson scratched his trimmed white beard as the black cat slept on his lap. Peterson's brown pants were clean except for the cat hairs on them. His boots and grey short-sleeved shirt were old.

He felt he didn't need much anymore to keep him happy.

Jim Peterson didn't care for lavish saddles or a new rifle. When he was young and in the army he liked new rifles but not anymore. He found he felt better when he owned few possessions. He knew the happiness he got from owning a new possession would be temporary until he bought some other shiny thing. His happiness came from small things, such as watching the sunrise over the hills or watching the cats play on his front porch.

The black cat nudged its nose against the old man's freckled hands. Peterson looked up and saw a man on horseback. The man rode slowly on the dirt road. Peterson squinted and the wrinkles around his eyes and leathery skin bunched together.

A visitor was rare.

The rider slowed, dismounted and walked up to the porch. Peterson sat in the rocking chair and slowed the chair to a halt. Peterson squinted. "Can I help you?"

"What, don't you recognize me?" said

Simon. "All those years, and you don't even recognize me?"

"I knew it was you," he sighed. He refused to explain, which caused Simon to watch the old man and try to read his face.

Simon spat on the dirt and put his boot on the wooden porch. He looked around and pushed the brim of his worn hat up to see the old man. Simon was half the age of Mr. Peterson, yet Simon looked much older. He looked older with his long and unkempt hair flowing down to his shoulders and with the sun damage on his face.

"Jim, I don't feel good around here," said Simon.

Jim Peterson nodded and petted the black cat. "How come?"

"It just looks like you're like some man who comes upon some wealth and now thinks he's better than everyone."

"I'm the same as everyone. I don't have wealth," said Peterson. "We're all the same in the eyes of the Lord."

Simon snickered and wiped his nose. "That right?"

Jim Peterson stared at Simon. "I changed." The word's came from a deep and stern voice.

"It looks it." Simon took his boot off the porch. Peterson watched as Simon looked at the field of corn about to be harvested and the pigsty and the land beyond that was mostly an open plain with oak and cedar and prickly pear cactus. Then Simon wiped the sweat off his forehead, as the sweat stung his eyes and stained the long-sleeved shirt that was partially dusted with dirt. "You got good land."

"Been working the land for twenty years."

"All that time?" asked Simon. "Thought I'd see you in some saloon somewheres."

"I don't drink anymore."

"No?"

"I'm not like that anymore," said Peterson. "I moved on. It wasn't good for me. Nothing good came from it. I live in peace now."

Simon squinted at Peterson, as if he said something strange. "I didn't think I'd see that day. Old Bull stopped having fun."

Simon shook his head.

"Those days weren't fun."

"If you ain't sinning, you ain't having fun. Now, I wanted to chat with you awhile, but it sounds like you're too tight for talk. A drink would help—"

"You're not welcome here," interrupted Peterson. His voice grew loud, but still remained calm.

Simon's mouth dropped open and then his boot left the porch and landed on the dirt. His right hand hovered near his Colt, but gradually he hooked his thumb into the jeans and looked casually to the sky. "I don't want to argue."

"Me neither," admitted Jim Peterson. The old man grew calmer and now his mind focused on being kind. He tried to get his mind off the past, as it was done and those days were gone. He only felt tempted, but he realized he'd never go back to his old ways. "Want some water or tea?"

Simon smiled wide and showed his brown teeth. "That would be kind of you, Bull. Water."

"Call me Jim," said Peterson. He got out of the rocking chair, but in his age it took a lot of effort. He used a wooden cane to walk around. "I forgot how I even got that name: Bull."

"I'll give you a hint. A bull is the most dangerous animal on a ranch. You get near it, it can easily kill you. Most cowboy deaths are from bulls."

"Fighting," said Peterson. "You could have just said fighting."

The old man went inside and came back with a glass of water. The water was stored in a container inside the house after Peterson had fetched water from his well earlier that day.

Simon drank all of the water. Some of it

dripped down his handlebar mustache and on to his sweat-stained shirt.

"Thirsty, huh?" said Peterson.

"It was a long ride."

"From where?" The old man stood and watched the horse.

Simon's saddle was pitiful. You can judge a man fairly just by the condition of his saddle.

"Oh, just out east. I was in San Antonio. Doing jobs here and there. Same as always. Nothing much to report."

"Report," said Peterson. "Now that's a word from the past."

"Private Simon Steiner, reporting for duty, sir," he said and saluted sloppily.

"First Sergeant Jim Peterson. At ease." The old man felt good from the salute, yet he still felt odd and wondered why Simon, of all people he had led, was visiting him after all these years. "Good times."

"It was all right for a while," said Simon, almost sighing.

"All right? You seemed happy. We were on the frontier. We helped protect that one family from Apaches. Remember?"

"Yes, yes. We saved them."

"We did good work," said Peterson. He tried to remember what else. "And, of course, that was when we drank too much." He admitted this, and then he tried to remember what else. It was something terrible Simon did. It was so long ago...

Simon said, "That's when I started living. I got all sorts of ideas in the army. That's before I moved down here to San Antonio."

That surprised Peterson. It was a big town though. It would be difficult to run into someone you knew. "It's a good place to live. The town is growing fast."

"It's good and all, but—"

Jim Peterson frowned, knowing the time had come to hear why Simon stood near his home. Of all people, Peterson didn't want Simon to be standing there. The old man could always tell when someone wasn't right in the head, and he always knew that there was something wrong with Simon, something sinister. Even right after meeting Simon in the military, he knew something was off. But he could never get to the bottom of it. All he knew was that drinking brought out that evil. Simon always used to beckon Peterson to drink with him, and, somehow, Simon would get Peterson into drunken fights.

Everything went blank after that. Jim Peterson said, "But what?"

Simon nodded at the land. "I'm looking to get a little land around here. I got big plans."

Jim Peterson squinted at the horse and then at Simon's dirty clothes. It was the same Simon; Peterson knew that. He just tried not to judge him at first, as he thought God wouldn't want him to judge others. He thought he had to at the moment, especially when the issue concerned what he owned and what he thought was important to him. "That's all you got, Simon: big plans and no action. A man takes action. Haven't I always—"

"Yes," interrupted Simon. "Yes, you've always said that. A man does this. A man does that. Can't you see I'm taking action now?"

"You aren't the type to take action. You said you were going to find gold out west. What came of that?"

Simon sighed. "I tried, didn't I?"

"I don't believe so. A man doesn't give up. He keeps digging. He might give up when he's a few feet from striking gold, which is what most do. How long were you out in Colorado?"

"It doesn't matter," said Simon. He tried to build up Peterson and get the old man to follow his idea. "What's more honest than gold or anything else? Farming. You hire some men to do the farming and you got yourself the good life. Sit back, relax and watch them work. Don't get bossed around or nothing. Be your own man. Like yourself."

"First you need money to hire the men."

"Well, I thought you'd help."

"I don't have much to offer," said Peterson. "I can't even afford workers. I do all the work myself. Borrowing things here and there, but I do the work."

"You got five hundred acres of perfect land for farming. You, what, only use a few acres for yourself?"

"I'm not selling. This land is my daughter's." He meant he gave the land to her in his will, and his daughter hadn't seen the will yet.

"Why doesn't she use it?"

"That's her business, not mine." The black cat jumped off the old man's pants and walked to the yellow corn field. The green stalks lined up perfectly and rose almost as high as a man's head. The old man stood up from his chair and looked Simon in the eye. "So you've just come for my land, huh?"

"I can put it to good use," said Simon. He looked up at the sky and thought of what he'd do with all that land. He could live a wealthy man and become respectable. He could drink all the whisky and rum and go to the brothel every day. He could smoke the best cigars and live every day as if it were his last. All these thoughts went through his head and made him smirk. A man can do so much with good, fertile land. With San Antonio growing, Simon thought it would be worth more as the years went by. He wondered why the old man didn't just sell most of the land.

"You got dust-covered clothes," said Jim Peterson, interrupting Simon's daydream. "You look like you just came out of a brothel and—"

Simon stopped smiling. "That was four days ago. I'm respectable now."

"Four days," repeated Peterson.

"You don't believe I could handle a little land."

"You wouldn't be able to handle growing an apple tree."

Simon pointed to his chest with his thumb. "I can do it. I'm respectable."

"As respectable as one of my pigs," said the old man, gesturing over to the pigsty and the dirt on the legs of the pigs.

Simon stared down at his pants and the dirt on them. Then Simon breathed heavily and pointed a thin finger at his former First Sergeant. "You watch your mouth. You can't tell me what to do anymore."

"You're asking for some land. I have the right to deny you that land." The old man shrugged. It was like talking to a child, but Peterson was still careful. He tried to remember Simon's past and his tendency for violence. "I'll tell you what I tell to them traveling salesmen selling me that snake oil. Get."

Simon raised his voice and when he did so, Mr. Peterson could smell the traces of whisky and cigars. "This land isn't even used. I got some men that'll work on it and make it blooming like flowers in spring. But I guess you don't want that, old man."

Peterson breathed slowly and raised his chest and neck. "I may be an old man, but old man isn't my name."

Simon lowered his hat after staring into Peterson's eyes. It was the same gaze he saw back when Peterson was middle-aged and hardened by war with the Indians in Kansas and Colorado. It was a threatening gaze that showed he was unafraid.

Simon lowered his hands that were hooked to his pants. His right hand gripped the revolver in the holster near his hip. Then, while the old man looked on, he gripped and aimed the revolver near his waist. The barrel, and the darkness within the barrel, was all Peterson saw.

"How about this, huh?" said Simon. "How about I just take it? We done it plenty of times.

In the army, we took food, rifles, hides—you name it."

"Those were Apaches that killed travelers. They killed entire families."

Simon watched Peterson's eyes. They were motionless, unblinking, as they looked at Simon. Simon looked away and then cocked the revolver.

"You pull that trigger you'll be a dead man. My daughter knows my past and all about you. She'll know it'll be you." Now Peterson remembered what Simon did.

"What? What does she know about me?"

"She knows about you and that Apache girl you—"

"Don't say that! Don't you say that again!" Simon lowered the gun and walked back and forth, like a caged animal does when nervous. "You're lucky, old man. You'll die within a few years. I can wait. I can wait all my life."

"You'll never get a piece of this land, Simon. You can't even replant a flower or harvest a field."

"You ain't doing nothing with it!"

"More than anything you could do with it. You best crawl back into the nearest saloon or brothel. I don't want you back here."

Simon holstered the revolver and hesitated

before mounting his horse. The horse galloped away and left a fine layer of dust in the air.

Jim Peterson sighed and held his right hand to his heart. He felt the heavy thumping until it slowed. He collapsed onto the porch and, after a few minutes, reached for the glass of water. A cold sweat ran down Peter's cheeks until the white beard absorbed it. He used his cane to sit back down in his rocking chair.

It had been about two decades since he first saw Simon. He thought of what he said: about the Apache girl. That was an awful mess. After Peterson reported what he saw, Simon was kicked out of the military for that. Then put in jail. What a mess. Jim Peterson left the military soon after; not just because of Simon but also for all he saw. Those images never left him. That was back in 1866. The old man didn't think he would live this long. He didn't think he would be alive to see 1899, when the west was almost tamed. People called the United States tame, but Peterson never thought of any country as tame.

The black cat with the big eyes came around the corner of the house and rubbed its head against Peterson's pant leg. The old man was calm and even smiled a little, which was odd since Peterson rarely smiled. He glanced at the cat and said, "Now we got a problem."

CHAPTER 2

HE APPEARED LIKE A MIRAGE. THE silhouette of Cord Cordeu on his horse emerged atop a large hill just west of San Antonio. A dark valley was behind him, and just ahead the morning sun brightened the green hills and woodlands and the open fields dotted with prickly pear cactus.

Cord took off his flat-brimmed Stetson hat and combed his short hair to the side. Then he wiped the sweat above his lip; it was an odd thing to do; Cord was not used to a shaved face. He only shaved before finding work in a new town.

He got off his horse and stood on the hill. He saw various farms, ranches with wooden fences and corrals. The dirt roads were busied with people on horseback and in stagecoaches.

There was a river that looked green from that distance, and along the river were tall cypress trees that casted shadows on the slow-moving water.

San Antonio was a big town. It was not bunched together like most towns. It stretched for miles. Farms and ranches spread across the town, making it seem like there was life behind every little hill and oak tree.

Cord looked behind him, but all he saw were oak and cedar trees on the dark hills. Then he looked down from the high hill and saw the wood and brick buildings and the intermingled strings of electric lights fading as the sun brightened the land in the east.

There were so many people. The last time Cord saw that many people was when he lived in New Orleans for a short while. With that many people there had to be work. Cord worked on the Northern Pacific Railway up in Washington, on a crabbing boat in Louisiana and recently as a cowboy and farmer in New Mexico and West Texas. He felt his experience was enough.

Cord stood motionless, then turned to his horse and spoke to it. "Well, Lightning. We better get down there. Food is low, water is low. I know you're hungry." The horse eyed the man after Cord rubbed its long neck. "Maybe it's just me. I'm the hungry one here."

Cord stopped then. Talking to his horse was a sign that he had been alone for too long. And when he wasn't busy he thought of his past. That's when he thought of his wife...

Cord mounted his horse and started riding down the hill. He brushed off the dirt from his button down shirt and grey pants. The boots were black and worn. Same for the Stetson hat. He wore a bandana around his neck, a reminder of his cowboy days, which helped prevent dust from getting into his lungs. The saddle scabbard held his Winchester rifle, which he glanced at to see its condition. He would often use the rifle to kill animals to eat.

Then he took notice of his lean forearms that were visible from his rolled up shirtsleeves. The hunger showed in his gaunt cheeks and lean body. Hunger showed all over his body, but it also kept him going. A hungry man was a focused man.

He thought he'd get lucky; as a migrant worker, he always got a job, whether it was picking fruit or planting corn.

He rode along a road that had deep ruts from the big wheels of carriages and stagecoaches. When he made it to a farm, he saw a middle-aged man walking along the edge of his cornfield. Cord waved to the man to get him to stop.

"Howdy," said the farmer.

"Howdy. I'm looking for a job. Know anyone around here who needs help?"

The farmer took off his hat and pointed north with it. "Follow this road and look for a house near the creek, just as the road bends right. The Gibson's own that land. They're looking for someone to work the fields."

Cord nodded and glanced up the road.

"Of course, there's work further in town."

"That's all right. I'm more comfortable farming than anything else. Thank you."

Cord made his way over to the farm. It was a peaceful ride.

Bluebirds and cardinals sang in the trees and flew overhead. When Cord turned his head he saw in the forest a sleeping deer. Then a squirrel crossed the road and climbed a tree.

The heat caused beads of sweat to drop down Cord's nose. He could smell the stench of horse in the humid air. Cord wondered if the bad smell came from him as well. Probably so, he thought.

Then he saw the Gibson's house and the green stalks of corn behind the house. Cord got off his horse and knocked twice on the door. As he waited, he heard the grasshoppers in the fields.

A woman opened the door. "Can I help you?"

Cord took off his hat and held it in his hands. "Is this the Gibson's place?"

"Sure is. What can I do for you?"

"I'm looking for work. Heard you was searching for a field hand or something like it."

The woman relaxed her shoulders and nodded. She held out her hand. "I'm Sarah Gibson."

"Nice to meet you. I'm Cord." He shook her hand and looked past her at the wooden flooring and the half eaten apple sitting on the dinner table. He licked his lips at the sight.

"Cord, you said?"

"Yes, ma'am."

"Lenny, my husband, needs someone to help him work the fields. Know anything about corn?"

"Yes, ma'am. I was a farmer for a while."

"Where you from?"

"I just came from New Mexico. I was a farmer, then a cowboy there."

She smiled and showed her white teeth. Sarah sounded excited and happy over just talking, and Cord assumed it was her normal personality. "Sounds like you're a good fit. I'll show you to Lenny," said Mrs. Gibson.

The two walked around the house and then to the field. Lenny Gibson was in the field when they walked up to him.

"Len? Found someone who's interested in the job," she said. Her voice was unusually high pitched and she was in her twenties in age. Lenny Gibson was bald and wore a flat-brimmed tan hat and blue overalls. Lenny was about the same age, and had a chipper attitude similar to his wife.

"Howdy," said Lenny Gibson, dropping a shovel and his glove to shake the hand of Cord. "Strong grip there." Then Lenny looked down at the hand and quickly judged Cord. He looked at Cord's lean body and the shaved face and the traces of dirt that Cord missed when cleaning his clothes the day prior. He saw the marks on Cord's face from the recent shave and the gaunt cheeks from long days with barely enough food. "You know a little about farming?"

"A little," admitted Cord. "I know about cotton and corn."

"Good, good," said Lenny.

Mrs. Gibson walked back to the house, humming when she was away from the men.

"I'll have to admit. I haven't had good help in a while. Had some men here a few months ago that were always drunk on the job or failed to turn up. Well, one day they just disappeared."

Cord put on his hat. "You don't have to worry about me, Mr. Gibson."

Lenny squinted and saw the hot sun behind Cord's hat. "You look capable. Are you hungry? We can eat and then I'll show you what to do. When was the last time you were on a farm?"

"Maybe six months ago," said Cord.

"I'll just refresh your memory then. It's hard work, but the pay is fair."

"I don't mind work, Mr. Gibson. I just need a little money until I move on."

"Move on? What do you mean?"

"I like to go from place to place, finding jobs and earning enough until I find another town. It's been that way for years."

"Years? Awful way to live, if you don't mind me saying." The two men began walking back to the little house.

"It suits me."

"Don't want a place of your own?"

"No."

Lenny Gibson turned to face Cord, but Cord's eyes were on the dry soil below. "I won't pester you about it," said Mr. Gibson. "It's just —most migrant workers are, you know, just starting out or had a run of bad luck or—"

"I'd rather we talk about something else," interrupted Cord. "Mr. Gibson."

Lenny locked eyes with him. He could see that Cord had something on his mind but refused to tell. Maybe he would know some other time or never know. It wasn't important. All Mister Gibson wanted was an honest and hard worker. "It's my fault," smiled Gibson. "It's none of my business. I just like to know a little about the men who work for me."

"I can tell you about myself, but I don't think I have to explain my life and the actions I take. If the actions were wrong, I would."

"I can agree on that," said Lenny Gibson, opening the back door of the house and walking inside.

The men could smell food in the air. It was dark inside the house and a white cat was the brightest thing in the room. Then their eyes adjusted and saw it was not dark at all.

"Smells good," said Lenny.

"Mmhmm," said Sarah. "You always say so." Then Sarah turned to Cord. "Sit down, if you want. You look hungry."

Lenny Gibson watched Cord to see if what

his wife said would offend Cord, but he didn't seem to mind. It was a fact, and Cord knew it was easy to see he was hungry. Hunger showed all over his body, even in the eyes and the way he licked his lips when he saw the yellow ears of corn in the fields.

Once the food was ready, the three of them ate. Cord ate slowly. Food lasted longer the slower who ate; that was something Cord learned over the years.

They could tell he hadn't eaten a big meal in a long time. It was such a big meal that Cord closed his eyes after eating and almost fell asleep.

"Where you from?" asked Sarah.

Cord shook himself awake. "All over. I just came from New Mexico."

"It must be pretty there, with the mountains and all."

"Yes."

It was quiet. Lenny grabbed their plates and put them in the kitchen. "It's time to get out there," he said. "Come on, Cord. I'll show you what needs to be done."

Cord followed Lenny outside as they walked to the field. Lenny showed Cord how the corn was shelled using the corn grinder. Then he was left alone.

Cord led a horse drawn wagon around and tossed the ears of corn into it. The work was difficult and it took a lot of time. He worked until the sun was just above the hills in the west, then Lenny came over and looked at all the corn in the wagon.

"Good work," said Lenny. "You're much more capable than all the previous men. You hungry?"

Cord smiled a little. "Sure am, Mr. Gibson."

"So am I. Let's go eat. I'll tell you about the town. You got a place to live?" They began to walk back to the house under the fading light. Lenny guided the horse that pulled the wagon.

"Not yet."

"Oh," said Lenny. Then there was silence. "I don't have room in my house. I hate to not have at least a little room for you. There's a hotel in town, but it's very far."

"That's all right," said Cord. "I've slept on my bedroll for a while now. I can save up."

"Well, that must be hard to do. Reminds me of my pa that fought in the war. He would have to do things like that."

Cord nodded. "You get used to it. After sleeping on the ground for a while, a bed like the one you sleep on gets uncomfortable."

"That's awfully peculiar."

"Sure is. Once you're away from people for a while, normal things seem strange." Cord stood outside and wiped the sweat from his forehead and combed his hair to the side. The day was long and his muscles were sore from the work, but it made him proud of doing something honest.

"Here's your pay for the day," said Lenny, handing him the paper money and some coins. "Now, that's a half day's pay. You come back in the morning and it'll be even better. By morning, I mean right when the sun comes up."

Cord said, "Thank you," and put the money in his pant pocket. The sun was just a sliver above the west hills. The two men watched it as it painted the clouds. "I better get going."

"Don't you want to stay for dinner?" asked Lenny.

"That last meal was enough for the entire day."

"You got me there. I forget. I eat so much, but it just disappears. Working all day does that I suppose." Lenny pointed to the woodlands. "Watch out for coyotes," he said, and he hated saying it. He heard coyotes yipping and howling last night, and he didn't want to scare the man, only make him a little cautious. Coyotes were skittish around people, but it was good to know what wildlife lurked at night.

Cord waved and headed to his horse that Sarah had fed and given water and brushed. After his horse was brushed, it looked like a brand new horse. With money in his pocket and a clean horse, all he wanted was a better appearance. He wasn't sure what he looked like. Maybe, he thought, I look like an animal. Maybe that's why they seemed a bit cautious.

Cord walked into the dark woodlands. He could hear the nighttime crickets and hear an owl somewhere above his head. He hitched his horse to a big oak tree and spread out his bedroll on the grass after clearing away rocks.

He rested on his bedroll and looked to the sky. It was peaceful. The stars slowly came into view. An armadillo scurried out at the edge of an opening in the forest.

He was alone again, but that was by choice. It felt comfortable being alone, especially under the stars with only the natural sounds of earth in the background. The sounds and daily work kept his mind off the past. That was good.

I'm getting lucky again, thought Cord. Hopefully it lasts.

But he knew luck didn't last long. It was more of hope that kept him going, not luck.

Cord took out his Winchester rifle and

placed it under a long blanket. It was an old habit. The past lingered in his mind at times when he was not busy at a job or doing some sort of activity. When vivid memories of his deceased wife appeared, he closed his eyes and tried to dream.

CHAPTER 3

Jim Peterson walked a few miles to the Gibson's farm the next day. Bad things were on Peterson's mind, even though all around him were invitations to enjoy the day.

Birds sang in the oak trees and deer ran in wide-open fields covered in yellow and orange flowers. The sky in Texas, always so blue and expansive, was bright, almost blinding.

Peterson was cautious since Simon threatened his life. If it weren't for Peterson telling Simon that his daughter Sarah Gibson knew about Simon and his past, he would have been shot and killed. That's what Peterson thought.

That's why Peterson walked three miles to the Gibson's place—to tell his daughter and his son in law about what happened. Then he thought he'd tell the police and see what they would do. The law in San Antonio were diligent, but Simon was not one to obey the law and not someone you would find in the same place twice. He might escape them, which would resolve the issue for Peterson at least.

When he got there, Peterson felt his heart beat rapidly. He sat in a chair on the Gibson's front porch and waited for his heart to slow. The heat only made his heart worse. It was not a good kind of heat but a scorching and desert-like heat. The old man wiped sweat from his face using a white handkerchief, and then he rested. He was almost asleep when the front door opened.

"Pa?" said Sarah.

"Hmm?" He woke up and turned. "Sarah. I was just resting." He tried to get up, even using his hands to push his body up from the chair arms, but he couldn't.

"You stay there, Pa. I'll go get you some water."

Peterson waited and when she came out she handed him the water. He drank it all and wiped his beard. "Thanks. I'm just tired from that walk."

"You shouldn't have sold your horse. You make it too hard on yourself." She saw him slow his breathing and wipe sweat from his forehead. "You know, we can always lend you a hand."

"No, I don't need charity. I do fine. You give me plenty already."

"Well, all right. Why'd you walk all the way here?"

"To see how you and Lenny are and check on things."

Sarah wiped her hands on her long dress. "The farm is going well. We got a new farmhand."

"A Mexican?"

"No. He's white. Well, I guess he could be from Mexico. His skin is very dark. He was a cowboy after all. Said he was a farmer back in New Mexico. And a lot of other things."

"A migrant worker?"

"Sounds like it."

"I don't understand them," said Jim Peterson. "Why don't they settle down? There's plenty of work around here that lasts longer than a season. Work that can last a lifetime. There's farming, stores, lawyers, everything."

"Well, it looks like he's the type that doesn't stay in one place for long."

"I'd be careful about people like him."

"Why?"

"They're trying to get away from something," he said. "Could be trouble."

Sarah giggled. "Pa, it isn't like the old days. There's not as many train robbers and bank robbers as it was in your time. Or Indian wars and skirmishes. That's all in the past."

"It still happens," he said, staring at her bright eyes.

"Yes, but this man. Cord. He's a quiet man, but he's polite and works hard. I can't see him doing anything bad. You know, it's kind of like that feeling you get when you're around someone good. That's what I get around him."

Then Sarah stood up from her chair, as she heard talking behind the house. She saw Lenny and Cord walk to the house.

"Here they are," she said.

Peterson got out of the chair and walked to his daughter. He waved to Lenny, his son in law, and Lenny raised a hand and smiled with his crooked teeth.

Lenny shook Jim's hand. "Didn't expect you," said Lenny. "Thought I'd check in."

"All right," he said, then turned to Cord.

Jim Peterson couldn't see Cord beneath the Stetson hat, as his face was casted in shadow. It was a shadowy face that hid a lot. Peterson squinted and saw part of the face as Cord looked up at him. He held his hand out and

Cord took it. Then the old man saw his face and tried to see why Cord would choose to work the fields. Cord reminded Peterson of soldiers in the army that didn't need to be told what to do. "Jim Peterson," said Peterson.

"Cord."

"Just Cord?"

"Cord Cordeu," he said.

Peterson wondered if that name was made up. "Sarah said you came from New Mexico."

"That's right. I worked as a cowboy and farmer over there."

"That so?"

Sarah watched her father's strange expression. "Then I rode here for work," said Cord.

"Glad he did," said Lenny, taking off the straw hat and wiping sweat from his brow. "I needed the help. Cord here is the best worker I've had."

Jim Peterson nodded but didn't smile. He rarely smiled. Not because he wasn't happy. He always had a stern face with frozen lips, the way a man looks after seeing what he saw in war.

"Is something wrong, Pa?" asked Sarah. "You don't look well."

"Is it your heart again?" said Lenny.

"No, nothing like that." Peterson looked

away, and through the corner of his eye he saw Cord take off his hat and brush the hair to the side. Then Peterson began to smile a little.

Sarah saw the smile and said, "Are you all right?"

"It's Simon. That's the problem. He came to my home yesterday."

"Why?" said Sarah.

"Wanted a piece of my land. That's what he said. I said no and then he pulled out his Colt." The old man sighed. "He was always a problem. I'm sure after I sent him to prison for doing what he did to that Indian girl he committed even more crimes. Probably went in and out of prison for years. Now he's much older and crazier."

Sarah exchanged glances with her husband. She covered her mouth with her hand. A man threatening Peterson's life was one dangerous fool.

"How'd you scare him off?" said Lenny.

"Said Sarah knew about him and that people would know who the murderer would be. He got fidgety and left. He was always a coward."

"But why's he in the city?" asked Sarah. "Why'd he come all the way down here?"

"Work, I suppose. That's what he wanted my land for. Said he'd hire people and have them work the fields for him," said Peterson, shaking his head. "I told him I'm not selling."

"What did he do to this Indian woman?" asked Cord.

Peterson wished Simon hadn't appeared yesterday. Now bad memories came up. "He raped her." Then Peterson watched the reactions. It was quiet. Sarah and Lenny knew, but it was still hard to hear something like that. No one wants to know about terrible things that happen to people, but when you see something like that you don't forget it. People have a morbid fascination with violence. They hate to know about all the violence in the world but they like to know when it's close to them.

"Then I got him thrown in prison," said Peterson. "It was a long time ago, but now it seems just like yesterday. The memories came up as I spoke to Simon. That's why I wanted Simon to go away. The problem isn't really him. It's why he came to my home and how he found me."

"Well," said Lenny. "You said he wanted some of your land."

"Yes, but why my land. There's plenty of land around here."

"Maybe he thought you'd forget his past," said Sarah.

"He's a lousy drunk. I remember that. I

would drink with him, same as all the soldiers, but there was always a bad energy about Simon. The boy was never right in the head."

They all thought about why Simon was in town and how he found Peterson. It wasn't too difficult to do, but it still begged the question about why Simon threatened Peterson's life. It was a crazy thing to do, even for Simon, and it left many unanswered questions.

"Where does Simon live?" asked Cord, out of the long silence. It was a good question, which caused Sarah and Lenny to turn to Peterson to find out.

"I don't know. He only appeared yesterday. You could say it was a short visit." He wanted to go on about his heart trouble and him almost collapsing to the floor, but he refrained. To him, it was unimportant.

"He said he's living here?" asked Sarah.

"Yes."

"But you don't know where," said Cord.

"Without a horse," said Peterson, "I don't have much use to go on in search of him."

"Have you told the police?" asked Sarah. "Simon threatened your life. He can at least be questioned by the police."

"Not yet. I'm going to."

"It's a long walk," said Lenny.

"I can help you," said Cord. "I'm intrigued.

This man sounds like some bad people I used to know. I might know what places he'd go."

"I know where he might be," said Peterson. "Saloons."

Lenny pointed to the stables. "Take my horse, Jim. You'll need one."

"Thanks, Lenny. That would be helpful." His tone was rough. He felt a little desperate, but he shrugged it off. Peterson would get some supplies from Lenny anyway. The feed store was only a mile away, but Lenny Gibson gave him feed. That was the only heavy thing he would buy.

Jim Peterson said to Cord, "You sure about this? Simon might pull on us. I know that sounds strange, but it's still 1864 to him. He still lives like we're still fighting the Indian Wars. He is a wild animal."

"I've dealt with wild animals before," Cord assured him.

Peterson nodded. Peterson knew that was true since he hunted for food. But he couldn't figure what exactly Cord's aim in the situation was and why he was a migrant worker. It was similar to seeing a man in the army that is comfortable in his position even though he could climb a few ranks with ease. Cord seemed restrained and Peterson thought he would figure out why in time.

"Sounds like you two got it covered," said Lenny. "Need my help?"

"I'm sure we'll handle it fine," said Peterson. "Know how to use a rifle, Cord?"

Cord smiled a little. "Yes, sir."

"Good. How well?"

"I can shoot a target, if you'd like."

"That's all right," said Peterson. "I'll trust you."

Lenny took off his hat. "You think Simon will pull on you again?"

Peterson shrugged. "If he did it once, I bet he will again. I'd like to be ready. He could have killed me back there. If I hadn't said Sarah knew about him, he would have killed me. I could tell. He wanted to kill me." He scratched his beard after a fly buzzed around his head and landed on his face. "I have a lot of questions for him."

"Be careful," said Sarah. "You know what he's capable of."

"You know, I read the paper maybe ten years back and I saw him in the paper. It said he was guilty for robbing a train. He robbed it alone with just a Colt."

"Alone?" laughed Lenny.

"Too bad he did it alone. He could have gotten away if he had any sense and did it with a gang," said Peterson.

"They never last," said Cord.

"What doesn't?" asked Mr. Peterson.

"Robbing. Those gangs always get greedy and split up. Or they die or get thrown in jail."

"All that happened for Simon," said Peterson, "except death."

Lenny led his horse to his father in law and helped Jim mount the horse. Once Peterson was on the horse he looked around, almost out of breath. "It's been a while since I've been on a horse. Good view from up here."

"You two be careful," said Sarah.

Cord mounted his horse and said to Sarah, "Don't worry, ma'am. I'm sure this is nothing. We'll handle it."

Peterson touched his hat brim and rode away. Cord followed him to the dirt road as they headed east. The horses pummeled against the road and brought up clouds of dust. Peterson stared at the rifle in Cord's scabbard. Peterson had a Colt in a holster on his right side.

Funny, thought Peterson. I feel like I'm in the army again, trying to find where Simon went off to.

CHAPTER 4

With about fifty thousand people living in San Antonio, it would be difficult to find one man, especially Simon. Peterson knew this, yet he understood the saloons would be a good first place to start. Any dark place would be a start.

It was late afternoon when they rode into town and saw the electric lights on the various two and three story brick buildings. The market on Military Plaza was busy with many vendors selling goods. Women in long dresses, some wearing hats, browsed the goods. Some men wore suits and flat or curled brimmed hats. Other men wore long-sleeved shirts and dirty pants and waited behind tables as customers bought merchandise.

"Let's see the police chief," said Peterson.

The two hitched their horses to a wooden rail and left their horses next to the others. They walked up the stone steps and inside a big building.

The two men waited in an open area inside. When the chief of police finally came out, Jim Peterson and Police Chief Donavan Marcus shook hands and smiled as two old friends smile at each other. "How are you, Jim?" asked the chief.

"Fine," he said. He motioned to Cord. "This is Cord."

"Hello," said Marcus, and shook Cord's hand.

"Good evening."

"It is, isn't?" said the chief, glancing outside the many windows and seeing the lights begin to shine on the busy streets and carriages and stagecoaches. "The day went by fast."

"Always does. At least the older you get," said Peterson.

Chief Marcus smiled a bit and showed the dark creases around his eyes. He shuffled his boots to look outside for a bit, as if to see if someone was arriving. "Haven't seen you in a while."

"It's been a while," said Peterson, and he stopped the small talk there. He always hated small talk. "I have a problem. It's about a man who threatened my life. Pulled a gun on me."

The chief laughed and looked back at a deputy sitting behind a desk. "And he lived?"

"I wasn't armed."

"And how'd this all play out? Start at the beginning."

"I sat in my chair in the morning, same as always. A man comes up and wants some of my land. I say I'm not selling. He doesn't like that. He pulls his Colt and I tell him my daughter will know who killed me. Then—"

"How would she know?" said Marcus.

"This man is Simon. He's a boy—well, back then he was young—that I had thrown in jail for raping an Indian woman. Must have been thirty years ago."

"And he comes to visit after all that time?" asked the police chief. "To get revenge?"

"I don't know," said Peterson. "He wanted land, supposedly. Not revenge."

"He got neither," said Cord.

Chief Marcus said to Cord, "He certainly didn't." Then he said to Peterson, "He pulled a gun on you. You think he'll try to kill you?"

"I can't say. He's unpredictable."

The chief scratched his beardless chin. Then he took off his Stetson hat and scratched his black hair, as if it were a habit he had whenever he was thinking. "Well, the best I can do is question the man. See what he's up to."

"He'll be nestled below some bottle of whisky," said Peterson.

"Is he a heavy drinker?"

"Always has been."

"What does he look like?"

Peterson gave Chief Marcus a description of his clothes and his face and the Colt and gun belt and horse. The chief jotted all of it down and wrote down Simon's full name: Simon Steiner. Then Peterson, and much to the chief's surprise, took out a photo of Simon in army uniform and placed it on the desk where Marcus sat. "That's him, but much younger. He's in his fifties now."

The chief looked up at the old man and then down at the faded photo. "Well, I'm not sure if that old a photo would help, to be honest."

"I didn't need it anyway."

"All right then. I'll show the photo to all the men and if we see him we'll go and question him."

"He might be violent," said Peterson, and it was quiet after he said that. One could hear someone turning a piece of paper over in another room.

"Violent? Well, he did pull on you," admitted the chief.

"I believe I saw him in the papers about ten years ago. Train robbery. He was caught, but he shot at the police going after him. He didn't hang. Don't ask me why."

"He would have if one of those men had been hit or killed," said the chief. "Shooting at police," he murmured. He turned to the deputy behind him, who was watching them every now and then behind a desk. "We will be wary of him."

"So will we," said Peterson.

The chief looked at Cord's stone face and then at Jim Peterson. "Are you assuming he'll come visit you again?"

"No, I mean we're trying to find him ourselves."

The chief didn't laugh that time. He sat down. He blinked rapidly and leaned back in his chair. "And what do you plan to do when you find him?"

"Ask him some questions."

Chief Marcus glanced at Cord. "Is this your bodyguard?"

"No," said Peterson. "He works for my daughter's husband, Lenny Gibson. He wanted to help me out."

Cord's hat was pointed down and hid his

face. It was a funny thing; Cord going into a police station. No one would think Cord would walk into such a place.

Peterson tried to read Cord's face, but he found he couldn't. Cord hooked his thumbs into his pockets and looked around the place. "I feel like I've seen you before," said the chief to Cord.

"Maybe we've met."

"Hmm," said Marcus. "I could be wrong. Oh, well." Then the chief stood up from a desk and walked over to the deputy and handed him the information about Simon. "I assure you that if any of us see this drunkard we'll ask him why he would be stupid enough to threaten your life."

Jim Peterson didn't smile, as he didn't feel assured. Simon might skip town or be hiding out somewhere. "If you find him, can you come tell me? I wanted to ask him some personal questions."

"Sure, just write down your address. We'll keep him for a day or two," said Marcus.

"Assuming you find him," said Peterson.

"Of course. I just didn't want to promise anything."

"You don't have to. I know how it is. I'm sure you have more important things to do." Peterson wrote down the address and directions on a small piece of paper and handed it to Chief Marcus. "Thanks for this."

"Well, I haven't done much yet," said the chief. "If this man is how I picture him in my mind, then he is not suitable to live here. I'll be on the lookout."

Jim Peterson walked out of the building with Cord. They stepped out into the humid air and found the sky a dark blue and the sun setting just above the Staacke Brothers Building.

"What now?" asked Cord.

"We start looking. Follow me."

"Should I take my rifle?"

"No. We can handle him just fine."

There were hundreds of people in the market and on the street and sidewalk. The two men watched the bobbing hats and heads under the hot sun and heard the horses and the big wheels of wagons on the streets that smelled of horse. Peterson started down a street and Cord walked beside him. It seemed to Cord that the old man was walking aimlessly, but he wasn't.

Peterson knew a good place to start.

They came upon Buckhorn Saloon and walked inside. Peterson brushed against a lot of shoulders and tried to see through the moving heads. It was loud. He kept walking near the long bar while Cord walked around the tables.

The two met near the back of the saloon. "I guess he's not here," said Peterson.

Then Peterson saw a face appear and disappear. It might have been Simon. It was too crowded and smoky inside the saloon. Peterson began sweating; maybe it was the humid air or the crowd.

"Let's go out," said Peterson.

They walked around people to get to the front door. Once they were out, Cord said, "Is it always that crowded?"

"This day it is."

Peterson squinted his eyes and spotted a man across the street. The man kept walking on the sidewalk and turning his head to Peterson. It was Simon. Peterson pointed to Simon and said to Cord, "That's him. The man with the black hat. See him?"

"I'll go to him."

Simon bolted and ran around a corner. Cord ran behind a stagecoach and dodged two horses making their way down the street. He went down an alley and didn't see Simon. Then, once at an opening to another street, he looked around. The black hat appeared to his right, so he sprinted by two women in long dresses.

Simon disappeared behind the edge of a building. Cord turned around and tried to see the hat. He breathed heavily. A woman waiting outside a store said to Cord, "Running from something?"

"I'm looking for a man with a black hat. Did you see him come by here?"

"I don't know if we're talking about the same person, but he might have gone into this store." She pointed.

Cord noticed the furniture store. A chair and table were shown behind a wall of glass. "Thank you."

He walked inside the store that smelled of cedar and oak. It was fairly dark. A young man walked out near the back. "We're closing soon, mister."

"Have you see a man with a black hat walk in here?"

"No."

Cord kept walking around the furniture, trying to see if Simon was behind them.

"I said we're closing soon," said the boy. "I can't help you until tomorrow. I should have locked the door already, to be honest."

"I'm looking for a murderer," lied Cord. "It's a little important."

"He didn't say anything like that. He told me—"

Then Simon appeared behind a wooden dresser, opened the back door and ran out with his hat in his hand. Cord sprinted after him. Both men had big sweat marks on their shirts. The veins in their neck pumped with blood.

Simon turned back quickly. It looked like he smiled. Cord sprinted and avoided the horses and the crowds of people along the sidewalk. Simon pushed a man aside and ran behind another building.

They were now near a green river. Simon was far ahead, just a hatless head among the others; he held the black hat in his hand and walked briskly, trying not to gather attention. But Cord saw him. He ran over a bridge above the green San Antonio River.

Jim Peterson walked right in front of Simon and made him halt. Simon breathed heavily and stared at him with wide eyes. Peterson looked him in the eyes. With a stone face, Peterson reminded Simon of the army days and how Peterson would give him orders and lead them against Apaches that had massacred stagecoaches. It was an emotionless face, which caused Simon to want to think about what the old man was thinking. And not knowing his opinion of him made him almost feel like a child wanting the attention from a forlorn father.

"What do you want?" said Simon, turning to see if the man following him was close. "Why you looking at me like that?"

"I got some questions for you," said Peterson. "And I want you to answer them."

"I don't have to answer them."

"You do if the police come along."

"What do they got to do with me?"

Peterson licked his lips and saw Cord far away in the crowd.

"You don't even know what you did. You don't even know right from wrong."

Simon shook his head. "I just do things. That's it. I don't know what you want. I just want to be left alone."

"So do I. But I want to know why you want a piece of my land and how you found me. I want to know—"

"Mr. Peterson," yelled Cord about fifty feet away.

The words caused Simon to bolt. Peterson grabbed Simon's arm.

"Let go of me," he said, and watched Cord run around people and get closer and closer.

"Make me let go," said Peterson.

Simon's heart beat fast, even though he was motionless for some time now. He thought about hitting the old man. Why didn't he? He was the type to do so. But Simon only grabbed the hand around his arm and yanked it off. Then he was running again.

Simon found his horse and mounted. Cord followed and grabbed a hold of his leg but his grip wasn't strong enough and the horse galloped away. The horse brought up clouds of dust and disappeared behind a building under construction.

Cord placed his hands on his hips as Peterson stood next to him.

"What did you say to him?" said Cord.

"Some questions that he didn't answer." He sighed. "Let's head back. It's dark."

The stars were bright and the moon was out. They traveled back home using the moon and stars as light. Jim Peterson asked Cord if he had a place to sleep. When Cord said he slept in the woodlands, Peterson invited Cord to sleep in a spare room. Cord preferred to be alone, but he accepted. It was better than sleeping out in the wild. The bed was comfortable and the room was big enough for privacy. The floor creaked and the small house smelled of cedar. It was a big change to Cord. He was used to being alone. Now he felt part of a community.

CHAPTER 5

CORD WORKED LENNY GIBSON'S LAND IN the early morning. It was quiet, and Cord loved the quiet. Even when the birds came out he was glad to be at work, with his mind busy on the sounds of birds, the smell of corn and the feeling of sweat on his palms. It was good to be earning money again.

When Cord's mind wasn't busy he thought of his wife. He thought of when she got tuberculosis. He remembered her smile when he came into her bedroom with a tray of food. She was weak in those days. And he thought of the day when he walked into the bedroom one morning and she was not awake and smiling, and how he felt her limp hand in his while he sobbed quietly and how he felt alone in the world.

This memory only caused him to work harder.

Lenny noticed this and said, "Slow down there. It's not even midday. It's a long way until the sun goes down."

Cord kept at it and refused to slow down. It seemed like Cord already gained muscle and strength after a couple days of working the fields. He clenched his teeth and frowned. The sweat was bothersome, but his mind was far away from work and he didn't like that. Cord threw the corn into the huge bin.

There were thousands of yellow corn in the bin and it was growing fast under Cord's anger. Even his footsteps were rough like an irritated animal. The dirt plumed up in little clouds when he walked towards the corn bin.

It was too hot for such fast activity. Hot days are easy if you take it slow. But Cord was working hard and fast.

Lenny squinted at Cord but didn't warn him anymore. If the man wanted to hurt himself, so be it. It wasn't his problem. People have to learn from their mistakes. It's not good to protect him from himself. He'll hurt himself and learn from it. Lenny walked away.

After a while Cord stopped and looked up at the sun. He wiped sweat off his forehead and followed Lenny as the two went inside the house for lunch. Cord was quiet, as always. He didn't say much and his mind seemed to be on other things besides the present moment.

"Any luck finding Simon?" asked Sarah Gibson. She dished out food onto plates and set them in front of each man. They sat at the table and ate.

Cord nodded. "We found him."

"You did?" said Lenny, bringing up his head in a fast motion.

"He got away." He said it sadly, almost apologetically.

"What happened?" said Sarah.

"We found Simon in some saloon and then he saw us and started running. So I ran after him. Mr. Peterson cut him off and grabbed him. But he said he didn't get much out of him. Simon got away on his horse."

"What will you do now?" she asked.

Lenny said, "What can Cord do? They got lucky finding him. Boy like that will be in some hole somewhere. Now he'll be even more cautious. A snaky man like Simon ain't coming out for long next time. He'll watch every corner."

"Well," said Sarah. "I just think the police ought to do something."

"They're too busy to catch someone like Simon," said Lenny. "They're trying to find murderers and thieves. Simon threatened Jim's life, but Simon is one slippery fella. He won't be easy to find. If he had pulled the trigger, the police would do something quick. But he didn't, and that's the problem."

Cord felt the muscles in his back tightening, and then he dropped his eyes slowly and tried to stay awake. Sarah looked at her husband, but Lenny shook his head. Lenny shared enough, but Cord was still a stranger that was only here in San Antonio for work. Cord was told plenty, as Lenny never seemed to stop talking. Now Lenny was aware of this and tried to let it go.

A man can't be beckoned into speaking about his personal life; if he talks, he talks, but a man mostly keeps his feelings to himself. It was better to leave Cord to figure out things himself. It was obvious he was in pain, physical and mental, but it was best to let him figure it out. And if he wanted to talk, he'd talk, but the best thing was to leave him alone to think.

There wasn't a need to get acquainted with a temporary worker. Cord didn't seem to care much for talk or careless words anyway. He didn't care to talk about the weather or what was in the newspapers. He just wanted to be left alone.

That was fine to Lenny; he was fine doing all the talking.

"All right," said Lenny. "Time to go out again. Maybe we'll spot Simon out there in the fields." Lenny slapped the table with the palm of his hand, laughed and headed outside with Cord.

Cord tossed corn into the wagon bin and kept a steady rhythm to it. It was almost like a fun game, almost hypnotic. He enjoyed the monotonous work under the sun.

After a while Cord sat on the dirt and looked at the clouds. There were big white clouds in the sky, but down the road there was a lone grey cloud. It was odd seeing the grey cloud all by itself and with no other grey clouds in the sky.

Cord stood up and brushed the dirt from his pants. Then he saw a line of smoke that formed the cloud. Now it seemed the cloud and the smoke were closer than he expected.

Fire, he thought.

Cord ran over to Lenny, brushing his shoulders against the green stalks. "See that smoke over there."

Lenny turned his head quickly. Cord's excited voice made Lenny more alert. "Well, look at that."

"Should we ride over there?"

"Yes, but hopefully it's just a brush fire. I've burned dead trees before, but burning on a hot day like this doesn't make much sense." He put his gloves in his back pockets and nodded at the horses. "Let's ride over there and see what's going on."

Cord mounted his horse and rode a few miles down the road. The grey smoke turned black when he got closer. Lenny reared up and then the two of them saw the fire up close. They walked closer to the fire and stared at the fire in shock. Then they heard yelling and woke up.

"Why don't you help?" yelled Jim Peterson, frantically digging a ditch around part of his land. About five trees, several bushes and part of his crops were blooming in red flames. It smelled of ash and the fire made crackling noises once the men were near Peterson.

Peterson's forearms were black with ash and dirt. "The shovels are in the shed." Peterson tried to create a trench near the edge of the fire so that the rest of his crops could be saved. It was a frantic effort. There was a light wind that blew the flames. He could feel the fire's heat being passed in the wind.

Cord and Lenny pitched in and helped dig a little trench to keep the fire from spreading to the rest of the cornfield.

It was a dry day, even for the prickly pear out near the oak trees. The fire was slow but strong. It was too strong to douse with water. It would have to die out all by itself.

The flames were bright red and the smoke grew blacker with each new hour. Now the men tried to dig near the trees, as the cornfield fire was fizzling out. The trees burned strong.

The men waited for the trees to stop burning. There was nothing else they could do.

"How'd this happen?" asked Lenny. The men were out of breath. All three stood and watched the fire. They sweated from being near the flames and also because of the Texas heat. Luckily, the heat was lessening each new day.

Jim Peterson shook his head. "I don't know, but I bet it was Simon."

"Why would he do that?"

"Why would he pull a gun on me?" said Peterson. "Simon would do this. I know him well enough. Maybe it's a warning to stay away from him. He's scared. He could have burned my house down, but he didn't. This is just a little warning. This isn't a big deal to him, just a friendly warning."

Cord wrapped his hands around the shovel that was stuck in the dirt. "You didn't see Simon?" asked Cord.

Peterson squinted at him. "I know it was him."

Cord nodded in agreement. He could see Peterson was angry, and he didn't want to make him angrier. "Will you stop trying to find him?"

"No."

"You think it's worth it? He could kill you," said Cord.

"I don't think he would," he said. "I'm probably the closest thing he has to a friend."

Lenny snickered and wiped away the sweaty black ash marks on his face. "A friend don't burn down a friend's home."

"That's not how Simon thinks," said Peterson.

Lenny refused to go on. He, as well as anyone, couldn't tell Jim Peterson anything. The old man would do whatever he wanted to do. After all, Peterson was used to giving orders in the army. That attitude translated to the rest of his life.

Cord almost thought it was silly asking. "You want us to try to go find him again?"

Peterson said, "If you want to come along. I can't run. My back and my knees aren't worth much anymore. You don't have to come along, but you were a big help last time. I'd appreciate the help. After all, we almost had him."

"I'll help you find him," said Cord. "I'll try to be discrete next time."

"Good idea. We were too busy moving through the crowd. We just got to wait for Simon to pop up. He'll be around."

Lenny walked around the fire that was about the surface area of an acre. The fire was dying down, but it was at a slow pace. A river was too far to retrieve water from, and water thrown on the trees from the well would be almost useless, as the fire was thick on the old oak trees. The fire lessened in the next couple hours. The men watched it, but soon Lenny and Cord had to ride back to the cornfields to work again. Peterson thanked them and sat in a chair on his back porch.

Peterson watched the fire on his land and heard the branches crack and fall every once in a while. Now he was alone again. An entire acre was black and covered in ash. It was a sad sight, but he was glad he saved most of his crops. He wore a bandanna to prevent the ashes from getting into his lungs.

Peterson watched the flames on the Texas Acacia. Then he looked through the flames and he could have sworn he saw someone on the opposite side of the flaming bush. A dark figure was lurking in the woodlands, and once he saw the figure through the flames he knew who it was.

"Simon," whispered Peterson.

Jim Peterson stood up and retrieved the rifle from inside. He held the Henry rifle in his hands and searched the trees. He walked around the fire and tried to see Simon.

"I know you're out there!" He walked until he was in a shaded area. "Simon! Don't hide. I'll find you." His voice carried over the trees. Then there was silence. "I want answers! I want to know why you're here, why you want my land, why you threatened my life, and much more." Then Simon, more than one hundred feet away, mounted a horse and rode away. He was a small figure at that distance.

Peterson shot his rifle once at a burning tree trunk. It was enough to scare Simon, but Peterson thought he needed to do more than scare him. Peterson knew what he needed to do.

CHAPTER 6

Jim Peterson borrowed Lenny's horse and rode into town the next morning. He told the chief he saw Simon burn his crops and trees. It was enough to cause Chief Marcus to grow interested in the matter; he thought it was a petty squabble before, but now the news made him alert.

"You're sure this was him?" asked the chief.

"I saw him. He was far away, but it was him. No one else would do this."

"I believe you're right. You don't have enemies." Then the chief smiled.

Peterson rode back to his house and saw Cord waiting in the rocking chair on the front porch. Cord stood up.

"No, you stay sitting there. I've been riding all day," said Peterson.

"And I've been sitting for a while here." He got up and put his back against a wooden column. "Sarah said you'd be here."

"I was in town. Told the chief I saw Simon after the fire died down."

Cord frowned. "You saw him?"

"I saw him ride his horse away just as the fire was sizzling out. Can't forget that horse or the look of Simon." Peterson shook his head and sat in the chair on the deck. The cats came walking over to the old man from around the corner of the house. The cats licked their paws on the deck and waited for food. "I almost forgot. I have to feed the cats."

The cats were watchful of Cord, but not the black cat with the big eyes. It came over and rubbed its body against his pants. And after Cord petted it the other cats were more relaxed. "Look at that. That one doesn't like people, but looks like he likes you."

"What's this one's name?"

"I never named them. I don't want to get too attached. They're wild cats after all. They come and go through the years. The black one is a new one. It seems like the leader of the group. When he comes to the house, the others follow."

Cord petted the black cat's head and watched as Peterson brought out meat for the cats. He dropped the pork scraps on the wooden porch and watched as the cats ate with their heads close to the floor and their eyes darting from one place to the next.

Peterson squinted at Cord. "The chief is more serious about Simon now."

"Should be," said Cord. "That fire could have killed you."

"True." No one could predict Simon; he might get up and leave tomorrow, but Peterson doubted that. Once Simon had a grip on something, he didn't let go. "How's the Gibson farm?"

"We're making good progress. I got today off because of it," said Cord.

"Good." Peterson took off his hat and set it on a table beside him. The black cat jumped on his lap and purred. "You fixing on leaving soon?"

"In a few months, maybe."

"Plenty of work around here. A city this big has plenty of jobs."

"I like to go from place to place."

"Why?"

Cord stared down at his boots. "Well, sometimes I just have this feeling of wanting to get away. I go with it."

"You can do that but still live in one place. It's called a vacation."

Cord smiled a little. "I don't like to own a lot of things. I don't need a house or a lot of things tying me down. I just need my horse, my rifle and the clothes on me."

Peterson said, "I don't like possessions either, but it doesn't mean you cling to them. I have cats, but if one is gone I'll know he'll be all right."

"Gone?"

"If one dies," said the old man, "I think the cat would be in a better place."

Only a muffled sound came from Cord.

"Don't believe in things like that?" asked Peterson.

"I used to. My wife, Lara, believed in God."

Peterson said, "I just like to think that the men I killed in war went to hell so that I won't have to see them again. Some of them were, I'm sure, good men, but I'll assume the men, such as the Apaches we dealt with, were punished in some way. I've seen some terrible things. I saw people of all ages scalped. That was out in New Mexico. Now the natives are all in reservations or dead—the violent ones are dead, I mean. We only fought the killers." He petted the cat on his lap. The cat slept. "Tell me about your wife."

It had been a long time since he spoke about her. Cord wasn't sure if that was a good or bad thing. It was difficult to think about. But he felt comfortable speaking to Jim Peterson about her. "She was beautiful, brown hair, brown eyes—"

"No," interrupted Peterson. "I mean, tell me what she was like."

"She was kind, a good person—a much better person than me."

Peterson said, "And? What else?"

"When I met Lara, I didn't have my life together. I didn't know what I wanted to do with my life or what kind of person I was. She helped straighten me out, but it was too late. I was too busy on the railroads, working here and there, always away. When she got sick, I thought it was best to move from Montana to New Mexico. Some sick people moved south to warm areas and seemed to feel better. We did the same. But it only got worse. I quit my job and worked as a farmer and cowboy, scraping by here and there. But the warm climate didn't help much. She only got worse. One day I walked into the bedroom. She was asleep and wouldn't wake up." Cord's face turned away. Then his voice changed, and it sounded like he held back.

Peterson nodded slowly, understanding what he felt. "My wife, Marguerite died two years ago." There was a factual tone to his speech. He thought his wife was in heaven, and that thought comforted him.

But Cord didn't believe in such things, so how do you comfort a man who lost his wife? Peterson only saw Cord's hat and the back of his hair. He saw his shoulders against the wooden pole and part of his face staring at the green hills in the west.

Peterson said, "I've seen terrible things in the war. I still have memories that come up every now and then. Bad memories. If I held on to them, I would be in pain every minute of every day. The past can kill you, if you let it. It might seem impossible to do, but you have to let go of the past if you want to live. Right now, you'll think it's not possible, but whether you believe in an afterlife or not, you have to make a choice: live now or never. It'll be a little here and there. Maybe you work a bit, smile at the good memories, and move on to something else. But you'll get better over time. I did. What would your wife want? She'd want you to live. It doesn't always mean moving on. You'll have the good memories to smile at, then you'll keep going. What else can you do besides keep going on? That's the only thing I know; I know I have to keep moving or I'll miss out on life. I won't hear the cardinal over there singing or feel the warmth that the sun brings or smell the wildflowers in spring."

"I move all the time. I keep going," said Cord, behind his back.

"Physically. Not in your mind."

"Then how did you move on?"

"Marguerite was able to accept death, so she moved on before I even tried to move on. It wasn't so sad. She and I were old. We knew we'd have to die soon. We lived fully, so there was no fear near death. I guess you can say I moved on because she did before she was even gone."

"How should I move on?" asked Cord.

"How would your wife, Lara, answer that question?"

"She'd probably want me to find another wife," he said. He turned his body around and faced Peterson.

"You got your answer."

Cord shook the man's hand and walked to his horse. He rode away, not knowing where he was going. He felt calmer than the previous day. His wife was on his mind, but this time he thought of the good memories of her and how he felt good around her.

Now Cord's mind was on Simon. Simon pulled his gun on Jim Peterson and burned down part of his land. Things were getting worse. Cord was focused on Simon's continual threats aimed at Peterson. He didn't know why Simon wanted Peterson's land, besides him saying he would farm on it. And why he thought it was a good idea to burn part of his crops, but he did know what Simon looked like and what kind of places he frequented. Cord thought there was more to it. Simon could buy land anywhere else. Why'd he want Peterson's?

Cord rode into town to find Simon.

THE SUN SET AS CORD RODE INTO SAN Antonio. He hitched his horse near First National Bank and walked on the road. People crossed the road and walked home or into dimly lit saloons. Visitors went inside the hotels. The crowds were large, and the city was dark except for areas lit by street lamps.

It was hard to see the faces of people in clear view, and Cord knew there was slim chance he would see Simon. Knowing this, he headed for a saloon and walked inside. He drank whiskey and had his elbows on the bar. He kept his hat on and didn't look around too much. It was fairly quiet until an hour later. Two groups of five men each played cards at the tables. A few men, including Cord, were sitting on the wooden stools.

Cord watched the horses ride by outside. It smelled of cigars, whiskey, horse and sweat inside the saloon; everyone was used to it, and to even question the smell would be odd. Questioning the smell would be like asking why someone who works outside all day smells.

Cord waited another hour and left the saloon. It was worth the try. He walked to his horse and on the way he overheard two men talking ahead of him. He could hear them speaking quietly, unaware that Cord was walking not too far behind them.

"...for all that?" one of them said.

"That's all I had to do," said the other. "Got paid one hundred dollars for it."

The first man frowned. "And he didn't see you?"

"Well, no. I mean, kind of. It doesn't mean he'll do anything about it. He's an old man. There's nothing he can do. He'll die soon anyway. Why does he need anything? He's lived long enough. He doesn't even use all his land. That land, I tell you, is worth hundreds of thousands of dollars."

"How do you know?"

The other man stopped, looked to the left and saw no one. A carriage went by, and once it did he felt safe. Cord listened intently and leaned his back against a wooden support beam.

"The man who paid me said this. I kept asking him why he wants me to do all this for him. He finally told me the land is worth two hundred thousand dollars."

"Sweet Jesus. That's a lot of money. You sure?"

"Yes," said the smaller man.

Cord noticed the two men were not walking straight; he could see it in their boots and the way their boots pointed every which way. He saw the smaller man of the two hold the wooden railing and vomit. The other man turned his head to the street as Cord walked into a dark alleyway. They turned back to see if someone was listening.

"What was that?" said the smaller man after vomiting.

"A stray cat or dog," said the taller man, who was red headed and stood almost seven feet tall. "Listen, you said you need help, right?"

"If you can handle it."

"Sure, I can handle it, but I need to know what's the risk."

"No risk."

"No risk?" repeated the taller man.

"I've done the risk. All we gotta do is—" The man looked around. "First, I have to know if you're capable. I have a job for you."

"What is it?"

"I'll tell you later. It's too late for business. I'll just say there's good money in it. Three thousand."

"I don't even know what to do with that much money."

"Our money," said the smaller man.

"I thought you just said I get three thousand."

"No! That's half and half."

"Why didn't you say so?"

"I'm saying so now," he said. "All right. I'll let you know tomorrow."

Cord peeked his head out from the shadows and saw under a streetlight that it was Simon. He saw Simon's wrinkled shirt and the dirt on the back of his pants. Then, when Simon turned to the left, he saw the handlebar mustache. It was Simon. Cord saw Simon's Colt Peacemaker near his waist.

Cord had his Winchester in the rifle scabbard on his horse, but he only wanted to use it if he had to use violence. He saw Simon mount his horse, but it was a struggle for the drunken man. The other man, who was much larger and wider and had red hair and a red shirt with black stripes, walked away with a grin on his face.

Cord walked back to his horse and mounted. He followed Simon down the street. It was a pitiful sight, as it almost appeared like Simon was about to fall off his horse.

Cord thought of restraining him, but he thought it wasn't time. What if he got away? Then Simon would never be in town again. He'd be gone forever. Cord wanted to see where he was going. Even Simon had to sleep. His home ought to be somewhere in the area.

The streets were almost empty. Simon was the type to roam the streets when no one else was around. Cord knew the type. He met people similar to Simon—the type he hoped he would never meet again. Simon stared up at the stars and the moon. The city and its lights were behind him, yet so was Cord.

Cord gripped the rifle to be sure he could reach for it quickly. And when he brought his hand up he noticed his palms were sweating. Then he looked up and couldn't see Simon.

He looked in all directions, but he couldn't see anyone, only the branches of trees that moved with the wind. Then he heard a shot, a loud crack in the trees that made Cord's heart jump.

Cord fell off the horse. His left boot was

stuck in the stirrup, but he didn't even think of it. The horse trotted away from the loud gunshot as Cord's head dragged against the dirt. He tried to reach for the Winchester, but he could only reach his knee. As the horse slowed, Cord's eyes darted in all directions to see who shot at him.

A man walked out from the woods and breathed heavily. He made the horse stop by grabbed the reins. And then he kneeled down to Cord's face that was upside down. :

"That's what happens when you follow me," grinned Simon.

The man's wicked smile and brown teeth were all Cord could see. Then Cord saw darkness and felt something rushing out of his leg.

CHAPTER 7

When Cord opened his eyes, his body felt stiff as metal. His head lay against the dirt. He turned his face and saw a small fire and a man on the other side of the fire.

"Howdy," said the man opposite to Cord.

Cord tried to stand up, but he couldn't. His hands and feet were tied with rope. And when he moved his hands to try to get free he could feel the rope tight against his wrists. His leg was poorly bandaged after being shot. There was no bleeding, which Cord was happy about at least.

"What is this?" said Cord, raising his voice above the crackling fire. Then he realized what happened and within a few seconds he put it all together. "Simon."

"Howdy," said Simon, chewing on bacon.

He grinned and walked around the fire. The fire faintly lit Simon's face.

Cord looked around and couldn't even see trees or bushes. There was no moon or stars visible. There wasn't even the sound of crickets; it was odd not to hear the crickets at night, especially in Texas. He looked for his horse.

Simon stood above him. Cord couldn't see the face, but he did hear the fire echoing.

"You followed me," said Simon.

Cord didn't answer.

"You won't talk? I can make you talk. I'd rather not hurt you, but I can burn you with this here piece of metal. I'll just put it in the fire and—"

"What do you want?" interrupted Cord. "Why am I tied?"

Simon snickered. "You—"

"What's that on my leg?"

Simon wiped his mouth of grease. "I shot you there. And don't worry one bit. I took out the bullet and cleaned the wound. You're good as new."

"I won't even be able to walk now," said Cord.

"I used a little pistol I got from a woman. One of them pistols you can hide in a hand. It doesn't do much." Simon sat and stared at Cord. He picked up sticks behind him and threw them in the fire. "Now you know my name. I wanna know yours."

"Cord Cordeu."

"Cord?" He studied Cord and his clothes. "And what is it with you? Why are you working for old man Peterson?"

"I'm not working for him."

"I seen you chase after me the other day and follow me in the night. He must be paying you for doing his work."

"No," said Cord. "I'm just helping him out."

"Out of the goodness of your heart?"

"Sure."

"All right. You won't say. Why are you here? I mean, what's your job."

"I'm a farmer."

Simon held his stomach while he laughed. "A farmer man? Well, I guess I shouldn't laugh. It's what I was thinking I'd do."

Cord tried to break the rope around his hands, but the rope was too tight. There was no use. He watched Simon take off his hat and place it on the rocky ground beside Cord's hat.

Simon sat crisscross with his hands on a spare string of rope, playing with it like a child plays with a carved wooden horse.

"A farmer for the old man, huh?" asked Simon.

"No, for the Gibson's."

"The Gibson's?" The last name sounded familiar. He went through it in his mind, but it had been a long time since hearing that name. "Sarah Gibson," he whispered.

"I'm working for them."

Simon nodded. The rock walls were casted with shadows of the two men. The fire was dying down. "A farmer."

"You sound disappointed," said Cord.

"I thought you was out to kill me. Like a bounty hunter."

"No, just to see where you were heading."

Simon frowned and wiped his giant handlebar mustache of bacon grease. "Why?"

"To see where you live."

"Why'd you want that?"

Cord pushed his body up using his elbow. Now he sat up with his hands tied behind his back. "Mr. Peterson wants to ask you some questions. That's why. And since you burned down part of his land, the police chief wants to find you. I don't know why you're making all this trouble. You're only making things worse."

Simon squinted at him. "He made trouble when he threw me into prison. He's in the wrong!" He calmed himself. "A man don't need all that land. Why can't he share a little? I gotta live in a cave to scrape by." He almost laughed.

"A cave. And Peterson has all that land. I could use it."

"It sounds like he doesn't want to sell," said Cord. "So why not let it go?"

Simon looked away. It was quiet for a while.

"I heard you and that red headed man talk," said Cord. "I know you're working for someone."

"That right?"

"You just want money, huh?"

"Who doesn't?" said Simon. "I can work the entire day and never live comfortably. How am I suppose to sit still for more than five minutes? What I make in a day, some men make in a minute. Well, I thought, you get a little bit of some good land and you'd do all right. He's got five hundred acres. Five hundred. And he's just holding it. Greedy, I tell you."

"Then buy someone else's land."

Simon crawled over to Cord and sat next to him. Cord could smell the liquor on his breath. "Look, you're what, working for the Gibson's until you can buy a place of your own?"

"Right," lied Cord.

"There's a man I'm working for. He told me not to give anyone his name. Said he'd give me three thousand dollars to get Peterson to sell his land. This man is very wealthy. Told me Peterson's land is worth so much that only he would be able to buy the land."

"How much is the land?" said Cord. "And don't tell me a lie like you did to that red headed man."

Simon smiled a little and nodded. He understood Cord now. In Simon's mind, this was someone just like him. "It's worth about three hundred thousand. That's what the boss says."

Cord shook his head. "How?"

"That land backs up to town. People have been trying to buy part of it for years, but Peterson ain't selling. He's holding onto it. Greedy, I tell you. My employer just wants me to get Peterson to sell. My employer wants to buy it and sell it in parts. Some of it he was gonna develop. He didn't tell me much else."

"And how do you plan on getting Peterson to sell?"

"Whatever I have to do," said Simon.

Cord was silent. He doubted everything Simon said. He remembered he was listening to someone who failed at robbing a train and had been in prison multiple times. Cord said, "You going to untie me now?"

"No."

"Why not?"

"Are you working with me or not?"

"I'll think about it."

"That always means no."

"So what now?"

Simon scratched his hands and glanced back at a tiny opening out of the cave. He got up and grabbed a rag and blindfolded Cord.

"What are you doing?" Cord shook his head and struggled to get away.

"Look, I like you. I just don't wanna kill you. I'll set you in some place, but I can't let you knowing where you is."

Simon pulled Cord by his arms and then put Cord on the back of the horse after a few tries. Then Simon tied him to the horse and rode away. It was a bumpy and long ride for Cord.

Once the horse slowed, Cord tried to see through the rag. He could hear the nighttime crickets again, which made him feel better.

Simon helped Cord off the horse. Cord fell to the dirt. His ankles and wrists were still tied. He struggled on the ground like a beached dolphin. "What are you doing?" asked Cord.

"Nothing." Simon mounted the horse and looked down at the man. "I'm just leaving you here. I don't want you following me. If I see you again, I'll have to use a better gun. Not some little kid gun." Simon turned and drank from a canteen. "I can't do nothing but pity you. I can't see a man like you farming. I can see you robbing a train or bounty hunting, but not farming." Simon shook his head and rode away.

Cord lay on the dirt and listened as the sound of the clopping horse died away. Now he could only hear the crickets and the sound of something slithering through the wild grass around him. He brushed his head against the dirt until the rag around his eyes dropped to his mouth, then finally to his neck. He breathed heavily and saw a rattlesnake nearby.

Cord pushed the dirt with his boots and slithered away. His hands were tied behind his back, so he couldn't push his torso upright, especially when a rattlesnake had its head widened and its tail vibrating. Once Cord was twenty or so feet way, the snake crawled back into a crevice inside a rock enclosure.

Then Cord tried to notice any landmarks. There was no road. He saw oak trees far a part from one another. The moon was bright and illuminated the land. A few clouds moved in front of the moon every now and then.

Cord searched for a sharp rock to cut the rope. It would be an awkward motion, but he thought he would try to bring his hands forward. He sat and dropped his hand below his butt so that his hands were now in front of him. He didn't know how he would cut the rope around his wrist, but he thought he'd try anyway. If he wanted to walk, he had to cut the rope around his ankles at least.

It took a while for him to scrape through the grass and dirt to find a suitable rock. He found one farther away, near the wild flowers. He cut the rope around his ankles and then around his wrists, but it took an hour. The rope was thick and the rock was not sharp.

Cord walked aimlessly, using the moon and stars to guide him. He felt the damage the little gun made on his leg. Then he felt pain on the back of his head. He ached all over, and he didn't know how his head was damaged.

He rode his horse back to Peterson's house. The incident with Simon only deepened Cord's involvement. The police would have to be told about what happened. The Gibson's and Peterson would now be on the edge, always on the lookout for Simon and his mischief.

Now there was no turning back. Cord felt compelled see to it that Simon would be put in jail. It was attempted murder, abduction and arson.

Cord saw Peterson's house and the partially blackened land ahead. It was home, for now, and he wanted to keep it safe for Peterson.

CHAPTER 8

"Two months and still no sign of Simon." Peterson drank a glass of tea and wiped his beard with his shirtsleeve. "Nothing."

Cord stood with his shoulder against a wooden beam. It was sunny and warm in the morning. Summer ended and fall began. The harvest was almost over. Trees were losing their leaves, so now the hills were only green with oak and cedar trees.

The crickets chirped near the crops and vultures flew low to the ground and circled in the west hills. "Simon is probably gone," said Cord.

"Or still in that cave you told me about," said Peterson. "The chief said he hadn't seen him. It almost sounded like he doubted your story."

"I think he believed me. The doctor believed me, and the police chief was there to see the damage in my leg and on my head."

"He thought you were delirious."

"A little."

Peterson listened and heard a sound coming from the crops.

The old man still had good hearing, but his eyesight wasn't what it used to be. It was blurry far away, but that didn't matter to him. He judged a person as a blind person judges a person: in how the person acts and talks. His poor eyesight was neither good nor bad to him.

The sound came from the cats. The black cat led the other four cats to the front porch. Then Peterson got up and went inside. He came out with the food and fed the cats that waited patiently. Two of the cats were play fighting.

Cord walked up to a tortoiseshell cat and tried to pet it, but the cat clawed at him in the air. "All right," he said. "I won't get near you."

"Don't worry about that," said the old man. "It was like that to me when it first came here. It clawed my hand and made me bleed. I didn't mind it. It's what I would have done. Can't trust every stranger you meet. But once I fed the cat it seemed to open up to me after a few months."

Cord said, "If you put it that way, I guess I'm just like a cat."

Peterson sat in the rocking chair. "I wanted to ask you something. Two months ago you said you'd be around for only three months. That right?"

"Right."

Peterson nodded. "Where will you go next?"

"Wherever my horse takes me."

"I'm sure that's an adventure."

"Sometimes you get shot though."

"Of course. You'll meet someone like Simon," said the old man. "But you didn't have to go after him, you know."

"I wanted to," said Cord. "You gave me a place to sleep. Best thing I could do was repay you somehow."

"That was dangerous," Peterson said to him. "I sound like a mother. What am I saying? Still, we don't have answers. We know he's working for someone. Someone who wants my land. But there have been about three different men who wanted my land. And I don't think they're the type to hire some criminal to burn down my crops. Nothing adds up."

"Well, we ought to go looking for him. Maybe he'll turn up."

"I doubt it. The police were on the lookout for him for two months. So were we. We headed into town just after you came back. Couldn't find him."

"That's because we went into town," said Cord. "He lives in a cave. We know that. He's more cautious than ever before. We have to find this cave."

Peterson struggled out of his chair. He used his wooden cane to walk to the edge of the porch. When he was near the front steps of the porch, he turned and said, "We can try for a while. You remember the direction he went when you followed him?"

"Yeah. But he might have led me over there just to shoot me."

"That's what I thought. I'll go borrow a horse from Lenny. When I come back, we'll head out."

They rode east during midday. The sky was clear blue and the sun blinding. It was not as hot as two months ago. The air was crisp, and a light wind blew from the north.

A cave was an odd thing to find in that region. There were caves, but they were far away from roads and homes and not many people knew about them. The two men didn't expect to find anything. Simon could have been hundreds of miles away.

They broke away from the road and traveled along a river lined with cypress trees. A white bluff appeared high above them and it was almost blinding under the sun. The river moved slowly and there were fish seen in parts of it. The fish huddled and swam together, and when Cord and Peterson rode near the water the fish swam away into a shaded area.

They searched for caves along the river and on the hills for two hours. They found nothing.

"Care to head back?" asked Cord.

"I thought I'd say that. Thought you wanted to find Simon."

Cord took off his hat, combed his sweating hair to the side and stared up at the sun for an instant. "Not in this heat."

"How about one more hour?"

"Sure. We rode all the way here. Might as well."

They found a dark opening into the limestone. The two men left their horses behind and walked inside, but it was a small cave with nothing inside but bones and fur.

Cord kicked the bones with his boots. The bones were months old. When he tried to find another opening, his hands only felt the rock wall. He sighed and walked outside with Peterson.

Peterson put his weight on the cane and nodded down the river. "We can head further."

"All right. At least we found a cave."

"Who knows what killed whatever that was," said Peterson.

"The bones back there?"

"Yeah. My guess is coyotes. But I doubt they'd bring the carcass back to a cave."

Cord mounted his horse and turned to him. "What are you saying?"

"I'm saying it's strange. That's all."

They continued and found nothing. No caves or any sign of some wild man living in a nearby cave. Not finding him wasn't a bad result since Simon had disappeared for two months. Peterson didn't believe Simon was gone. He believed Simon might have given up, but he thought that he wasn't gone.

The men traveled to Peterson's home in the late afternoon. The sun was forgiving for the rest of the day. Big clouds huddled in the west and they promised rain; it was a good sign. Rain was rare in San Antonio. The crops needed the rain. The problem was the chance of a flood.

"Rain clouds?" asked Cord, noticing the old man take off his hat and squint his eyes at the dark clouds in the west. The clouds looked menacing over the hills, spreading out wide, like storm clouds over the ocean do. He could see the grey lines coming down from the dark clouds and he could see the birds fly in different directions. Peterson always noticed what the animals did right before a storm; that's how he knew what was going to happen.

The deer pranced away. The squirrels hid in their homes. The armadillos went into bushes or to higher ground.

"It looks like it," said Peterson. "We better ride faster."

Cord rode faster and then looked up at the black clouds. As he looked closer, he noticed the clouds looked strange.

"You see that black cloud there?" asked Cord.

Peterson's eyesight wasn't great, so he couldn't see the black clouds clearly. "Not yet. Let's keep going. We're getting close to it."

They rode on and soon they found the black cloud was made of smoke, and the cloud was above Peterson's house. Cord and Peterson found the road and then they could see the giant cloud of smoke rising in the air.

That's when they saw Peterson's crops on fire. All the crops were on fire. Some volunteer firefighters were using a plow around the crops to prevent the fire from spreading.

There was nothing Cord or Simon could do; the crops were already in flames. The pigsty was safe, and so was the shed and house. Peterson got off his horse and used his cane to reach the firefighters.

"What happened here?" said Cord to one of them.

"We don't know, sir. We got here as soon as we could. All we saw was the fire and the crops burning. We did what we could," he said, and walked away.

The firefighter monitored the fire with the others. They walked around the fire. Peterson watched as his crops burned, and then he turned to see the rain clouds blowing from the west. He and Cord knew one thing: Simon was still around.

Peterson stared at the fire with his mouth open. He brought up a hand and covered his mouth. An entire harvest destroyed within a few hours. It was a dry and hot day, so the fire spread quickly.

The rain poured down and doused the flames within the next two hours. The water pelted the tin roof of the house and made a sound similar to bullets hitting metal. Cord and Peterson waited for the fire to fizzle out.

Peterson sat in a chair on the back porch and rested his cane on his legs. He breathed heavily and felt his heart. "We know Simon is around," said Peterson. "Somewhere."

"At least we know he's around."

"I'd like to give him two acres and see what he does with it."

Cord frowned and almost smiled at Peterson. "Are you joking?"

"Yes." Peterson's stern face and constant frown was still present. He breathed calmer. "We'll have to tell the chief about this."

"I think he might already know. We saw the smoke from a long ways away."

"Yes, he might." He looked for the cats and wondered where they live. He tried not to worry about them. "I imagine you're leaving in a couple weeks."

Cord looked down at his boots. "I might."

Peterson shook his head. "I kind of envy you. You going off to wherever you want. I always wanted to do that."

"You still can."

"I can't really get around much, Cord. My knees and my back hurt. I just have to sit down always. Riding horses seem to make things worse."

"Why didn't you say so? We rode for a long time today."

"I wanted to find Simon. I didn't worry about the pain in my back and knees. I needed to find him," he said. "But it looks like he found us."

Cord looked at the oak trees dripping of water and the rain plopping up from puddles of water. Simon could be watching them from the trees; Cord thought about that. He tried to see a figure out from behind a tree trunk, but it was dark outside. The sky was black. Thunder echoed over the land and the sky flashed white with lightning.

"It's about time to sleep," said Jim Peterson. But he didn't make any indication that he was getting up and going to bed.

"Are you watching for Simon?" asked Cord.

"Yeah. Why does he want my land so much? It's just land. It's nothing special."

"Someone thinks it's special."

"Yeah, and they should have thought better of it," said Peterson. "I'll shoot him next time I see Simon. He almost killed you, remember?"

"I remember," said Cord.

"Dragged you off to his little cave," he said. "Are you sure you don't know where it is? It's somewhere around here."

"I don't remember how I got there. When we left, I was blindfolded. Couldn't see anything."

The thunder roared above them. They felt

the thunder shake the ground and rattle the window shutters. Peterson couldn't see anything, so he walked inside. He sat down in a dining room chair, tired and yet not able to sleep. There was an arsonist somewhere out there, and he knew the fire was spreading each time.

Cord sat in a chair opposite Peterson and listened to the rain against the windows. The room was dark except for a coal-oil lamp on the table.

"Are you giving up?" asked Peterson.

"On what?"

"Catching Simon."

"No. I think we'll find him."

"What if he doesn't come back for two months? You'll be gone. Won't you?"

Cord folded his arms and looked outside. It was so dark he couldn't even see the pigsty or the shed in the south. He was glad to be in the house and not on a bedroll out in the rain. "I don't know, Jim."

Peterson looked outside with him, but there was nothing to see except for flashing lines of lightning in the distance. "You know, I never had a son, but I always thought I'd have one." He touched the chin of his white beard. The beard was cotton white, but sharp as cactus spikes. "I never had one. A daughter was a surprise to us, Marguerite and I. Sarah was easy to raise. She was never trouble, but trouble is what I'm used to. I raised a bunch of boys in the army and taught them all I knew. You can say I raised them. I tried to teach them how to be good men. When one man goes off and commits crimes, you wonder if you did something wrong."

"Simon was probably like that before you met him," said Cord.

"Could have been. But you can teach them how to be civilized, even if they were criminals before. I failed at that."

"You can't tame a rattlesnake."

Peterson grinned. "Yeah? That's true. Maybe that's all there is to it."

Cord leaned his elbows on the table and listened to the thunder that was heading southeast. It was a faint sound. The rain slowed and the pelting against the tin roof lessened. "I remember what you said about moving on. I'm going in to the city tomorrow."

"For what?"

"To find a woman."

"To court a woman?"

"That's right."

Peterson laughed and used his cane to stand up. In a cheerful tone, he said, "Good!"

CHAPTER 9

CORD WORKED ALL DAY ON THE GIBSON'S farm. The harvest was almost over, so the Gibson's were happy. But Cord didn't think much of it; he'd keep working somewhere. He thought it was time to move to another city, but now he wasn't sure if he should stay or not.

Another month, he thought. I want to find Simon. He's been terrorizing Mr. Peterson long enough.

Cord mounted his horse in the late afternoon and rode to the city. He hitched his horse in front of a law office and walked the sidewalk. He walked by two women in long dresses who smiled at him but he said nothing in return. He smiled back and went on. When he turned back, he saw the two women go inside of a carriage.

It had been so long since courting a woman he didn't know what he would say. Women were beginning to feel unfamiliar to him, and he thought that was a bad sign.

He walked inside a saloon and ordered whiskey at the bar. Then he propped his elbows on the bar and drank alone. After a while he got tired of smelling sweat, horse and manure- bottomed boots and headed outside. It was getting dark, so he walked inside of a restaurant and sat down at a table with two chairs. It was quiet and he liked that, so he stayed and ordered food. After eating, he smoked a cigar and looked around. There were about three others eating, and they all minded their own business.

Then he heard a noise outside that sounded like two dogs fighting. He turned his head and looked out the window. There was a woman and man across the street. The man was yelling at the woman as he held her arms. She struggled to get away, her head veered back from his face. Cord squinted at them, went outside and walked into the alleyway.

"What's going on here?" asked Cord.

"Mind your own business," said the man. He looked over the shoulders of the woman.

Cord noticed the hands around the young woman's upper arms were so tight that they left red marks on her skin. The woman turned her head towards Cord.

"Help!" she said.

Cord said to the man, "Let go of her or I'll have to make you let her go. And I don't want to have to do that."

"Do something then!" The bald man let go of the woman. She tumbled to the ground and looked up at Cord. The bald man walked sideways and kept his eyes on Cord.

Cord looked behind them and saw the street dark and poorly lit. A stagecoach went by and a couple walked into a hotel.

Then Cord squared up and punched the man on the side of his face. The man fell to the ground and then gradually pushed his body up from the dirt. He held on to the side of the building beside him and with the other hand felt the blood near his eye.

The woman leaned against the building and slowly backed away. She saw the bald man on the ground brush dirt from his pants and stare back at Cord.

The bald man pulled a four-inch long blade from his coat pocket. "Come here, woman! I ain't asking again."

"I don't have to do that. I don't want to! Leave me alone," she said, folding her arms and watching what Cord would do. Her eyes were wide and her breath erratic, yet not as erratic as the bald man's.

Cord noticed the person he punched was a middle-aged man like Cord, yet he looked desperate and hungry for something. When Cord looked back at the woman in the red dress, he figured out what he was hungry for.

Cord stood with his hands to his sides. He didn't even stare at the knife, which the woman found odd. Cord smiled a little, and she found that even more odd and, in a way, thrilling. He put his fists up and kept his eyes on the knife.

"Walk away," said the man with the knife. "I'm not gonna ask you again."

Cord didn't respond. He waited.

"Ain't nobody around, mister. If I kill you, no one will find out," said the bald man.

"I'm here, you idiot," said the woman.

"You're next," he said to her.

Cord pointed his finger back at the woman behind him. "All she'll do is get someone to carry your body away, 'cause I'm not going anywhere."

"If that's how you want it."

The man with the knife hunched over and made a stabbing motion for Cord's stomach. Cord moved his body to the side, grabbed the hand with the knife and punched the man in the nose. The man stumbled back and didn't seem bothered by the blood streaming down his face.

Then the man rushed Cord and cut Cord against the arm and leg. Cord grabbed the knife once he tried to slice him again and then clutched the man's neck with his free hand. Cord then pulled the knife closer until it was close to the man's neck. The man head-butted Cord.

The woman gasped and looked for anyone on the street. No one was around that part of town, but she yelled for help anyway.

Cord stumbled to the ground and gradually stood up and held his hand to his forehead. The man with the knife gasped for air and it sounded like someone who gasped for air after almost drowning. Cord felt the thump on his forehead and then walked towards the man.

The man with the knife yelled out and almost stabbed Cord in the belly, but Cord once again moved to the side. But this time he grabbed the arm and twisted it. The man screamed in pain; his neck grew stiff as Cord twisted the arm and then broke it. The knife dropped to the ground.

The bald man fell to the floor and felt his broken arm. With the man's face to the mud, Cord grabbed the knife and put his knee against the man's back. He held the knife to the man's neck as the woman watched with her mouth open.

Cord breathed heavily. He could feel all the deep knife cuts in his skin, but he didn't think about that.

"I've killed a man before," Cord said to the man on the ground.

The man was silent. His arms were to the side as Cord turned back and noticed the woman. Then his breathing slowed and his face grew more relaxed. "But I'm not like that anymore," he reminded himself.

Cord put the knife in his pant pocket and pulled the man up. A deputy ran behind and the woman signaled him down. The people that were in the restaurant across the street came around the corner and formed a small crowd.

"Did you hear a scream?" asked the deputy.

"Yes," said the woman. "That man tried to kill that other man."

"Which one started it?"

"The bald man. The other one saved my life," she said.

The deputy walked forward and handcuffed the man who almost killed Cord. "You're coming with me. Hope you have a good reason for this."

The bald man refused to answer.

"That's what I thought," said the deputy. "What happened here?" he asked Cord.

Cord told the deputy the story and the deputy then thanked him and yanked the bald man away. The crowd gradually separated until it was only Cord and the woman.

She said, "What's your name?"

"Cord. And yours?"

"Ann. That was an awfully brave and stupid thing you did," she said.

Ann and Cord walked together until Ann sat down on the stairs in front of St. Joseph's Church. Cord sat down beside her. "Are you all right?" he said. "Can I walk you home?"

She placed her head between her knees and cried. She wiped the tears with her fingers. When Ann turned to Cord, she noticed his shirt was cut up and his skin bleeding. He didn't lose sight of her eyes. Strangely, he felt safe near her.

"You need a doctor," she said.

"Probably."

Ann grabbed his hand and led him away. He didn't resist and followed her. She led him to her apartment that was on the second story of a red wooden building. He stood and looked around the room. It was brightly lit. The bed had red covers. The chair in the corner was red. Even the wallpaper was red.

She likes the color red, thought Cord.

"Sit down. I can bandage you."

He sat in the chair in the corner of the room and looked outside the window at the street. At that moment Cord forgot all about admitting he killed a man and that he said it in front of Ann. He wondered if she cared about that, but he felt he already knew; he was sitting in her apartment.

"I can't believe you did that," she said, walking out from a separate room. She carried white bandages and alcohol. Shaking her head, she kneeled between his legs that were spread on the chair and started unbuttoning his shirt. He was uncomfortable at first but slowly he unbuttoned it and watched as she poured a clear liquid on the wounds. He bit his teeth hard.

"Sorry," she said. "I should have told you it would hurt."

Then she wrapped his torso wounds in a white material and as she did so her face was close to his. He could smell her, but he couldn't tell the exact smell; to Cord, the smell of women was an exotic smell that was much stronger than simply smelling flowers.

After she was done her hands were on his legs. He stared down at her hands and then at her face. "This will be free," she said. Ann started unbuttoning her dress.

"I don't know about this," he said quickly.

She lowered her hands. "What do you mean?"

"I've never been with a woman that's, well —a woman who is in your line of work."

She smiled and her teeth were the whitest Cord had ever seen. "You don't have to, if you don't want to."

He straightened up in the chair. Her hands glided down to his knees. "I'd rather get to know you," said Cord.

She stood up and sat on her bed.

"I know I smell like a dead horse and look like a wild man. But I—"

"You don't," she interrupted.

"Well, that's good."

"I'm flattered. Not many men want to get to know a whore. If they do, it's just a ruse. They just want to use you."

"I'm sure I'm not the first to ask," he said.

"No, but you're the first man to ask that I like," she assured him.

"Why do you like me?"

"Well, you saved my life, for one. And you fought a man with a knife while you were unarmed. That takes a lot of courage. Not many people do something like that. I never saw anything like that before. And because I feel good around you."

"Can we see each other again?"

"If you're all right with what I do for a living."

He frowned and realized he wasn't all right with that. He had loved one woman and one woman only, and that was his previous wife, Lara. He wasn't sure what he was getting himself into, but he couldn't resist Ann. "I don't have much money," he said.

"I'm not the type to care about the wealth of people, just if they're good enough to know."

"Am I good enough?"

"Yes," she smiled.

Cord walked to the window curtains and looked outside at the moon. "It's late."

"You sure you don't want to stay a while?"

He shook his head. "I don't feel right about it."

"It's not right or wrong. It's just a thing you like to do."

"I don't think so," he said. "It's wrong."

"I'm wrong? Because that's what I do."

"No, I wasn't saying that."

"I do what I have to do," she said.

"I know."

"You said you killed a man."

He was silent and stared out the window

for a while. He kept that part of his life in the past, and he didn't want to speak about it. "That was a long time ago."

"You aren't perfect yourself."

"No. I never said I was. Look, forget what I said. I just never met someone like you before. I just don't even know how to act around you."

"You don't have to do anything. I can do it all."

"No, I don't mean that." He shook his head and walked to the door. "This was a bad idea. I should have just stayed home."

"Wait," she said. She walked over to him. "You can see me again."

"Are you sure?"

"I'm sure." She looked down at the blood on his shirt. "I'll be here. I can cook for you or something."

"Okay," he said. He had not felt this good in a long time. He nodded and said, "Good night, Ann."

"Good night, Cord."

He walked down the stairs and then to the street. He tried to remember how he got there. Despite the cuts and bruises he felt great. He looked up at her window and memorized the address to the place. Then he found his horse two blocks away and rode back to Peterson's house.

He admitted to killing man. Cord thought about how he admitted it so easily, but he remembered he was caught in the moment. And he forgot about the woman behind him. He thought she would have run for help. And— he tried to stop making excuses. The excuses weren't helping. He told himself that he was a changed man. The past only made him aware of what he shouldn't do, and he knew exactly what he should do now.

CHAPTER 10

CORD GOT HOME LATE THAT NIGHT.
Peterson didn't see the scars on Cord, as Cord
managed to sneak inside in the middle of night.
Then, after going to his room, he got rid of his
ripped shirt and pants. And then he lay down
to sleep after drinking some whiskey he had for
the pain; the whiskey came from a canteen
Cord had. Like the feeling after waking from a
good dream, he wanted to never forget Ann
and how he felt around her.

Chief Marcus rode to the Peterson house
with a deputy beside him. It was late morning.
Peterson sat in the rocking chair with the black
cat on his lap. When the chief walked closer
the cat jumped up and ran up a tree.

"Didn't think your cat was skittish," said

Marcus, staring at the oak tree and the cat on a high branch. "Sorry about that."

"That doesn't matter. The cat's like that."

"This here's Deputy Hernandez." He pointed at the deputy with his finger and then got off his horse and walked to the front porch.

Hernandez shook hands with Peterson.

"We heard you had a little fire," said Chief Marcus. "Saw it, too."

"That's right. Simon burned down all my crops."

"Simon," said the chief, nodding and staring around the land at the black ground. "He's come back, huh?"

"No idea why."

"Are you sure it's land he wants? There's gotta be more to the story."

"Cord said it was land," said Peterson. "I'm sure he told you the story after he was pulled into Simon's cave."

"He did. But it's been two or three months since then. We assumed he was long gone. Now he's back."

Cord leaned against a wooden beam. "He wants to scare Peterson away."

"But Peterson don't scare easily," laughed the chief. "We're concerned that he'll do something worse to you. This man twice caught your land on fire. We think it might be the house next."

"Could be," said Peterson.

"You don't sound worried."

"I'll be here, waiting for him with my gun."

The chief's smile faded as he straightened his back and stared at his deputy for a quick moment. "We thought so. But I wanted to offer you protection."

"I don't need any," said Peterson, shaking his head. "He burned down my land when I wasn't here. Don't think he'll kill me."

"And when you leave he might burn down your house," said Marcus. "I can put two men here for one week. They'll take turns on duty and watch for this idiot."

"Simon isn't much of an idiot." Peterson stood up and used his cane to walk to his pigsty. The men followed him. "He sometimes is, but he can be smart. After all, he hasn't been found in two months. Cord and I went after him to try to find his cave, by the way. That's when Simon showed up."

Chief Marcus looked back at his deputy and then at the blackened ground. The black cropland looked like the remnants of a war zone. "You don't want our help?" he asked Peterson.

"I got Cord," said Peterson.

"I thought he worked for some farm away from town."

"Yes, but he sleeps here at night. If Simon comes back, it'll be at night. We'll be on the lookout for him."

Marcus put his hands in the air. "All right. I won't ask again. I'm just afraid this will only get worse." The chief and deputy rode down the dirt road and disappeared.

Cord prepared for his ride back to the Gibson's. The harvest was almost over, and he didn't know what he would do for work the rest of the year. He had a lot of things on his mind, and he knew Peterson did too.

"Where are you going?" said Peterson to Cord.

Cord mounted his horse and looked back at the old man. "Work, of course."

"Where were you last night?"

"In town. Why?"

"Just curious," said Peterson.

"You sound like my pa when I would sneak out at night to see a girl."

"So that's what you did."

Cord blushed and turned away.

"That was it, huh?" asked Peterson.

"I said I was going to find a woman."

"What kind of woman?"

"Just a woman."

"This wasn't at the whore house, was it?"

"No," said Cord. "I don't go to them."

"Good. I've seen a lot of men who get ruined from those places. Some of them get violent and can never leave. Don't know why, but they end up destroying themselves."

"I've heard it."

"Tell me about this woman," said Peterson.

Cord was about to joke and say, 'Well, she's a whore.' But he did not think of her in that way, even though every man would call her a whore. He couldn't see her being that kind of person. "Her name is Ann."

Peterson listened intently and leaned his weight on the cane, like a father does when he hears his son has decided to make a big decision in life.

"I saw her getting harassed by a man. I fought him and left it at that."

"Fought him? That explains the bruise on your face. And the ripped shirt you got on your bed."

Cord felt his face. It felt numb, but he wasn't sure if it was from fighting or drinking. "He pulled a knife on me."

"I guess you won."

"The police came and took him away."

"And the woman is all right?"

"She's fine. I made sure she was all right before I headed back."

Peterson fed his pigs and leaned his elbows against the fence. "That's good. It gets real nasty at night. Don't know what brings out all the bad in people during that time. Maybe they were like that even during the day and they're just more comfortable at night."

"I think you got a point," said Cord. "This man won't be on the streets for a while. He cut me up but Ann took care of the pain. She bandaged me."

"Yeah? Sounds like you had yourself a good night."

"You can say that."

"You're going to see her again?"

"She said she wanted to see me again," said Cord. He hung his head, unsure of what he agreed to. It had been so long since he courted a woman, and he didn't know whether Ann was the type to even marry him. I'm already thinking about marriage, he thought.

"What is it?"

"I think I'll need to get a job somewhere around town. If I want to see her again, I'll need to be closer."

"Well, there's plenty of work there. The city is growing fast. It won't be too long before

San Antonio reaches one hundred thousand people."

Cord listened to the birds chirping in the trees and saw the sun was high above them. It meant he was late for work. "I have to go."

They waved to each other. Jim Peterson watched Cord go away and disappear behind the curve of the road. The black cat jumped down from the tree and Peterson waited for it and the other cats to bask in the sun on his porch. He sat in his chair and watched the trees. He felt he was being watched.

Later that day Peterson put his land up for sale and waited to see who would want to buy his land. It was a test. If someone wanted his land so badly, Peterson thought he would come out in the open.

CORD RODE INTO TOWN THE NEXT DAY. He searched for Ann. He walked by a saloon and then turned back and went inside. He ordered whiskey to calm his nerves and then looked at himself in the mirror behind the bar. He saw that his beard had regrown. His cheeks weren't gaunt like they were when he rode into San Antonio two months ago.

"I've seen you before," said the man sitting next to him.

Cord turned to hear him. "Excuse me?"

"You was up in New Mexico. You knew Hugh Beckwith, didn't you?"

"I don't know what you're talking about," said Cord. "Must be someone else."

Cord paid and walked out. The man talking to him followed him outside. He was a talkative fellow and seemed to not be able to keep quiet about anything. He raised his voice too loud whenever he spoke and it caused Cord to want to be far from him.

"Come back!" said the man. "I wanna talk to you."

Cord turned into an alleyway and the man persisted. Cord stopped in the middle of the alleyway and turned to the follower.

"I'm Joe Cobb. I was a friend of Hugh."

Cord stood motionless and nodded. He looked around for people but no one was close enough to hear them.

"Hugh," said Cord. "That was a long while ago. Do you know my name?"

"Yes, you're Cord," said Joe Cobb, who looked sad but also excited about seeing someone from the past. "That all didn't end well, did it?"

"No. It never does. I just didn't know that at the time."

"What never does?"

"Fighting. It just leads to more and more fighting."

Joe was unarmed, which surprised Cord. But he didn't know what Joe wanted and what kind of person he was. "You know about Hugh, how he died?" said Joe.

"Didn't know he died."

"He tried to rob a bank somewhere here in Texas and got shot. Think it was in El Paso."

Cord shook his head and took off his hat and combed his hair to the side. "I was going to say I didn't expect that, but that was Hugh. He wanted more and more money. He turned ugly after a while."

"Yes, well, how about you? What are you doing around here?"

"Working."

"What kind of job are you planning?"

"No, not that. I'm working clean jobs now. I'm a farmer, sometimes a cowboy. I take what I can get."

"That really what you been doing?" Joe wore no hat. He felt his buzz cut hair, as it used to be long and he had just cut it recently. Then he wiped his face of sweat using a handkerchief.

"That's smart. I was thinking that was an awful shift. But most of the Seven Rivers Warriors died. It seems like they are all forgotten already."

"That happens," said Cord. "We'll all be forgotten eventually."

"Truth be told. Well, I guess you'll be around town and—"

"Don't tell anyone about this," interrupted Cord. He walked until he was a head length away from Joe Cobb. Then he pointed at Joe's chest. Joe looked down at Cord's finger and then at his eyes. Cord's lips were slightly turned down. "I don't need any more trouble than what I got already."

Joe Cobb stared at the bruise on Cord's face. "I won't tell. I promise. I was friends with Hugh, remember?" He talked quickly and looked over Cord's shoulder to see if anyone was watching.

Cord nodded and patted Joe on the shoulder. "Good. You're all right."

"You—you served your time, didn't you?"

"I'll see you around," said Cord. He walked away and turned his head to say, "Remember, don't tell anyone I'm here."

Cord walked across the street and into another alleyway. He was relieved after the encounter with Joe Cobb. He fled to Texas to leave his rotten past, but now it seemed to follow him.

Cord turned back and saw a big red headed man leaning against a support beam with one eye watching Cord. It was the largest man he had ever seen, in height and in muscle.

The big redheaded man followed him into the alleyway and Cord made it out of the dark alleyway and blended in with a crowd walking the wooden boardwalks. He turned back and saw the redhead peer over the heads of people and spot him.

Now Cord picked up speed and tried to lose him. It was a big town. He thought he could lose him in the crowds.

The redhead walked around people and acted as if no one could spot him. Cord walked into a saloon and then went out the back door. He thought he lost him there. Cord walked up the stairs to a second story building and then climbed the railing and grabbed the rim of the building to climb to the flat roof. He lay on his belly on the roof and waited. He was cautious of poking his head out from the rooftop.

After a few minutes, Cord looked around all sides of the building and tried to see the redheaded man. There was no sign of him. The wagons and stagecoaches and horses went down the streets. It was getting dark and the electric streetlights were turning on. Cord could see the lights in the building windows and he could see the streets thinning out until there were only the late-night folk on the streets.

Cord climbed down from the roof. He did so slowly under the dark. The alleyway was entirely black and unlit. He walked to the street and peeked out. He saw a few women on the sidewalk and a man crossing the street. Then he felt a hand on his shoulder. The hand dug into an area near his collarbone and prevented Cord from making any action.

"Found you," said the redheaded giant.

Cord couldn't speak. The hand dug into a spot that caused the victim to freeze up and close his eyes. Cord fell limp to the ground. The redhead pulled him up from the arms. It was such a fast motion it was like Cord weighed as much as a cat. To the redhead, he weighed nothing.

"Don't you run again."

The redheaded man pulled him back into the alleyway but now Cord could move better. He elbowed the redhead in the nose but that only angered him further. Cord hit him again, but this time his elbow went into the redhead's eye.

Cord was set free as the redhead held his

damaged eye. Then Cord ran to the open street and tried to find out where he stood. He was still new to the city. Nothing looked familiar. He ran on the sidewalk and turned back. The redhead started sprinting towards him, his nostrils flaring and his mouth turned downward in disgust and pain.

Cord turned right on a brick street and searched for his horse. "Lightning," he yelled out. Sometimes his horse Lightning would nay when Cord said his name. But he heard no sound.

He took another right and ran faster. He wasn't sure if even three men could restrain the man chasing him, so he felt he must escape by horse or he would get caught. And he wasn't sure what would happen to him if he were caught.

Cord turned back but he couldn't find the redhead anymore. He kept running and then looked up and saw the apartment building where Ann lived. He was about to go upstairs to her room, but he felt he might lead the man chasing him to her place.

He walked and tried to breath slower and calmer. His clothes and hair were sweaty. He tried to listen for running but all he heard was a horse clopping by and a wagon somewhere on another street. The sound of the horse seemed to echo through the valley shaped street lined with two-story tall buildings. Even Cord's breath sounded loud to him.

He walked and kept his eyes on the dark alleyway. He walked the streets for several minutes and tried to find his horse. It was two blocks away; he could see Lightning from that distance. The horse waited.

If I can get my rifle, thought Cord, I'd have a much better chance.

Cord leaned his back against a store window and noticed the moon moving out from the clouds. He could hear laughing near his horse. Then he spotted a man and woman walking together.

He left that spot and then heard footsteps behind him. The redheaded man wrapped his arms around Cord's stomach and pulled him into the alleyway.

"Get your hands off me," yelled Cord. "What do you want?"

The redhead didn't say anything. He pushed Cord against the brick wall and punched him in the face. The punch felt like a rock being shot from a cannon. Cord barely moved on the ground; he clawed his way to the street but the redhead knew he couldn't do much anymore.

Cord's body was limp when the redheaded

man pulled him up by the front of his shirt. "I got a message."

Cord's bottom lip was bleeding and so was his cheek. Just below the eye was a purple bruise. "Go ahead," said Cord.

"Think you're funny, huh? Can't do much now, can you?"

"I don't have much money on me."

"I don't want your money. I got a message from Simon. He says to stop searching for him. Don't try to find him. If he spots you, you're dead. This is just a friendly warning."

"A friendly warning for friends."

The redhead punched Cord in the gut. Cord coughed and spit blood.

"Sure, we're friends. Don't let me catch you again. I don't want to have to kill you. It's too much trouble."

"Wouldn't want to trouble you," said Cord.

The redhead let go of Cord's shirt. Cord's body fell to the dirt. The redhead spit on the ground and shook his head in disgust.

"Look at you."

Cord tried to get up, but he was too exhausted. His head felt scrambled, and he could barely see through his right eye. His ribs hurt and his face was busted up badly. He coughed and spit blood. His face was against the dirt and when he turned he couldn't see the redheaded man anymore. He was gone.

Cord lay there on the ground for half an hour and then gradually stood up. He walked on the street and sometimes held his hand against the glass windows of passing stores. He found his horse and slowly made his way home.

Cord hunched over on his horse as he neared Jim Peterson's house. He was about to pass out but he held on a little longer. The purple bruise near his eye and the opened wound caused him pain, but his mind wasn't on the pain.

Peterson walked outside the front door and spotted Cord. Without saying a word, the old man helped Cord get into the house. Cord shuffled his heavy feet. It took a while to get him to the bed since Peterson used a cane.

"I don't have whiskey, but I have some medicine," Peterson said to him.

Cord drank the foul-tasting medicine and lay on his bed. Peterson wiped the blood from Cord's face using a wet towel, then he sewed the opened wound on the cheek.

"Who did this?"

"Not Simon, but someone who works for him." Cord's voice was a whisper.

"Why'd he do this?"

"We both know," said Cord. He turned his face to the window. He could hear the crickets in the night and he could see the moon half visible in the clouds. The medicine made him drowsy. The room seemed to vibrate, so Cord closed his eyes.

"Simons wants me to stay away."

Peterson shook his head and frowned. He looked worried. "That won't happen."

"No."

"We'll find him. We know he's scared. He wouldn't have sent someone to hurt you if he wasn't scared."

Cord opened his eyes and found the room still moving. Then he closed his eyes again.

"You just rest, son," said Peterson, using his cane to stand up. He walked to the window and looked outside at the black crops and the partially burned trees.

The tree branches moved in the wind. He could hear the tree branches and the leaves brushing against one another. But he could see no sign of Simon. He was out there, somewhere, and Peterson and Cord knew it. It was just a matter of getting him to stop hiding like a mole rat.

There was one solution to getting Simon's employer out from hiding.

"I put my land up for sale."

Cord woke up after hearing the deep voice. "Why'd you do that?"

"How do you catch an animal? You put down some bait. I have three men interested in the house. I've heard of two of them. Never heard of Livingston. The other two are men that are known to buy out land over town. Livingston, Sinherst and Felville are the ones interested. I'm visiting all three tomorrow."

"To do what?"

"See if one of them is working with Simon. I have a feeling one of them knows Simon. Maybe it's Sinherst. He has a big manor far east of here."

"What are you going to do?"

"Ask them questions. I can always tell when someone lies." Cord lay with his head against the pillow. He watched as Jim Peterson turned around to face him. "Why'd you go into town anyway?"

"To see Ann."

"Ann, right. I forgot. Was this fight after visiting her?" He said it quickly. "You might have led Simon to her."

"I never got to her. This giant followed me. He must have been seven feet tall and three hundred pounds. He could run faster than me. There was no way to escape. I tried to run to my horse. My rifle was on my horse. But he got me first."

Peterson nodded. "At least she's safe."

"Yes," Cord whispered.

"How did this man find you?" asked Peterson.

"I don't know."

"He said not to go after Simon, but you said you were going to see Ann."

"That's right. I just wanted to see Ann. I gave up on finding Simon. I guess he thought I was trying to find him." Cord yawned and closed his eyes. The medicine almost made him sleep. He could barely see out of his right eye, as the skin around it was puffed up. He could feel sharp pain but the pain came and went. It was not so bad.

It looked bad, but Peterson had seen worse when fighting the Apaches thirty years ago. Peterson had seen men and women scalped, and he thought for his entire life he wouldn't see anything worse than that.

"Simon ought to come out from hiding. I have the bait set. House is for sale. Now he ought to come out for a chat," said Peterson.

"Maybe. He took it pretty far this time."

"He took it too far when he burned my crops and shot you and now almost killed you." Peterson held his chest. He felt his heart beating slowly. Then it went back to normal. His face was covered in cold sweat. Peterson regained his composure and tried to see if Cord was watching him.

Cord was almost asleep on the bed. He was about to talk about his past with the gang he ran with but he realized it was the medicine about to speak.

"Are you feeling all right?" asked Peterson. "How's the medicine?"

"It's working. It's making me a little tired."

"It'll do that. You'll feel better in the morning, until you see a doctor. I got money for you." He dropped ten dollars on the table next to Cord's bed.

It was a good amount of money and Cord was surprised to see that much from Peterson. "Thanks." Cord looked at him through squinted eyes. "You'll need someone if you want to visit those three men."

"You're too weak to even work tomorrow. I have a revolver. I can manage. I've been in the military, remember?"

"What was your rank?"

"Sergeant Major."

"I don't know what that means."

"I just led some men," said Peterson. "I call them men, but they seemed like boys. Most of them came from farms. Raised them like my own children, but I wasn't easy on them. I never was easy. You're not going to make a man by being soft on him."

"You're pretty soft on me."

Peterson smiled a little. "You're already a man."

"A good one?" asked Cord. His voice was quiet, as he was near sleep. His eyelids twitched as he tried to stay awake.

"Yes. A good one."

Cord watched Peterson as he moved towards the bedroom door. Under the drowsiness and deliriousness of the medicine Cord closed his eyes and said, "Good night, pa."

Peterson paused near the bedroom door and hesitated before he spoke. "Good night, son," he said and walked back to his bedroom.

❧

CORD WOKE UP IN THE LATE MORNING AND tried to stand up. His legs were wobbly and he felt dizzy, so he sat down immediately and held his hands on his head, as if doing so would make his throbbing head better. It was another hour before he could manage to walk, eat and find his horse. He stared up at the sun just above his head and then he put on his flat brimmed hat that had fallen near his horse during last night.

Cord rode to a doctor that Peterson talked about. Peterson wrote him directions. After he was given medicine and his wounds sewn or wrapped up, Cord rode back home after a couple hours, ate and decided to see the Gibson's.

He rode to the Gibson's, as the harvest was almost over. Cord's job was almost done, but it wasn't on his mind. His mind was on the throbbing headache and the pain that he felt all over his body. It felt like he had just fought a grizzly bear.

And that was just a warning, thought Cord.

Cord knew the fire was a warning. Now it was a beating. Things were escalating quickly. With Peterson going off to town, he wondered if the old man would be all right. He noticed Peterson coughing and having trouble walking. He didn't know the state of his health but Cord could tell Peterson was in bad shape.

He knocked on the front door and Sarah opened it. She gasped when she noticed Cord's bruised face. "What happened to you?"

"I want to tell you and Lenny what happened at the same time. Could you get him? He out back?" Cord leaned against the doorframe.

"I'll go get him. You can sit down at the table," she said to him.

Lenny and Sarah walked inside through the back door. Lenny took off his hat and tried not to stare at the bruises on Cord's face. He sat down and looked down at the table. "Well, I guess I know who did this. It's Simon."

Cord nodded. "In a way."

"Tell us what happened," said Sarah.

"I went into a saloon and when I came out I noticed I was being followed. I tried to get away but someone managed to find me. He was a giant redheaded man. I didn't stand much of a chance."

"No one was about?" asked Lenny.

"Some, but they were too far. I was on an empty street. It doesn't matter though. It would take more than three men to restrain that man."

Sarah gave him a glass of water. "Does pa know about this?"

"Yes. I told Mr. Peterson. He sewed my cheek and gave me medicine."

"You haven't seen a doctor yet?" said Lenny.

"I have."

"That's good. Are you in pain?"

"I am, but I thought I'd head out here and warn you two. I just wanted to tell you two about what happened. It just seems like every time I try to do something I get shot, pulled into a cave or attacked at night." He tried to see if they were disappointed, as he felt defeated. Lenny and Sarah looked worried instead. "He gave me a message from Simon. Said to stop trying to find him and stop helping Peterson."

Everyone was quiet for a while. They could hear finches singing outside on oak tree branches. But even the peaceful sound of birds chirping couldn't ease their anxiety. Lenny talked about eating lunch, so they all ate and sat around talking about what happened.

Sarah said, "I wish we could just find Simon and throw him in jail. Maybe have policemen go after him."

"It's not that easy," said Cord. "It isn't like those dime novels. The bad guy sometimes gets away."

Cord could tell Sarah was worrying and trying to see what they could do. It was a fire before, but now it was violence. Cord held his head and tried to make things still. The medicine was wearing off.

"Well, thanks, Cord. You've been doing a lot for us lately. Not just for Sarah and I, but for

Jim. You're the hardest worker I've had. You've been doing so much good around here it makes me wonder about you. Why are you doing all these things?" asked Lenny.

"I don't know," said Cord. "Maybe to make up for the bad things I've done."

Lenny chuckled. "You ain't bad. You're good. I can tell. If you done bad, well, that don't make you bad, 'cause you're changing and doing good now. You're helping out." He shook his head and noticed Cord's bruised knuckles. "You should have died. Just look at you."

"Right," Sarah said. "You need to take it easy."

"It's a good thing the harvest's almost over. Now you can settle down for a while," said Lenny.

Cord nodded. "I guess so."

"Plenty of jobs in town," said Lenny, "if you got the itch for more work. The money will be enough for a while."

"Thank you. I should be fine."

"So you'll be staying in town?" asked Sarah.

"I think so. I got someone I'd like to see."

"What do you mean?" she said.

"I wanted to see about Ann. She's a woman I met in town."

"Look at you. Already got yourself acquainted with someone." She smiled and folded her arms. "I guess she likes the quiet type."

"I guess so."

"Don't hold out on us," said Lenny.

"Well, I don't know much about her. I helped her when some man was harassing her."

"See, you are good, doing something like that," said Sarah.

"Any fool does good from time to time," said Cord.

"I don't know." Lenny shook his head and leaned his elbows on the table. "It takes a man to fight for his woman."

Sarah smiled and looked at her husband, causing Cord to think that Lenny might have fought for his own wife.

"I think you're right. Well, I'll be seeing her soon," he said. "I wanted to see her last night but that red headed man really got me good. I was on my way to see her."

"Don't go to town," Sarah urged Cord. "It's not worth it. You don't know how many people Simon's got working for him."

"Who knows how he got someone to work with him," said Lenny. "It's a shame the police can't do much about it. The city is growing fast. They might not have the time for it."

"Sure they do," said Sarah. "They're just too lazy."

"I wouldn't say that," said Lenny.

"It's true. I heard of a robbery in town where the robbers got away. That shouldn't happen in a town like this. It shouldn't be so easy for a robber to hide, especially in a big town."

Cord said, "I'll be careful. I just wanted to see Ann."

"After what just happened to you?" said Lenny. "You ought to stay in Jim's home." He chuckled a little. "Even after those fires it's still safer than going into town."

Cord said, "Well, now that Peterson's land is for sale, maybe Simon will disappear and all of this will blow away. I thought of it this way: Simon probably gets some money if his employer buys the land."

Lenny and Sarah frowned at each other. It was an outrageous statement. Peterson was selling his land? He never wanted to sell. "He did what?" said Lenny.

"Peterson wanted to draw them out and see who is the one in charge of Simon. Simon told me he's working for someone, but he didn't say whom. Putting the land for sale is one way of finding out."

Lenny shook his head. "I just can't see any good coming from it."

"Anyone interested so far?" asked Sarah.

"Three men. Peterson rode out to talk to them today."

"Today," said Lenny, raising his voice. His eyebrows rose in disbelief. "The man who is in charge of the one that beat you to a pulp?"

"I didn't think it was a good idea either," said Cord. "But I don't see any other choice. Like you said, Sarah, the law isn't doing much for us. They wanted to watch Peterson's house for a while, but that would just keep Simon away temporarily. He'd just wait it out. That wouldn't do much. We need to do more than wait. Peterson is tired of that. I think that's why he's taking things into his own hands. He wants to find Simon and make him pay."

"How would we make him pay?" said Lenny.

"Whatever the law says. He might hang. He's dangerous. You saw that fire. You see my face. He could have killed Peterson with that fire. He could have killed me."

"But he didn't," said Sarah.

"Right." Cord scratched his beard and glanced outside. It was a little past midday. He assumed Peterson would be back at the house soon. "We have a lot of questions that need answers. Simon has the answers, but the source is his employer. Simon talked to me about it, remember?"

"Why did he?" asked Lenny. "Why even share that with a stranger?"

Cord shook his head. "I don't know. Simon said we were similar."

"About as similar as a dog and cat," said Sarah. She stood up and took her plate to the kitchen. Cord got up as well, and he took the rest of the plates to the kitchen and helped Sarah wash the dishes.

"I don't see how Simon can live in a cave," said Cord.

"It could have been temporary," said Lenny from the table.

"Could be."

"Then again, no one is like Simon. He isn't right in the head. Pa told me that a long time ago. He told me the stories about Simon," she said. She was about to go on but stopped.

Cord said, "I thought we were being careful, but I guess not. Now I'll be even more careful."

"Maybe you should hold off on going to Ann," said Sarah, placing a hand on Cord's shoulder. "You almost got killed."

"I'll be all right." He walked to the back door and looked out the windows at the sun. He held on to the wall to keep him from falling. He felt dizzy. "She was in trouble once before. I want to make sure she's safe at least."

"Be careful," she said. "You said you would be, but it's been awfully dangerous lately. Reminds me of how it was when I was a child, when it was wild out west." She walked behind Lenny, who was sitting in a chair and watching Cord. "Makes you think it's still like that."

"This is just one man," said Cord. "He can't do much. He can't even fight me himself. He has to send someone. Anyway, I'll be all right," he assured them.

Cord walked slowly to the front door. Lenny told him he didn't have to work that day. It would take one more week to finish all the work, so there was no rush. Cord nodded and went out.

Lenny and Sarah watched Cord ride down the road, his body barely having the ability to stay upright. His shoulders rolled forward and his hands barely held the reins as he rode back to Peterson's home.

CHAPTER 12

IN THE EVENING CORD RODE BACK TO
Peterson's house. The sun was down. The
moon and stars were the only lights that lit the
road. He could see Peterson's horse, which is
the horse Peterson borrowed from Lenny. The
horse was hitched to a wooden pole.

Cord hitched his horse and walked inside
the house. As he stood there, he held his back
against the wall and glanced around the main
room that contained a dinner table, a small
kitchen and one leather chair.

Cord could feel that the pain in his head
was getting worse. It came sharp like a scorpion
sting but gradually lessened until the pain
came back once again. He held his head and
tried to see clearly. The right eye was swollen
and his ribs were sore.

Cord walked into the bedrooms and came out to the main room again. There was no note informing Cord where Peterson went, so he walked out back and searched the area. He thought he must be out on a walk, but the old man never went out for a walk. He was always in his chair petting the cats or out back in the fields.

He couldn't find him, so he went back inside and ate dinner, thinking he would come back later. He assumed Peterson was walking outside. He looked outside and searched the trees. He called for the old man but heard nothing. He walked around the house and then walked far into the trees in every direction except the west, which was a view of the road and the hills.

Cord struggled to walk back to the house. He found the medicine Peterson gave him. He drank the medicine and lay in bed. The medicine made him drowsy and forced him into a deep sleep.

In the morning Cord woke up and looked at Peterson's empty bed. He walked quickly to the front door and saw that Peterson's horse was still there. Cord looked around the lot. He searched the shed and the pigsty and the trees around the land. He called out Peterson's name.

He mounted his horse, rode to San Antonio and came back with the Chief of Police, Donavan Marcus. Deputy Hernandez came along as well. They dismounted from their horses and stared at Peterson's horse and the burned crops that were now ashes that blew away whenever a warm wind roared from the west.

"And you haven't seen Peterson since yesterday?" Chief Marcus asked Cord.

"No, sir. He said he was seeing some people, but his horse is here." He shrugged. "I searched around, but I couldn't find anything."

Hernandez walked behind the house; his eyes were focused on the ground.

Marcus stood next to Cord and said, "If Simon sent a message to you by almost killing you, then I doubt he'll be nice to Mr. Peterson."

"You're right about that."

"Let's walk around," said Marcus. "Maybe we can see if there are any signs of where he went."

Cord walked to the east and ended up at the tree line. The police chief walked south and Hernandez north. They looked for horse tracks and boot prints.

"I got something," yelled Hernandez.

The others walked quickly over to the deputy and found what it was; it was two separate lines, similar to what one sees when a person shuffles their feet in the sand or snow. Then there were two large boot prints, one wider than the two long lines and the other keeping a steady pace. The tracks led to the dark woodlands.

"What is it?" said Marcus.

"Tracks," said Hernandez. "They look like someone was dragged away."

"You sure?" the chief asked him.

"I'm sure. Look at that. They go into the trees over there." They followed the tracks until the tracks faded into a rocky area of prickly pear and thorny bushes. Cord walked ahead and picked up Peterson's wooden cane. He turned around as the other men walked up to him.

The chief nodded. "I was afraid of that."

"What do you think happened?" asked Cord. He held the cane as if he were presenting a ceremonial sword.

"We both know, son. Simon and that redheaded feller you told me about took him." Marcus wiped the sweat from his forehead and pointed back to the horse. "I don't know what they'd want from him. He's selling his land. Simon wanted land, didn't he?"

"That's what he told me," said Cord.

"But Simon goes and does something like

this." Marcus took the cane from him and inspected it. "There's no blood. That's good. He's probably all right. If they wanted to kill him, they would have done so. Bunch of idiots. We'll have to get the dogs to find him. I know it seems nasty but the good thing about this is the dogs can pick up Peterson's scent and bring us to him."

"Sure," said Cord.

"Don't look sad. We'll find him."

"I'm all right."

"Well, it didn't look that way. The dogs will lead us to him."

Marcus carried the cane and said to Hernandez, "We don't know what we'll find. Get Deputy Matthews. We'll need one more man, just in case."

"You think he's using Mr. Peterson for ransom?" asked Cord.

"I believe so. If they took him, Simon wants something. Either he or his employer want to bargain, and I can't have that happen." Marcus saw Cord's face and tried to read it before speaking to Hernandez. "It might get violent."

"Yes, sir. I'll go now." Hernandez walked back to his horse.

"Remember the dogs," called the chief.

"I will."

Marcus patted Cord's shoulder and smiled

a little. It was a reassuring and forced smile, and it looked unnatural for Chief Marcus. "He'll be all right. Mr. Peterson was in the army, you know. He can handle himself."

"I know. He told me about his army days."

"Then you must know about Simon's past."

"Some of it."

"Then you better have that rifle on your horse ready."

❧

CORD, CHIEF MARCUS, DEPUTY Hernandez and Deputy Matthews rode horses in a grass field as the two bloodhounds sniffed the dirt and followed Peterson's scent.

The dogs' ears flopped around as they sprinted and slowed whenever they raised their noses and picked up the scent. Sometimes the dogs would bark and then immediately run, so the men tried to keep up in all the excitement.

The four horsemen followed the dogs for more than an hour, and at that point the men began to think the dogs were lost and unsure of the scent.

Cord wiped the sweat above his lips and looked at the dogs sniffing the ground and air. Cord reached around and felt his back with his hand and touched the spot that caused him pain ever since he mounted his horse that day. His face bruises were lessened, but it was his back that caused him pain.

They came upon a river lined with tall cypress trees that had some of their roots above the water. The last rain wasn't enough to bring the water line to its normal level.

Chief Marcus looked across the river and then down below the moving water. He saw it wasn't too deep. The dogs swam across and the men followed on their horses. The dogs had their long ears dripping with water, and the horses' bodies had a horizontal mark on their coats, just above the stirrups, that showed the depth of the river.

"Look ahead," said Marcus, leading the way and turning his head to the men.

The dogs halted and barked at something up ahead. The dogs were excited and howled, like the sound a dog makes when it sees a predator nearby.

Marcus got off his horse, kneeled down until the knees of his pants were green from the grass and held up a bandana. It was a clean bandana. The dogs sniffed it and Marcus allowed the two bloodhounds to pick up the scent and keep running.

"What is it?" asked Cord from his horse.

"I think it's a bandana," said the chief.

"I never saw Peterson use a bandana before," Cord said.

"That's what I was about to ask. I was going to ask you if he wore one."

"Might have used it to blindfold Peterson," said Cord.

"Could be right. Look at that. The dogs are going on." Marcus mounted again and led the line of riders into the forest.

The dogs walked around a cedar tree and brushed their bodies against the branches. The area was so thick of cedar and oak trees that the horses kept hitting their bodies against the branches. The men had to hold back the branches to keep the branches from hitting their faces.

Cord thought it was part of Simon's plan. It would make it difficult to travel in an area of thick brush; it would slow them down.

The men tried to keep up with the dogs. The dogs didn't have trouble finding their way around the trees.

An hour later the men rode down a steep valley, across a dead creek and into the trees again. Then the dogs stopped and barked.

Chief Marcus got off his horse and walked up to the blood- hounds. "You got something?" He tried to look for anything on the ground, but there was nothing. Then he turned and saw two horses. He motioned for the men to be silent, and once the men saw the horses they all dismounted and grabbed their rifles or revolvers.

Cord reached for his Winchester from the rifle scabbard and followed the two deputies. When he caught up with the others, the dogs were quiet. There was no sign of a cave. The men branched out and looked for an opening to a cave.

The chief walked near the horses and pulled away oak branches. When he did so, the branches fell, as they were cut recently, and he realized he found the entrance. He walked up to the men.

"All right. Here it is," he said, breathing heavy and perspiring. He said to Cord, "You recognize these horses?"

"That one with the saddle is Simon's. I saw it when I chased him with Peterson in the city."

"What about the other horses?"

"I haven't seen them before," said Cord.

"Good." Then he faced his deputies. "Be alert. We don't know what we'll find. Watch your fire. They probably have a hostage."

The men nodded and held their rifles ready.

The cave entrance was about four feet tall and a few feet wide. They had to duck their heads to enter. Deputy Matthews walked behind the chief and used a lantern to show the way. Their footsteps echoed once they were farther in.

Cord could hear water dripping somewhere. The ceiling opened up and now the men didn't have to bend down any longer. The boot echoes were louder.

The room was poorly lit. The men could only see Deputy Matthews and part of Chief Marcus. The ceiling height and walls were unseen.

Then there was a loud crack. The lantern Matthews held fell and broke and the cave went into complete darkness. Matthews yelled, "They're here."

A shot went off somewhere near Hernandez and then there was a loud groaning. Cord dropped to the floor and tried to see in the pitch dark. He heard scuffling and yelling, but even if he found the noise he didn't know who needed help.

Deputy Matthews lit a match and frantically tried to find the source of the noise and yells. The light showed the redheaded man choking Hernandez and then quickly pulling out a knife from his waist.

Cord aimed and shot the redheaded man.

The body went limp. Hernandez pushed the dead body off of him and gasped for breath.

"Everyone all right?" said Cord.

"Chief?" called Deputy Matthews. "Chief, you there?" There was no reply, which made Matthews search for him using the small light from his match. Cord checked on Hernandez.

"Where's Simon?" asked Hernandez, who was still trying to breath normally.

"I don't know. Deeper into the cave maybe," said Cord.

"Oh, God," said Matthews. "Come over here! Hurry."

Cord helped Hernandez up and then the two walked to Matthews.

"What's wrong?" said Cord.

Matthews kneeled beside the chief and moved the burning match to show the chief's fatal head wound. "He's dead," said Matthews. "He got shot in the head."

"I didn't see anyone else," said Hernandez.

"Me neither," said Matthews, covering his mouth and shaking his head. "This is worse than I thought."

"Simon must have been here," said Hernandez.

"I heard a shot, but not coming from there," said Cord. He looked around and tried to see. His eyes weren't adjusted to the pitch-black cave, but he could hear something coming from a long ways away.

Hernandez looked down at the chief and then he took off his police hat and held in to his chest, just what Matthews did. "They murdered the police chief," said Hernandez. He and Matthews stared at the body in disbelief. It was unreal to see the body of the police chief.

Then Cord said, "Hear that?" And the men gradually woke up from their stupor.

"What?" said Hernandez.

"Listen."

"I hear it," said Matthews.

Cord asked for a match. Then he walked to the sound with the lit match and found Peterson in the far corner of the cave.

The old man's hands and feet were tied with rope. A cloth tied around his mouth muffled his voice. "Jim?"

Peterson made a sound that sounded like a sigh of relief. Cord took out a small switchblade from his boot and cut the ropes and took off the cloth around his mouth. Peterson breathed heavily and pointed to the entrance of the cave, yet no one saw any light from where he pointed. "Simon ran around you and left. If you leave, you might be able to get to him."

"Simon was here?"

"He shot the police chief. I saw it. I saw the whole thing." The old man had trouble getting up. He pushed his hands against the cold rock and caught his breath. Then Peterson held his neck and closed his eyes tight, as he felt pain in his back and neck.

"He killed the police chief," said Cord again, still in disbelief.

"He wanted to use me for ransom," said Peterson.

"I thought so. Where do you think he went?"

"I reckon to Felville's house. He's his employer. I heard everything. I suppose there was no use holding anything back. He told me he would get some money if he convinced me to sell the land. Felville would put in the highest offer and Simon would get about ten thousand. That was the idea. Not sure what his plan is now," said Peterson.

Matthews walked over to them. "Thank God you found him. I'm taking back the chief. You two can go on ahead. A few other men will come to Felville's house. Hernandez can tell you where he lives, if you want to come along."

"You think he'll have more men there?" asked Cord.

"I don't know. I didn't expect to get shot at,

so we might be surprised again. You go on ahead."

Hernandez and Matthews carried out the chief as Cord lit the way with a lamp he found in the corner of the cave. Peterson struggled to make it out, as the entrance was narrow and steep, which made his knees hurt.

The sun blinded them as they walked out of the cave. Deputy Matthews and Hernandez put the chief on one horse and the redheaded man on the other.

Hernandez said, "We better play this smart. Go on home. We'll handle this."

"You're going to Felville's house?" asked Cord.

"Are you sure Simon works for Felville?" Hernandez said to Peterson.

"Yes."

"All right," said Deputy Hernandez to Cord. "We're going to Felville's place in two hours. If you want to come along, you can. But it probably won't be pretty. I can't guarantee your safety."

"I'll be fine."

"Then see you there."

CHAPTER 13

Jᴛᴍ Pᴇᴛᴇʀsᴏɴ ᴛᴏᴏᴋ ᴛʜᴇ ʀᴇᴅʜᴇᴀᴅᴇᴅ ᴍᴀɴ's horse and rode home with Cord Cordeu. On the way home Peterson held his heart and tried to breath slower. He looked up and saw the short hair on the back of Cord's head and saw the sun blind and warm above their heads.

It seemed the heat was slow to blow away in the fall. Peterson thought it would be snowing up north in Kansas and New Mexico, two places he used to live. He closed his eyes and remembered the snow.

"You all right, Jim?" asked Cord, slowing his horse to ride alongside the old man. "You look like you're about to pass out."

"No, not really." He wiped sweat from his nose and above his lip. "I haven't been well, Cord. I've been dying."

"From what?"

"My heart is giving out. I don't have long. I can feel it."

Cord squinted his eyes and looked at the old man. Peterson's mouth was open. He barely opened his eyes, as if they were heavy.

"Don't talk crazy. We're almost home."

"I got something on my desk. A letter. It's a letter I want—"

"Hold on there. Tell me when we're there."

Peterson was quiet for the rest of the ride. Cord put his arm around Peterson and helped him inside the house. He took him to the bedroom and sat him on the bed.

"Thank you," said Peterson.

"You go on and sleep."

"I don't want to. I just want to stay up and say something to you before you go."

Cord leaned his shoulder against the wooden doorframe and waited. And as he waited Peterson looked out the window at the cats coming out of the woodlands. The cats pounced on the grass and ran to the back porch.

The backdoor was slightly ajar, but not enough for the friendly black cat to open. The black cat used its claw to open the screen door. It was one of those doors that didn't need a doorknob, as it opened whenever there was a strong wind.

The black cat walked into the bedroom. And then the black cat nudged its body against Cord's jeans and purred. Peterson said, "Look at the letter on my desk, son."

Cord picked up the letter and read it. After he was done reading it he said, "What is this?"

"My will."

"You're giving me half of your land?"

"Other half to my daughter. They'll probably sell it, which is fine."

"I don't need your land. I'm doing all right. You didn't have to—"

"It's yours, son. I'm giving it to you."

"I don't know what to say," said Cord.

"Felville wanted to pay $250,000 for it. I thought he was joking. But an oil tycoon with that much money doesn't joke about business. He wanted the land."

"Why didn't you sell?"

"I'm about to die, Cord. I don't need money where I'm going. It doesn't mean much to me. For you, it might make a difference."

Cord shook his head and sat down on the desk chair. His hands were shaking. "You look all right to me. Are you sick?"

"It's my heart. Just part of old age, I guess. It doesn't matter."

The black cat brushed its body against

Peterson's pant leg and then jumped off the bed and onto Cord's lap.

"You've been here for months, but I feel like you're family," said Peterson.

"Family?"

"You've done good around here. You nearly died to see that woman you met. You could say it was for doing what you thought was right. Not many people do that anymore. It's rare." Peterson looked down at his hands. They were old hands, wrinkled and calloused and freckled with brown spots. He began to feel they weren't his hands anymore. "It's a big difference from your past, isn't it?" He glanced up and saw Cord peer at him from the corner of his eye.

"What do you mean?"

"You know what I mean. You think a price on your head goes away?"

"What?"

"I'm not turning you in, son."

"Then why bring it up?"

"Seven Rivers Brothers. Was that the gang you ran with?"

"Seven Rivers Warriors. It ended a long time ago."

"Wasn't that long ago."

"They all died or walked away. The ones that survived are now ranchers, cowboys and such." Cord stood up and breathed slower. "I'm not like that anymore. I haven't done anything like that in a long time. Nothing can make me go back there."

"You're not going there, of course," said Peterson.

Cord stared out at the window. It was getting dark and he had to leave soon. Simon killed the Chief of Police and now nothing would prevent him from getting caught. Cord wanted to see the end of it.

"But that wasn't all. You killed a man, didn't you?"

"Yes," said Cord quietly. "A man who tried to rob my wife and I on the road. I was lucky he missed when he shot at me."

"He shot at you?"

"He was a gang member who was backed by the local law. I heard word I got a bounty on my head, so my wife and I fled the state and lived in El Paso for a while, until my wife passed away. We lived there together for a month. I guess I'm not very good at hiding since you know about me."

"I saw your bounty poster years back. Call it chance or whatever you like, but I knew it was you when I first saw you."

"How come you didn't turn me in and why

did you let me, a man with a bounty on his head, live here with you?"

"I could tell you weren't bad. I could see you were in pain," said Peterson. "Then I learned it was about your wife that passed away. That explained some of it."

"I think about her all the time."

Peterson lay down on the bed and closed his eyes tight. He put his hands on his chest and felt his heart beat. "Do you think about Ann?"

"A little. I just met her."

"You almost got killed trying to see her."

"Hopefully getting attacked is a one time thing." Cord put the letter down on the desk and looked outside. "I have to go."

"You don't have to."

"I want to. I want to see the end of all this. I'll be back tonight." Cord went outside and mounted his horse. He rode fast to Felville's house. He bent over a little to try to ride faster. It had been a while since his horse Lightning ran fast; it was a good change from standing around for most of the day. In an hour he saw the electric lights of the Felville Manor and waited for Hernandez and Matthews and the rest of the police officers to show up.

FIVE POLICE OFFICERS SURROUNDED THE Felville manor. The manor was a two-story brick building that had a seven-foot high fence around the house and the garden in the back. The police officers had opened the front gate and watched the outside doors and windows of the manor.

Cord left his horse outside of the fence and held his Winch- ester in one hand. "Good to see you," Hernandez said. "I'm sure Mr. Peterson likes you coming here for him."

"He does."

Hernandez stopped walking and pointed to a horse. "Is that Simon's horse?"

"Yes."

"He'll be around. Be on the lookout. Don't be afraid to shoot him. He'll be hanged for what he did."

"You all right?"

"No," said Hernandez. He held a Colt in his right hand and frowned at the big manor that looked like a small castle. "The chief was well-liked. He was a good man. Seeing him die so suddenly was unreal. He didn't deserve that." Hernandez walked on until he found the door.

"I'll be right behind you," said Cord.

"Good. There might not be a reason to

shoot. He might surrender. We'll take it slow. Don't want any civilians getting shot."

The front door opened. A man in a suit noticed them and stared at the police officers around the manor. "Can I help you, gentlemen?"

"We're here for Mr. Felville. He's wanted in connection to the murder of Chief of Police Donavan Marcus."

The butler said, "A murder?"

"Is Mr. Felville here?" asked Hernandez.

"He's in the library," said the butler, and opened the door wide so they could enter.

They followed the butler upstairs and found the library where Felville was reading. The library was a big circular room with artwork on the ceiling. Felville put down the book as Cord and Deputy Hernandez entered the room.

"Is everything all right?" asked Felville, his tone concerned and his eyes wide. He looked out of the second-story window and saw the police officers watching the manor.

Felville wore a suit and had a black beard and short hair that was pulled back and greased. He kept his distance and noticed the rifle Cord carried. Cord's eyes met Felville's. "What is this?" He sounded almost annoyed and confused at the same time.

"We understand Simon works for you. Is this correct?" asked Hernandez. The deputy had his Colt holstered, but his right hand was near the revolver grip so that he would be quick to draw the gun and shoot.

"Why do you ask?"

"Simon Steiner shot and killed Chief Marcus. He's wanted for murder."

Felville looked down at the wooden floor and then scratched his beard. "Murder?" he whispered.

"We understand he's been working for you."

"Well, uh—yes. Yes, he's been working for me. Little things here and there."

"Like burning down Peterson's crops?" interrupted Cord, his voice loud and clear. The voice echoed in the big library and caused Felville to frown at the loud voice.

"What do you mean? What is this, this 'burning down' you're saying?"

Hernandez and Cord exchanged glances. The event was in the San Antonio *Express* newspaper.

"Twice Simon has set fire to Peterson's crops. By your order. It's best to just admit it. We know he's here. We saw his horse," said Hernandez.

"He's here? Simon's here?" Felville looked

outside the window again and saw Simon's horse. It was an odd thing to see because Felville had stables and Simon's horse was left outside of it. "Oh, no."

"What?" said Cord. "What's the matter?"

"Did you or did you not tell Simon Steiner to burn Jim Peterson's land and abduct him and torture Cord and threaten his life?" Hernandez shook his head. "Who knows what else?" he said, partly to himself.

"I did not," said Felville. He scratched his beard and turned away, which caused Hernandez to wrap his hand around the grip of his Colt. Felville sat down on a red leather chair with carved wooden legs. "I wanted the land. It's a good piece of land. Prime location. I offered $250,000 a few years back but Jim didn't care to sell. I wanted to buy it, divide the land and sell it in pieces. I saw an opportunity. Simon Steiner said he was good friends with Peterson. I trusted his word and he worked for me. I told him to persuade Peterson to sell. Persuade," he reiterated the last word. "I didn't tell him to burn down crops. I said nothing of the sort!"

His voice rang out clearly and made the men quiet for a while. "That's all you said to Simon?" asked Cord.

"Call me desperate or whatever you like. I

wanted the land. I saw he wasn't using most of it. I offered him so much money that the money could be passed down for several generations. I told him this. Why not sell? But he wouldn't have it. Simon was a way of getting him to sell. But I should have known Simon wasn't to be trusted."

"He killed the police chief," said Cord. "You can say he was a lot of things."

"Of course." Felville rose quickly to his feet.

Hernandez, still unsure about Felville, watched every move- ment from the man. The deputy didn't trust anyone; that was the result of trusting the wrong people. He looked at Felville, who looked around the room and then at the side doors of the library. The library had two double doors to enter and two side doors that went into a bedroom and an office. It was situated in the back center of the manor.

"If you saw his horse, he might be in the house," said Felville, stepping back to the window.

A side door flung open as Simon appeared with a revolver in his hand. He grabbed Felville and aimed the revolver at the man's head. Hernandez aimed his Colt at Simon, yet only half the man's face showed. The other half was behind Felville's head. Cord brought up his Winchester and had Simon in his sights.

"Let him go," yelled Deputy Hernandez. "No one else has to die."

"You know that's not true," said Simon.

"Put down the gun," said the deputy, walking to the left of him as Cord walked right.

Simon aimed the gun frantically from Cord then to Hernandez. He breathed fast and had blood on his shirt. Simon pulled Felville back near the window and stared out at the police officers.

"It's over," said Cord. "Should have left the city when you had the chance."

Simon laughed and pressed Felville closer, as Cord and Hernandez were getting closer. "All I wanted was a piece of land to farm."

"You don't farm," said Cord.

"Then ranching. Raise some livestock."

"We both know you don't do anything like that."

Simon smiled and his brown teeth were visible. "I can do anything I want." He looked back again and saw his horse was being led to the front gate of the manor. Simon cursed silently to himself.

"If you shoot him, we'd just shoot you. You'd die anyway," said Cord.

"Don't say that," urged Felville.

Simon said, "I'm leaving. You won't see me again."

No one said anything for a while; it felt like minutes, even thought it was for a short moment.

"Why'd you have to mess everything up?" Simon whispered into Felville's ear. Felville, almost unaware of Simon's absurd statement, ignored him. Simon noticed the open door he came from and looked from the black room on the opposite and then back at the men inching forward.

"I got money in this drawer," said Felville. "Right desk drawer. It's four thousand dollars. Take the money and leave."

"Open it," said Simon. "Hurry up."

Felville opened it. Simon still had his left arm around Felville. He handed Simon the money. Simon pushed Felville forward and ran through the door, into a bedroom and down the hallway.

"I'll try to cut him off," said Hernandez.

Felville stayed frozen on the wooden floor as the men frantically ran in different directions.

Cord could hear heavy footsteps in the hallway. He turned a corner and a loud crack, like lightning striking a tree, rang out from the hall. The shot hit the doorframe near Cord and made a hole in the wood. Cord's heart beat rapidly; he tried to calm himself. It had been a long time since he had been shot at.

"He's coming out," yelled Deputy Hernandez, hoping the policemen outside could hear his voice.

Simon ran down the spiral marble stairs; his footsteps sounded like horse hooves on a brick road. Then Simon looked up. Hernandez poked his head out. Simon shot once and missed. Cord ran down the stairs and tried not to fall.

The back door opened. Cord heard three more shots, and as he ran outside he saw the smoke in the air and two police officers staring down at Simon's dead body and the four thousand dollars scattered on the grass.

CHAPTER 14

Deputy Matthews was one of the men who shot Simon. Matthews stood above the body. The other officers didn't speak, yet Cord knew what they were all thinking.

Deputy Hernandez patted Matthews on the back and said, "Good work. The chief would be proud." The men walked back to their horses and began to leave the area.

A wagon came by to pick up the body. It was nighttime and the crickets were loud in the tall wild grass near the Felville manor. When Felville came out, Cord told him what happened and said, "Simon was going to hang anyway."

Felville said, "Yes, of course. It was necessary. I just didn't expect to hear gunshots and see gun holes in my home today."

"Mr. Felville," said Hernandez. "Do you know if Simon worked with anyone else?"

"Not that I know of."

"Are you sure? He never told you of anyone?"

"No," said Felville. "He talked very little to me. He only said that it wouldn't be long until Peterson would sell." He shook his head. "I shouldn't have listened to Simon. I shouldn't have even tried anything."

"You didn't know what kind of person Simon was," said Cord.

"Definitely not," said Felville, covering his mouth as he saw Simon's body transported by wagon out of the front gates and down the road.

Cord and the police officers mounted their horses and rode away. Hernandez rode alongside Cord and made sure the other men were far before speaking to Cord. Hernandez said, "The chief wanted me to look into you, you know."

"What do you mean?" said Cord.

Hernandez said, "He was suspicious of you and told me to find out where you're from and what your past life was about."

"I'm from New Mexico," said Cord. "I've mentioned that, I thought."

"Yes, but you didn't mention you murdered someone." Cord slowed his horse to a halt and looked at the other police officers about thirty feet ahead. They didn't turn back. When Cord saw Hernandez with his hands relaxed and on the reins, he felt a little better. "The man I murdered tried to rob my wife and I."

"I know. I said I looked into it."

"Why'd you bring that up?"

"Sorry if it brings up bad memories," said the deputy. "I think the chief would want me to let you go free. He'd want me to clear your criminal past, whatever it involved. Only a good man would help an old man like Peterson and avenge an innocent man's death. The chief would want me to help you in some way, but it's not just for him. I wanted to do this. You don't have a bounty on your head anymore," said Hernandez.

"Do the other men know?"

"No, they don't."

"I don't know what to say," said Cord. "This changes my life. I always thought I'd get caught. I was used to looking over my shoulder."

"Well, don't worry about it anymore," said the deputy. "You're clear. No one will come for you. I made sure of it. If they do, give them this." He handed him a piece of paper that explained the bounty was void.

"Thank you," said Cord.

"You shot that redheaded man in the cave, didn't you?"

"Yes. It happened fast."

"I was curious."

"I better go see Jim."

"Jim? Oh, you mean Mr. Peterson. Well, I'll leave you be. We have a lot of bodies to bury and a lot of work to do. We'll need a new police chief and that won't be easy to find. No one stays as the chief for long. Well, the last chief was the one who lasted more than five years."

Cord said goodbye and rode back to the Peterson's house. It wasn't as dark as Cord thought it would be, as the full moon was bright. A raccoon's eyes glowed in the night and a possum crossed the road further up the road. And when he made it back home he felt at ease. He felt light and free, like the owl flying to another tree.

Having no bounty on his head meant he could stay in one place and not have to look over his shoulder every day. He wouldn't have to hide his rifle under a blanket, like he used to do while traveling, or check to see if someone was staring at him in a strange manner. He could find a permanent home, but he didn't know where he would find this type of home. He wanted a place of his own, yet now that Peterson gave him half his land he wondered if that meant it included Peterson's little house. He thought so. The house wasn't much, but it was all Cord needed.

He saw the house further up the road. As a child he would be happy walking home from school, and this same emotion rose inside him as he saw Peterson's home up the road.

CORD WALKED INSIDE THE HOME AND gently shut the front door. Peterson walked out of the room using his cane; he was hunched over a little and gradually raised his eyebrows to hear the news.

"Simon's dead," said Cord.

Peterson looked neither glad nor sad. "How'd he die?"

"We found him at Felville's house. Simon ran and shot at us. And then Deputy Matthews and some others shot Simon. He died quickly."

"It didn't have to be that way," said Peterson. "He chose it. He killed the police chief; there was no coming back from that." Then Peterson remembered Felville. "What about Felville? Is he going to jail?"

"I don't think so. Hernandez questioned him. It's true Felville had Simon working for him, but all he told Simon was to persuade you to sell. Maybe Hernandez will ask him more questions, but he is innocent so far. It might change."

"I think that's about right. He seems smart but not a crook. Those two don't go well together."

"What about me? Am I a crook?"

"Nonsense," said Peterson. "Why are you asking?"

"I killed a man, remember?"

"In self-defense."

Cord said, "At least I don't have a bounty on my head anymore. Hernandez said he got rid of it. I'm free for the first time in years."

"You're free to do what you want, huh?"

"I don't have to look over my shoulder every minute. That's what I mean."

"Good," said Peterson. He took a few steps to his bedroom and then stared out of the window at the field of ash and the trees that casted shadows under the bright moon. He found himself worrying about re-planting crops and then he laughed it off.

"What's funny?" said Cord.

"Nothing. Call me free as well. I don't have Simon threatening me." Peterson walked over to Cord, opened up his desk drawer and took out a key. He handed the key to Cord.

"What's this?"

"A key to the house."

He looked at the key under the moonlight streaming in from the windows. It was a sign that he could move on from his past and live again. Cord put the key in his pocket. "Thanks, Jim."

"You know you called me Pa not too long ago."

"When?"

"After you got tortured by that redheaded man we killed," said the old man. He sat on the bed and noticed the bruises on Cord's face. "It was the medicine, I guess."

"Oh." Cord scratched his neck and backed up to the doorframe.

"Don't be embarrassed."

"I'm not."

"It looks like it. Plenty of people say something like that when they are on medicine."

Cord smiled out of embarrassment. "I don't even remember my pa. He died from tuberculosis when I was young."

"What about your mother?"

"She raised me. She was a good person. Kind, intelligent and hard working. Penelope was her name. I write to her. She lives in Louisiana and remarried when I left to go west."

"How's the man she remarried?"

"He's fine from what I hear. She can't really lie, so I could tell her letters were the truth." Cord nodded at the will on Peterson's desk. "When did you write your will?"

"Not long ago, of course, since I gave you half the land. That includes the house. I don't think Sarah and Lenny will mind not inheriting a little cabin and some pigs."

"A cabin is better than sleeping on dirt. It's a lot for me."

"I thought so. You don't need much to be happy. I used to think I needed this and that, but now I don't think that's true."

"What about a big manor like Felville's? Wouldn't you want that?"

"No, I would have to dust the house pretty much every day, all day. Have you seen his house? I think people call it a manor or mansion. Whatever you call it, I feel like I wouldn't know what to do with it. Even with ten horses I wouldn't do much with them. I'd just sell them."

Peterson wrapped a blanket around his body and then took it off. He felt either too hot or too cold, never in between.

"I was thinking of why Simon killed the police chief and burned your crops and sent someone to fight me." He shook his head and frowned at the idea of Simon being a murderer, among many other things. "I don't understand him. What causes someone to be like that?"

Peterson crossed his arms. "If you're asking what causes evil, then I'm afraid you'll be busy wondering about that until you die. I can't read Simon's mind. When does someone become evil: at birth or over time? Is it a gradual process? Was there some tragedy in childhood that changed them and molded them into the person they are today? I don't know. I think it's far more complicated. Evil lives with evil. Evil follows one another. There's no rational thought from them, because committing evil always leads to consequences, whether it's in life or the afterlife. And they don't tend to think of consequences like normal folk. They need money, so they rob and kill an innocent person. They don't even understand it when they're being hanged for murder. They can't comprehend the morality of their actions." Peterson lay down on the bed and closed his eyes. "Do you believe in Hell?" asked Peterson.

"I'm not sure what I believe."

"That's all right. Maybe if you do good you'll be all right, no matter what happens after we die. I like to think I'll see my cats after I die."

Cord smiled. "I'm sure you will. That's not a big request."

"Had a few dogs, too."

"I'm sure you'd see them too."

"I better. If not I'll be pretty mad."

"Did you see bad things when you were in the army?" asked Cord.

"Yes, and I tried to try to understand why men and women were scalped by some of the natives. I just realized it wasn't worth thinking about it. All I focused on was protecting settlers and people riding west to California or wherever they were headed. I did my job as best I could. That was all I thought about. If you worry about morals and evil, you will panic when you have to shoot an Apache riding towards you. Now the violent Apaches are gone. The other Apaches are in towns and cities or in their reservations. Everything is far different than it was thirty and forty years ago. It changed fast."

"You think we're civilized?"

"In a way. We have law and order now. It doesn't mean there won't be crime. As long as there are people like Simon there will always be crime."

Cord stood up from the desk and heard the old man snoring, his belly rising and falling. He waited for Peterson to say something else, but Peterson was asleep.

Cord walked back to his room and grabbed the house key out of his pocket. He set the key on a small table by his bed. Now he felt his life was starting over again.

He thought about seeing Ann.

CHAPTER 15

THE SAN ANTONIO *EXPRESS* AND CITY newspapers across the country wrote about the murder of Police Chief Donavan Marcus. It made national news and caused a commotion in San Antonio. Residents complained that it was unsafe in the city. Once learning that Simon lived in a cave like an animal, people suddenly assumed that caves were somewhere in the vicinity.

Cord wasn't listed by name in the local paper; he was referred to as a friend of Jim Peterson, but he didn't mind. He'd rather be on the outskirts of the crowd than in the center.

Cord picked up the newspaper and put it on the kitchen table. Then he rode to the Gibson's for his last days of work. On the way there Lenny and Sarah were riding together on a single horse, going a little faster than a trot, their heads bobbing along the way. Sarah sat behind Lenny and peaked her head out and spotted Cord. After noticing Cord, Sarah waved him down.

"Have you read the newspaper?" asked Cord. His horse faced the opposite direction of Lenny's as they spoke.

"That's why we're riding to pa's house. We wanted to see if he's okay. Is he hurt? Did Simon hurt him? What happened?"

Sarah spoke fast and tried to conceal her anxiety.

"He's all right," Cord assured her. "He's not hurt at all. I just left and he was asleep."

"Good," said Lenny. "About time this whole thing ended. I was sick of putting out fires."

"So was I. And getting shot at."

Sarah's eyes widened. She slapped her husband's shoulder. "I didn't know we had a gunslinger working for us." She sounded happy and excited about it.

"I'm nothing like that."

"You just said you were shot at. You must have shot at Simon. Didn't you?"

"Yes, but I missed. The police officers killed

him. I might have killed the redheaded man back in the cave, but I'm not sure. It was dark. It doesn't matter either way. All that matters is it's over."

Lenny used his thumb to point back at where he came from. "I finished the harvest. I guess you'll have enough money to tide you over for a while, until you find another job."

"I should be all right," said Cord. "I guess I'll go into town now."

"All right then," said Lenny. "We can talk some other time. Stay safe out there."

Cord said he would, but he felt safe already. The city residents were afraid now that the police chief was murdered; they assumed it was violent and unstable, but it was far from the truth. It was just as it was before Simon entered the city. Cord rode by The Alamo and a chapel with an old bell that rang. The bell's sound reverberated through the streets and caused those that were walking across the road or along the sidewalk to look up at the sound, as if by habit, such as what one does when hearing a bird singing nearby. Then the people walked on.

Cord hitched his horse to a pole and walked along the sidewalk. It was late evening and the street was busy with people leaving to head home. Some women wore colorful hats with a feather or two that was pinned into the hat; their long dresses were still unfamiliar to Cord.

The women Cord saw in Louisiana, when he worked on a crab boat, wore different clothes; so did the women in New Mexico. But his eyes turned away from the women and were fixed up at the light coming from Ann's bedroom window.

Cord took off his hat and combed his hair as he looked at his reflection in a store window. Then he walked up the stairs and knocked on her door. His heart pounded, and he felt it and thought that was a good sign.

The door opened and there stood Ann. She had on red lipstick and a red dress with little frills at the end. "Oh, Cord."

"Hi, Ann."

She smiled and then looked behind him. He stood, without having the words. And then she opened the door wider for him and said, "Come in."

"Thanks," he said, holding his hat in his hands and viewing the room like before. It had rugs, which was an odd thing for Cord to see. That was a luxurious oddity to him. "How are you?"

"Good. How about you?" She closed and locked the door.

As she walked over to him, Cord tried to grin, but it was forced in his nervousness. "I'm all right. Well, I guess I'm more than all right. Have you read the newspaper?"

"No, I don't read the papers much. It's always depressing. I read about who was raped and who was murdered and I get into a terrible mood. You know what I mean?"

"A little. I guess I'm numb to it, having read the newspaper here and there."

"What did you want to tell me?" She sat in a chair in front of a vanity set as Cord stood near the window that overlooked the street.

"The police chief was shot."

"Oh, that? I've heard. You don't need to read the newspaper to know that. Word gets around."

"The man who shot him was terrorizing a friend of mine," he said. "I went after him with the police. He's dead. Simon was his name."

"It was an awful thing he did. I couldn't figure out why he did it."

"He was sick," said Cord. "Simon tried to get Jim Peterson to sell his land because Felville promised to give Simon money for convincing Peterson to put his land up for sale. That didn't work out, so Simon assumed 'persuade' meant burn down crops and nearly kill him. He thought doing so would cause Peterson to want to sell, but Peterson doesn't scare easily. Nothing worked, so Simon thought holding Peterson hostage for a ransom would be a suitable way of getting money. That didn't work either. We got to him just in time."

"You killed the man who killed the police chief?" She walked over and sat on her bed with her hands behind her back, pressing against the red comforter.

"No," he said. "I shot at him but missed. It was the police officers that shot him three times."

"That's awfully brave. First you save my life. Now you shoot a murderer. What else do you do? You never told me much about you, except, well, you said you killed—"

"That was self-defense. I didn't tell you before," he interrupted.

She was quiet and stared intently at him.

"Look, Ann. Aren't you tired of your job? Aren't you just sick of it? You must get disgusting customers, don't you? You probably are forced into things. I don't even want to think about it," he said, walking back and forth on a rug with an elaborate design. He thought the money she made was plenty, and he thought maybe she liked the job because of the money. And that the money made up for all the pain. "Don't you want to let go of your life and get away?"

Ann laughed a little and sounded cheerful. When she smiled there were dimples on her cheeks. She never lost sight of Cord's eyes, and she looked at him as if he were the only thing that was important.

Ann looked down and said, "Yes, I've wanted to do something else for a while. But I don't know what else I'm good at. I'm in the oldest profession. It's been around because it works and pays well. I charge whatever I want really and—"

There was a loud knock on the door. A man yelled, "Ann. Let me in. I've been itching for you. Come on. Open the door. Let me in. I see the light under the door. I know you're in there."

Cord was quiet as he walked to the door; Ann didn't stop him. As he unlocked and opened it he saw the bald headed man he saw in the alley, the one that harassed Ann. Cord frowned at Ann in disbelief. "Who is this man to you, Ann?" asked Cord.

"You," yelled the stranger. Ann stood up quickly and the stranger pointed a finger at her. "I thought I told you to stay away from this feller. I told you he was no good. He's a murderer. He said so himself. I heard him. You heard him. What else is there to say?"

The bald headed man had a big beard that was unkempt. He had a short-sleeved shirt and black pants with grey suspenders. His eyes were wide, darting to and fro Cord and Ann. His back foot was far behind the left one, as if he were in position to brawl and stay on his boots. Cord could see him in plain view and he could tell he was no good.

"Leave," said Cord.

"I own her," said the man.

"Who is this?" said Cord to Ann.

"My—my past employer. Logan," she said quietly. "But I don't work for him anymore. I work for myself now."

"Your what?" said Cord.

"That's right," said Logan, pointing a finger at him. "You're lucky I don't break your face against the wall here."

"I'd like to see you try."

Ann covered her mouth and walked to the far side of the room. Logan swung first; his arm flung wildly and missed as Cord stepped back. Cord almost jumped as he stepped back fast. Logan's body flung forward and then he regained his stance, but it was too late, as his movements were jerky and slow.

Cord punched with his left and hit Logan

in the jaw. Then Cord hit even faster with his right, this time in the eye, and forced Logan to fall to the wooden floor and create a loud bang and crack, almost like the sound of a great tree being felled.

"Don't try it," said Cord. "Or I'll have to hurt you for real next time."

The back of Logan's head touched the wooden floor. A cracked wooden board was below the bald man. His fat belly took heavy breaths as he touched his face and felt the blood flowing and coming from his nose and busted lip. "Damn you," said Logan.

"All right," said Cord. "Go on now. If I see you again, I'll hit even harder."

Logan slowly pushed his body from the floor and held his back to the wall for support. He walked a step forward and made it seem like he was about to fight again, but he touched the wallpaper instead and made his way to the stairs.

Ann walked near Cord and pulled Cord out of the hallway and back into her bedroom. Then she closed the door.

"I have some explaining to do," said Ann, her back facing Cord.

"Go ahead."

"He was my employer. I worked for him in

the past. That's all. I don't work for him anymore."

"It didn't sound like it," he said.

"I know it doesn't, but it's the truth. I may be a lot of nasty things, but I'm not a liar." She walked close to Cord and held his hands and stared up at him.

"You were saying you wanted to do something else," he said. "Well, what about doing that? Why hasn't a man married you yet? I mean you're the prettiest woman I've seen in the city. Why aren't you marrying some rich man or something? Why are you a prostitute?"

"My love isn't for sale. I do what I want. I don't want some rich man telling me to clean this, wash that or cook dinner. I just want to be myself. I never found what I had in mind. Sure, I've been married before. He was rich, but it was just all about money to him. I was just a prize for him to show to his friends, like one of his hunting trophies. He was always gone. I just wanted to be with someone who loves me for who I am, not for my looks."

Cord felt her small hands in his. She was about his age, yet she seemed younger than other prostitutes he had seen on streets of big towns. They always appeared old and wretched, and they repulsed him.

Cord didn't think she had any business

doing what she was doing. It was a waste to him, and he could tell she thought so as well. And that maybe she wanted to change, just as he had changed.

The way he looked at her reminded him of how his wife looked at him when he brought in food to her bedroom when she was sick.

"I love you for who you are," said Cord.

Ann kissed him once and then said, "What do you do? Like I said before, I don't even know you. You came around out of no where, twice." Her voice was gentle and calming.

"I had a wife. Lara was her name. I had known her since I was fifteen. About five years ago she got real sick and gradually weakened. I took her to doctors everywhere, but nothing helped. She gradually got weaker. I was desperate. I joined a gang and rustled cattle for money. The medicine was expensive. I didn't have a choice. But that gang fell through. Lara died and that's when I started drifting from place to place. I did kill that man, but he tried to rob my wife and I while we were going to the city one day. Then a bounty on my head complicated things. The man I killed was part of a rival gang that was connected to crooked cops. Then I was a farmer, trying to hide out. I rode east from El Paso and hoped my past didn't follow me. It always seemed to," he said.

"I lost my father in the war," she said. "We've all lost something. But you don't have to go on about it. I just don't think it's good to avoid what's bothering you. It comes back in different ways, sometimes in bad ways."

"A deputy in San Antonio got rid of my bounty for helping him catch Simon. But I still don't feel as great as I did when I was with my wife. I guess I'm just afraid if I move on I'll forget her, and I don't want to forget her." He stared down at his fiddling hands in hers.

"Every man is scared of something," she said. "It usually takes a woman to get him to admit it." Ann hugged him, pressing her ear to his chest.

"I have a home and two hundred and fifty acres of land now," he said. "I'm not rich, but I know I want you, Ann."

"I want you to," she said, pulling her head back and looking up at him. She looked around the room. "The only problem is I have a lot of things to move."

He smiled. "I live there with someone. Jim Peterson is his name. He gave me his house in his will and a bunch of land," said Cord, shaking his head. "I told him about you."

"That's all right. I'm not in a hurry. I'd love to meet him," she said.

Cord and Ann spoke for a while longer and

then Cord left to go back home. As he left he felt better than he had felt in months. It was as if a huge weight was lifted. He began to smile. His head bobbed about as his horse trotted down the road.

CHAPTER 16

IT WAS DARK OUTSIDE WHEN CORD WALKED into Peterson's house and shut the door. He was careful not to wake the old man.

He peeked into Jim Peterson's bedroom and saw that the old man was on the floor. Cord hurried to him and helped him get onto the bed. Then Peterson lay down with his head against the pillow.

"I told you. I'm sick."

"All right. I'll get a doctor."

"Get Sarah, will you?"

In an hour the doctor arrived. He was a man with silver hair combed to the side. He wore glasses and was quiet. He checked Peterson's pulse as Cord looked on.

Sarah and Lenny Gibson watched Jim from behind the doctor.

They appeared worried, but Peterson told them not to look at him that way, that he had to die anyway. There were no more surprises to Peterson. It was only death. He looked forward to it. "I lived long enough," he told them. "Marguerite is waiting."

"What's wrong?" Sarah asked the doctor.

"His heart is giving out," he said. "I'm sorry. The best thing you can do is speak to him one last time." The doctor gazed out the window and waited.

Sarah kneeled down by the bed and grabbed her father's hand. Peterson pointed a crooked finger at his desk. "My will—my will is in that drawer."

"I don't need to see that now, pa," she said. "That can wait. I just want to be here until—" Tears streamed down her face and she wiped them immediately.

Cord took out the will and gave it to her. She read it and shook her head. "I don't need all that land."

"Then sell it," he said.

"I forgot how much land you had. Two hundred fifty acres is a lot of land," said Lenny, reading the letter over his wife's shoulder. "What do you think is the worth?"

"Two hundred thousand or so for the entire

five hundred acres," said Peterson, his voice barely a whisper.

"Good Lord," said Lenny, exchanging glances with his wife.

The money meant they didn't need to work anymore. That amount could be handed down for generations. It was good land in a good location.

"It's generous, very generous of you, Jim," said Lenny. He then nodded at Cord. "You saved Jim's life. The land isn't even enough to show our thanks."

Sarah cried a little. "Are you sure the land is worth that much?" she asked.

"I got different offers," said Jim Peterson. "They were close to that."

"Well, it's quite a surprise," said Lenny.

That was all they spoke about the land. Their attention turned to Jim, whose breathing was barely noticeable.

Peterson's eyes were glossy as he thought of his cats. But then he saw Cord and realized he would take good care of them for him. Everything will be all right, he thought.

"I love you," said Sarah, still kneeling by the bed.

"Love you," he said. Peterson motioned with his hand for Cord to come near.

Cord bent over and placed his ear near Jim Peterson. Peterson's voice was a weak whisper.

"Did you see that woman of yours?"

"Yes, I'd like to marry her."

"Good," he said, raising his voice a little. "You aren't running off now again? You're staying?"

"No," said Cord. "No, I'm staying right here."

"Good. My cats," he said. "Someone needs to care for them."

"I'll feed them," said Cord, now kneeling, as his back was hurting from bending over. He took off his hat and tried to smile. "I'll feed them for you."

"Will you promise me something?" he asked Cord. "I want you to promise me— promise me—" He coughed, which made the doctor turn around.

"Do you want water?" asked Cord. He could feel his throat tightening. His heart felt like it was bleeding, and he didn't know why. But then he remembered it was how he felt right after his wife passed.

"No, no. I just want you to promise me. Promise me not to go back to your old ways. Can you do that? Can you do that for me?"

Cord turned his head at the Gibson's and

then back at Peterson. "I promise. I don't want to go back to who I used to be. I've changed already. I'm not who I used to be, but I think that's a good thing. I'm better than the man I once was."

"You sure are," said Peterson.

"Glad you think so."

"Then I have nothing else to say. Everything is in its place," he said. He glanced outside at the full moon and the stars; they seemed brighter than ever before. As he closed his eyes his heart slowed to a halt and he died in peace. Sarah sobbed and the other men looked on.

The black cat with the big eyes used its claws to open the slightly opened back door to the house. It walked slowly over to the bed and jumped on it. Then the cat curled up near Jim's feet and slept.

◈

IN A FEW DAYS CORD AND ANN WENT TO Jim Peterson's funeral in San Antonio. Ann met the Gibson's and spoke to them about what they read in the papers, about Simon, the police chief murder and Jim Peterson.

Cord rode with Ann to his new house.

Cord was somber as he watched Ann walk into the bedrooms and make her way to the front porch that overlooked the west hills. He followed her outside just as the sun was setting.

"You can sit down," he said, pointing at the rocking chair.

"Thanks. How are you feeling?"

"Fine."

"Were you close to Jim?"

"I suppose so," he said. "We helped each other out. He gave me medicine once and supposedly I called him pa."

She smiled. "Some people do that to teachers. I guess that means you were close to him."

"Yeah."

"It sounded like he was a great man," said Ann. "I wished I had met him."

Cord turned his head at a sound coming from behind the house. He walked around the corner of the deck and saw the five cats coming towards the house. Their tails swished about, as they knew it was time to eat. Some mewed on their way over to Cord.

The big black cat led the way, and it rubbed its body against Cord's jeans, wrapping its tail around him and looking up at him with its yellow eyes.

"Time to eat, huh?"

Cord went inside and came back with bits of chicken. He fed the five cats and then rubbed the head of the black cat and said to it, "A cat should have a name. How about I call you Jim?"

THE WANTED

CHAPTER 1
THE STRANGER RETURNS

THE STRANGER STOOD BEHIND A CROWD AND watched as a loose rope fastened around an outlaw's neck.

Town Marshal Jim Courtright, a lean man with calloused hands and a six-shooter near his waist, tightened the rope. The marshal wore long hair and a handlebar mustache, and the mustache and his expression remained motionless and stoic. His deputy stood by and studied every movement the marshal made.

The marshal's boots scuttled in the dirt as he went and faced the crowd. The sun shined in his face and illuminated the bead of sweat about to fall from the tip of his nose. In the back of the crowd he recognized the stranger. Of all people, he did not expect the stranger to witness the hanging.

In the shadow his hat made the stranger looked just like any man in the crowd. His hat and forearms were dusted with sweat and dirt. He wore a long-sleeved shirt rolled up to expose his sinewy yet strong and hairy arms. The collar was open and showed a bit of chest chair. The hair on his sun-darkened arms was flattened by sweat, and near his hand was a Colt Peacemaker in a worn holster near his waist. The Colt caught side-glances from onlookers, especially the miners that populated the town. Dust had coated his full, unfurled beard and clung to his boots and pants. His pants would appear black if not for the dust from his long journey. The grey eyes were steadfast and were fixed on the rope about the outlaw's stringy neck. On impulse the stranger touched his own neck and once he found himself doing so he noticed the deputy and marshal staring at him, both confused, speechless and cautious of his being in town. Courtright kept his eyes on the stranger and watched for any movement from him. But, at that distance and situated at the back of the crowd, there would be no trouble from him.

There were murmurs in the crowd. Outside the stables the crowd stood and waited for the outlaw to swing down from the rafters of the stable. The outlaw stood on a wooden ladder, and he stood so high his head was above the rafters of the livery barn. The horses nearby were all quiet except one that whinnied in his stall.

"I hear he killed Ron McAlister," said one woman in the crowd.

The stranger stood behind this woman and listened to her as she spoke quietly to a portly man with a pocket watch—an oddity in that town—that hung out from a front breast pocket. The portly man and the woman appeared out of place among the crowd made up mostly of miners. The stranger figured the couple was not from that town. Next to the couple a boy who stood alone without a hat looked around at the crowd until he noticed the stranger staring at the man about to be hanged.

Most of the Lake Valley crowd consisted of miners; their clothes were drenched in sweat and the dirt clung to their faces until beads of sweat carried the grime on their cheeks to settle into their beards or mustaches.

Behind the stranger was Lake Valley, New Mexico. The town was in a wide plain, and nearby a great hill with a rock formation resembling a crown stood barren and high in the sparsely clouded sky. At the top of the hill, one could see the entirety of Lake Valley. From that hill one could see plains of yellowed grass. There were no trees.

Wooden buildings spread far apart from one another in the town that boasted three churches, a post office, various stores, hotels and more than ten saloons. In the foreground a train could be heard going down the tracks. Black smoke rose from it and flowed back to the rear. As the train went by, people turned their heads to hear it. It was an automatic response.

"We all know why we're here," said the marshal in a tone that resembled both a sigh at what he must do and seriousness in the matter. A hanging in Lake Valley was rare. His voice bellowed above the heads that moved left and right to get a glance at the outlaw that stared down at his feet. It was dark inside the stables, and people could not get a good look at the man about to be hanged. "Walden Nealey shot and killed Ron McAlister," continued the marshal, "the owner of McAlister Farms. Nealey and two others, who have yet to be identified, helped him steal twelve of Mr. McAlister's horses, injured three of McAlister's men and—" He paused and looked back at Walden Nealey to see his reaction. "And took his fifteen year old daughter."

Some women gasped in the crowd. Heads shook from curled brim hats set upon the locals and people that were passing through the town. The stranger stared at Walden Nealey and caught Walden glancing at him. There was no emotion in either face. The stranger turned and spat on the ground and kept his eyes on the man about to die. If there was any fear of death in the man's eyes, the stranger couldn't see it.

"We've proved by the account of Ron's wife, Elisha, that you were there at his farm, at that hour and had shot Ron McAlister in the chest." The marshal turned his head to the priest and nodded at him.

The priest stood next to the outlaw. Walden wore no hat and yet his long hair was flattened in the top from wearing it earlier. He smelled of carrion and looked the figure of someone who was halfway to hell. The priest stood on a stool, held his hand on the outlaw's leg, as he was standing on a tall stool, and said, "May the Lord have mercy and look down—"

"I don't need your words," said the outlaw, shaking his leg to rid of the priest's hand. In the shake he made he had almost slipped off the stool and hung himself. "Get on with it." He looked at the marshal and refused to look at the crowd again.

The priest stepped back and quickly walked away, shaking his head for the man's soul and his actions in life.

"Well," said Courtright, watching the priest walk back to his church. He looked up at Walden. "Do you have any last words?"

Walden Nealey looked down at the crowd and heard whispers and coughs from the silver miners. There were big sweat stains under his arms and near his neck. The shirt he wore was scratchy, and he felt an itch made from the rope and which could not be rid of. "I didn't shoot him. I swear! But I won't say who did, and you'll never find him." At once Walden Nealey jumped from the wooden ladder. A few women gasped; one of which closed her eyes and turned away.

The rope tightened as the life of the outlaw disappeared from his eyes. It was an immediate death.

Walden's feet dangled a few feet above the dirt. The body twisted slowly and in each twist there were sounds of the rope squeaking while the body turned. The deputy grabbed the ladder and set it against the wall. The horse that was whinnying before grew silent; its nostrils widened and contracted as he looked at the dangling man.

"No," said Jim Courtright to his deputy. "Bring that ladder, Kim." He turned to the crowd that began walking away. The miners frowned as they went away, though they were not saddened by the death of the man. The women appeared sickened by the death, but none appeared to feel sorry for the murderer. It was a death he chose. And, in many towns, it was a swift death for a man doing the devil's work.

Jim Courtright climbed the ladder while the deputy Kim Fleck helped bring Walden Nealey down. Deputy Fleck was strong despite his young age, and the carrying of the man appeared easy from where the stranger stood.

They carried the body away to a flat and raggedy wagon meant to carry goods about town and not much else. The deputy put a flour sack over Walden Nealey's head, as there were children that were not allowed to visit the hanging. They did not want the little ones to see. Hiding behind houses and stores the children peaked out to see the body taken away. It was a curious and rare sight for Lake Valley. To some a hanging was an exciting thing to witness, especially if their life was monotonous and dull.

Jim Courtright put the ladder in the wagon and turned to see the stranger walking away. The stranger was the last to leave.

"Jake," called Jim Courtright. A light breeze blew through the streets and cooled the sweat on the marshal's face. He wiped the sweat and studied Jake.

Jake half-turned to the saloon, disinterested in the marshal.

"I don't know why you're here, but I think it's time for you to go," said Courtright.

"Why's that?" said Jake. He now faced him, though he folded his arms to show he was not there to fight.

"You've been in and out of jail since the first time I saw you. That's what."

Jake nodded. "I've been a cowboy for more than five years. I'm not going back to my old ways."

"I hope not," said Courtright. "It's not how it was ten years ago. You'll get hanged this time. You won't get lucky again."

"I know it. I came for the hanging, and that's all."

"That's an odd thing to do based on previous events," said Courtright. He motioned to Kim Fleck to help him move the body to the cemetery near the church. The wagon stumbled away on its wheels and made crunching sounds against the little rocks on the ground.

Jake headed for the saloon. His throat was dry and filled with bits of dust, and a drink was long overdue. The saloon was an adobe building with small windows to let in the sunlight. Little squares of light shone on the floor and illuminated the darkened glasses behind the bar. The barman was playing seven up with two miners when Jake stepped inside. Jake's boots creaked against the wooden floorboards and made his presence known.

"What can I get you?" said the barman, standing up and walking to the liquor.

"Whiskey," said Jake. He paid and sat on a stool to drink alone in peace. In the mirror he saw himself, crude looking and unwashed with long hair that was pulled back under his hat. He set his hat on the counter and in the mirror he saw the red marks the hat made against his forehead. His forehead was pale compared to the dark tan on his neck and face and hands. It had been some time since he shaved.

A woman walked on the street outside and looked in the saloon. She had a long white dress and wore no hat and near her side was a man who smiled as the sun shined on his face. She walked inside and noticed Jake sitting at the bar.

Jake did not even look to see the visitors. He only rotated the glass of whiskey on the wooden counter, listening to the glass move against the wood and seeing the liquid slosh about.

"I haven't seen you around," said the woman to Jake. The man she walked in with stepped back and ordered a drink. "Can I buy you a drink?" Her voice was cheerful.

Jake held up his glass of whiskey without turning.

"How about after that's done?" she said.

Jake nodded. "Only one more. I have business after this."

The woman sat down beside him. She had a strong perfume on that enveloped the room and caused the men at the poker table to smell its sweet aroma. "What kind of business?"

"I suppose you can call it hunting."

"Suppose?" interrupted the man beside the woman.

"Yes," said Jake.

"What brings you to town?" asked Martha.

"The hanging."

There was a pause. The woman noticed Jake was a cowboy. He looked the part. Hard-working men were her customers, though she liked something in Jake, something that told her this was a dangerous man that was perhaps running from the law. Aloof, Jake was not interested in her beauty; that put her off, as every man looked at her when she entered the room. But in a way she liked someone who had the gall to not notice her. She was, after all, in the oldest profession and was interested more in different customers than the carcass-smelling miners she would often get. She took a liking to him and said, "What's your name?"

"Jake."

"I'm Martha," she said. "This here's Heinrich."

Heinrich did not speak, but he bowed slightly, and the bowing caught Jake's attention and caused him to straighten up in his stool and look them over. Martha had long blonde hair and blue eyes and was in her late twenties. Heinrich sat down and drank whiskey, though farther away from Jake and Martha.

Jake glanced outside as chickens made sounds nearby and miners walked the streets. The streets outside were zigzagged. There was no real structure to the town, except perhaps in law, and that was only because of Jim Courtright. There was money in the silver mine, but it did not seem apparent. And the lack of structure was apparent in the houses that were setup without any pattern. The buildings were not lined up in a row, such as along a straight street. The only thing that appeared straight and moral was the law in Lake Valley.

"Did you see the hanging?" Martha asked. "We hadn't had one in a very long time. I saw it from a long ways away. A bit scared of it, to be honest. Frightening, don't you think?"

Jake shook his head and scratched the hair on his upper neck. "I don't think so. No, it wasn't like that to me. Living is much harder than dying. Death is immediate. It takes more courage to live than to die. That man, whoever he was, had it coming. He certainly didn't appear frightened when he jumped off that ladder."

Martha showed her bright teeth. "Well, I guess that's true. I hadn't thought of it that way. Wouldn't it take a lot of courage to take your own life?" She rested her right elbow on the bar and tried to look at the stranger's eyes, though Jake was more interested in the whiskey than her.

"Does it take courage to die? That's what you're asking? Not as much as living takes," said Jake.

"And where do you do your living?" she asked.

"Kansas."

"You're not giving much. I'm afraid you don't want to talk to me."

"I don't know why you'd want to talk to a man like me. Shouldn't a young man about town be more to your liking? I am here for one thing and one thing only. Now, I don't want to be rude. But I would like to sit and be alone. I won't need your services."

"My services?" said Martha. "You think that's all I care about? Why, I do not court men for service. They come to me. I thought, 'This is a strange and curious man. I should say hello.' I have never in my life heard someone say something as bold and rude as you. Services!" She stood up, embarrassed. The two miners playing poker were looking at her and Heinrich. "You are not an old man, if that's what you think," she said to Jake. "And my services do not come as easily as that."

"Why don't we go Martha?" said Heinrich, finishing his glass and standing in the light near the door that was left open during daylight. "Enough games."

"I say whether we go or not," she said, facing Heinrich.

Heinrich left the saloon without another word.

Jake watched her without showing any expression in his face. The beard hid everything, even a slight smile. The barman went to play cards again. The miners gradually went back to their game. Jake put his elbows on the bar and went right back to his whiskey. Martha hurried out the door without turning back.

Jake sighed, finished his whiskey and walked back outside in the sun. Now his stomach gnawed at him and growled. If he had wanted peace, he was making enemies fast. That was not what he wanted. He wanted to see the hanging and then speak to the town marshal, but it appeared the marshal was not in the right mood. That was expected. He would speak to him when the right time came.

Jake found a place to eat. He sat at a table that had a window near a nameless road. Outside he saw a white dog roaming the town, sniffing the air and staring cautiously at people walking the town.

The owner of the place that served Jake steak and potatoes was a large bald man who frequently looked outside the window with Jake. He understood Jake and left him alone, though he could tell he was a stranger and was lost.

Perhaps the stranger was looking for someone. The owner of the little restaurant thought he could help.

"I see you're new here," said the owner whose name was Douglas and who was a former slave. He used to be a cook as a slave back in Louisiana. Now he was old with wrinkly skin and lived a peaceful life as a business owner. Sometimes a drunk would challenge him to a fight, and every time Douglas won the fight. It did not look like he was a fighter, yet as a slave he was sometimes used as a boxer for his slave owner on account of his massive size and strength. This was, of course, partially due to him being a cook and having the best food to eat. Most slaves were not fed well, yet the boxing slaves had great size and power and were given the best food.

Douglas went towards the window and put his shoulder against the wall, staring out at the dog outside. "Do you need help finding somebody? I know the area well."

"I don't need help," Jake said. "But thank you."

Douglas folded his arms. Jake finished eating and paid for the food.

Then the front door of the restaurant swung open and Martha stood there, her eyes wide and angry. "There he is," she said. She pointed her thin finger at Jake, who was now standing with his hands to his sides. He sighed when Town Marshal Jim Courtright stepped inside the room with his deputy.

"I knew you'd be trouble," said Courtright. "But I didn't think you'd bother Miss Martha."

"What's the problem, Marshal?" asked Douglas, stepping forward.

"This man, Jake, is disturbing the peace.

He harassed Miss Martha." Courtright took a few steps, and the floorboards creaked as he did so. His deputy Kim Fleck was close behind, but Martha distracted the deputy and caused the deputy to be more interested in the woman than the job at hand.

"He's a pretty quiet fellow to me," said Douglas. "I can't see him doing wrong."

Jim Courtright laughed and when he laughed his stomach shook and his mustache rose a little as he smiled. "This man, Douglas, has gone to prison before. I advise you to stay away from him."

"He has?" asked Martha, turning around. Her frown disappeared, and curiosity replaced her expression.

"Ten years ago was the last time I know of. Who knows what happened after he got out," said Courtright. He motioned for his partner to take Jake's Colt Peacemaker.

Martha grabbed the deputy's hand to hold him back. "Wait a minute. You two know each other?" she asked the marshal.

Jim Courtright watched Jake's hands. Jake was disinterested, staring outside the window at the dog that was walking down the street, sniffing the area, breathing in the dust that blew up from the road and hovered above the soil. "We understand each other," said Courtright.

"I would call it that. He was a train robber. That's why he went to prison for five years."

Jake now looked back. The memories came back vividly, but they never went away. It was just a temporary blot that sometimes resurfaced. He squinted at the marshal and then at Martha. "Are we going to jail or what?" asked Jake.

"If you knew you'd have trouble, why'd you come back to Lake Valley?" Martha asked Jake.

"I came for the hanging."

"No one comes all the way from Kansas for a hanging," said Martha, frowning. Her anger subsided completely. Anything said by Jake before now was forgotten. "Why this hanging? Did you know Ron McAlister?"

"Know him?" said Jake. "He was my brother. I'm Jake McAlister."

CHAPTER 2
RUSTLERS

"It would be a lot easier if we'd let the girl go, Donavan," Hansford Vorris said to him.

Donavan spit into the fire and ignored the statement. The fire crackled in the night. Below the mountain were bare hills scattered across the land with plains of grass and dust and not much else. No trees were in the vicinity. There were more mountains near the horizon, yet in the night they were black figures and barely visible in the moonless night.

Donavan leaned his head against his bedroll and looked up at the clouds that hid the stars. Then the two men heard the muffled screams of the woman. She was on her side and her hands and feet were tied with rope. The rope had long rubbed and burned her wrists, causing pain, yet she was not conscious of the pain, only survival, like a fox with an injured foot and surrounded by wolves.

Hansford touched his own mouth as he looked at the woman with the handkerchief tied around her mouth. He could tell the woman was saying something to him, trying to ask for help, but he could not figure what the words were. They were muffled words. He rotated a small rock in his hand nervously. Never had he stolen a person; it was always horses or cattle. And then Donavan had to go and shoot that old man at the ranch. What a mess.

Hans felt he himself had killed the man, that man whose name was still lost to him, even though it was Donavan Nealey who murdered the man.

"Settle down," said Donavan to Hansford. "I see you're as jumpy as a cat that just woke up. Sleep. It'll do you good."

"Sleep? After what we just did? How can I sleep? Hell, who knows where your brother is."

"He's dead," said Donavan.

"And you don't sound worried at all about that."

Donavan opened his eyes across the fire

from where Hansford Vorris sat. Slits of white showed and nothing more.

The fire separated the two men, though Donavan could see Hansford clearly. Donavan was in the dark, farther away from the fire. It was comfortable to him at that distance. "He's smart. He'll be all right. He wanted the girl for us. Well, we got her."

"That was your plan," said Hansford.

"No, that was Walden's. He wanted the girl. A little entertainment could help us out. Have your first try at her. You earned it. You did good. It was Walden's fault for getting shot in the leg and caught. But you did all right. You always do."

He cared nothing for the compliment. "We never done anything like this before," said Hansford. His mind was mixed up. The white rock in his hand had darkened from the sweat of his palms. "What if we get caught? Will they hang us?"

"They hang horse thieves, don't they?"

Hansford nodded and shut his eyes. His face now glistened with sweat. The fire showed this, and Donavan noticed it.

Hansford had short hair under his hat, parted cleanly to the side. He had light stubble, having shaved recently because of the heat. In the winter he grew a beard, as the cold and snow were unforgiving sometimes, especially up in the mountains to the far north. Recently it had become too hot for a big beard. He had sweat marks under his arms that showed right through his long shirt. His brown pants showed some dirt on the knees, but they were fine clothes and not as dirty as they used to be.

"But we won't get caught," said Donavan, watching young Hansford sweat and look off in the distance. He could tell the young man was nervous, even though Hansford had stolen cattle and horses plenty of times before. Hansford's experience is why Donavan even invited him to steal the horses from the McAlister Farm. Despite Walden's doubts about Hansford, Donavan knew the young man was bold and not afraid to steal from those that had too much for their own good. "They didn't see our faces, right?"

"No. No, I don't think they did."

"Then we're all right." His tone was lighthearted, yet his attempt to reassure Hans was wasted.

Hansford nodded, yet doubt crossed his mind several times. "I guess so. I've stolen horses many times before. But it was always from Mexicans near the border. Hell, they steal from us, too. It was almost like a game sometimes. Mexicans steal our horses, and then we go over and steal theirs, except it was most likely ours and a little extra for the trouble they caused us. But I never stole from a white man before."

Donavan pushed a hand against the ground to stand up. He drank whiskey, and it showed in his breath, even from a good distance away. He could not walk well, even as he walked a short distance to the girl. He picked up a lock of the girl's hair and smelled it. "She smells good, too."

Hansford frowned from a distance, watching Donavan. Donavan kneeled down, his long hair falling to his shoulders. He wore a big beard, which helped hide his face though not by much. Donavan then touched the girl's shoulder and she squirmed, saying something through the muffled handkerchief.

"What are you doing over there?" asked Hansford, speaking loudly over the crackling fire. It was dark and he could not see that far from the fire. There were too many clouds that hid the moon.

"What do you think?" Donavan said to him. "I'm going for one." He unbuckled his pants.

"What about your wife?"

Donavan halted, sighed and said, with a harsh tone, "Forget about her. She's probably been sneaking off while I'm gone. I didn't think you'd bring up such a fuss, Hans. If I had known you'd pester me like a woman, you wouldn't have come." But he knew that was untrue. Hansford did a better job at rustling than Donavan and Walden, and both knew it.

"I say we let the girl go."

The girl turned her eyes to Hansford. The young man was now standing. He had an 1875 Remington Revolver in his hand, at the ready, cocked back. The finger was on the trigger. The hands were still sweaty, and the rock he had fiddled with was on the ground near the fire.

Donavan looked at the rock and the hand. Hansford stepped away from the fire and listened as the tied up girl breathed deeply, her chest rising and falling, her eyes wide. She stopped moving and stopped trying to wiggle out of her hands. Now her eyes were on the revolver that Hansford held in his hand.

"Forget about the girl already, Hans! There's no going back. Understand? She would turn us in. She sees our faces."

"Can you see me?" asked Hansford.

"What? What are you talking about?"

"Can you see what I got in my hand?"

Donavan said, "I'm pretending not to. I'm hoping you will not do something stupid like try to scare me with that gun of yours. We both know you're not shooting that thing."

The young Hans looked down at the girl, and he watched her eyes that appeared to say something, that appeared to urge him on. Then he knew what the eyes truly said. The eyes focused on the Dragoon near Donavan's side. In Donavan's hand was the Dragoon, hidden near the side of his body.

"Drop the gun, son," said Donavan, his pants still unbuckled, yet he stood now, swaying in his drunkenness. The belt was on the ground, though he had grabbed the Dragoon in time.

Hansford looked at the girl. From the fire he saw she was very young, with blue eyes and blonde hair. She pleaded with her expressions, with the nodding towards Donavan, signaling to the young Hans to kill the man. She sensed there was some good in Hans.

"What would you do after you—did what you were about to do?" asked Hansford.

Donavan sighed. It was unimportant to him. "I don't know. Hell, just let her go."

"There's Apaches in these hills," he said.

"I don't see what that has to do with letting her go. She'll live, won't she?"

"You were going to—no, I can't. I can't watch, let alone listen to that," said Hansford.

He brought up his revolver, and just as he did so Donavan brought up his Dragoon. Although his shooting hand was slippery with sweat, Hansford pulled the trigger and shot the man in the chest. Donavan's gun went off, though he had missed. The sound from the guns was deafening, especially from the Dragoon. The girl had closed her eyes. There was a ringing in Hansford's ears.

Hansford kept his revolver pointed at Donavan as he walked to him. He then crouched and checked for a pulse on the man's neck. There was none. He left the body, took out a big knife and cut the ropes that tied the girl's wrists and ankles. She took out the cloth that was in her mouth. Hans did not even look back at her. He simply sat back down, as if in shock, and watched the hills and mountains once more.

The girl stood up, ironed her dress with her hands, as it had ridden up from Donavan touching her body. She then stood there, not knowing what to do or where to go. She could be in Mexico for all she knew; yet it did not take long to ride from Lake Valley to where she and Hansford were.

"Is he dead?" she said, looking at the dead body but not wanting to get closer to check if he was dead.

Hansford said, "Yes," without turning. "Sit down if you want."

She stood there awkwardly.

"Go on. Sit. I killed the man who wanted to hurt you, remember?"

The girl sat down on the ground near the fire. She folded her arms near the fire. The sweat from Hansford's face was drying, as the night was cool even in the summer. She was cold, so she sat closer to the fire. "I'm Delilah," she said.

"Hansford Vorris," he said. "People call me Hans."

"Why'd you do that? Why'd you kill that man? You must have known him a while."

"No, I met him several months ago, him and his brother. They wanted help rustling. Well, I had stolen some cattle when I lived along the Rio Grande, so I thought I might help them out and get paid. I suppose the money is mine now." Hans pointed at the horses down below the mountain that were still drinking from a river. "It's time I take them to the buyer."

"You don't sound excited," said Delilah. "That means you get paid three times as much. The other two are dead or caught."

"Sure."

"You were awfully brave," she said,

watching Hans stare blankly at the fire. "I—I won't tell them you were here. I'll say you're dead," said Delilah McAlister.

"You don't need to do that. You just go on home. You know the way?"

She squinted her eyes at the road below. The terrain appeared familiar. She could see the road that led to Lake Valley in the distance. "I know it."

"Then go on, and don't stop for anything. There's Apaches in these hills. That's why we rode this far. Just take that horse there," he said, motioning to Donavan's horse.

"I'd like to see my father again," she said.

Hansford nodded. "Yes," he said. "That would be good." He could not tell her that he was probably not alive. A man getting shot like that would not survive. He could not tell her that her father was dead. Did she see Donavan Nealey shoot her father? No, he thought, otherwise she would be crying or acting out in anger. She had probably heard the shot and then felt Donavan grab and carry her out of her bedroom.

She idled, standing up and wanting some sort of reason for all of the events to happen. But she could not find a reason. Not everything needs a reason. It was time to head home and not search for why this had all happened to her family rather than another one. The morality of it was too much for her to think about as well, such as why bad things happen to good people.

"Hold on," said Hansford. He stood up, grabbed Donavan's Winchester and gave Delilah the rifle.

The girl stared at the rifle without grabbing it. "You're awfully trusting of me. I would have liked you to kill that man sooner." She finally grabbed the rifle and put it in the scabbard on the horse. She then mounted with the help of Hans.

"I never shot a man before," he said.

"For a man to shoot, you shot the right one." She looked down from atop the horse. "I hope I won't hear about you getting hanged for stealing horses."

"I made it this far," he said.

"Don't push your luck. I've seen some men get boastful after winning a poker game and then lose it all."

"You sound like a mother," he said, smiling. "But there's some truth to it. I'll be careful. I work best alone or with good friends, such as the ones back in Texas."

"It sounds like you'll keep doing what you just did."

"No, I won't. I don't think I can. Stealing

from Mexicans was far different than stealing from your old man."

"That 'old man' might want his horses back," she said.

"I'll be long gone after getting paid. You can find them near Silver City," said Hans.

She rode off without saying another word. He watched her until the horse and rider disappeared behind a hill.

Hans hesitated as he stared at Donavan and then eyed a small shovel on the horse. Instead of digging a grave he would let the vultures and land animals pick at him. Hansford knew his past, and most importantly he knew Donavan would leave him to die as well. After all, he let his brother die.

With his boot he covered the fire with dirt and rocks. Then he mounted his horse and rode down to the river to gather the horses.

With only Hans it would take the rest of the night to lead the horses to Silver City. As he began his way back he tried to see the girl again, but she was already gone. Nothing could be seen in the night except dark shapes of mountains that were frequently mistaken for storms on the horizon.

He went on as the night turned colder by the hour. The sweat on his skin dried.

The money would be good at least, though

it cost two deaths. And if they were on his trail, it might cost a third.

Hans brought up his black bandana from his neck to cover his face and watched the hills for Apaches. Nighttime Apache ambushes were common in that land. It took another hour for his heart to slow down to a comfortable pace.

CHAPTER 3
QUESTIONING

MARTHA SAID NOTHING ELSE AFTER JAKE McAlister introduced himself. Jake frowned at the woman and then at Town Marshal Jim Courtright.

This was a waste of time to Jake. They were blocking the door and keeping him from finding out what exactly happened to his older brother.

Douglas, the big cook, stared down in sadness. Everyone in Lake Valley had heard of Ron McAlister and the good he did around town. His death was a shock. "I'm sorry to hear that," said Douglas. "Ron was a good man."

Jake nodded in appreciation.

"I didn't know you were—" said Martha, half in apology.

She walked out of the room, but before

doing so Courtright said, "Was he harassing you or not, Martha?"

"No, it was nothing, just words," she said.

Courtright let her go. The deputy, Kim Fleck, stood nearby and loosened his shoulders after the miscommunication was cleared. Fleck still kept an eye on Jake, just like Courtright did.

"What are you doing here?" said Courtright. "You came for the hanging. It's over."

"I wanted to ask you some questions about what happened to Ron," he told him.

Jim Courtright brought up his chin and motioned outside with his hand. "Let's go to my office." Courtright signaled to his deputy that it was all right. Jake used to be a wild one, though now his energy seemed draining, as if he was just barely keeping up. Courtright felt he wasn't a threat. It didn't appear like Jake would cause trouble, but those that appear tame sometimes end up being trouble.

In Jim Courtright's office Jake sat down in a wooden chair as Kim Fleck sat outside the building and surveyed the land. It was his position, and it gave an impression that the law was always watching the town.

Courtright poured Jake McAlister whiskey after asking him what he wanted. Then he poured a small one for himself. "What do you want to know?" asked Courtright, leaning over the desk. He drank and wiped his mustache with his shirtsleeve and put away the bottle below the desk.

The wind picked up outside and had brought up dust that tapped against the windows. It was difficult to see how fast the wind went except by the way the grass swayed or by the way the wind moved across the sky, as there were no trees around Lake Valley. Along the western sky were grey clouds hovering low and moving fast.

"I just want to know what happened," said Jake.

"How did you hear about it in the first place? I assume you hadn't spoken to Ron after what he did to you."

Jake took off his hat and combed back his hair. "No, I hadn't. Not for ten years."

"Then why come back?"

"I felt like I needed to say goodbye," said Jake.

"A little late for that," he told him, but not in an unkind way. It was a matter of fact. "But you still hadn't answered my question. How'd you hear about it?"

"Elisha told me."

"She sent you a telegram?"

Jake nodded.

"She would be kind enough to do so," said Courtright. He leaned back in his chair and watched outside. The storm moved fast. The silver miners were watching the storm as well; they did not want to get stuck in mines that filled up with water. The rain itself was a welcome sight. There were dark rain clouds in the west that moved fast over the hills. "First time she'll be a widow."

"How is she taking it?" asked Jake McAlister.

"What you expect. Hard. She still has her daughter missing. I sent word to a few places about what happened and to be on the lookout for the horses and the girl, Delilah."

"Know what they looked like?"

"The rustlers? No. Elisha said she only heard one of them yell. It was dark because of the clouds. And no one lived nearby except a few of Ron's workers, so there are no witnesses except one or two of Ron's men. They told me they couldn't see the faces clearly. At least we caught one of them, Walden Nealey, but that's cause he got shot in the leg. He gave nothing. He wouldn't turn anyone in."

"Then we have nothing to go on," said Jake, sighing. He adjusted his hat and touched his beard. As he brought his arm up to his hat he smelled himself, and his smell was so foul it unsettled him. If he were on a drive, it would be normal and not even a thought. But he was far from his usual doings. In a town like that, he felt he shouldn't smell too bad.

Jim leaned his elbows on the desk and tried to see Jake more clearly. There was nothing in Jake's face. The big beard and the dull eyes hid everything. It was the deep voice, a whiskey and grainy as sand type of voice, that expressed his emotions—the ones he cared to show, which were not many. He was a rough-looking man; a beard as mangled as a bird's nest, and the skin was dark and leather-like. This was a far different man than the one Jim Courtright saw more than ten years prior, though during that time he was just a loud-mouth stranger in a violent town, a man who was a notorious train robber and who had not yet been caught.

Jake McAlister stood up. "I figured that's how it would be."

"You better head over to Mrs. McAlister's house," said Jim Courtright. Right after saying her name he forgot she was a widow and now Miss McAlister. He glanced outside with Jake. "There's a storm coming. You might be able to get out there in time."

"You didn't even ask what I've been doing

all this time," said Jake, turning around from facing the window. "Aren't you curious?"

"If you aren't robbing trains or banks anymore, it's none of my business," said Courtright.

Jake opened the door and went out. He held onto his hat with his left hand, as the strong wind almost blew his hat off his head. He walked to his large white horse, a mighty horse that was envied by whoever saw it. And when the man neared it the horse turned its head and almost seemed to nod. The horse was hitched near the saloon, and this was after the horse had been fed and cleaned in the town livery.

The horse was clean and yet the rider was dirty as could be. Jake hesitated before mounting his horse, not sure of going to the McAlister Farm or not. A lot of memories were formed there when Ron and Jake were growing up; it was a house owned by their father, Ambrose McAlister. Those memories seemed as far as Kansas was, so he wanted to see it and touch the walls and see the stable and the creek where he used to play as a boy. It brought up some excitement in him, but it quickly died out when he touched his beard and glanced down at the hair peaking out from his shirt that was unbuttoned near his neck. He buttoned it up and searched for a place to bathe.

It was best not to see Elisha McAlister while looking like a dog that had been playing in the mud. So he went to a little hotel, as he had no place to sleep and it was better than sleeping on a bedroll in the wild. He took a bath in his room. From his beard and skin and hair the dust immediately panned out in the water. The clothes were washed and set out to dry. He had another pair of clothes to wear once he decided to visit the McAlister Farm. He cleaned out his beard, in which small bits of grass clung, and smelled the soap. When he did so, he felt his beard.

After the bath he stood in front of a small mirror and shaved his beard clean off. It took some time, as it was a lot of beard. Once Jake was done he felt his smooth face, which was an odd feeling. He appeared younger, handsomer, which surprised him. He figured he would look worse, but this newfound appearance was to his liking.

He put on clean clothes and picked up his gun belt on the bed and looked into the mirror once more. Then a sound outside made him turn his head. He went to the small window and looked first at the rain clouds moving over the land, and then at the dog he had seen earlier. It was a white-haired dog with shaggy fur, but the fur was not as long as dogs with hair that gets in front of their eyes. It was a medium-sized dog and bigger than a fox at least. Its mouth was opened, its tongue dangling, and then the dog made the sound once more. Its nose sniffed the air and it howled once again.

Jake saw it in the middle of the barren street. There were no sounds except the howl, but then more howling came into play. This howling rose from the mountains or perhaps beyond in the plains. As Jake heard it again and again he knew it came from wolves. Jake supposed wolves were once the dog's kin, though because of their differences they were left to only speak from afar.

The man walked outside, passed the hotel owner that was asleep in his room and found the dog just outside the hotel. The white dog slept; then it opened one eye as Jake was near and growled at the man.

"No?" asked Jake to the growling dog. "I don't like to be touched either."

After taking a few steps back the dog calmed, though it did not blink or leave its eyes from the man. The tail was still and the big ears pointed up.

"Stay right there," he said.

Jake went inside the hotel and came back

with some meat. It was a big slab Jake took from the kitchen in the hotel. He dropped it right on the wooden porch. The meat slapped against the porch and the dog stared at it in curiosity.

The white dog walked over and sniffed the meat cautiously. Once it was found to be good, the dog nibbled at the meat and then chewed and swallowed it.

Jake smiled a little and sat down on the far side of the porch, letting the dog eat in peace. It appeared wild, without an owner, too aggressive for anyone in that town. In a few minutes the dog was done eating and began licking its nose and paws. Jake kept his back to it and stared at the rain that he could now see from across the land. The storm was far in the distance and had not reached Lake Valley yet. Farther in to town there was laughter rising out from the saloons. Drunken miners walked back to their beds in big wooden houses built to house groups of them. The lightning flashing in the sky brought out some excitement in the miners and the wolves howling to the north.

Jake mounted his horse and looked back at the dog one last time. Then he made his way north to the old McAlister house, his childhood home. Near the edge of town the man glanced back at the flickering lights from coal oil lamps being doused near the windows of homes. He saw the white dog following him. For a white dog in a dirty mining town, it was as clean as his horse.

He slowed his horse. The horse and Jake turned their heads back at the dog. The dog waited, walked a few steps and turned back with them, as if his being there was typical. "You just want more food, don't you?" said the man.

The dog turned back, licking its nose and then staring at the black clouds now spreading out near the horizon.

"We better go," said Jake. "All three of us."

Jake continued again and left the town and made it to a road that had stagecoach tracks imprinted on it. The nighttime sky and clouds hid the moon, so the land was hard to see. In an hour Jake made it to the house, though it looked different from his childhood. The stables were expanded. There was even a new building that looked to be another barn, and there were pigs in a fenced in area and a chicken coop a little farther from the pigs.

It was a one-story wooden house with a wide wooden porch where stairs led up. He saw a glow from lights near the shut curtains from a mile away. He halted and looked back at the white dog. Then he saw from the west a lone rider. In the pitch-black night he could not see the figure clearly. For all he knew it was an Apache scouting out a new place to pillage and perhaps even burn down. But that was unlikely. The Apaches were mostly in reservations, though the land was still wild and unpredictable. And it was best not to judge the land and its people lightly.

The rider rode fast from the west hills, crossing a little creak that was almost dried up from frequent droughts. The rider's horse stormed through the water, its hair flying up, nostrils widening.

Jake was so far that his presence was unknown. It did not appear the rider cared who was about. When the rider was close to the front porch, a woman from inside the house came out, almost running down the steps. The woman from the house embraced the rider.

Jake trotted to the house, but by the time he got there the rider and woman were inside. Then a drop of rain fell on Jake's hat, and then another and another until the ground of dust became mud. Muddy water poured into the creek from the hills and rolling plains. A sound of thunder from the west caused the dog to walk to the front porch and curl up into a ball. The sound of the dog on the creaking floorboards must have been heard, because the woman inside the house came out with a lantern in her left hand and a rifle in her right.

Then Jake dismounted and said, "Hi, Elisha."

"Who is it? How do you know my name?"

The woman was perhaps fifty years old, with wrinkles near her eyes and mouth. Her skin was pale; though the only skin showing were her hands, neck and face. She wore tan pants, brown boots and a long-sleeve buttoned shirt like the one Jake wore, but hers was tighter and appeared almost new. Her figure was lean yet strong. To Jake she did not change from more than ten years ago. The only change he could see was the new wrinkles.

"Jake," he said. "Can I come to the steps?"

"Jake?" she said. The name did not sound familiar. "Come to the steps, but stop once you reach the bottom step."

He did as he was told, leaving his rifle and horse behind. The dog was near Elisha's boots. She looked down at the dog, but his eyes were closed and he was already asleep. For some reason he did not appear to mind the voices or the sound of thunder cracking against the sky.

Jake walked closer and when he was near the steps he stopped and let Elisha get a better look at him. After all, it had been ten years since he had visited her. Ten years certainly changed him.

Does she remember the telegram? he thought.

Elisha held the lantern higher and then saw the man in clear view, but it still was unclear to her who he was. "Jake who?" she asked.

"Jake McAlister."

She brought the lantern down to her side and remembered the telegram. It was a heavy lantern, but she lowered it mostly because she wanted to see the look of his clothes and boots. The clothes were clean but drenched from the rain pouring down on the land. He got under the roof that covered the porch and part of the steps and stayed there.

"I didn't think you'd come," she said. "When I sent that telegram, I thought you'd ignore it."

"I thought of doing that. Part of me thought I should come."

"So you came because you thought you had to?" she asked.

"No. Maybe at the beginning it was like that. Not anymore. Can I come in? I wanted to talk for a bit, if that's all right. I'd understand if you don't want that."

She frowned. Behind her a girl of about

fifteen came from a hallway and said, "Is everything all right?"

"Yes," said Elisha, without turning her head back. "You go take a bath." She kept her eyes on Jake, studying him. The young girl disappeared inside.

"Was that Delilah?" he said, in surprise and in a serious and deep tone. He heard of her being taken from one of the rustlers, and he understood what happened to women who were stolen. "Is she all right?"

"I believe so," she said. "She just got back. She said she managed to get way. But—that is beside the point. I can't have you here if you're hiding from the law like you used to do. It happened once before, and it will never happen again. God knows you—"

"I'm not running," Jake said. "No, ma'am. I am not like that anymore. I am a cowboy in Dodge City. You have nothing to worry about. I'm not running anymore."

She lowered the rifle, as her arms were no longer tense. She took a deep breath and relaxed. "I thought you were in trouble. A man riding to your house in a storm wanting shelter is not usually a good sight."

"Can I come in?" he asked again.

"Yes," she said. "But you will have to excuse the rifle. Ron—" She choked back tears, went inside the house and put the lantern on a table. She covered her face with her free hand, breathed deeply and placed the rifle on the dinner table.

"I understand," he said. He walked inside and shut the door.

"Put your horse in one of the stables," she told him. Thunder shook the house. It sounded like a crack and then the echo of the crack seemed to stretch across the land.

Jake went back outside and led his horse to a stable and then went back inside and shut the door. When he had returned he saw Elisha at the dinner table. There was a small kitchen, yet the living room with the stone fireplace was large. Two leather chairs were there, and a buffalo fur rug covered the floor. There were pictures on the walls, but he did not go to view them.

Jake took off his hat and put it on a rack on the wall. As he did so he saw what looked to be one of Ron's hats.

"Come sit down. You must be tired," she said, sitting back in one of the four chairs. She herself had sleepy eyes that barely opened.

"Happy Delilah is all right," said Jake.

"Thank the Lord she returned safe. She escaped," she said.

He doubted that.

"I'm glad to hear it. Last time I saw her she was as tall as my knee."

This caused Elisha to smile and remember her daughter's childhood that did not seem too long ago. Time moved fast, and that was especially felt in the last few days. "You never came back," she said.

Jake leaned back in his chair. "He turned me in, Elisha. Because of him I spent five years in jail. Five. Now, I don't know about you, but a brother doesn't do that. I would do anything for family. Anything. But he had to do that." He shook his head. "What was I supposed to do? Come back and visit him and say, 'Hey, brother, remember me? Yes, thanks for sending me to prison.' There was nothing to say. I felt he abandoned me right then and there. When I saw the state marshals waiting outside, I knew it was Ron that turned me in. There was no way they could have found me. He even admitted it to me in a letter that I never responded to."

"What did he say in the letter? I never heard of any letter he sent you."

"I read the letter when locked up, but it doesn't matter," he said. "It definitely doesn't matter now."

She got up and poured a glass of water. Jake noticed Delilah peaking out her head from behind the doorframe of a bedroom. He refused to look, though he could see her in his peripheral vision.

Elisha put down two glasses of water. "All this rain is making me thirsty. It hasn't rained in weeks."

"Is the farm handling it?"

"It does all right."

"You must have workers, don't you? How many acres is it now?"

"About seven thousand," she said. "The workers live north of here."

He combed back his wet hair. The light from the lantern on the dinner table lit his face and his eyes. A little spark of fire showed in his eyes from the single flame in the lantern. Elisha looked him over finally, as she was a bit tense around him. "You look almost the same as ten years ago," she said.

"Well, I just shaved off a big beard," he said, touching his face. "It feels like I should have something on my face, to cover up, but I'll get used to it."

"It suits you."

He drank his water and wiped his mouth and nodded at the living room. "This place looks just like it was when I was a child."

"We added some stables and various other things. But it's almost the same."

His face fell somber suddenly, as if he thought of something that needed to be done.

"Did you really ride all the way here from Dodge City?"

"I tried to get here fast," he said. "I did see the hanging in time."

Elisha scratched her hands, uncomfortable to hear about hanging and murder that many were used to hearing about.

"And I saw Jim Courtright and spoke to him a little about what happened. I wanted to know what you saw. Were there three men?"

She closed her eyes and nodded. Then she stood up and pointed to the west. "I heard a scream, so I went to the sound. That's where I saw two men rounding up the horses. Then I saw a man grabbing Delilah. I went outside, but as I went for the rifle I heard a shot. When I came out I saw two men leaving, one with Delilah and one man shot, limping away, staring back with a revolver in his hand. That man fell down behind the stables and hid. I then saw Ron on the ground, holding his chest, taking his last breaths." She paused to wipe away tears with her forearm. "He told me he loved me and Delilah very much and then he died right there with his head on my lap."

Delilah came from her bedroom and stood there in the living room, trying to find out who the man in the house was, especially at that hour, and why her mother was crying. "What's going on?" said Delillah.

Elisha wiped away the tears and said, "This is your uncle, Jake. Don't you remember him? It was a long time ago—"

Delilah walked closer, standing cautiously from a distance. She stared at Jake after he lifted his head. "I remember," she said, a little cheerful but not her usual cheerful self, especially after recent events. "Where have you been?"

"Kansas," he said. "I've been a cowboy for many years. I came back, well, to—" He looked at Elisha and then back at the girl. "I came to find out what happened. That's all."

Delilah sat down at the table with them. "There's not much to say. We were attacked in the night. The marshal said he caught one of them. But mother didn't want to see the hanging. Was he already hanged?"

Jake nodded. "He's dead." There was a pause. The two women did not appear to show emotion to the death of the man. "But there were three of them. Is that right?"

"Yes," said Elisha.

"That means two are still out there, somewhere. Courtright said he sent word to forts and towns nearby to let them know about it. That won't do good," he said, speaking of experience. "They could be in Mexico by now."

"You plan on finding them?" asked Elisha.

"That's the first part of it," he said. "Then having a talk with them. Do you have any enemies?" he asked Elisha.

She touched her face and thought about it. Does everyone keep track of their enemies? "No. We've always treated people right."

Jake looked at Delilah, who was looking at the raindrops on the windows on the east of the house, the ones not covered. She looked nervous. "What happened out there? How'd you get free?" he asked Delilah.

"I don't think this is the right time," Elisha told him.

"It's fine," said Delilah. "I just managed to get free in the night, stole one of their horses and got here."

"How'd they manage to take you away? You look strong enough to fight off one man alone."

She blushed. "Well, I—I was tied up."

"With rope?" Jake asked. He noticed the red marks around her wrists.

"Yes." She saw his eyes and held the wrists behind her back.

He leaned back in his chair. For some

reason she lied to him. He wondered why. "You were tied up? It's difficult to get free from being tied up."

"I guess they were amateurs," said the girl.

"They planned this all out. They knew what they were doing. They would know how to tie a rope."

"Are you calling me a liar?"

"I am saying it doesn't make sense," he said.

"I don't understand all this talk," said Elisha. She looked curiously at her daughter. She, too, felt it odd she returned so easily. Not many questions had been asked except the question of if she was hurt. There were so many things that happened recently that Elisha felt almost sick.

"I don't either," Jake said to her. He turned to Delilah, who was breathing heavier than before. She had been standing from a distance, but Jake said, "What really happened? Tell us. I'm here to find the man who killed your father. Don't you want that?"

"Father's dead?"

Jake looked at Elisha.

"How does she not know?" Jake asked Elisha.

"She didn't see it," said Elisha. "She thinks he is at the doctor in town."

"Oh, God no," said Delilah. She collapsed

in a chair near the fireplace and covered her face with her hands and cried. Her back was turned to Jake and Elisha in the kitchen.

Jake walked to the fireplace and crouched near the fire. "Your father was a good man," he said.

"You don't think so. You're lying yourself."

"All right. I lied."

There was a silence. He felt the heat of the fire and smelled the burning wood.

"And yet you want to find his murderers," said the girl.

"He may have turned me in and sent me to jail, but he's still my brother. I don't want murderers to get away with it," he said. "If I was you, I'd tell people what happened, no matter what. It will help me find him. Don't you want me to help you?"

She dropped her hands and then wiped the tears. "Yes."

"Then tell me. What happened?"

She told him everything. Jake then got up and got his hat near the door and put it on. The hat was wet from the rain that still poured outside, but he did not mind. It sounded like lightning struck the ground nearby. The sky flashed white every few seconds. He could see through the windows the creek whenever the sky flashed. It was now full.

Elisha said to him, "You should probably go." Before Jake touched the doorknob she said, "What are you going to do?"

"There's a man out there who had something to do with Ron's murder. I intend to find him."

"And what?"

"Ask him some questions. He's involved in your husband's murder. Wouldn't you want him dead?"

"I don't know," she said. "I don't want revenge. I want justice."

"What's the difference? Either way, he'll be dead, whether it's by the law hanging him or a bullet."

"It's not like that anymore. You can't just shoot a man and get away."

"We'll find out."

He went outside and could not find the dog. It was not on the porch. When he went to retrieve his horse from the stables he saw the dog sleeping near the horse. The dog opened its eyes and after Jake mounted his horse the dog followed him once again.

CHAPTER 4
THE OUTLAW AND THE MISTRESS

Hansford Vorris drank at the saloon and overheard talk about rustlers near Lake Valley. This caused Hans to turn his head and try to listen over all the loud laughing and talking in the room. He sat on a bar stool and watched as more and more men entered the saloon.

The room was poorly lit, and outside only the moon lit the muddy streets. Hans finished his whiskey and paid and then moved through the crowd, brushing shoulders with men, to hear the conversation better. He walked near the table where he heard the news of rustlers. Two men were playing poker, drinking and smoking. Slow-moving smoke filled the room. The smoke could be seen through the glow of the lamplights scattered across the room.

A black-haired man with a big beard and sleeves rolled up to show thick forearms said: "That's what I heard. There were two of them that got away."

"How do you know that?" asked another man, who had short red hair and a stubble forming on his cheeks.

"I know someone who works—well, I guess I should say worked—for Ron McAlister. He gave me the news. From the telegram he sent it sounded like he—Bob—was a bit angry."

"Why do you say that?" said the red head.

"Said they were 'bastard rustlers.'"

They laughed. The black-haired man put down the cards and lost but showed little worry in his face.

Hans stood near the table and said, "Mind if I play a game or two?"

The black bearded man nodded. "Not at all. Sit down. This is Fred," he said, pointing his hand to the red head. "I'm Samuel. What brings you to town?"

"Work, mostly," said Hans.

"Same for us all. Plenty of work around here. Mining seems to be popular, especially up near Fort West."

"Don't kill the man," said Fred. "There's Apaches near there."

"In a reservation," he said.

"Not all of them. Some still kill travelers, burn stagecoaches, raid villages."

"Don't listen to him," Samuel said to Hans. "There's plenty of bastards that are white and do the same."

"Not raid villages," said Fred, putting in some money to the center of the table.

"Well, there could be. There'd be no survivors to say what happened."

Samuel shook his head and sighed. The conversation seemed ridiculous to him. "What's your line of work?" he said to Hans.

"I do a bit of everything," said Hans. He looked at his cards and put down some money. He was cautious about spending his money, as he was not sure whether there were men searching for him. He would need plenty of money if he had to hide out somewhere. If they have my name, he thought, I will have to come up with a new one.

"I heard about those rustlers as well," said Hans.

"Oh?" said Fred. "Were you friends with them?"

There was a pause. Then Fred laughed, and Hans caught on and grinned, yet he perspired, as the room was hot and he was unsure of his presence in the town. But it was his home, for now, and he knew there were plenty of places to hide in a big town. Maybe, he thought, I should stay away from here for a few months and wait until this all goes away. But he knew it would not go away unless he moved far away, just as he had done before on the Texas border.

"What do these bastards look like?" asked Hans. "I want to know in case I see them."

"It wouldn't say," said Samuel. "The message from my friend Bob was short. I'm sure we'll find them in the next month or so. The horses are probably branded."

Fred shook his head. "That is unlikely."

"What?" said Samuel, unable to hear over all the laughing and cheering in the saloon.

"I said the law probably won't find them. How do you track down horses when a storm wiped away all tracks?"

Samuel put down his cards and drank. He shrugged. "You don't know everything there is to know. They could have laid low for a while, stayed put and then traveled in the night again. That's what I would do."

"Still," said Fred. "It's hard to catch them."

"Not if everyone in the area is on the lookout for the man's horses," said Samuel. "We have to look out for each other. It sounds like McAlister was a good man. He got shot over some horses. Hell, that's a bad way to die. I wouldn't wish it on someone. It just happened. Maybe we will get some description on the horses and the men soon. Ah—" Samuel took a cigar that was hanging out from his mouth and said, "Now I remember. It said he was a young man, white, about 25 to 30 years of age, short hair parted to the side and had a light stubble." He pointed a thumb at Hans, who was resigned but listened intently to the talkative men.

Fred smiled and so did Hans, but Hans felt anxious, exhausted and dizzy. Samuel patted Hans on the back. "Are you all right, man?"

"I just feel a little sick."

"Well, don't get me sick," said Samuel. "I'm just joking. You don't have to stay for us. We'll talk all night like this."

Hans smiled apologetically, nodded goodbye and left the saloon. He went behind the saloon and vomited on the ground. A man came out from a back door, noticed him and mumbled "drunken fools" to himself as he went back inside the saloon.

A stray cat sat on the roof of an opposite building and looked down at Hans curiously.

I helped kill a good man, thought Hans.

He got up and stumbled drunkenly away. By the time he found the street he was breathing hard and listening to hitched horses breathing. Hans sat outside a two-story wooden building on the steps and tried to devise a plan. In a few minutes he left his spot and walked the streets. The dizziness left him. Walking the streets helped him feel better. Hans found a house and climbed the side roof, crouched on the roof and went to a window.

There was a faint glow of light coming from the opened window. The white window curtain blew in the wind and sometimes blew outside of the window when a strong breeze came by. Hans looked inside and saw a woman sitting on the edge of her bed.

"Bonnie," he called to her.

Bonnie still sat on the bed. Hans couldn't see what she was doing. She had on her nightgown. Her hair was long and brown, and her back faced him. He could see, after moving the curtain with his hand, that she was brushing her long hair.

"Bonnie," he said again.

She turned quickly, frightened. "Who's there?" she said. She went for a pocket pistol that she had beneath the bed.

"Hansford," he said.

She opened up the curtains and saw his face. She smiled and said, "What are you doing? I could have shot you right there."

"You're not that stupid," he said, crawling inside the room.

"Not that stupid," she repeated. "I wonder why I bother with you."

"Maybe because of my good looks."

"I'm not sure that's why," she said.

He stood up in the bedroom and looked down at her. They embraced, and then she pulled him closer and kissed him. "I missed you."

"Is he here?" asked Hans.

"He had business somewhere."

"Where?"

"It doesn't matter," said Bonnie. "We have time."

Bonnie sat on her bed and looked him over. "Why are you sweating?"

"It's hot out."

"Not to me," she said. "In the day it is, but not at night."

Hans looked outside the window. He could not see any horse except his own. In the distance he saw a big dog near his horse. The horse was sniffing the dog, its tail swishing.

"I've done something stupid," he told her.

"Again?"

"I'm serious, Bonnie." He paced the room. He felt his palms, and they were sweaty, just like they had been before he killed Donavan Nealey. He wiped his palms against his shirt and looked up after he heard faint voices coming from the town. The house he stood in was along the main road yet farther from town. Mountains stood black in the distance.

"Tell me what happened. You seem jumpy as can be."

He sat down on a wooden chair in front of a mirror and turned the chair to the window. "I stole some horses."

"That's not too bad."

"I was with some bad men. I knew there was something wrong with them. I had a bad feeling around them. But I didn't think much of it. All we were doing was stealing horses. Well, it was just that. One of the men took a girl."

Bonnie frowned and sat crisscross on her bed. Her back was straight, but after she heard him mention the girl she leaned forward, waiting for an explanation. "What happened to her? Is she all right?"

"She's fine. Well, the last time I saw her she was riding back to her home."

"What else?"

"I killed a man. I killed the man who was about to rape the girl. Before that I saw Donavan shoot the man whose horses we were stealing."

Bonnie covered her face with her hands. Then she looked up at him. "What will you do?"

"I don't know," he said. "I'm not sure if they know my name. If they do, then I got to leave town, maybe forever." He sat there, head down, thinking of his next move.

She walked to him and sat beside him. "You helped that girl. You're not bad. Everyone does bad things, but that doesn't make them a bad person. You feel regrets, so that means you know what you did was wrong. Stop your fretting. We'll think of something." She stopped and listened to a wagon outside and then said, "I haven't seen you in a while. Is this why?"

He shook his head. "A little. I've been working."

"You'll keep your secrets," she said.

"Not all of them. I just told you my biggest one. I hadn't killed a man before, you know. I never had to. I have fought men. But I've never killed one." Hans put his hands around her and pulled her close. He felt better now that she was close to him.

"How many men did you work with?"

"Two. All dead but me."

"You killed the man about to have his way with a girl. Is that right?" said Bonnie.

"Yes." He tried to look out the window, but the white curtain blew in front of it. The wind whistled outside.

"Then you did good. You saved her." She

took off his hat, was about to put it on her head, but smelled the hat and thought better of it. She hung the hat on one of the bedposts. "You can stay here a while, until this all goes away."

"When's your husband getting home?"

"I don't know, whenever you hear the front door open," she said.

"I don't see why you're with him." He shook his head.

"If you'd stay longer, maybe we'd know each other long enough to leave this town together. But you always leave and I don't see you for several weeks."

"I can't help that. I have things to do."

"And what exactly are these *things* you do? I bet you're married yourself."

"No," he said.

"Then what?"

"You don't need to worry yourself about my comings and goings. We aren't married, are we?"

"No, but it's about time we get married."

Hans smiled.

"See, you want to, too." Bonnie showed her white teeth. Her pale skin was shown in the moonlight coming from the window. Hans touched her hand and then the hand glided to her stomach and then up to her neck.

After a while Hans lay in Bonnie's bed

with her head on his chest. He touched her hair as she heard his heart thump in his chest. The voices outside died down so that it was only crickets chirping outside.

"I have to go soon," he said.

"Why?"

"I don't want to get caught in your bed and get shot. That's why."

"Then shoot him first."

"I'm surprised you said that," said Hansford.

Bonnie lifted her head and placed the back of it on the pillow. "I know someone who wanted a divorce and her husband didn't like it. She was beaten so badly she couldn't eat for a week."

"Would your husband do that?"

She did not answer.

"Would he?"

"He has a tendency to drink a lot, and when he drinks too much he gets angry."

"What happens then?"

She refused to answer. Instead she kissed him and used her fingers to comb his hair to the side. He put his arms around her waist. "I'm in love with an outlaw," she said.

"We're both hiding things from each other," he said.

She looked away. "Why would someone

who visits me every few weeks care about what happens to me?"

"Don't say that. I told you things I will never tell anyone else. I care enough to do that. I care enough to see you instead of other women."

"You could lie and see other women," she said.

"I could, but I wouldn't do that. I'm not that type."

"You are. You sleep with another man's wife."

"It was not planned. It turned out that way," he said.

"Just like that rustling business you mentioned."

He sighed. For a while the memory was hidden. Now it brought up his fear of getting caught. In his mind he did not think it was fear. It was something else, a fear to be told he had something to do with the death of a good man.

"I was just about to forget that."

"I'm sorry," she said. "I'll get your mind off it. I hear there are Apaches attacks north of here. They say there is a small group of them attacking people on the roads."

"Where is this?"

"Somewhere near Black River. I couldn't get much out of anyone. No one seemed to want to tell me what happened. Then later on I overheard someone in the store talk about it. There was a man who escaped an Apache attack somehow, but he had an arrow in his side. He died after making it here. He managed to pull the arrow out, but that ended up killing him because right after taking it out he bled inside. Mr. Stevenson at the store told me this. He said the town doctor told him everything."

"Terrible," said Hans. "I thought we were through with Apaches attacking us."

"I guess not. They're still around. Just because there are reservations it doesn't mean they're all in them," she said.

"It makes me cautious out there."

"Be careful if you go near there."

She got close to him again, and he put his arm about her. "I'll be all right. If the law finds out I'm in Silver City, I'll have to leave."

She brought her head up. Her eyes widened. "Will you take me with you? If the law comes, will you take me with you?"

"I don't know what'll happen, Bonnie."

"Hans, you and I can be good together. I won't slow you down. I bet you're wanted already. Well, I don't care. I'll come with you and we'll just ride. We'll ride and never look back."

He laughed. "You're talking crazy, Bon.

There's no price on my head. I just told you the man I killed was Donavan Nealey. And that was in the middle of nowhere. They might not even find him. They don't have my name. I'm the last one left."

She relaxed a little and put her head on his shoulder. "What if it happens? What'll you do?"

"What if what happens?" he said. He listened to the sounds outside.

She acted like his entire life would change and that he would have to be on the run again. That business back in Mexico could return. He didn't want that. When Juan Gonzalez and his men tried to kill Hansford, his boss and the others, he felt unready to die. He did not want to die for stealing horses. He was not sure what was worth dying for, but he knew it wasn't for a horse.

"What if they find out your name?"

"That won't happen."

"But what if it does?" she said.

"There's no reason thinking about what could happen. A million things can happen. You'll just keep worrying about which one of those things will happen. Just a waste of time. I'll tell you what will happen. They won't catch me. I'll be away for a while. I'll come back and—"

"And?" she said, hoping he would take her away.

"I don't know. I haven't thought that far ahead before. I've always done one thing at a time."

She got up and put on her nightdress. She then sat on the end of the bed with her arms folded. "You must not love me if you don't want to run away with me."

"Of course I love you, Bon," he said, sitting up.

"Then why won't we run away together?"

"Because I don't want you to get hurt," he said. "There are men after me. Who knows what they'll do? They might hang me. God knows what they do to rustlers. They hang them, and they don't waste time doing it."

"You don't have to look out for me. I can shoot a gun. I can ride a horse. I can cook. I can chop wood, plant a garden." She smiled a little, though she spoke in an almost sad tone. "We can live in a little house. I don't need much. This house is big, but I don't need it. I am happy with even a little."

He crawled on the bed until he sat beside her. He took her hand and held it in his hands. "The next time I come back we leave. Day or night. I have enough money to tide us over for a long while. We can live north of here, maybe Socorro or Los Lunas. We'll figure that out later. I'll find work there, something clean, and stay out of trouble." He stared at the floor, thinking. "We'll be together."

She hugged him. "What about my husband?"

"He won't mind. He'll find someone else real fast."

"He is violent. He might find us. He has the money to hire people to find us."

Hans could tell her mind raced. "We'd be too far. If he finds us, we go all the way to California."

"We can go there instead," she said.

"Maybe," he said. "A train runs through Rio Purco. It can take us far west. I don't know how far it goes, but it ought to take us out of the state at the least. That would be a start."

"When will you come back?" she asked.

"I don't know. I still don't know if the law will figure out my name. If they know my name, then I will have to give myself a new name. There's too many things to think about."

The two turned their heads and heard the front door open.

"Bonnie, I'm home! Tell me you have something to eat. I'm starving," yelled the man's voice downstairs.

"Oh, God, it's him," whispered Bonnie to Hansford.

"Bonnie," yelled the man named Enor. Enor was in his fifties, a heavyset man with a blonde beard that was beginning to gray, and was climbing the steps. The steps creaked loudly.

"Get on the roof through the window. I'll throw your clothes out for you. Quick. You don't have time," she said, her eyes widening, heart pumping fast. If they'd get caught, the entire plan would end—end in the death of Enor or Hans.

Hansford ran to the window. There was a small section of roof just outside the window that Hans had used to get to her bedroom. He stepped out to it and was naked from head to toe. He felt cold outside in the middle of night. He saw his shirt thrown out from the window. He put it on fast. Hans kept his body away from the window. Then he saw the pants and other garments and the gun belt and finally the hat.

The voices were calm inside the house. This calmed Hans. For a while he waited outside and tried to hear any shouts. When he realized it was fine he walked back to his horse.

CHAPTER 5
VULTURES

Jake McAlister stayed the night in a hotel in Lake Valley. When the sun climbed above the mountains he mounted his horse and left town in a quick pace. The white dog followed.

The rain would have covered all tracks by now, so Jake rode aimlessly west. If I were them, he thought, I would head for the buyer as soon as I could.

But there was no telling who the buyer was. The two nearby towns he knew of were Hillsborough and Silver City. Delilah, he remembered, mentioned the Black Range to the north. She had lied and said she was never told the name of the man that saved her.

With the facts Delilah provided, he decided to head to Silver City. If he did not

463

find any trace of the last man, he decided he would simply go back to Kansas.

The man is probably long gone by now, he thought. But I can at least find those horses in Silver City.

Jake wondered why Donavan Nealey and the nameless other man went to the Black Range. Those mountains were known to have rogue Apaches hiding in them. It was not wise to go there, especially with stolen horses. But as he thought about their plan it seemed to make sense. No one would think they'd head to the Black Range. There was maybe a village there he did not know of, but that was all.

The land changed the more he rode away from Lake Valley. Ponderosa trees, pinon and wildflowers came into sight. The dreariness left the land, but the summer heat remained.

Jake took off his hat and wiped the sweat from his forehead using his shirtsleeve. He could see green mountains covered in tall trees. Even the smell changed. The air smelled of pine.

Jake found a river and let the horse and dog drink from it. There were fish in the water swimming fast. He could see them in the clear water that splashed against large boulders that were like islands in the river.

The dog barked at the fish. It was then that

Jake realized he should probably give the dog a name. He sat near the riverbank and said, "Bud. I'll call you Bud." The white dog turned his head, but not in the man's direction. But looked around cautiously. Anything could hide in the dark shade of the green mountain trees, especially Apaches. Jake, too, looked about.

"Bell and Bud," said Jake. He named his horse Bell after the outlaw Tom Bell.

In another hour he saw black vultures circling far in the distance. He rode in a valley, yet he could see ahead the scavengers in the sky. Something big must have died, because there were more than ten vultures in the sky. At that distance the vultures were small black figures in the blue sky.

Jake decided to take a look at it. It was off the path, so he traveled around trees, brushing against them, and finally found the vultures were upon a hill overlooking the land. More vultures appeared to see the sign in the sky, as Jake could see them flying from a distance to join the others.

Jake was careful riding up to the top of the hill, and once he got to the top he could see a man, alone, standing above a dead body. Vultures were standing nearby, their big black wings spread wide, almost awkwardly, attempting to scare the man away.

The man near the body stood up quickly, as his back was turned to Jake, and said, "Who are you?"

For a moment Jake was unsure of the man. Jake looked at him. The man near the body wore nice boots. His pants were dirty near the knees from digging his knees into the dirt next to the body. He was bald and had a crooked nose.

Jake noticed a badge on the stranger's chest. "Jake, and you?"

"Reubin Conway. U.S. Marshal." There was a silence. The marshal stared down at the dog and then looked behind Jake to see if there were others. "You're far off the path."

"I wanted to see what happened here."

"Where were you heading?"

"I was on my way to find the man who had something to do with the death of my brother," said Jake.

"I'm sorry to hear that. What was his name?"

"Ron McAlister," said Jake.

Reubin smiled and took off his hat, now relaxed knowing he was no trouble at all. "Then we are hunting the same man. Ron was a friend of mine. We knew each other in the army."

"I might have heard him speak of you a while back," said Jake.

"He was a good man," said Reubin. "This body though—" He used his boot to touch the boot of Donavan Nealey. The eyes were pecked out already. The rest of the chest caused Jake to stand back, as the smell was strong. The wind did not help either; it only carried the smell to him.

"Who's that man?" Jake asked the marshal.

"I was just figuring that out." He used a piece of cloth to cover his nose. Then he searched the pockets and found a soggy cigar and coins and a flask of rum. The Dragoon pistol was left. He found the cartridge lodged inside the body, taking it out from the chest using a long stick nearby, and put it on the rocks. After pouring water on it he held up the cartridge and said, "Looks like a .44."

"Could be anything to me," said Jake.

"It's a guess." The cartridge was smashed, as it had hit a bone, broke it, and was lodge in the body. "We know it wasn't Apaches at least. At least not the ones with bows. I guess I'm showing my age. I've lived in Kansas City for years now." He pointed his thumb back. "But we do know horses are around here."

"How do you know?"

"Their droppings are over there," said Reubin, pointing down the hill. He grabbed the revolver and the gun belt from the body and put the coins in his pocket. He eyed the boots, scratching his beard, contemplating taking them and maybe selling them, but he left them. Old habits from the old days. It was not worth it. The boots were not worth that much. "There were maybe ten or so horses, maybe more. The only problem is we don't have clear tracks. The rain didn't hit too hard in this area, but it hit hard enough to wash most of the tracks. Maybe we can find a trail, maybe not."

Reubin stood up. The sun had darkened his face and skin for over sixty years. He squinted down the hill and pointed southwest. "Silver City is that way. Maybe they went there."

Jake nodded and said nothing.

The marshal put his hat back on. "What about you? You're really after these rustlers?"

"I am," said Jake. "I believe only one of them is left."

"How is that so?"

Jake told him what Elisha and Delilah said to him back in Lake Valley. U.S. Marshal Conway listened and frowned at different parts. When Jake finished the marshal said, "Then this man here is probably Donavan Nealey. And we have one out there, alone. I guess he liked money, because he didn't want this man to have half." The marshal searched the area again. Farther away he found the ropes used to tie up Delilah, which made him certain that it was Donavan on the ground.

"I think he wanted to protect that girl I told you about," said Jake, watching Conway search the area.

"You really believe that? He could have had a go at her himself. These men don't have any morals. No respect even for each other. There's a string of blood leading across the entire county because of them. We'll probably see even more blood."

"We? I would think you'd have men with you."

"I will have. I am meeting them in Lake Valley, but it seems my path has diverged. I read a telegram from Jim Courtright. He told me a little. I figured they'd head out this way. If I understand enough, I may know where those horses will be. They're either in Silvery City or in no place I can find them." He mounted his horse. An 1876 Winchester Rifle was in the scabbard, and he had a Remington Revolver near his waist as well. He was quite large, but he had swung onto his horse with ease and surprised Jake at his quickness.

"Do you think you can find them so quickly?" said Jake

"No, I can only follow the tracks, if there are any. I can't promise anything. Some just get away, especially rustlers. I don't see much in the way of tracks. I can only tell you I'll try. Ron was a friend back when I lived around these parts during my army days. He saved my life more than once when we were young. That was when Apaches seemed to poke up from behind every boulder you saw. Well, we've found the bastard who killed him at least." He pointed to the dead body of Donavan Nealey. He spat on the body. The vultures got close to the body now that the marshal was clear of it. "Now we just need to find the last one. What did you say he looked like?"

"The girl didn't tell me much. Only that he was young," said Jake.

Reubin grumbled something to himself. "Well, let's go on now, Jake. Those horses may be close."

"What about the body?"

"Leave it for the buzzards," said the marshal. He spat once more.

Jake mounted and followed him down the hill. The dog ran ahead of them. "What's that dog of yours doing?"

"Bud?"

"Whatever his name is," said the marshal.

"He seems to be finding the tracks all right. Look at him."

Up ahead they saw the dog sniffing the ground, looking up and finding here and there a scent, a trail. The men went faster and caught up, but as soon as they did so Bud was already ahead, barking back at them as if to tell them to hurry up.

"He's found a trail," yelled the marshal. "Your dog here has found a trail." He sounded as excited as the dog. "We'll find the horses in no time."

Jake and the U.S. marshal rode for a long time. Jake could not tell how long it had been, but as they followed the barking dog and tracks they came upon a ranch in a wide plain. The ranch was alone. There were horses in a corral and stables and a house. "Call your dog back. I don't want him to get too far ahead of us."

Jake said, "Bud. Come on back."

The dog's ears perked up by the sound of Jake's loud voice coming from behind. He had not realized he had a name, but he turned at the sound of Jake's calling. Bud saw the white horse remained behind, so the dog walked back and rested for a while on the ground.

The marshal saw the tracks led to a ranch about a half mile ahead. "If these are Ron's horses, they will be branded. Regardless, we saw the tracks. They lead here."

"You think they'll fight?" asked Jake.

"If they're dumber than dirt. You'd got to be pretty stupid to try to kill a U.S. marshal," he said, looking around. "This ranch seems far out. I don't see the road anymore. This would be a fine place to get killed."

"What about your men in Lake Valley?"

"What about them?"

"We can wait for them," mentioned Jake.

Conway scratched his beard, as he would usually do when thinking. He sighed, almost in an angry manner, and grabbed his rifle from the scabbard and put it across the pommel. Jake glanced at his own rifle, the Winchester, but left it in the scabbard.

The sun was falling, and soon it would be below the mountains. The decision had to be made. "Let's go on," said the marshal, riding ahead.

Jake followed and caught up with him. When Jake was beside him the marshal said, "I know you used to rob trains."

Jake said nothing. He wasn't sure what to say to that. After some time he said, "That was a long time ago. I've been a cowboy ever since I got out of jail."

The marshal nodded. "I know."

"How?" said Jake. The decision to leave Lake Valley when he was younger was immediate. He never told anyone.

"Your brother told me to keep an eye on you, see where you went. Well, I did, but you were a hard man to find. I saw you in Dodge City about three years ago."

Jake said, "I didn't think he would do that."

"Well, he did," said the marshal. He looked over at Jake, who was frowning and staring in the distance in confusion. "Can you shoot all right?"

"Yes. Why?"

"They might get angry we're gonna take those horses back," said the marshal, half smiling. He had almost a wild look in his eyes, as if he did not care whether he died. But soon the look disappeared and he was left to squint at the house coming into view.

The two men could see a person walk out from a small house. At first sight, the man from the house, who was carrying a pale of water, was carefree and whistling. But after spotting Conway and Jake he dropped the pale of water and went back inside. Jake grabbed his rifle. He thought he would be shaky after all the years of never pointing a gun at a man, but his hands were steady and dry. His heart was calm. He was not sure if that indicated he had accepted death and if he had any regard for his own life.

The bucket of water was overturned. The marshal dismounted and did not knock on the door. Instead he carried his rifle and went to the back of the house. He tried to look inside a window, but he could not find anyone.

There were footsteps heard inside. Conway then spotted a man walking in a hallway, picking up a revolver from inside a drawer.

"This is U.S. Marshal Reubin Conway. Open up," he yelled.

The man inside loaded his revolver with cartridges, and as he turned he saw the marshal point the rifle at him. "Put it down," said Conway.

But the man grabbed the box of cartridges and ran out of the room.

"I'll go to the other side," said Jake. He crouched below the windows, walked to the front door and went to the other side of the house. As he did so he heard horses whinnying.

The marshal yelled again, saying he was a U.S. marshal. He put his back against the house and saw in the rear, near the stables, two men hiding behind the horses with rifles. "Two in the back," yelled Conway to Jake. As he yelled out the two men near the stables shot their rifles and hit the house. Conway was at an odd position because he was right handed and he was on the left side corner of the house. His entire body would be visible when he would shoot. He peaked over the corner of the house and again he was shot at. Conway cursed them Then he heard shots coming from Jake, who had used the entire minute to go for better cover behind the trees. Jake shot twice and hit one of the two men. The man who got shot groaned on the ground, holding his stomach in pain, cursing and yelling out in pain.

The front door of the house banged shut. Conway turned and saw another man, the one who was loading his gun inside, aim at the marshal. But Conway was faster and shot him first. The man fell to the ground and was still. Conway turned his attention back to the stables and listened for any shots.

The loud groaning from one of the men at the stables died down. It was silent again.

Conway peaked over the corner of the house and saw Jake walking forward and shooting. The last man mounted a horse and rode away.

Conway cursed and ran back to his horse. Jake did the same but was a little faster. The last man had a good distance between the two. "Is that all of them?" Conway yelled while riding behind Jake.

"I think so. That man I shot looked dead. Are you shot?"

"No. You?"

"No."

Conway focused on the man ahead, weaving into and out of openings around the trees, brushing his shoulders against the pines. "We better split up. I'll head left. You go right. We want him alive."

Just as he spoke the last man turned and shot his revolver at them.

Reubin Conway cursed again. Jake and Conway split up.

Jake was not sure how to keep the last man alive. He rode faster and faster and saw the man's shirt whenever there was an opening in the trees. He shot but missed. The dog, Bud, was running far behind, not as fast as the horses.

Jake heard another shot and heard a yell behind him. He slowed his horse and went back to the sound.

"I got him," called the marshal.

Jake went to the sound of his deep voice. He found the last man on the ground with his arm bleeding. The man held his arm and squeezed his eyes shut in pain.

Conway dismounted and took the man's guns away. "I was thinking, 'There's no way they'd start shooting.' The stupidity of criminals amazes me." He crouched near the wounded man. "Why'd you start shooting?"

The last man refused to say anything. He kept groaning in pain.

"What's your name?"

"Hal," said the last man. He turned to Jake and then looked around, as if for an escape.

"Well, Hal, tell me what you know and I'll get a doctor for that arm." He pointed to the bleeding arm that had stained the shirt.

Hal breathed heavily and put his head back against the dirt. Conway went back to his horse as Jake kept his rifle pointed at the outlaw. Conway got the rope he would use to bind Hal's hands and ankles.

"What are you doing?" said Hal.

"You're not gonna talk, so I have to bring you to jail," said Conway.

"No, no. I'll be hanged. You can't do that. I'll tell you everything if you let me go. I won't last long with this arm. Just look at it."

Conway saw the arm. "All right," he lied. "It's a deal. What's the MF brand stand for?"

Hal lowered his eyes. "I forgot his name. A man came by and sold us those horses."

"Us?"

"Henry owns this place," said Hal. "I'm his cousin."

"What about the man who sold you the horses? What did he look like? Describe him."

The wounded man let go of the hand holding onto his bloodied arm and took a look at the damage. "Young, short hair, he had a light stubble, brown pants." Hal closed his eyes. "Not sure what else to say."

The marshal slapped the man on the face, but Hal's eyes barely opened. He had lost a lot of blood. Conway opened up the shirt and noticed he had been shot in the gut as well. He tore off some of the shirt and used it as a tourniquet to reduce the bleeding. Then he poured water over the man's face.

Hal opened his eyes so that only a slit of white showed. The marshal got close to hear the man's whispering voice.

"What else do you know?" said Conway.

"Henry kept saying—"

"What? Tell me his name."

"He talked about the man's gun. Henry always knew his guns. It was a 1875 Remington Revolver. And—" But there was nothing else he could say. The marshal stood up and looked around to get an idea of where to go.

Hal's eyes closed. His hurt arm stopped fidgeting and was still. A fly buzzed around the man's face. He was dead.

Bud the dog finally caught up with them. He barked at the man on the ground and, realizing he was dead, sat still on the ground, panting after the long run.

"We know a little about him," said Jake.

The marshal nodded. "Not enough. He could be anyone and anywhere. But at least we found the horses. Let's go to Silver City. I'll send word to Elisha, and she'll send her workers to come get these horses."

Jake looked up and saw vultures already flying in circles overhead.

"We'll have to clean up all this mess," said the marshal. "The town isn't far. Maybe we'll find more about him there. Someone must have seen him." He sighed at the sight of the dead man on the ground. "I'll let the law know in Silver City. Five dead men already, the Nealey's and these three. If this last man knew what he was doing, then he's as dangerous as the Nealey's and the men they trusted—like these men that almost killed us." He looked at Jake. "Thanks for the help. I might have been killed if it weren't for you."

Jake helped Conway put the dead man on the horse. They went back to the little house to find the other bodies just as the sun fell below the mountains.

CHAPTER 6
THE SEARCH

HANSFORD VORRIS SLEPT IN THE COUNTRY at night. It was safer that way. From where his bedroll was he could see Silver City and Bonnie's house.

In the morning he took out his field glasses and tried to see anything unusual in town. As he did so he saw a posse of lawmen ride out from Silver City. They traveled east and their horses picked up a cloud of dirt doing so. He lowered the field glasses, ate with his dog and went down to town to get his horse from the livery.

He hitched his horse in front of a store and went inside to buy a new blanket. If he had to leave with Bonnie, she would need something to keep her warm at night. He wondered about a horse for her, but that was too much. They could ride together if it came to that.

Hans walked the main street and overhead a conversation between two women. The women wore long dresses and boots. One spoke about the lawmen leaving town.

"Who knows what? After Dan Tucker left us, it's been awfully quiet. It cleaned the town up."

"For now," said the other woman. "You just wait. It won't last."

"Why say that? Do you hear any shots?"

The woman, who was middle-aged with brunette hair, said, "Well, no. But it doesn't mean it's safe in the area outside town."

"If we're safe in town, that's good enough for me," the other said. "Apache attacks is what I used to care about. That and outlaws shooting up the town. Both are gone."

"I suppose so, but that posse we just saw isn't a good sign," said the woman.

"No," said the other. "No, it's awfully strange. I hope it's not about the Apaches up near the Black Range."

The brunette shook her head. "I almost forgot about that."

"Hard to do that. I thought you'd remember that and keep talking about it for days, maybe weeks."

"It's better than what you talk about: what drunken man you shooed away or some other such nonsense," she said.

"If you don't want to hear it, tell me. I'll be happy to sit in silence."

"We both know you can't do that."

Hans went across the street and loitered for hours. There was a feeling in him he had not felt before. This crept up on him. I have to leave soon, he thought.

But he stayed still and waited to see if the lawmen would return soon. He had always left suddenly and without much of an aim. Work kept him moving from place to place, working at a saloon here, gambling there and rustling down near the Rio Grande River in Texas. The only reason he stayed in Silver City was for his woman, Bonnie, who he frequently thought about. She was the only woman he felt understood him. It was more than that. They understood each other, even without words, like how someone can feel the others pain.

This feeling to escape, to run away with her, arose as swiftly as the horses that left Silver City early in the morning.

Later that night Hans was in the saloon. If there were conversations about the law trying to catch a rustler from Lake Valley, he would have to leave with Bonnie and never turn back.

If it was safe, he thought of staying even longer. The commitment to stay with a woman was new and almost frightening. It was a lot of responsibility to him.

He met the men he played poker with before, Samuel and Fred. Hans played a game with them, yet he seemed preoccupied. He constantly tried to overhear conversations. He glanced outside the windows to see if the lawmen had returned. They had been gone all day, and soon the sun would disappear.

"You haven't said much of a word," said Fred to Hans. "Something wrong?"

"No, I was just thinking."

Fred and Samuel exchanged glances.

"A man's business is his own," said Samuel. "But you can trust us, if you want." Smoke came out from Samuel's lips. The smoke floated in the air, and the loud saloon, busied with miners and ranchers and travelers, erupted with laughter and talking. "You've been troubled. I can tell. Is it about a woman?"

"You can say that," he said.

"I told you it was," Fred said to Samuel. "You told me it wasn't. See? It's always a woman."

"A woman," said Samuel, bringing his bearded chin up in reflection, "really complicates a man's life. First you don't want any part with a woman. You want her to come and go, maybe have a short talk with her. Some company for a bit. Then the next thing you know you're helping her pick out what curtains you both want for your new home."

"I might be in the middle of that road," said Hans. "I might have to have a new life."

"A new one?" said Fred in a cheerful voice. "What's wrong with the old one?"

"The old one was dangerous. I risked my life too many times than I can count. It's too hard a life to live forever. Eventually you have to settle down, but I never thought when that time would come."

Samuel drank some whiskey and belched. "Sure, there's a time for everything. Sounds like you've been thinking a lot."

"I have. I've been alone to think about it."

"Don't think too much," said Samuel. "Sometimes thinking can be a bad thing. Thinking can be a sickness at times. You start thinking so much and start thinking about your past, your future and all these things when you really should be living. Thinking isn't living." He slapped the table. Men from other tables looked on, smiled and went back to their games and drinks. "Thinking is foolish. I say live, not think. If you love this woman, then love her. No thinking is involved with love. It's with the heart, isn't it? You love with the heart, not your mind. Isn't that true?"

"Yes, I guess so," said Hans. He widened his eyes, as this was not what he expected. His mind was off the men that were perhaps following him. For now he was drinking and listening. Running like a wanted man could wait.

"Well, then. This woman you love—" Samuel paused. "What was I saying?" he said to Fred.

Hans could tell Samuel was very drunk. His words were slurred and his head moved unnaturally whenever he spoke, as if the head felt heavy. He was sounding happy though, and that was fine by Hans.

"About women and thinking," said Fred.

"You love this woman, without thinking. So you go and love her and stay with her. If you love her, then make sure she loves you too; otherwise, you're in trouble. Does she love you?" he asked Hans.

"She said she did," he said. "The only problem is she's married."

Samuel was quiet. Suddenly he slapped the table with the palm of one of his hands again and laughed. "That complicates it, does it? No wonder you're looking out the window so often. A man is out to kill you."

"Should we let him look out the window?" asked Fred. "When the guns are pulled, I want to be out of town or at least on the floor. That would be kind of you, Hans, if you let us know if you spot him."

"I haven't seen him lately," said Hans.

"Good," said Samuel. "This woman of yours. She's as strange as you. She loves you but stays with this man."

"She says she'll leave him," he said. "But that he might hurt her. He is a wealthy man. He might try to hunt me after we leave together. He has the money to have men find me."

Samuel scratched his beard and thought about it. "This man could kill you, yet he does not love this woman he married, since you say he might hurt her."

Fred drank his whiskey and put the glass down on the table. It would have made a loud sound as he put down the glass, yet the voices in the room drowned out most sounds. "I got it. You must confront him." Fred sounded almost as drunk as Samuel.

Hans glanced out the windows and saw the lawmen had returned. He saw them through the windows. A wagon pulled by two horses went slowly down the road. The wagon creaked loudly and was covered in a large blanket. Peeking out of the end of the blanket were boots.

Samuel ignored Fred's statement and looked outside with Hans. "Look at that."

The saloon got quieter, but there were still a few voices. The people inside the saloon looked outside at the wagon carrying the bodies. About five lawmen rode horses and appeared alert despite their tired faces. People went to the windows to see what the silence was about.

"That's a sight," said Fred. "Three dead. I wonder what happened."

"Who knows," said Samuel. "Look how many men they had to get. Maybe the law killed the three. Or maybe it was Apaches."

After the wagon went by the noise inside the saloon returned.

"What do you think happened?" Hans asked.

Samuel and Fred could not say. No one knew. The saloon grew louder once again, and everyone went back to drinking. Smoke drifted in the air and made it hard to breathe.

If I am found, I will die, thought Hans. I will be hanged the day they find me.

He kept glancing outside. In a few minutes the town marshal and a deputy went inside the saloon. Hans pushed his hat down to hide his face. But that was not necessary. It was dark inside the saloon, as the sun hid behind the clouds and would fall below the mountains soon. There were long shadows of the buildings that stretched across the road, just as the mountain shadows blanketed the land.

Hans got up and tried to get closer to the lawmen. He could hear them asking questions. Then he saw the town marshal look in his direction. Hans looked away and tried to act calm, but inside his heart pounded hard and fast and he was sweating in the dark and crowded saloon. He felt the room was too thick with smoke. He coughed and turned to the back door of the saloon. The deputy stood near the front door of the saloon, watching the men leaving, especially any that carried a revolver on him.

Then Hans heard a description that fit him, which was spoken by the town marshal.

It was so crowded he could leave without notice. Hans made his way through the crowd slowly and walked out the back door. He then walked quickly to his horse down the street. He rode to Bonnie's house and looked to see if her husband's horse was there. It was not.

He banged on the front door. It felt like he waited there for a long time. He kept looking back from where he came.

Bonnie pushed aside a curtain to see Hans. She opened the door and smiled. As he walked inside, she saw his worried face. Her smile faded. "What's wrong?" she said.

"Remember I said we might have to leave for Los Lunas?"

"Is it time?"

"Get your things. We can't take everything. We can buy you new clothes and whatever else."

Hansford Vorris went to the front and locked the door. He looked out of the windows, pushed aside the curtains and saw men exit the saloon. He then saw two men on horses ride into town, and one of them had a badge on his shirt. But Hans could not tell what it meant. From that distance he could not read it. The man was large, bald under his hat, and appeared to have the look of some importance. As soon as he saw him he got his mind away from it.

The other man, clean shaven and forties in age, accompanied him. For a moment Hans felt he recognized the man.

"There's more of them," he said.

Hans turned and noticed Bonnie was gone. He went upstairs and saw her packing things into a suitcase.

"We can't take everything," he reminded her.

"I know, Hans."

He could tell she was frightened. She packed quickly and threw some things on the bed that were not important. Certain things she looked at momentarily to see if the item was important.

"It'll be all right," he said. "We'll be gone within five minutes. They won't know where we went."

"Will they find us?"

"They won't know. They might think you took a train and went to California. For me, they'll think I left town and went to another state or country. Los Lunas is just the beginning."

"Maybe it's nice there," said Bonnie. "Maybe we can get married."

She finished packing. He went over and touched her shoulders and kissed her. She smelled nice to him, even though that was just her natural smell.

"You don't have to go," he said.

"You love me, don't you?" she asked.

"You know I do," he said, looking down at her near his chest. "That's why I'm asking you to leave with me."

There was a loud bang at the front door.

Hans turned to her. "I thought your husband was gone."

"I thought so too. Maybe it's my friend."

"Bonnie, let me in! Why the hell did you lock the door? Have you gone crazy?" said her husband, Enor Philips, from outside the house. He banged on the door again.

"It's him," she said. "We can go out back. I'll tell him—"

"Don't unlock the door. We don't have time," said Hans. "Let him wait."

"He probably saw your horse," she said.

"My horse is in the back."

She went downstairs and said, "Just a minute."

Then Hans grabbed Bonnie's luggage, went downstairs, opened the back door and saw Enor a few feet away.

"I knew something wasn't right," said Enor. His mouth was turned down in disgust. He breathed heavily and saw his wife behind Hans.

Bonnie stood behind Hans and said, "I'm leaving, Enor. I'm unhappy."

"I don't care. You're married to me. It's a contract. If you want to leave, you will have to find a lawyer. And we both know you don't have the money. You're mine. I own you."

"A piece of paper means nothing," said Hans. "Move out of my way."

Enor stood taller than Hans, even though Hans was taller than most men, and he was double Hansford's weight. Enor studied Hansford's width and height, looking him up and down to measure his strength. "You're bold. No one speaks to me like that."

"It's about time they do," said Hans. "Find another slave. Bonnie is with me now."

Enor looked over Hans to see Bonnie. Enor's lips were turned down still. His nostrils flared as he took in deep breaths. "Have you gone mad, woman? Is this true?"

"I love him," she said. "And I don't love you."

"I give you this house, dresses, jewelry, everything you want, and this is how you repay me?" said Enor.

She was quiet. Hans kept his eyes on the man. Time was being wasted. The law could find him any minute, and then all this would be for nothing. Hans put the bag down. Then Enor pushed Hans against the doorframe.

Hans swung at Enor and hit him on the chin, but that did not appear to do much. Enor only blinked after being hit.

Hans felt a pain in his hand and stood back, circling the big man, away from the house.Hans hit with his left and then with the right.

Enor stumbled back but did not fall down. He yelled and almost jumped forward in a fury. He picked up Hans with his giant hands and pinned him against the wall of the house. There was a noise that was similar to the sound of cracking wood. Hans kicked him in the knee, and the big man went down and cursed.

Bonnie stepped around and looked to see if lawmen were about. She could see down the road that the town marshal and his deputies were going door to door in search of Hans. They were coming down the road. When she turned back Hans was on the ground, his nose bloodied and his cheek cut. Enor had a small knife in his hand. Hans touched his stomach and saw his shirt cut and the stomach slashed. Hans cursed and felt the blood on his cheek using his hand. Then he looked down at the hand.

"Get up," said Enor. "Get up and fight."

"You want to kill me?" said Hans. He breathed heavily and tasted metal in his mouth. He could feel the stomach bleeding; he hoped it was just the skin that was cut and not the muscle. He stood up and held the wall of the house. Now his heart thumped as if he were running. The fear of death was unimportant to

Hans. It was the fear of leaving Bonnie with Enor that mattered to him.

"The marshal," said Bonnie, pointing to the road.

Hans faced her.

"A wanted man?" said Enor. His eyebrows rose.

Enor slashed Hans again on the shoulder and cut him worse than before, as Hans was turned to Bonnie. He fell back again, turning to crawl back in the dirt. They'd hear the gunshot, so he went for his knife and took it out from his boot. As Enor came back again Hans displayed the knife and before Enor could realize what was happening the knife had pierced Enor's belly. The blade went through until only the hilt showed. Enor fell over and said, "Help! Someone. I'm dying."

Hans covered his mouth and slit his throat. As Hans looked up he saw Bonnie cover her mouth. "I had to," he said. "You saw him take out the knife." Hans looked over the corner of the house and saw a deputy coming for the house. It did not look like he had heard the yells from Enor. The deputy walked slowly.

Hans picked up Bonnie's luggage and secured it to his horse. "We don't have time. We have to leave now."

Bonnie nodded absentmindedly and was in

shock at seeing the body. She took Hansford's hand and mounted the horse. "Is he gone?"

"Yes, he's dead. Did you see what he did to me?" said Hans.

"Yes. I didn't expect that. Are you all right?"

"I'm all right."

They went through the forest behind the house and traveled using the moonlight as their guide. In a few minutes Hans turned back to see if he was followed. There was no one. He heard sounds of wolves in the mountains, but they were faint howls and not a concern. Wolves were usually skittish and rarely seen.

As Bonnie put her hands around Hans she felt the cuts and pushed herself back. The palms of her hands were stained. "Oh, God. How bad is it?"

"It's not bad," he said. "I'm fine."

"No, you aren't. You're hurt."

"I'm fine. It hurt at first. The cuts aren't that bad."

"Stop," she said. "Let me see them."

He did not slow down. "We have to keep moving."

"Stop right now," she said.

He slowed the horse near a river. He dismounted and held out his hand to help her down.

She then took off his shirt with his help and made him turn so the moonlight showed the wound better. Clouds every now and then obscured their sight, so she waited and saw the cuts. "I have something," he said, and went to his satchel on the horse.

He began to wrap the wound, but Bonnie stopped him and said, "Go in the water," she said. "Let me put water on it."

"Why?"

"To clean it," she said. "We have nothing better. No doctor in the forests, is there?"

After he splashed water on the wounds near his shoulder and stomach, he closed his eyes in pain. She dressed the wounds and put his shirt back on. And after doing so he touched her hands and said, "I love you, you know."

"I know," she said.

"Those men in town...the marshal and his deputies were looking for me."

"I know."

"How?"

"You said they might be after you, and when I saw you tell me you had to go, I knew you figured out they were on your trail," she said.

"I don't think they know my name."

"What do they know?"

"My Colt, my appearance, my age. They're

questioning people in Silver City now. I gave two men my name." He let go of her hands and looked down at his boots. "Those men might give me away."

She sat on the ground with him. "That doesn't mean they know where we're going. Did you tell anyone where we were going to go? Did you tell them about Los Lunas?"

"No one," he said. "Did you?"

"No."

"We'll be safe there. Maybe for a while. They might send word to the entire state," he said. He remembered what he saw earlier that day and was cautious about telling her about it. "I saw three bodies in a wagon today. The marshal and his men were coming from the east. Those bodies must have had something to do with me, because right after that I saw a U.S. marshal ride into town. I saw him speak to the town marshal. I overheard who those three men were. This is worse than I thought. I don't even know how they died. I didn't get to know about that part. Maybe Donavan Nealey gave one of those men my name."

Bonnie put her hand on his shoulder that was not hurt. "Don't worry. That might be something else. Besides, we'll be in Los Lunas, far away from here."

"You're right," he said. He took a deep

breath and watched the path from where they came. "There's nothing to do but keep riding. This is off the road. We can head east; that's where the road is. From there we head north. We better stay here tonight."

She looked around. The dark trees in the night and the shadows across the land unnerved her, as if some beast might jump out of the shadows and attack them. "Here?"

"Yes," he said. "This is a fine place. We can see pretty far along the river. We'd be able to see if a rider is coming."

She stayed put as Hans got out bedrolls. He put down a bedroll for her and went to look around.

"Where are you going?" she said.

"I want to look around. Yell if you see anything strange," he said. He saw her eyes looking all about. He could tell she was nervous and scared. He grabbed a revolver and put it under a bedroll. "You see this? Cock it back to shoot. Only aim a gun at someone you want to kill. All right?"

"Right."

"I'll be back in five minutes. I want to survey the area. They shouldn't have followed our tracks. As far as we know, they will knock on Enor's front door, wait and then go to another house. They might not find the body for another day or two. We have time. By then we'll be long gone."

Hans walked away and carried his rifle and field glasses with him. He went up a large hill and used his field glasses to see any movement. There was nothing but dark mountains and plains. It was difficult to see anything at night, so he could not tell if there were others in the area. He went back down the hill and walked along the river. There were fish in it, but they were small and looked motionless. When he went back to Bonnie he made sure to come from the river so she would not get fidgety and pull the Colt on him.

She breathed in deeply when he returned. "Couldn't see anything unusual," he said.

Hans got out his bedroll and lay down on it. He then closed his eyes. Bonnie was surprised he could sleep so quickly and be so relaxed out in the wilderness. She felt a bear or wolf might come upon them. But his relaxed nature comforted her and gradually she left her bedroll to lay with him. He opened his eyes to see what was the matter. After he found her near him he held her close as they slept in the mountains.

CHAPTER 7
PATH DIVERGED

Jake McAlister, U.S. Marshal Reubin Conway and the local lawmen banged on the doors in search of the rustler. The trail led to Silver City, yet after a few hours there was no sign of him. And no civilian had seen the man except two men who said he was planning to leave the town soon. Jake assumed the man already did. The two men said the rustler didn't give them his name.

The U.S. marshal stood there beside the street in the early morning as a stagecoach went by. "Our trail ends here," he said to Jake.

"What do you think happened?"

"He took the money and rode far from here," he said. "Smart move, if you ask me."

"And the horses?" asked Jake.

500

"Elisha sent some of the workers to get them. They're on their way back to her."

"That's good."

"More than good. Most people don't get their horses back. And if they do it's through killing the rustlers. Maybe some of their own would get killed as well. If I hadn't followed the trail—" He looked at Jake. "If *we* hadn't followed the trail, they'd be long gone and I would have been killed by those men you helped me kill." He patted Jake on the shoulder. "But now I'm not sure what else to do except keep searching the town and asking folks if they saw anything. If they saw him leave town in a certain direction, we could get something to help us out. Otherwise, we'll be here for a bit."

"That doesn't mean you're giving up, right?" asked Jake.

"I don't give up," he said, looking at him. "The trail ends or they disappear, but I still keep my eye out for them. If they're crafty, they could leave the state and never be heard from again. But outlaws like attention; they don't stay quiet for long."

Jake nodded. "I'll keep looking around."

There was a scream coming from the east. It sounded like a woman's scream. Conway and Jake were not far from the noise, so they ran over to where the scream came from and saw a woman walking, covering her face and nose.

"What's that smell?" said Conway.

"Are you all right, ma'am?" Jake said to the woman, who was staring straight at the ground in fear, almost in shock. "Ma'am?"

She said, "There's a man behind that house. He's dead."

"Where?"

Conway already followed the smell and found the body. "Over here, Jake."

"Do you know the man?" Jake asked her.

She kept looking around.

"Did you know him? What are you doing over here?"

"I went to see my friend, Bonnie," said the woman. She was still frightened. Gradually she looked up and smiled a little, but Jake could not tell why she was partially smiling. "I guess she made it out."

"Made it out?"

"She wanted to leave town," said the woman named Evereth.

"Why?"

"She didn't like it here." Evereth looked back at Conway examining the body. "And she didn't like her husband."

"Will you be all right?" he said.

"Yes," she said. "I just need to sit down a while." She sat down on the front porch.

Town Marshal Hilmer Debolt walked over and asked Jake what the scream was about. Jake told him, and the two walked behind the two-story house and found the body and Reubin Conway kneeling beside the body with a piece of cloth covering his mouth.

"Who is this man?" Conway asked the town marshal.

"Enor Philips," said Debolt. "He's a local businessman."

"Was that his wife on the porch?"

"No. That's Evereth."

"What was she doing all the way back here, behind the house?"

"I don't know," he said. "I'll go ask her." The town marshal went away after seeing what happened to Enor.

Jake got closer to the body and said, "Stab wounds?"

"It looks like it," said Conway. "Whoever did this was in a hurry."

"Why do you think that?"

"He's got money in his pockets," he said. "So this isn't a thief. We know that at least. This man's got plenty of money in his pockets. No, the person who killed this man wanted to get away fast."

"Do you think it was our rustler?"

Conway shook his head. "I don't know. There's no connection. What does this Enor have to do with a rustler? They're on the opposite sides of the street, so to speak."

Reubin Conway then went to the front door, as he heard a noise near there, and saw Hilmer Debolt knock on the front door. There was no answer, so Debolt broke the window, unlocked it and went inside. They searched the house.

Jake noticed clothes at the top of the stairs, dangling from one step. He went upstairs.

"Keep that Colt ready," Conway said to him. "The killer could be here. I doubt it, but you never know. I've contradicted myself plenty of times before. Best be prepared."

Jake went to the top of the stairs and picked up the piece of clothing. It was a strange piece, but he soon realized it was a woman's clothing. Then he saw more clothes in a bedroom. In the room the clothes were scattered across the bed and floor. He went to an opened window and saw the curtain blow in the wind. He looked outside and tried to see if they had left recently, but near the body there were no horse tracks. Maybe they took a stagecoach and then a train, he thought.

He sat on the bed and then heard the loud

boots against the stairs and the floor as Conway entered the room. "Well, that explains it. She was ready to leave."

"Evereth said she wanted to leave town."

"Maybe her husband got in her way," said Conway.

"Maybe."

"You don't think it?"

"She'd have to be pretty strong to kill a man like Enor," said Jake. "There were bruises, too. Those bruises come from someone who knows how to fight hard and well."

"I saw them. That's right. My idea is she had some help."

"Could be the rustler."

"I think it might," said Conway. "But we saw no tracks. They might have taken the road going west." He took off his hat and scratched his bald head. "This woman and the rustler...it could happen. I just think we need more information. We don't even have his name. This woman, Evereth, doesn't even know his name. But she said Enor's wife, Bonnie, mentioned a man she would see from time to time. This man fits the rustler's description."

"Do you think he stole her?"

"It's possible," said the marshal.

Conway glanced out the window and then went outside with Jake. They searched for tracks, but there were none. That was strange to both of them. But it was not too strange. The house was on a main road that was traveled by the thousands. Their horse tracks would mingle with all the others.

"I'll keep asking around," said Conway.

Jake watched the local lawmen carry the body of Enor away and put it on the wagon. Then the wagon went to the cemetery while one of the wooden wagon wheels squeaked every few seconds.

There were tall trees behind the house, and the trees were so close together Jake's shoulders brushed against them. He touched one pine branch and felt its needles, and then he looked down. There was a horse track. He looked back and found the other tracks had been hidden, covered so that no one would come that way. "He's good," Jake said to his dog, Bud, who followed him the entire way.

Bud sat and stared at Jake.

"We better go," he said to Bud. "They're out there."

Jake got his horse and followed the trail, and as he made it a mile out he looked back. He wanted to go it alone. It was only one man and maybe a woman. And by the time he made it back to Silver City this rustler and his woman might be out of the country. He was so focused on the trail he forgot to go back and bring Reubin Conway with him.

"Bud," said Jake. The man got down and pointed at the tracks and took out one of the woman's clothes he had put in his pocket. "Smell this? Find her. Find the woman." He put the clothing next to Bud's nose.

The dog smelled the clothes and started running down a hill. Jake mounted his horse and tried to catch up to the dog.

Bud kept running, sniffing the air, stopping to pick up the scent again and continuing once more. This process took hours, and even though there was a slower movement from Bud he still had energy. They went through mountains covered in aspen, mesquite and various oaks.

The dog stopped at a river and drank from it. Jake let his horse drink as well. And then he got down and drank himself. There were small fish in the river, and they swam away once Jake put his hand in the cold water. He looked down the river and then saw Bud sniff something and bark at the man to get him to come over.

"What is it?" said Jake.

He looked down and saw nothing.

"What?"

Jake couldn't find what Bud was barking about. He crouched and tried to see. But then he spotted the remnants of a fire. It was covered well. Only the dog could find it, as the charred wood was buried under dirt. Bud dug his paws in the shallow soil and showed Jake what he smelled beneath the soil. Jake picked out the wood that was blackened by the fire.

"That's them, huh?"

The dog wagged its tail.

Jake knew it was the woman, the rustler or both. He did not want to assume too much. Either way, they were in mountains that only the Apache seemed to inhabit. And the Apaches that liked those mountains were the ones that refused to go to the reservations built for them. These were Apaches that could not be contained and which were violent and burned stagecoaches and massacred families traveling the roads.

"Come on," he said. "Let's go on."

He mounted and continued to follow the dog. In a few hours he stopped to eat.

If they were traveling, thinking they were smart, I can catch them, thought Jake. I can find them in a day.

Then they went on, but before night he heard a scream. The scream echoed in the valley he rode in. Beside him was a river, and while near the river he heard the scream once again. The scream was off the tracks, but Jake disregarded the tracks and rode faster and faster. The scream was loud and caused the man's hair to stand up, as the scream echoed over and over again in the deep valley.

Once out of the valley Jake saw a burning stagecoach. Then he saw Apaches in the distance, mounting horses and riding away in the trees. Jake's heart beat quickly. He pulled out his rifle and listened for the scream. But there was no sound. He rode in the trees and was careful not to be spotted by any remaining Apache. He saw a road and the burning stagecoach. He dismounted and walked closer to the stagecoach. Three bodies were on the ground. Two had arrows in their chests and one had a mark in his head made from a tomahawk. Jake held the rifle tighter, breathing heavier now, and then he went around the stagecoach. He could feel the fire on his face, even from a good distance away. He couldn't see any Apaches.

"Help," a voice called.

Jake turned around, raising his eyebrows. "Where are you?" he said.

The sun was going down, but it was near the horizon. There were shadows in the trees, and it seemed night when looking into the forest from where the voice called out. It sounded like a woman's voice.

"Over here," she said.

He went to the voice. "Come out. I can't see you."

"Will you help me?" she said.

"Of course I will. I just rode from Silver City. We can head back there."

She walked out. Her dress was ripped. She held her hands over the ripped parts. Tears ran down her cheeks. She was shaking.

"I'll get you something," said Jake. But then he watched the trees. "Are they gone?"

She nodded. "The others?" she said. "Are they—are they dead?"

"Dead."

He went back and gave her a shirt to put on over her dress. She put it on and looked at the burning stagecoach and then at the white dog, Bud. "That's Bud," said Jake, motioning to his dog. "I found him wandering the streets of Lake Valley."

She made no sign of understanding. She looked down at her shoes. Her ankles were scratched and there were bruises and marks across her arms and legs. Some of the markings looked to be from nails.

"I stabbed one of them," she said. "But there were too many. They surrounded me and—"

"You don't have to say. It's all right now. We'll get you home. Do you have a home?"

"The home I had was with my pa."

"Your pa?"

She pointed at the stagecoach, but from where they stood her pa was on the other side and could not be seen. He was dead.

"What's your name?"

"Agatha," she said. "Agatha Stafford." She was in her late twenties. She trembled and kept looking into the trees.

"I'm Jake McAlister." He led his horse to Agatha and said, "Come on. I can take you to Silver City. I'll let you figure out what you want to do once you get there. For the time being, we have to leave this place. There might be more of them around, and it will be night soon."

Agatha kept looking into the dark forests, as if to see if more Apaches were waiting. Jake saw her and touched her arm to try to lead her out of the forest and back to his horse. But she pulled back in fear and trembled.

"They're gone," he said. "All right? Come on. We'll tell your mother what happened as well."

"I don't have a mother. Pa was it." Her eyes teared up.

Jake sighed. "I'm sorry. I guess you just got me now."

She hesitated, glancing down at the dog

and the stagecoach. The clouds turned violent from the sun setting below the mountains.

"You can trust me. I've done bad things, but I'm not a bad person. I'll get you out of here." He held his hand out.

She grabbed it and mounted the horse with him. Then they began to ride back to Silver City. As he looked back he saw the stagecoach still burning. The woman riding behind him still shivered.

CHAPTER 8
HUNTED

"When will we get there?" asked Bonnie.

She kept turning back. The two rode together on Hansford's horse and were on a small trail that would lead to a main road heading north to Los Lunas.

"Won't be long." said Hansford.

"Are you all right?" she said.

"Yes," he said. "I might have to sell my horse."

"Why?"

"There's a train we can take in a town called Cutter or Aleman. I don't think they take horses on them," he said, smiling back at her anxiously. His horse was a friend to him. Seeing him go was not a good thought. It made him even more nervous.

"That's okay," she said. "You can buy another horse, can't you?"

"It's not the same thing."

Bonnie could tell he was angry, so she let it go. Nothing had gone to plan. The nerves of both of them were tight. They slept little and ate little. The trail Hans tried to cover might not have worked. And Hansford knew if those men back in Silver City worked together they could maybe find him. He was not out yet. And his name, face and gun, were possibly plastered on the walls outside saloons.

A big bounty, he thought, could be on my head right now. Then it would be up. But it couldn't end that way, he thought. There had to be a reason for all the things that had happened.

They came out of the Caballo Mountains. It was a dry place with few trees and plenty of yucca and grama near the streams from which the two drank. Food was running out.

"We should have followed that road north," she said. She pressed against him and felt safer there than she had ever felt. She tried not to touch the cuts on his chest.

"It would take too long and we're almost out of food. They would catch up with us. We can't, Bonnie. The train will be faster. We're almost there."

"How do you know?"

"I've read about a train robbery once on that track," he said. "It was about five years prior. Just east of where we are now. Aleman, I think."

"And that's where we're going?" she asked.

"If I'm where I think we are, yes."

She frowned, as the sun was blinding. She had been inside for too long, and now she felt the back of her neck and her arms were browning under the hot sun. The back of Hansford's neck was very tan. She thought she would become tan like him soon.

Looking back she saw deer on the plains; they were blurry at that distance; standing motionless, they were hard to see from far away.

They found the train tracks. The horse went over them. A booming mining town called Cutter came into view. It was busy with wagons and folks roaming the main road. Along the streets were wooden buildings and a few adobe houses.

"Will we be safe here?" she asked.

"I don't see why not."

"I mean about the law," she said, almost whispering, as they were on the main road and people were nearby. There were hotels and saloons. Cowboys and miners were walking to the saloons. In the distance she could see thousands of cattle on the plains.

As Hans looked around he noticed a sign saying Cutter Saloon and realized he was not in Aleman. He looked for lawmen, but he could not find any.

"We'll be in and out," he told her. "I have to find when the train leaves. Then we'll be in Los Lunas before you know it."

She nodded.

"Don't look so worried. They might not even know my name," he said.

"You said they knew what you look like."

He found the livery. He asked a man there where he can sell his horse, and the man pointed him to a rancher who was in town. Mr. Yale was his name. Hansford sold his horse to him, as it was a fine horse and Yale had the money.

Hans walked with Bonnie to the train station. Hans asked the man selling tickets when the train would arrive, and he told him it would be another hour. He pointed to a clock on the wall and said, "Two o'clock sharp. Do you need tickets, sir?"

"Yes," said Hans.

He paid for the tickets and waited with Bonnie on a bench. On impulse Hans tapped the heel of his right boot against the floor.

Bonnie noticed and touched his knee to get him to relax. Then she noticed a sign just outside the booth where the man selling tickets worked. It was a wanted sign. She got up and walked to it and saw there were a few other wanted signs.

An old man with a white beard came over, as he noticed Bonnie looking at one wanted sign, and said, "Have you seen that man?" he asked Bonnie.

"No," she said. "No, I believe I haven't."

"Well, that's a shame. It looked like you were very interested in him, like you had seen him."

"Oh."

"He is a handsome man," said the old man. "I suppose that's why you looked at that photograph." He looked around.

About ten others were waiting for the train. Hans had his hat down, pretending to sleep. He could not sleep, but he pretended to calm him down and make it seem as though he were not an outlaw on the run.

"He is," she said. "But I thought I might have seen him in Silver City. He looked a little familiar."

The old man nodded. "That's where he killed a man. Supposedly he killed a lot of people. He also stole horses from a man called Ron McAlister."

"Sounds like he made some bad choices," she said.

"That's a gentle way of putting it. A man like that doesn't deserve to live in civilized society. Men like him are a thing of the past. Time is changing. Men like that will be caught immediately in the future. We'll be so packed into towns that a man like that will be found soon after committing the crime."

"You believe that?" she said.

"Certainly. This man won't last much longer. He'll be found." The old man took out a pocket watch from his vest and looked at the time.

"Did you know the man whose horses were stolen?" she asked.

"No. I read about him in the papers. It sounded like he just tried to defend himself. Shot one of the rustlers at least. But he ended up dead. Too bad. It shows that any of us could have been in his position. I suppose I felt like he was one of us, like a neighbor, so I've been keeping my eye out for this man." He pointed to the wanted sign. "We'll find him. And once he's found he'll be hanged."

The old man walked away and squinted his eyes to see if the train was arriving soon.

Bonnie sat down again and whispered to

Hans. "That poster," she said, looking around, "over there. See it?"

Hansford pulled up his hat and said, "Yeah."

"That's you."

"Me?"

"Go over and see," she said.

"If I'm on that poster, I wouldn't want to show my face anywhere."

"Should we get a stagecoach?"

"It'll take too long," he said.

"But it's safer. We might get caught if we take the train."

"We can get caught either way."

"So what do you want to do?"

Hans stood up. Bonnie tugged at his shirt, but he shrugged and put his hand down to indicate it would be all right. He looked at the bounty and saw it was him. But there was no name. It said he was wanted for murder and rustling. The girl, Delilah, might have said his name by now. He wondered if the two men in Silver City, Samuel and Fred, gave his name away. I trust people too much, he thought. I'm in the wrong line of work.

But there was no name, so he settled for a while and watched the people around him. They didn't seem to notice he was the wanted man on the poster.

He sat back down and stared at the ground, half in a daze.

"Well? Did you see it?" asked Bonnie.

"I saw it all right. I see I'm a dead man."

"Don't talk like that," she said, touching his shoulder. "Oh, is this your hurt shoulder?" She held her hand just above the shoulder.

"Yes, but you can touch it. I haven't felt much in the past day. I've just been running nonstop with you. Now we're running again. I can't live like this forever," he said, looking at her.

"Will we leave the state?"

"I don't think we have a choice. We'll head to Los Lunas and try to find a train that heads west. Who knows how far west," he said. "Maybe we'll have to go all the way to California. They wouldn't think we'd get that far."

"Do you have the money for it?"

Hansford picked up the satchel that sat between his boots. He had his rifle with him and his revolver. Some people glanced over at him and saw his weapons, which was an odd sight to some people who kept to the big cities and were only passing through the small towns by train. They were used to trains and not horses, and newspapers and top hats instead of revolvers and curled brim hats.

"We might see someone who recognizes me," he told her. "If that happens, we'll have to do something desperate."

"Desperate?" she said. "Don't tell me you'll kill someone again."

"Did I have a choice last time? It was my death or his. Isn't that how it was?"

"Yes," she said. "Yes, I guess so. But I don't want to see any more of that. I'm sick of that. I don't want anyone else to get hurt."

"Me neither. I didn't wish any of this to happen, but it did. All we have to do is move on and keep moving on."

Some people walked over to see the train arriving. The train and the black smoke behind it came into view. It could be heard from far away.

Bonnie picked up the luggage and Hans carried the rifle and the satchel slung around his shoulder. He had one free hand still so he grabbed one of the suitcases Bonnie was holding. She smiled at him, but he was too nervous to smile back. He was thinking how far those wanted poster go and if he'd see them in Los Lunas.

"I'm happy you're here," he said to relieve her.

She squeezed his hand as the train hit the brakes and screeched slowly to a halt. People came out of the train. Train workers went by and checked to see if all the luggage and things were taken by those getting off. People began to board. Hansford and Bonnie were the last to get on. They found a couple seats and sat down. Hans stowed his rifle away but kept the satchel between his boots. He tried not to look around, even though he felt people were watching him from behind.

The train took off. It slowly gained speed until it was moving fast. "We'll be there in no time," said Hans, looking out the window at the moving landscape. "Look at how fast we're going."

"I haven't been on a train before," said Bonnie.

"It's fun, isn't it?"

She nodded.

Bonnie turned around and saw that the old man that she had spoken to earlier was watching Hans. She did not say anything about it. There were many stops along the way, and the old man might be off. But in each stop Bonnie watched people get off while the old man remained. His eyes were almost black in the darkening interior of the train. The sun was going down. People got on the train after each stop. It was almost full before they reached Los Lunas. As they were slowing down to Los Lunas, almost coming to a halt, Bonnie told Hans about the old man eyeing him.

"We'll be here one night," said Hansford. He looked outside. The dark sky and the clouds moved with the stars that hovered above the mountains. A few people got off. Others waited for the aisle to clear.

Hans got up and turned to see the old man, but he could not find him. Hans helped Bonnie carry the luggage.

They got off the train during the night and looked about. Hans found a hotel for them and paid for one night. The room was on the second story of an old wooden building. There were stairs on the outside that went to their room. Hans used the key and let Bonnie go in first. Then he looked about outside.

"What are you doing?" asked Bonnie from inside. She sat on the bed and smiled. "Isn't it nice?"

"What?"

"The room—isn't it nice?"

Hans closed the door and locked it. He put the luggage down and moved the curtains with his hands to see outside. He still had the rifle in his hand.

"Sure is," he said. He could see lights on near the windows. A woman came out from one house holding a light, calling to a cat that ran inside the house.

"You don't sound excited about it."

He looked back at her. "I got wanted signs of me. If I don't sound excited, it's because of that."

She did not respond. Instead she lay with her head against the pillow, closing her eyes.

"I'm sorry," said Hans. "I'm just nervous. You said a man was looking at us. I guess I'm paranoid." He looked outside again, hesitated and then said to her, "I'll be back."

"Where are you going?"

"To look around."

"Be careful," she said.

He went outside and down the stairs. Then he walked the streets and found one poster outside of the sheriff's office. It was a poster of him. He turned and looked around. There was no one about, but then a man walking on crutches surprised him and said, "You seen that man?"

Hans turned around. "No, why?"

The man on crutches had one of his pant legs tied up, as the leg ended at the knee. He lost the leg in the war. "Just wondering. $1,000 is a lot of money for one man."

Hans studied him. "Yes, it is."

"Wouldn't want someone like that to get away," said the war veteran.

"Assuming the wanted posters are right. The man could have gotten mixed up with the wrong people. Maybe he's taking the blame for others," said Hans.

The war vet nodded and looked away. "Those are nice boots. You must make good money with boots like those."

"Sometimes."

"What kind of work?" he asked.

"I think you know," said Hans.

The vet laughed and said, "Then care to share some of the spoils?"

Hans thought about it. He gave the war vet twenty dollars and saw the man's eyes widen. "That's a lot. I didn't think you'd give that much."

"And what do I get in return?" asked Hans.

The old war vet combed back his white hair that went back to his ears. He looked around. "What would you want?"

"A little information," said Hans. "If there are rumors about me, let me know. I'm staying at the hotel over there. I leave in the morning. I need to know if they're close. Do that and I'll give you more."

"More?" His eyes widened.

"Yes, but don't make up anything. I'll know if you're lying."

"I don't lie."

Hans started to walk away.

"What if I don't hear anything?" asked the veteran.

"Then maybe you can repay me some other way. Just keep me alive, will you? I don't feel like getting hanged."

The veteran nodded in agreement. "It's a deal."

Hans went back to the hotel and went up the stairs. He noticed the door was locked, so he knocked and said, "It's me."

She opened the door and watched him go inside. Then she saw the war veteran staring at her from far down the street. She closed the door. "There's an old man staring at us."

"Don't worry about him," he told her. "He's all right."

"What do you mean? Who is he?"

"He recognized my picture on the bounty."

"Will he turn us in?"

"No."

"You can't trust a stranger like that. What happened? What did you tell him?"

"I gave him some money," he said. Hans sat down on the bed and began to take off his boots.

"And?"

"And I think he won't turn me in."

"Why? It's a $1,000 bounty. Why wouldn't he turn you in?"

"Not everyone is greedy. Sure, he wants money. Maybe he knows this is a small town with maybe a sheriff and two deputies. If I were him, I'd think if I turned in someone, especially the man who killed people, I'd get killed by the man with the bounty on his head. That man would kill the law and come for me. But he isn't stupid, and he's not begging either. He's not a beggar. He was asking, not begging. Well, I gave him money. He knows I'll give him more, and he knows a little more money is better than a whole lot and a quick death."

"He's scared of you," she said, locking the door and looking out the window. "Is that it?"

"No, he's not scared. He's just sure that the man on that bounty is capable of more. He's right. I've done some bad things, Bonnie. I think a man who's been at war can tell when another man has seen and done awful things. He understood me. That's what I'm saying. We understood each other."

"What is this, some 'man talk' I'm supposed to ignore?"

"No." He sighed. "Come over here."

"I'm not coming over there until you explain."

"I already did," he said.

"It wasn't enough."

"Look, he's out there still. You can wait another hour. If the law doesn't show up, it'll prove what I said is true. You'll see. That old man on the crutches won't do anything."

"You seem so sure of yourself," she said.

"I'm tired of your attitude," he said. "Can we not argue?"

"You think you always know what to do, but you don't. You're like a lost dog who gets into fights, makes love and runs off to fight some more."

"Sure, that's what I am."

She frowned at him. "You're putting us in a bad position," she said. "You have to think about both of us, not just saving your own skin."

"I have always thought of both of us," he said, raising his voice. She stepped back at the sound and hoped no one had heard outside.

"All this running is so we can be together and so that I don't have to rustle horses and worry about getting killed. I never knew what to do until now. All the time before I was just drifting without any aim in life. I thought that was a comfortable life. No one told me what to do. But now I'm thinking about you and me together." The veins in his neck disappeared after almost straining and pleading for some understanding. "That man out there understands. That's all I'm saying. He knows I just want to leave. Now that he saw you he probably understands more. I told him it was a misunderstanding—that poster of me. He knows I will die if found, and he thinks my life is more important and his life more important than any amount of money. That's what I mean."

She sat down on the bed with him. She took his hands in hers, but as soon as she did so he got up and looked outside. There was no movement in the streets. Some of the lights near the windows had gone out. A dog barked somewhere.

"Why don't you come to bed?" she said, opening her eyes.

He set his rifle on the dresser and took off his gun belt and put it on the table beside the bed. Then he lay on the bed with her. "What happens now?" she asked.

"We'll get tickets in the morning. Hopefully the train comes early. Then we'll head west," he said. "I don't even know how far the train here will take us. It'll take a while to get to California."

She took his hat and wore it on her head and smiled. Hans grinned and pulled her close. "We both smell, don't we?" she said.

"That's what happens when you're an outlaw."

"I'm an outlaw?"

"You are now."

"I haven't thought about it," said Bonnie. But she tried not to think about the death of Enor and the $1,000 reward for bringing in the rustler alive. California was what she thought about; that and its ocean and the mountains along it. She had heard of California, but it sounded more of a paradise, more fiction than true.

Hans felt her against him and was happy. He put his hands on her waist and kissed her, and then she forgot everything bad that had happened.

In the morning Hans woke up and saw Bonnie was not in bed. He looked for a note and saw she wrote that she was going to get food from the store she saw yesterday. He then relaxed, put on clothes and his gun belt, and looked out the curtains. Near the opposite side of the street he saw an old man, the one on the train, talking to what looked to be lawmen. Hans felt his heart beat fast as he saw the old man point directly at the room where Bonnie and Hans had stayed. Hans paced in the room, feeling the palms of his hands sweaty. He rubbed his hands together and then wiped them on his shirt.

"Calm down," he said. "They don't know your name."

He looked out the curtain and saw the sheriff and what looked to be his deputy. "Come on down," yelled the sheriff. "We know who you are." The sheriff and deputy separated and carried rifles. One watched the door and the other watched one of the windows.

Hans didn't want to kill them; if he did, he would be found no matter what state he fled to. He paced in the room again. The only exit he could find was the front door, and that was right where the sheriff was. He turned back and saw a back window. He grabbed the satchel and looked around the room for anything else he needed. He then crawled on the roof, just as he used to do when visiting Bonnie in the night, and jumped off the roof of the first floor, right above a porch. There was a loud bang as he hit part of the stairs and mud, and he fell to his butt and got up immediately. He walked the streets in search of Bonnie. When he walked into the store, a person at the front desk looked at him and frowned, as Hans sweated profusely and breathed heavily.

Hans saw Bonnie looking at produce and touched her shoulder.

"What's wrong?" she said. "You're sweating."

"They've found me." He looked outside.

"Oh, no."

"We have to go. Now."

They went outside, but there was no train and they had no horse. "Do you know when the train gets here?" he asked Bonnie. "No, I went straight here. I don't know."

"Let's go to the train station."

As they turned someone yelled, "There he is."

Hansford turned and saw the sheriff and deputy run for them. "Get on that horse there."

Bonnie did. It was the deputy's horse. Hans ran by, pulled ten dollars out of his pocket and gave it to the injured war veteran that sat on the steps outside a building. "Now's your time," said Hans. "Distract them for us, will you?"

Hans and Bonnie rode away on the deputy's horse. The war vet hit the back of the sheriff's horse with his crutches, which caused the horse to gallop out of town.

Hans and Bonnie rode west and turned back. There were two people behind them, but they were small at that distance. Dust picked up as they went.

They rode on the desert-like land. In an hour Hans slowed down.

"How does it look back there?" Hans yelled to Bonnie.

"I can't see anyone." After a few minutes she said, "Where are we going?"

"The railroad went northeast, and then connected to head west in that direction. So the railroad should be northwest of here. We'll go west and then north, and at that point we'll find it and head west until we find another place to get on a train."

They rode a little faster until Hans could see the railroad ahead about a half mile away. Hans felt relieved, especially when he turned back and saw no one in sight. When they reached the railroad, they followed it. Buildings could be seen in the distance.

CHAPTER 9
DEPARTED

Jake McAlister and the woman he saved, Agatha, went back to Silver City. He heard her cry for a while, but as they neared the town the cries lessened.

He helped her get off the horse in the early morning. She looked around the town with crazed eyes. "It's all right," Jake said, noticing her expression. "Nothing can hurt you here."

Bud the dog licked her calf and she smiled a little. But as soon as the smile disappeared, she was back to being paranoid.

"Let's go to the doctor."

Jake took her to the doctor and in an hour she was out. Jake had been sitting outside the doctor's building when she walked out from the building. Gradually people began to appear on the road.

"Here," said Jake. "I thought you might want this, for now."

The gift was a dress similar to the one she was wearing. The dress she wore was torn up, ragged and dirty. The end of her hair was fringed from the fire.

She grabbed the dress and said, "Thank you." It seemed she was getting better, more cheerful. "Your name is Jake?"

"That's right."

"You're kind to help me," she said. "Most people would look the other way or run from Apaches. You're very brave."

"Do you have money on you?" asked Jake.

She shook her head.

"I guess I knew that. Well—"

"I feel a bit helpless, to be honest. I'm usually the one doing all the work," she said. "This dress, even, is not like me. I'm used to pants. I worked a bit on my father's ranch. He had men he hired, but I would still work some, not knowing what else to do. This dress was more for the occasion."

"What occasion?"

"We were heading to San Francisco; thought we'd start a new life there. We sold the farm and went west, and well—you know how that turned out." She pointed at a hotel. "I guess I can stay there awhile, until I relax some."

"Will you head to San Francisco still?" he asked.

"I think so. We sold the ranch. There's nowhere else to go. My father wanted me to go to the university there, even though I'm twenty-five and never had much education except through books."

"I'm about uneducated as they come, but isn't books how you learn?"

She smiled. "You're right. What am I saying? I'm not myself."

"That's a normal reaction to what happened to you," he said. "I'll walk you to the hotel if you want."

"I'd like that."

They went to the hotel across the street, just as the street was getting busy with wagons and horses and men and women walking. Agatha felt embarrassed to be seen with the torn dress and the shirt given to her by Jake over her. She got a room and changed into the new dress. All the clothes she liked to wear had been burned in the stagecoach fire. She wondered if Jake had told the law about what happened to her. After changing into a new dress she went outside and found Jake sitting in a chair, his eyes closed and sleeping. The dog, Bud, was sitting on the floor and sleeping beside him. Bud lifted his head when she came closer.

Agatha touched Jake's shoulder to wake him. "Jake?"

He breathed in, as one does when woken up in deep sleep, and said, after looking at her, "You look nice. That dress suits you."

"Thanks," she said, crouching to pet the dog on the floor, who had woken up after hearing her footsteps. "Did you tell the sheriff about what happened?"

"Sheriff?" asked Jake. "Oh, it's a town marshal in this place. I told him. He sent some deputies over there. They've been busy lately. There were three rustlers dead, a businessman dead and a wanted man that escaped this place. They sure don't get a break." He paused and looked outside at the bright street. "There was a stagecoach attack up near where you were not too long ago. The Black Range." He shook his head, not sure what to say after what he saw. His face turned somber and serious. He could picture the stagecoach fire in his mind, the yellow flames, the men with arrows in them. "Your father will be buried wherever you want him to be buried."

"We're from Chloride," she said. "It's a bit far to bury him there."

"I understand."

"Where are you from?" she asked.

"Dodge City. How is it in Chloride?" he asked.

"The mine is the only reason people live there," she said, her mind now occupied. "Mother owned a store there. After she passed, my father and I wanted to move west."

Just then U.S. Marshal Reubin Conway walked in, looked the room over and found Jake McAlister sitting in the chair, his face tired from sleeping too little. "There you are," said Conway, frowning as he usually did. But this time he waited a while to speak, trying to figure out Jake. "I heard you went away."

"I found the trail," said Jake.

"All right," he said, pausing.

"I was too far to come back. I thought there was only one man, so I figured I could find him."

Conway nodded. "He was the one who helped kill your brother. It's a normal reaction. You want revenge, whereas I want justice. Well, thanks for telling us. There are a few deputies on the trail you told them about. They are following it as we speak."

"You think we'll catch him?" Jake could not

tell whether Conway was restraining anger or not. Jake knew it was his own fault. I shouldn't have followed the trail alone, he thought. More men could have kept on the trail.

"I don't know. His trail is getting harder to track," said Conway. He looked outside the hotel windows and saw the sky turning grey and black over the mountains. "That trail won't last long." He turned back to Jake. "I can't be riding across the entire state forever. There's a point where the trail ends. And that point might be at a railroad."

"What do you mean?"

"If he takes a train, he's gone. There's not much else to do. We have his face on posters, but only on the far west side of the state."

The door opened quickly. A deputy came inside, found Conway and said, "We have word up in Los Lunas that a man matching the poster was spotted. He was with a woman. They escaped the town and went west."

"West?" asked Conway. "On horseback?"

"Yes, sir."

"There's nothing west of Los Lunas except mountains. They must be desperate. And with a woman? This might be Bonnie Philips and the rustler. It's possible. It's likely she had help killing her husband, and he has killed Donavan

Nealey. He is not shy of violence. It has to be him."

"We think they might be looking to get on the railroad north of there and head out of state," said the deputy.

The marshal sat down on a bench and took off his hat. His bald head showed and it was tan in the light coming in from the windows.

"Sir, what should we do?"

"When did this happen? When did this man and woman leave Los Lunas?"

"Last night."

"Then they're gone by now," said Conway. "Regardless, have some men in Manuelito or around those parts have a look at each train that goes through there today and tomorrow. Make sure he's not taking his time."

"Yes, sir," the deputy said and left the hotel.

Jake stood up and looked at Conway. "I guess this is it," said Jake to the marshal. He held out his hand.

Conway looked at the hand absentmindedly. He then opened his eyes wider and took the hand and shook it. "Well," he said, getting up. "I better get back to it. I'll send word to Arizona. Maybe they'll find him. But I doubt it. It was more likely we'd find him around these parts." He sighed and opened the front door. Over his shoulder the marshal said,

"Your brother was a good man," and shut the door.

Jake sat down again. Agatha walked over and sat down beside him. "What's that about? What happened to your brother?"

"He died," said Jake. "Some rustlers took his horses and killed him. We got the horses back at least."

"I'm sorry."

"We almost had him," said Jake. "He was right in this town."

"Who?"

"The last rustler we were after," he said, "who had helped kill my brother. We could have found him, but we didn't. It was my fault. If I had told the others about the trail, I could have helped you and had the deputies and Conway continue on the trail. It was my fault."

"I'm sure they'll find him." She put her hand on his shoulder, as he looked sad staring down at the floor.

He was surprised it took a while to notice her hand on his shoulder. Jake stood up and looked at the restaurant down the street. The street was now bright under the morning sun, and the warmth returned to replace the cold night.

"Are you hungry?" he asked her.

They ate, but in all that time Jake was

thinking about where the rustler went. He felt disappointed in himself for going it alone. But he had almost always gone at it alone. It was automatic. It was his nature to be alone. He preferred the quiet and despised the noises of the cities. He had been to Kansas City, Missouri and could not handle all the hundreds of thousands of people roaming the streets. It was too much. Everyone was always in a hurry and talking about things that didn't matter. They complained and talked too much. In the small towns and villages, it was slow and peaceful. It was in the small towns he could think again. You didn't get bumped into every time you walked the street. To Jake the rural land was the only place he could be happy. He could only live when alone. But sometimes he thought whether another woman could come into his life, yet in those moments of thought he remembered his wife who passed away.

"You're awfully quiet," she said.

"I'm just thinking that in a day or two I'd head back to Kansas," he said.

"And do what?"

"Be a cowboy again."

She almost laughed, but held her hand over her mouth. Jake looked over at her, surprised she was getting along well. Maybe, he thought, it won't always be on her mind. And the longer time goes by the longer the time it would be without thinking of the bad memory. Maybe she would think about it everyday. But in a few months it would be once a week and eventually once a month. But he knew not every memory is forgotten. He realized the memory won't change, but the reaction to it can.

"I'm sorry," she said. "But you don't seem to fit the part."

"Why not?" he said, partially angry.

"You look like someone who is maybe a retired army general," she said, holding her fork up in the air while thinking. "Maybe someone else. I just can't see you doing it."

"What if I had a big beard that made me look like a mountain man?"

"Did you have a beard?" she said.

"Used to. I shaved it not too long ago."

"Why?"

"I had to see my brother's wife, and I didn't want to look that ragged. I don't really know why I thought I had to. I had the beard for maybe a year, trimming it every so often, but not by much."

"Why?" asked Agatha.

"Why what?"

"Why have a beard that big?"

He leaned back in his chair and had to think about it. "I think I first grew it after my wife died," he said, looking out the window. He put his hand on the curtain to move it away.

Rain came down in the north sky. He saw the storm moving slowly to the southeast.

"I'm sorry," she said. Now, finished eating, she studied the man across the small table. He was in his forties, though she could tell he acted older. His movements were slow and controlled. When he took his hat off, it was slow and not jittery like a man dying for a shot of whiskey after a long ride. They were calm movements that made Agatha think of a man who takes his time. She felt his calmness had made her calm as well. "What was her name?"

"Cleo."

"How did she pass?"

"She was sick for years," he said. "The doctors couldn't help her. It was cancer."

"I'm sure she's in heaven," said Agatha.

He nodded slowly, knowing those words didn't mean much to him. He paid and walked out of the restaurant with Agatha. Her face was full of color now, and her energy returned. Jake said, "Well, I guess I'll make my way back home." He put out his hand for her to shake.

Agatha quickly said, "Already? It's so sudden."

"I have no reason to stay here," he said. He put his hand down and looked back at his dog,

Bud, who was about to be fed the leftovers Jake had.

She fiddled with her hands. "I'd like to see you again," she said.

Jake noticed her then. "Again?"

"Yes," she smiled.

"Are you saying you've taking a liking to me?" he said, not sure what else to say.

"Yes," she said, blushing.

Jake looked back at his dog and then at her. "When would you like to see me again?" he said. "Tonight?"

"That'd be wonderful."

He smiled, yet this time the smile was not forced. He felt glad, and this was the first time he had felt happy in a long while. Then he said, "I'll see you at the hotel."

They went their separate ways. She stood there, watching him walk away, curious of him. Then she went back to the hotel.

Jake mounted his horse and rode to a river he had heard about. Not knowing what else to do all day, he decided to fish. As he rode out of town he noticed the wanted poster of the rustler. He stared at the poster a long time and then left the fringes of town. In an hour he found a spot where the water was dark below the shade of a tree's branches. He looked up at the storm in the distance, but the storm did not bother him. He took out a fishing pole from his horse and fished for a while. He caught two trout and put them away in a satchel. Sitting beside the river with his dog and horse, he felt sure that everything would be all right.

CHAPTER 10
THE ESCAPE

HANSFORD VORRIS RODE ALONG THE TRAIN track and looked up to see a town in the distance. The town itself blended with the desert landscape. Great mountains rose to the southwest, but they were clear of trees. Cacti were abundant. Across the land there were bushes with small leaves to survive the hot and dry climate.

Bonnie glanced down at the ground and realized, based on the vegetation, that they were far from home. It was the farthest she had been from home.

"Where are we?" asked Bonnie.

"Close to a town," said Hans, turning back to her. As he turned back he tried to see if the lawmen from Los Lunas were still following. He could not see anything. Still, he picked up

547

the pace and kept his eyes on the land and the people he would soon see in the town ahead. He wondered how far that poster he saw went. He felt he might see the poster even in California, but as soon as he thought all of this he shook his head. I'm thinking too much, he thought.

"What town?" she said.

"I don't know."

"Does the train stop here?"

He said, "I hope so." His throat was sore and his stomach gnawed at him. He could hear by the tone in Bonnie's voice that she was irritated. So was he. Looking down at the horse, he realized the things he once carried were gone. The rifle was left behind in the hurry. Bonnie's luggage was back at the hotel. His horse was sold. He did not care too much about the rifle, but it was the horse he missed.

"Can we get water here?" she said.

"Of course. We'll eat and drink and ask about a train. Watch what you say around here. We're from Texas going to California. That's all you have to say."

"Have you had to make up a story like that before?" she said.

"No, but I think it's best we take it easy here. Act like we didn't just steal a horse and are accused of murder and rustling."

They reached the town and saw a sign that mentioned Rio Purco. Hans slowed the horse and found a place to eat and drink. Bonnie and Hans ate and felt full afterwards. When the waiter came back to refill the glasses once more Hans said, "Does a train come through here?"

The waiter, a young man, said, "Yes, sir. You can catch the next one in an hour. Be ready though. They don't wait for stragglers. Those trains are always on time."

"Thank you."

The waiter left.

"What are you smiling for?" Hans asked Bonnie.

"We'll make it."

He tried to smile with her, but he couldn't. He was not that optimistic. The posters were still on his mind. "Yes," he said. "We will."

Bonnie put her fingers in the glass of water and washed her face. Hans watched her and then touched his own face and felt the hair on his chin growing sharp like needles.

Afterward they went outside. Across the street Hans saw men staring in curiosity. Then they went inside a saloon.

Hans then looked for any lawmen, but there were none. The town was so small there didn't appear to be any lawmen about. If there were, they were not seen by Hans.

Hans said, "Come on. The train will be here soon."

She walked beside him. The platform beside the train tracks had no benches. And on the platform dirt was blown like sawdust in the wind.

"How far until we reach the border?" she said.

He was tired of questions. "I don't know. I would say half a day or less. It depends on how many stops." Hans thought of something. He told her to come along. They went into a store. Hans bought a map and looked at the railroad and pointed a finger on the end of the map. "There," he said. "Here we are. The rail goes north and then west. See?"

"We aren't far at all," said Bonnie.

An old Navajo man in clothes similar to the clothes Hans wore came up to stand and wait for the train. His face was without hair, and he wore a flat brimmed hat with long hair down the back of his head. He appeared to not notice them. The Navajo only stared down the track at the train going slowly down the track.

Then the Navajo looked at them. "It will rain soon," he said, looking to the west now that showed no sign of a storm.

"Why do you think so?" asked Hans.

"I can feel it in my bones."

"Well, that's an odd way of putting it."

"When you understand you are nature, you feel it in you. You know when it will rain and snow." In his somber face, he then looked at the train arriving.

No one else was boarding the train but the three of them. There were several others inside as Hans and Bonnie sat down. An old woman and old man sat together and behind them was a business man in a suit and tie. The Navajo sat down ahead of them and looked out the window. As the train started up again the landscape moved fast. Rain began to fall and run down the windows. Hans was happy to be on the way out of the state.

Bonnie touched his hand and held it. "What do you think San Francisco will be like?"

"Is that where we're heading?"

"Where else would we go?"

"I don't know much about California," admitted Hans. "Only that there's a city called San Francisco on the coast. That's it. Do you know of any other cities there?"

"No," she said.

"San Francisco it is."

"We can both work, if we have to," she said.

"I'll figure it out once we get there," he said. Then, still sweating despite the sense of calm the rain brought, he worried about being caught. And as he looked outside, the moving land slowed to a halt. The train stopped. Some people got on, and some got off. There were many stops until they neared the border. Once at the border Hans noticed men in military uniform waiting for the train.

"The military," said Hans. He pointed to outside the window. Soldiers waited outside.

"What are they doing?"

"Maybe there's trouble ahead. Maybe there's been a derailment."

Once the train stopped, the soldiers, with their rifles in their hands, surveyed the people inside. One commanding officer held what looked to be a large piece of paper, and as he went down the aisle he looked up and studied the people sitting. There were about twenty passengers now. One old man asked what the stop was about, but the commanding officer only said, "Is this your stop?" They were at the border. No one could see outside because of the storm. The wind and rain came diagonally from the black sky.

"No."

The officer said nothing else. He continued walking and found Hansford and Bonnie sitting in the dark. Hans looked out the window.

"You," said the officer. He held up the wanted poster in his hand and studied Hans. "Stand up!"

Hans moved out of the aisle and stood there.

"What's going on?" asked Bonnie.

"There's a wanted man about, ma'am," said the officer.

"We're from Texas," she said. "We don't know much about wanted men. In San Antonio, it's pretty quiet. Nothing like this happens, does it Hal?" she asked Hansford.

Hans turned to her, understanding what she was doing. "Yes. What's this man wanted for?" asked Hans.

The officer stood directly in front of Hans and stared at him. "Murder, rustling, robbery." The soldier then looked down at the wrinkled page and back to Hans.

"How far do you think it is to California?" she asked the commanding soldier.

He put down the paper and saw her smiling. "Should take maybe two, three days." He found he couldn't not smile when looking at her.

"Have you checked the others in the train? A wanted man might be about," she said.

The officer then woke up from his stupor and said to Hans, "You can sit down again."

The soldier continued down the aisle and questioned two others in the train.

Hans breathed again and tried not to turn back. After a few minutes the soldiers had searched the train and found nothing. Then people were let off again, and some got on. After a while the train was off again. Hans was quiet.

Bonnie turned to Hansford. "We made it," she said.

Hansford sighed and felt his heart slow as the train began to pick up speed. The train took them over the border into Arizona.

The rain stopped after an hour. Then the sun lowered to sit above the bare mountains. Hans and Bonnie got off the train. He carried his satchel, and the two stayed in a hotel for the night.

Hans looked out the window.

"Why do you look that way?" asked Bonnie. "We made it."

"I'm tired is all. I'll be happy once we're in California. Then I'll relax and go back to my normal self."

"Be your normal self with me right now," she said, crawling on the bed. When she reached him she put her chin on his shoulder. Then she helped him take off the gun belt.

In the morning they had set out to head to

the train station when they saw a crowd forming. There was a man holding up glasses of liquid in each of his hands. As he held up the glasses he yelled out they were cures. "It's the cure, ladies and gentlemen! Doctors across this great country recommend my formula." The man, cleanly shaved, wearing a suit, spoke wildly.

Hans and Bonnie stood behind the crowd, watching the man.

"By God, this is the answer you've all been waiting for! You're prayed for it. Here's the answer," he said.

A woman paid for a bottle and walked away. On the bottle it said "John Bean's Elixir."

The man stood on the back of his wagon filled with the elixir, yelling to the crowd about his elixir said to cure all illnesses.

"What's this about?" Hans asked a woman in the crowd.

"Another salesman," she said. "It's just alcohol, you know."

"What is?"

"The bottles he's selling... it's mostly alcohol in them."

"How do you know?"

"What do you think? I drank the stuff," she said and walked away.

The man yelled over the crowd. "Smooths

wrinkles, prolongs life, and gets rid of warts and other abominations you good folks receive!"

Bonnie said, "Come on, Hans. I've had enough of this."

After Hans and Bonnie left the area they heard a gunshot coming from behind them. Hans turned quickly, pulled out his Colt and looked at the crowd. People were running away. Some men with revolvers pulled them out. Then it was clear to see. A man had pulled out a revolver and shot John Bean, the man selling the elixir. John Bean felt his stomach and saw the gunshot wound and the blood. He put his hands over his stomach and looked at the crowd for an answer.

The man who shot him kept his gun pointed at John Bean. "You told me this would save my wife!" In his hand was an empty bottle of the elixir. He looked up and saw the wagon full of the elixir.

"Please, God, don't kill me. Maybe I can still live, just don't kill me," said John Bean.

"Shut up," he said, and punched John Bean.

"Phil," someone yelled in the crowd. "We can't let you kill the son of a bitch. That's murder."

"Then shoot me!" said Phil.

Phil grabbed a bottle of the elixir and

tossed it to John Bean. "There! Drink it. It prolongs life, don't it?"

There was no answer. The eyes of the salesmen were shutting. The hand on his wound slightly dropped. John Bean breathed heavily and looked behind Phil at the men with drawn revolvers. The guns weren't aimed at Phil, yet they were ready.

"Don't it?" said Phil. "Drink it. It'll save you."

"I am just here to make some money," said John Bean.

"You were doing more than that. What's in this anyway?" asked Phil.

"Herbs, antler extracts—" He coughed blood and felt the life going out of him. He knew he would die soon.

"What else?"

"Don't know. I just sell it."

"You sell it good," said Phil.

"What do you say you put the gun down?" asked Hans, coming up from behind Phil. "Phil, is that your name? The man's about to die. You taught him, all right. He won't come back again."

Phil turned, pointing his revolver at him. Hans had put his gun away before speaking, thinking Phil only wanted to kill the charlatan.

"I want more than that," said Phil. "I want him to die! I want to watch him die."

Just as Phil turned back, he noticed John Bean had pulled a revolver out of his pocket. The shot went off. Phil fell back to the ground and shot once more at John Bean. Both lay still. The men in the crowd put away their revolvers and checked on both. John Bean lay dead. One older man slapped Phil and found him still alive but unconscious. "Get the doctor," he yelled.

Hans stood still and watched the men carry Phil away. As he walked away he thought of all those bottles in the wagon. Beside him he saw Bonnie shaking. "Are you all right?" he said.

"That poor man and his wife," she said, shaking her head. "I can't imagine how he feels."

"He's not feeling much of anything at the moment. If he wakes up, he'll probably feel terrible. But I don't think he cares if he'll hang or not. He got what he wanted."

"I'm half-curious about what's in that elixir," she said.

"Nothing good, I imagine."

While in the train they saw out the windows someone cutting boards of wood.

"Won't be long now," said Hans to Bonnie beside him. "We'll be in California today." He smiled at her, feeling good. No one recognized him. There were no wanted posters. Everything was going as planned, which was back to how it used to be for him. He felt safe, even in the violence just witnessed back in that small dusty town in Arizona.

He wondered if the same people he met back home would be in California. All the people he met, no matter what town, were the same as the next. Big talkers, quiet talkers, merchants, outlaws, prostitutes, swindlers, businessmen, hard workers, drunk workers, Mexicans, former slaves—he saw each one in almost every town. But as he looked outside, the land changed so rapidly. There was no telling whether he would change as fast as the land passing outside the train window or stay as the rustler he once was.

CHAPTER 11
COURTSHIP

AFTER CATCHING TWO TROUT, JAKE McAlister went back to Silver City. He invited Agatha Stafford to eat with him that evening, which she was happy to accept.

"You know, you're the only good person I've met around here," said Agatha.

"There are others like me, if you go out and find them."

"I guess that's my problem. I don't like to go out."

"Well, that explains you staying in all the time."

Later on they walked outside to the porch of the hotel.

"Will you sit down with me?" she asked.

He sat down and suddenly felt nervous.

"What are your plans? Are you getting away soon?"

"I don't know," Agatha said. "Where do you plan to go?"

"I haven't figured that out either. I was getting a liking to this town and the people in it. I might stay put for a while and find some work someplace. I was born near Lake Valley," he said. "So this area is home to me. It's familiar at least."

"I think it'll be my home to," said Agatha.

She grabbed his hand and put it on her lap. Suddenly he felt uncomfortable. The face of his wife flashed in his mind, so he let go of her hand.

"I'm sorry."

"It's all right," he said.

She watched him stand up and lean against the wooden column.

"Did I do something wrong?" she said.

"No." But he didn't go on.

In two days, Jake and Agatha got to know each other. On the second day the town marshal came and told him that the rustler still wasn't found. Jake figured the man was long gone. He thanked the town marshal for telling him but still felt frustrated.

At least the horses were found, thought

Jake. I ought to go back to Elisha and tell her what happened.

But he realized there would be nothing to say. The girl, Delilah, didn't want to tell him anything. That's fine. He felt she protected the man. Maybe there was something he wasn't seeing and wasn't told about.

On the second day of Jake speaking to Agatha, she grew restless and became tired of her failed advances with Jake. He was alone, aloof and distant. He always appeared to be thinking. She felt that it was about his wife and that he needed time. Agatha did not have time. She and her father were going to California, and only a short trip in New Mexico stalled it. She always wanted to see the mountains, so she did.

Now it was time to leave. Nothing was keeping her from leaving.

Jake was kind enough to help her put a big suitcase into the stagecoach. She smiled. Jake always saw her smile at him, and he felt great each time she did. Her smile caused him to smile, and smiling had been rare since his wife died.

"You're going, huh?" he asked.

"Yes. I've lived here long enough. I want to see what California is like. What will you do?"

"I might stick around for a while in the city,

see if I can get work here. I don't have much stake anywhere. I go where I want."

"I've always dreamed of living like that," she said.

"It's not much of a dream, more of a way to live."

"Well, whatever you call it, I think it's almost part of America—everyone doing what they want to do. I suppose that's what my father would say."

"What will you do in California?"

"I don't know. Get married. Raise children. Grow old," she laughed. "I don't know yet. I guess I'm figuring it out like you."

"Well, you'll be all right. It's wild out here. I'm sure it's safer where you're going."

He held out his hand for her to shake. She smiled and kissed him on the cheek. He swallowed and stood motionless and pale.

"I'm sorry," she said. "But you look so nice, and I always wanted to do that."

"That's fine by me."

"Really? It doesn't bother you?"

"Look, Agatha. I think it's time to talk straight with you. I want to get to know you better. All this talk hasn't gone anywhere." He stepped closer and looked down at her after taking off his hat.

"I didn't think you liked me," she said.

"I always have. I'm just old—much older than you. I didn't think—"

"How old are you?" she asked, frowning. "You don't look much older than thirty-five."

"I'm forty," he said.

"That's fine," she said. "My father was sixty-five." She almost laughed.

"Was he?"

"You're not old at all. I almost want to see if you really are forty. You don't look that age," she said. "Anyway, there are more important things." She kissed him on the lips for the first time. "How about we go to California together?"

"But my horse," said Jake. "I'll need to sell him."

"No, you can bring him along. Some trains can store horses," she said.

Bud came close and sat between them, wanting attention. Agatha smiled and petted the dog. He liked the attention. "And bring Bud along too. We can all go. The whole family."

Jake called the driver to ask if he could take one more. The driver agreed, so Jake gathered his things and told Bud to ride inside the stagecoach. The dog jumped inside just as Agatha sat down in one of the seats inside.

Jake mounted his horse. Bud stuck his head out of the window of the stagecoach, his tongue dangling out of his happy mouth. Jake rode his horse and followed the stagecoach. From a small town they took a train. And from the train they took another and another until they were just at the edge of California.

"It was awfully kind of you to drop everything and come with me," Agatha said to Jake.

"It was an easy decision for me."

"You must have a home someplace in Kansas."

"I sold it before coming to Lake Valley. It wasn't much. I sold almost everything inside the house anyway."

"Why?"

"Everything reminded me of my wife and my past."

"Your past?" she said. "What's in your past?"

He began to regret speaking about it. He looked outside the window, but Agatha was near the window and he could not conceal his expression. "I've done some bad things."

"Like what?"

"Robbing trains," he said quietly, as the train was almost filled completely.

She smiled and laughed. "Oh, I don't think you did. You don't look the type."

"You don't believe me?"

"Well," she said, looking at him. She saw he was upset with what she said. "When did this happen?"

"About five to ten years ago, before all hell broke loose. That was when I had made a good amount, putting most of it away in the house I bought with my wife back in Kansas. But I was caught," he said.

"How'd you get caught?"

"I had just finished a job, but I got split up with the others when—"

"The others?"

"A group of men I'd do jobs with," he said, hesitating. "They are probably either dead or in jail. I'd be surprised if they'd be in jail. They were the type of men that fight until they die."

"You were armed while robbing?"

He looked at her. "Of course I was armed. I can't just ask nicely."

The idea of her loving a dangerous man caused her to be distant. She could not picture him as someone holding a gun to people on a train and yelling for money. "Well, what happened after you got split up?"

"I went to my brother's farm north of Lake Valley. I thought I would stay there a while. But my brother had informed the local law. It was too late for me. The next day, just before I was about to head back to Kansas with the money, I got caught. Must have been a dozen lawmen just outside the window. Probably even U.S. marshals out there, just waiting to get me. Somehow, I was not hanged. I figured my brother, who was always well known, had something to do with that. I was sent to jail for five years. When I got out, I cared for my wife, who was sick by then, and years later she died."

"I'm sure she's in a better place now."

He nodded.

"Were you afraid of telling me this?" she asked.

"No, I was only worried about what response you'd have. I've done some bad things in the past. But I'm not like that anymore. I just didn't want to hide anything from you."

She took his hand, smiling, looking out the window for a while. The sun was bright and made looking at the land difficult, especially because the inside of the train was dark and cave-like. "I don't mind if it's in the past. As long as you don't rob trains in San Francisco."

He said, "No reason to go back to my old self. Especially when in a place like that. I hear it's a big city."

"There's more than 200,000 living there."

"Much bigger than I thought," he said.

In a few hours they would reach San Francisco. They had traveled for days and stayed in small towns along the way, though they took separate rooms. They took their time and grew friendlier by the day. Once they reached the city, they were awestruck at the immensity of the city. Not knowing where to go, they went to a five-story hotel and stayed there while they searched for a place to live.

CHAPTER 12
OLD WAYS

Hansford Vorris and Bonnie lived in San Francisco for six months. At this time, Hans worked as a construction worker. With the city growing so fast he had no trouble finding work. He quickly grew at his profession and worked diligently on the construction of Arctic Oil Building Works warehouse owned by Ernest Ransome.

Ransome told Hans his inventions and his idea of reinforced concrete, saying that it is the way of the future and that not even fire could destroy his buildings.

"You have big ideas, Mr. Ransome," said Hans. "But I'm just a low-wage worker. I would think you would speak about your ideas with other engineers like yourself."

Ransome smiled, though his lips were completely hidden in his beard. His head was almost bald, yet his eyes showed his emotions, especially when he smiled and the wrinkles showed near the eyes. He wore a suit and a loose tie around his collar. "I do that as well. You could be one, if you wish."

"An engineer?"

"Sure, why not? What do you want to be? A young man like yourself has to have big dreams."

"I like working here," said Hans. "Working my way up in the construction business would be my goal."

They stood near the bay. Large rocks were in between the water and the Arctic Oil warehouse. They could hear the water against the boulders. Seagulls were heard far above them.

"Would you like to have more responsibility?" said Mr. Ransome.

"Yes, sir."

"Then you'll have it. You have the drive. I can tell. Most of these men need someone like yourself, you see, not me. You'll do well."

They spoke for a few minutes more. Then Ransome shook hands with Hans and went away.

In the evening, Hans went back to a small

place he and Bonnie rented. It was the third floor in the south of town. He had to walk a good distance, up and down steep hills, from the south of town just to get to work. The walking had made him stronger and happier. Everyone seemed to walk in the city, even from far distances, especially those like him, who were low-wage workers trying to make a decent living.

Bonnie saw him out the window walking the street and waited for him to come up the stairs.

"What is it?" she said. She saw him smiling, whistling as he went inside the room.

"I am the manager now," he said.

She smiled and kissed him. "I'm proud of you."

"And you? What have you been up to?"

"The grocery is the usual. It's up and down."

"Hopefully more up than down," he said, putting his coat on the wall hanger.

It was fall and the trees were now changing colors. The coldness caused his cheeks to redden slightly, though it was hard to see under the dark tan he had from being out in the sun all the time. The wind in the city caused the cold to feel worse than it really was. It was always windy. He wore no hat anymore. Only his short hair combed neatly to the side showed.

"You look like a manager," she said, winking at him.

"Maybe we can live in a better place now."

"I'm fine with living here."

He looked outside the street. He did not like the area. Sometimes he saw strange men in groups walking in the evenings. It did not comfort him, though he realized it could be paranoia. They were like the men he had seen when rustling in Texas.

"A nicer neighborhood," he said, "would do us good. Nothing fancy. Just something that is safer."

"Is this about those men you've been telling me about?"

"What else would it be?"

"You worry too much," she said.

"Maybe. It's not worrying though. I'd call it caution."

"Sounds like worrying," said Bonnie, putting down dishes on the table. She had brought food from the grocery store she worked at and began to cook.

"Maybe I should see what they do," he said quietly, mostly to himself.

"Be careful, whatever you do."

"Now it sounds like *you're* worrying."

She laughed, and he smiled at the irony. "Sure," he said. "I'll follow them."

"Are you going to bring that revolver of yours—to make peace with them?"

"I don't know," he said. "But maybe I should. I wear a coat. I can hide it easily."

"Don't go back to your old ways. We're through with that, remember? I don't want to see you in jail—or worse, in a grave."

In the kitchen she watched him nervously. Hans looked outside the window at the city and its lights blinking. He could see ships in the bay and the wind moving the trees along the street. Then he saw the men walk by. There were three of them wearing big coats, laughing, horsing around. They were in their twenties, like Hansford, but they looked much older. One was bald with a flat nose, one had large ears and a thin face and body and the last one was mid-sized like the bald one and had a scar on his cheek. Hans watched them go by until they disappeared in the night; only their voices echoed along the street.

"I'll be all right," he said.

After eating Hansford went outside and buttoned his coat, as a cold wind blew through the streets and ruffled his hair. He walked and sometimes heard laughter, the same laughter he had heard from the three men earlier.

He followed the sound and saw the men surrounding a woman, who was frightened, cowering in a dark alley to another street.

"What's going on here?" said Hans. His voice was deep, stern. The men turned to him.

The woman began to run, but the bald man grabbed her.

"If you touch her again, I'm going to have to hurt you. And I don't want to go back to jail," said Hans.

The bald man, still with his arms around the woman's belly, smelled the woman's hair. She struggled, tried to elbow him in the stomach, but her attacks did nothing.

The thin one and the other with the scar came forward. The one with the scar sized Hans up. "There's three of us. Why don't you get out of here? No one has to die here."

"I'll leave once the girl is home."

"Are you her mother?" said the thin one.

Hans smiled at him, and the thin man took this as an insult.

"Help me!" said the woman. The bald man put his hand over her mouth. Hans looked passed the two men at the woman.

Hans stood still and waited. "Come on," he said. "Get on with it."

The man with the scar said, "I seen you

and that pretty wife of yours. Once we're done with you, we'll go over and visit her."

Hans clenched his fist and hit the man in the jaw. The man tumbled back to the wall and banged his head against it. The thin one came forward but was more cautious. He brought up his fist and hit Hans in the stomach and ribs. Hans hit once then twice in his face. The man with the scar jumped on the back of Hans and put his arm around his neck, squeezing it. Hans still stood, yet his feet were getting wobbly. He fell over, his face reddening. Then he elbowed the man with the scar and kicked the thin one coming towards him.

"Kill him," yelled the man with the woman. The woman could barely move. She was held tight by the bald man. He looked around. The other side of the alleyway was far away, empty and silent.

It was so dark Hans could not see very well, but he managed to pull a knife from his boot and stab the scarred man in the leg.

The man with the scar yelled out in pain. Hans sliced him on the shoulder. The thin man tried to grab the knife. Hans hit him hard with the left, then, gripping the knife so that it pointed perpendicular, he hit straight at the thin man and knocked him unconscious.

Hans breathed heavily. The bald man with

the woman said to the man with the scar, "What are you waiting for? Kill him."

Hans felt the bald man was the leader. Just as he looked at the bald man, the other one pulled a small revolver from his jacket. Hans dropped the knife immediately. His jacket had come open during the fight. He found his revolver, just as he had always found it, pulled it out of the holster and shot. There were two shots. Hans shot first and hit him in the chest. The other man shot the wall. The man was on the ground, silent, as still as the alleyway.

The bald man with the girl kept turning back to the end of the alleyway.

Hans stood there with the gun ready. "You armed?" asked Hans.

"Yeah. I am."

"Put down the gun real slow."

"What will you do?"

"I haven't figured that out," admitted Hans, breathing heavily, feeling his bruised throat. "I can't kill an unarmed man."

"No. I guess not," smiled the bald man, licking his lips, looking for an escape, figuring it out.

"Let go of the woman."

He still had his hand over the woman's mouth and chest. "All right," he said, looking at the thin one who was knocked out. "All right. You win, bud. You win."

"Don't call me bud. Just do it."

The man let go of the woman. Hansford shot the man in the foot.

"Jesus! You shot me," yelled the man. He fell over and held the foot. "You said you wouldn't kill unarmed men. You bastard. You—"

"Stop whining. I said I wouldn't kill one. I said nothing about shooting."

The woman was near the wall, breathing heavily, looking at the bald man on the ground who was yelling out in pain.

"Get me a doctor. I need a doctor," said the bald man.

"I'll get you one," said Hans.

The police came and got a report by the woman and Hansford. The full moon was out, shining bright, reflecting off the ocean when it was all done. The woman thanked Hans, and the police escorted her home. The two surviving men were locked up that night and the one Hans shot in the chest was carried away.

Hansford walked home. Although he saved the woman, he felt sick at what he did. He promised his old ways were in the past, but they had followed him like an old habit. He was about to go inside his home, but Bonnie already opened the door and stood there, scowling. Gradually her face lightened as she saw the marks on Hansford's face and neck. "What happened to you?"

"Found those three men I told you about," he said.

"Come inside. It's cold out."

They went upstairs. She helped him walk up. "What happened?"

"Found a girl with those three men. She was about to get—well, she was about to get hurt. I didn't want that. Nobody with the right mind does. I fought them. One of them died. The other two the police took away."

Hans sat down and then collapsed on the bed, his arms out so that his body was in the shape of a cross.

"You're a brave fool. You could have died. They could have stabbed you or shot you."

"Almost did die."

She sighed and took off his shoes and helped him out of his coat. She helped him out of his clothes, and then lay close beside him. She then got up and gave him a glass of water. He drank it all, so she got more.

"How's the woman?"

"She's fine," he said. "She was real scared and shaking, but the police walked her home."

"What was she doing up late at night?"

"She said she liked to walk at night. Can't blame her. It was a nice night. The moon was so bright you could see everything. Everything except that alleyway she was stuck in."

He lay down on the bed with her. "Are you all right?"

"A doctor looked at me," he said.

"How about that head of yours? The head that always worries."

"I used my gun, and I haven't used it in a long time. It brought up memories, bad memories. I almost wished I had used the knife to kill the man, not shoot him. But there was no choice. I did what I had to do." He turned to her. "I feel I might be going back to my old ways, when I had violence in me."

"Everyone has violence in them. They just keep it inside." She put her hand on his neck. "You did what's right. That's all. You don't regret saving someone's life, do you?"

"No," he said. "I just wish it might have went some other way. What other way? I don't know. Maybe I just need to sleep."

"You'll feel better in the morning. Sleep will help you relax."

Hans closed his eyes and said in a tired voice, "I love you."

She kissed him, and they slept. In the

morning Hansford walked to the warehouse. He caught many glances due to his bruised face, but after telling one person what happened the news spread so that everyone looked at Hans as a tough, brave and even more respectable man. It was at this time he earned the nickname "Gunfighter" among the workers.

CHAPTER 13

PAYMENT FOR WORK

JAKE MCALISTER STAYED IN THE EAST OF town with Agatha. They had married and lived together for six months, but during the first week of being in San Francisco he had not found work to suit him. He was not sure what a cowboy would do in a city.

This is how Jake found work during the first month: Walking on the street one day, he found a "Help Wanted" notice on a door and decided to see what it was about. It was at a gun store. It had weapons from the 1840s all the way up to 1884. There were even knives and swords and some things that shipped from China. The inside was an elongated, thin room, and the building was situated in the part of town where most Asians resided. Above the shop were three floors of apartments. The street outside was always busy. Jake learned that area was called Chinatown, which was named about thirty-five years prior.

Jake shook hands with the manager, Li Min, who was the sole person who worked there, and accepted the job. For months he helped Li Min with everything. Li liked the honest nature of Jake and immediately liked him. Jake had told him some of his history, even about the hunt for the wanted man who rustled his brother's horses.

Li Min told Jake about his own history one day when they were alone in the store. Business had been growing, which is why Li wanted someone to work with him, someone who knew about guns.

"You work with me, but you don't know me," said Li Min.

"I figured you'd tell me if you wanted to."

"Now is a good time. You've been working hard for me unlike some I've had working here at my shop," he said.

"I wondered about how you got here and your family," said Jake.

Li Min sat in a chair and folded his arms. "You told me your history, so I should tell you mine. I usually keep it to myself, even among people I know. But you have shared, and I can feel your pain from what happened to you and your brother. I once had a brother. Zhang. He was like me but in one aspect he differed. He was wild and did not like authority. He did not like to be spoken down to. This ended up being his downfall." Li paused. "He and I worked on the railroad a few years. Very dangerous. Very high chance of death. We could fall easily to our death. Well, one day Zhang spoke out against the conditions and our very low wage. We still get paid very little. Why do you think I have my own shop? Anyway, one day we were building over a gorge of maybe five hundred feet. Zhang was down below the rail and I did not see what happened but somehow he fell straight to the bottom. I could only hear his scream. It was a foggy day. I could only hear his yell in the fog. When I ran down the long road to reach the bottom, I found him and cradled him in my arms. I carried my brother back home and did not say a word to my boss. I could not work on the railroad anymore. Too many die for too little pay."

"I'm sorry," said Jake. "It's good you got out in time. You could have died too."

"I've thought of that," he said. "But sometimes the screams my brother made through the foggy gorge makes me want to die. Then I could be with my brother. Why would that be a problem?"

"Depends on what you believe happens after death."

Li Min nodded but did not smile. He never smiled much, even though he was reasonably happy. When he did show appreciation, he nodded.

"We understand each other. Not many understand me. I have seen many die at war in the Taiping Rebellion. When you have seen so much death, you aren't so afraid of it. It becomes familiar, you see, and that's why it's not so bad to be dead. Death is just another beginning."

A customer came in and bought a knife and went out. Customers came gradually through the day. There were many swords shipped from China that customers liked and bought.

Later that day Jake helped Li Min close the shop. "I need your help," said Li Min.

"What do you need?"

"You don't have to do it. It might be dangerous."

"I don't mind," said Jake. "You know my past."

"Yes, but you said you don't want to go back to how you used to be. I don't want to cause you to go back there."

"I don't rob trains anymore, so if we aren't robbing trains, then it should be fine."

Li Min nodded. "Good." He motioned for Jake to walk with him.

The sun was almost down. It was just above the ocean, shining in their faces as they went down to the houses near the water.

"There is a man who owes me money," said Li Min. "I know this already sounds bad. It is. He is a man who has refused to pay me. I loan him $100, but I end up finding out he doesn't want to pay. This is an untrustworthy man. I realized he cheated me, understand? He is a crook. I'm surprised he's still in the same part of town. He should have left."

Jake felt anger coming from Li Min, which was the first time he had seen him angry. Jake had his coat on, and he still had the gun belt and his Colt Peacemaker. It felt odd wearing that in the city, so far from where everyone seemed to carry a revolver—back east near his hometown.

Li Min stopped just outside an unpainted, wooden house on the side of a hill. "He's in here," he said to Jake. "But he never comes to the door. I have seen him inside."

"Should we tell the police?"

"The police don't help people like me."

Jake said, "What should we do?"

"Go out back. If he starts running, chase him. We might need to roughen him up."

"I don't want to do anything illegal. I just want the man to give you the money you let him borrow," he said.

Li Min nodded. "Okay. Just ask him nicely."

Jake went to the back of the house. He could see a light on inside, but he could not see through the curtain. But then, after Li Min spoke Chinese from outside the house, yelling through the front windows, Jake saw someone walk quickly by the curtain. Then he saw the person again. It was as if they were pacing inside. He could hear something breaking inside. Jake watched the back door. He saw it open slowly. A bald Chinese man with a thin jacket walked out and shut the door. In the darkness, now that the sun had set, he did not notice Jake waiting for him.

Jake stood there with his arms crossed. When the bald man noticed him, Jake yelled to Li Min, "He's out back."

Jake then saw the man run to the opposite side of the street. He was very quick, and Jake was not quick enough to catch him. He saw Li Min run past him and had almost caught up with the bald man. "Give me my money," he yelled.

Jake laughed as he ran. He felt he did not have the air to run fast. It was not like it was when he was younger. Li Min ran so fast, going left and right, up long stairs, down hills, and into alleyways, that he had lost sight of him. He then slowed down and breathed heavily. Sweat dripped down his cheeks from his forehead. "Where'd they go?" he said.

Then he heard a yell. Jake ran to the sound and found Li Min on the ground. He was holding onto his stomach while two men surrounded him. One had a large knife in his hand, and he stood very tall. He was a white man, though, and the man who owed Li Min money was standing behind him, waiting, looking at Jake.

"Who are you?" asked the man who owed Li Min money.

"Jake. Who are you?"

"Wang," said the bald man.

"Who's the big guy?"

"Paul," said Wang. "Paul works for me. You work for Li?"

"Yeah," said Jake. He looked down at Li Min and said to him: "What do you want to do?"

"I'm afraid I have to ask you to go back to your old ways today, just one last time," said Li Min.

Jake looked up and saw the bloodied blade Paul had in his hand. The liquid dripped to the ground and made a long trail. Jake turned and saw the life going out of Li Min's eyes. Li Min looked at him and nodded.

Paul then stepped forward, blade in hand, and tried to slice Jake in the face. But Jake had put up his arm and the knife went against the forearm and cut him deep. He recoiled and unbuttoned his coat. But there was no time to reach for the gun, as Paul had come upon him fast and hard, punching him with his freehand. The big fist knocked him in the eye and cheek and caused Jake to fall back. He crawled back, trying to find the gun, but a hand had reached his coat and pulled him around. Then his face got pummeled, and his bleeding forearm was disregarded. His face was getting bloodied as Li Min watched from farther away, helpless and dying.

Wang watched. His face was without emotion.

"Had enough?" said Paul.

Jake felt the life wasn't in him to do it, but he reached for the gun near his waist and shot the man in the gut. Jake then saw Wang's eyes widen beyond the body of Paul. "Pay up," Jake said to Wang.

Wang swallowed hard and perspired even though a cold chill ran through the city in the night. He turned and ran.

Jake shot him in the leg. Then Jake's arm collapsed and he lay there on the ground, tired and bleeding. He felt alive, and the fight brought back some youthful feeling in him.

He turned to Li Min and tried to walk to him, but he found he could not. He crawled to him and sat down beside him. They both leaned their backs against the wall of the alleyway.

"You did good," said Li Min.

"But we didn't get the money."

"To hell with the money. I'll be dead soon."

Li Min opened his shirt and showed the damage.

"I'll get a doctor," said Jake.

"No doctor can fix this, Jake," he said, and coughed. He spit blood and looked out of the alleyway lit only by the moon. He nodded at Jake and said, "I see my brother soon. I wonder what he'll look like, an old man like me or young again."

Jake managed to stand up but not without feeling sharp pain. "I'll get a doctor."

But when he returned with a doctor and a patrolling policeman Li Min was dead, his cheek against the ground.

CHAPTER 14
UNEXPECTED VISITOR

ONE DAY HANSFORD VORRIS WAS AT THE warehouse when he heard a knock on his office door. A man arrived, clean shaven, tanned and broad shouldered. He was about forty years old from Hansford's estimate. He did not look like he belonged to a city. He wore a cowboy hat, but this hat brought back memories to Hans and was not seen as a joke to him, unlike the others in the city.

"I saw the ad in the papers," said the man. "Heard you needed help."

"Come in," said Hans.

They shook hands. "Sit down."

The stranger found a seat. He took off his hat and put it on his lap. "Young man like yourself is doing well. When did you get here?"

"Seven months ago. You?"

"I'd say about six months back."

Hansford took out a bottle from behind his desk. The light from the windows illuminated the liquid and showed the hands of the stranger but nothing else. Hans looked at the hands. They were strong hands. He first judged a man by them, especially if that man wanted to work at the warehouse. He could not stand a man who could not get his hands dirty. And he saw those hands had something about them. This was not a beggar's hands though; Hans knew that.

The stranger was barely seen in the room, as it was fairly dark on one side. The light only stretched to Hansford's desk.

"Have you been working?"

"I was working at a gun shop owned by Li Min."

"What happened?"

"He died a while back."

"Sorry to hear," said Hans, pouring a glass of whiskey. "Are you a drinking man?"

"On occasion."

"Whiskey?"

"Sure," said the stranger.

He poured two drinks and pushed one glass to him. The stranger got up and grabbed it from the desk. Hans wanted to do that so he could get a better look at him in the light. And then he saw him. Of all people, he did not expect the stranger to be there, sitting across from him, as relaxed as could be.

Hans watched him drink. Suddenly he felt his heart beat hard in his chest.

"Something wrong?" said the stranger.

"You don't happen to be—never mind. I thought I recognized you."

"You recognize me? From where?"

Hans felt his hands shake with excitement. "Aren't you Jake McAlister, the train robber? I read about you when I was just a boy. I heard you robbed a train from President Andrew Johnson himself."

Jake scratched his neck and looked out the window to the side of the room. "That brings up memories, all right." Half-embarrassed, he tried to think of something else to talk about.

"Aren't you?" said Hans.

"Yes."

"How did you do it for so long?"

"Luck, I suppose. Blind luck. I should have died, you know."

"And what happened? I never heard what happened to you. You were in the papers all the time, and then nothing. Completely nothing. I thought you had died."

"My luck ran out," said Jake. "I got caught, thrown in jail for five years." He drank from his glass and put it back on the table.

When Jake did so Hans got an even better look at him. "What fool turned you in?"

"My brother."

"Oh," said Hans, his face darkening.

Jake eyed him and saw Hans lean back in the chair, smiling.

"Don't really know why," said Jake.

"Let's not think about that," said Hans, waving his hand in the air. "I'm just surprised to see you here." Suddenly he listened closer to the last name, "McAlister." The last time he heard the name was in Lake Valley, New Mexico. He tried to make a connection. No, that couldn't be right. Ron McAlister, was it? No, that couldn't be related. Then his thought was interrupted.

"Are you all right there?" said Jake, as there was a long silence.

"I guess you just brought back memories of my youth," admitted Hans. He was surprised at his own honesty.

"Yeah?"

"I used to live in Texas when I was younger. I lived on the Rio Grande. Sometimes we'd steal cattle and horses from Mexicans across the border. They'd steal from us first and then we'd steal them back. It sounds like a game, but it wasn't. I saw men die," he said, his face somber.

Jake nodded. "I know how it is. You pay the price eventually."

"Agreed. But we're getting better."

Jake squinted at him, trying to see what he meant. "We learn from it." He said it in a manner to see what Hans would say. But Hans did not go on with it.

"I think I remember Li Min," said Hans, pouring more whiskey for Jake and him. "Was he the one who got stabbed?"

"That's right. Someone owed him money. But he got stabbed. The bastard who killed him —well, I got revenge. I'll leave it at that." He looked down at his glass, got up and put it down on the table again. "Look, Hans, I don't mind if you won't give me the job. Maybe there's a big age difference. Maybe you think I can't do what those kids out there are doing. Well, I can. Maybe that sounds funny. But I can handle myself. I'm loyal to those that are loyal to me. And I expect fair pay."

Hans leaned back in his chair and looked up at Jake, who was standing there, his curled brim hat back on his head. He was a stern-looking man and a man to be taken seriously.

"You stood up for that man you worked for," said Hans.

"Li Min."

"You helped him get back his money."

"We didn't get the money. We couldn't—not from a dead man. Besides, he was dead. Li's wife sold the shop, and that seemed to bring in some money. She didn't want to keep it going. She kept her own store. Two stores was too much for her to manage."

"Right," said Hans. "But you worked for this man for months and still you went out of your way to help him, your employer. I say you are the right man for the job." He stood up and put out his hand.

Jake took it and nodded as a sign of thanks.

"It might seem random, but are you related to a Ron McAlister in Lake Valley?"

"He was my brother."

Hans felt his pulse rise. "Well—I just—I heard about the bastards that killed him. I thought the last name sounded familiar."

"How'd you hear about it?"

"In one of the papers," said Hans, sweating beneath his arms. He remembered the wanted posters back in New Mexico. He then said, "You start in the morning at seven."

"I'll see you then," said Jake and left. He closed the door behind him.

After Jake left, Hans sat down in his chair and breathed in. Then he put a hand over his forehead and wiped off the sweat and felt the cold room again. "He didn't recognize me."

He left his office outside of the Arctic Oil Works and looked back at the construction of the warehouse. He saw that work was going well. The warehouse would be finished soon. Then Hansford walked home and found Bonnie.

When he walked inside, she could see he was not himself. It looked like he had seen something terrible.

"How was your day?" she said.

He put his coat away and sat heavily in a chair near the small fireplace. "Strange," he said. But he did not go on.

"What do you mean?"

"You remember I told you about rustling cattle from a man in Lake Valley?"

"Yes," she said. "It's the reason we're here."

"That man had a brother, and that same brother came to see me today."

Bonnie's eyes widened. She came and sat in the chair beside him. "What did he say about it? Did you kill him?"

He shook his head, almost laughing. "No, he would've killed me if I had tried anything. The funny thing is, he didn't recognize me. He was very relaxed. I gave him a job and that was that."

Bonnie put her feet up on the chair and turned to him. He saw Hans looking into the fire, thinking. "Well? Will you tell him the truth?"

"The truth?"

"That you were one of the rustlers," she said.

"He would kill me, Bon. What are you talking about? That's crazy talk. Why would I do that?"

"Because he should know. It's the right thing to do."

"The right things to do? I wouldn't send a letter apologizing for every horse I've rustled. I would get killed. I'm sorry I had done those things; I feel terrible realizing all that I've done. But it's best to leave things be."

"You gave him a job?" she asked.

"He starts in the morning."

"You think you can keep lying to him?"

"It won't be brought up. I was the idiot for bringing up his brother, asking him if he was related to Ron McAlister. But that's how I knew." He paused and heard the wood in the fire crackle. "You know, I used to look up to him when I was young. That's the crazy part of it to me. He was a famous train robber. I would read about him in the papers. They could never catch him. He was one of the reasons I went down that road, rustling, fighting and so on. I wanted to be just like him. But reality set in, and I realized I couldn't keep that life up. He realized that too, but it was after he got caught and thrown in jail."

"How do you know he went to jail? Was it in the papers?"

"If it was, I didn't find it. He told me."

"Told you?"

"I asked him about it back at the warehouse," he said. "I was like a child at a circus, excited to meet him finally. Jake McAlister, right in my office. And he wants to work with me."

"How old is he? You said you looked up to him in the past, so he must be old."

"He's maybe forty years old," said Hans.

"What job do you have him doing?"

"Various things," he said. "He said he built his house back in Kansas, so he knows some about construction. Well, Joey will train him and he'll be busy at work."

"Sure seems odd for him to be here," said Bonnie. "What do you think brought him here?"

"I don't know." But then Hans stood up and paced the room. "What if he's on my trail? What if he's here looking for me? Could they know we're here?"

"Relax," said Bonnie. She got up and put her hands on his shoulders to stop him from walking around so much. "That's impossible. No one knows we're here."

"But what if he is here looking for me?"

"He would've recognized you," she said.

"Would he?" he asked, not believing her. "Has my appearance changed since then?"

"Since then? It's been about eight months since that's been over."

Hans looked outside and felt paranoid. "Maybe you're right. But what if he finds out who I am?"

"He won't unless you tell him."

Later that night Hans could not sleep. In his bed he listened for any sound outside. He was alert. He felt that Jake McAlister might be waiting for Hans to go home so that he could get his revenge. After overthinking for hours, he finally fell asleep.

CHAPTER 15
FINAL DECISION

BUD JUMPED ON JAKE AND AGATHA'S BED and woke them up. The dog licked Agatha's face and waited for pets.

"Bud, can't you let us sleep?" said Jake.

"He's just hungry," said Agatha, touching Bud's belly that was facing the ceiling. The dog rubbed his back against the bed playfully.

Later, after eating, Agatha asked about the new job Jake got.

"It's something," said Jake. "I don't know what'll come of it."

Agatha noticed he was smiling and acting strange.

"What?" said Agatha.

"Nothing."

"Tell me," she said.

"The manager there," he said, grabbing his hat and putting it on, "is a young kid. Maybe not a kid. But he's far younger than me. He seemed to like me."

"That's good. Maybe you can work your way up there."

"Maybe." He decided to not wear the hat and put it down on a chair. He looked outside the window at the sun coming from the top of the hill. "Hansford is his name. It's just strange. He looks familiar. I feel like I've seen him somewhere before." He shook his mind from the thought. "Anyway, love you."

"Love you."

He opened the door. Bud, the dog, whined. "I'll be back," Jake said to Bud. "Like always."

Jake then went to his horse, Bell, at the stable and fed him. There was no need for a horse anymore, he realized. But he still kept him and rode him around every once in a while, to the east of town, in the hills and sometimes down to the beach. And Jake gradually adjusted to city life, even though he once hated the cities. Now he enjoyed the city and walking the streets. "See you tonight," he said to his horse.

This became his usual routine as he went about his life in the city. He worked at the warehouse for Hansford Vorris for a month, and they got to know each other. Hansford treated him like an equal and a friend. Jake's disconnected and reserved attitude melted away around Hans, and the two soon became even better friends.

Later on, after getting to know each other, Jake told Hansford more about his brother, Ron, and how he died.

Hansford was curious and asked what Jake would do if he found the man who rustled Ron's horses. Jake said, "I don't know, something bad, something that might put me back in jail. I'd be angry," he said. "Who knows what I'd do? The man is probably long gone by now."

"It's a big country."

"That's for sure. He could be dead. Since he's a rustler, he probably got shot by a man protecting his cattle or horses. Who knows?" Jake shook his head. "I don't know. At this point, I'm not sure. I had almost forgotten about him. I'd ask him why. I'd ask him why he killed that man and saved that girl, Delilah. He's a curious one."

"Maybe he got mixed up with the wrong people," said Hans.

"Maybe. What do you think you'd do if you

found the man who helped kill your own brother?"

"That's a hard question," said Hans, scratching his chin. "I think I'd ask him some questions and see what kind of person he is. I'd want him to explain."

"Exactly," said Jake. "I'd do that. He can't be all bad. He did save that woman. Everyone does bad things; it doesn't mean they're a bad person. They can learn from it and be a better person. But this man—I just don't know about him. He definitely ran away with the money and succeeded; I'll give him that. But he killed two men who got in his way, Enor Philips and Donavan Nealey. That's not a stable man."

"No," said Hans, looking down. "No, maybe not."

"Anyway, enough talk. How about we go drinking?"

"I don't feel well," said Hans. "I think I'll head home."

"All right. Hope you feel better."

Jake went home as well. On a whim he decided to go through his old things he brought from New Mexico. In his satchel he took out a faded piece of paper. It was a wrinkled and partially wet piece of paper. He brought it to the light of the fireplace and looked at it. It was the wanted poster of the man who stole Ron

McAlister's horses and killed Enor Philips. Jake squinted at the picture for a long time. But after looking at it for a while he threw it into the fire.

There was a loud knock on the door. Jake turned and looked at his wife. "I'm not expecting anyone," Agatha said.

Jake opened the door. A large man in a suit stood there, cap in hand. He had a black beard that was partially grey. With his hat in hand, his nearly-bald head showed. "Mr. McAlister?"

"That's right," said Jake.

"I might know where the man who helped kill your brother is. Can I come in?" The man squinted, as the cold wind blew in his face and made his big nose red.

Jake opened the door wider. "Come in."

The stranger shook his hand. "Ray Philips." Philips said to Agatha: "Evening, ma'am."

"Evening," she said, sitting and knitting in a chair though still listening in on the conversation.

Jake shut the door and led him to the two chairs near the fireplace.

"Anything to drink?"

"Scotch, if you have it."

He poured him a glass and sat in the seat beside him. A table was in between the chairs, and Ray Philips set his glass on it.

"Where'd you come from?" asked Jake.

"New York," said Ray Philips.

"Are you a Pinkerton Detective?"

"No," smiled Philips. "I'm a banker. I came to proposition you. The man who stole your brother's horses is right here in the city. I managed to track him down."

"How?"

"People here and there gave me info," said Philips. "A woman in Silver City told me about Bonnie's plan to move to San Francisco. That sure wasn't easy info."

Jake frowned. He met Hansford's wife, Bonnie, but he was not sure of the connection. Jake and Agatha even visited Hans and Bonnie's home and ate with them many times over the previous two months.

"My brother, Enor Philips, was killed by the same man that helped kill your brother, Ron." He drank from his glass and put it down on the table. "He's your boss, Jake. He's Hansford Vorris. You've been working for him without even knowing it."

Jake tried to see the wanted poster in the fire, but it was already ashes. He put a hand on his head and leaned back in the leather chair. He didn't like someone stalking him, finding out where he worked and who he worked for. How'd he get this information? In disbelief he said, "What all did Hans do?"

"Murdered two men that we know of, rustled horses, stole a man's wife."

"A man's wife? Bonnie?"

Agatha came over near the fire and said, "That can't be. How is that possible?"

Philips leaned back in his chair and looked at Jake and Agatha. "That's right." He then put his elbow on the arm of the chair and said to Jake: "Look, there's money in it. Two thousand dollars if you help me kill him. I want it quiet. This same man killed your brother. He killed my brother. We're together in that aspect. You want him dead, don't you?"

Jake put a hand over his face and closed his eyes tight. Agatha folded her arms and watched for Jake's reaction.

"It's hard to take in," continued Philips. "I know. My brother was a hard man, but he didn't deserve to be butchered with a knife. I'm sure your brother didn't deserve to die either."

"What are you, an assassin now?" said Jake. "A banker thinks he can just kill someone out here in the city and get away with it. Funny. It's not like it was back east in New Mexico and the surrounding states."

"Don't play smart. I'm trying to help you, can't you see?"

"I'll kill him myself," said Jake, "for free." He stood up and put a log into the fire. "I don't need your damn money. And I don't need you stalking me to where I work, finding out where I live."

Ray Philips said, "I will find another man for the job. I suppose you don't like or need money." He got up and put his hat on, thought of the wind outside, and held the hat in his hand instead.

"I want blood, not money," said Jake, standing there, his eyes dark and his voice calm. "The hell with your money. This is personal."

"Same for me!" pleaded Philips.

"The man will pay, whoever gets to him first."

"Fair enough," said Philips, and went outside, walking the cold streets.

Jake collapsed onto the chair near the fire and put his head on his right hand. He looked into the fire. He couldn't think.

"What will you do?" said Agatha. She stood near the window.

"Did you hear the man?"

"Yes," she said.

"Then I have to confront Hans," said Jake. "I have to get to him before Philips does. Otherwise, he's dead."

Jake and Agatha visited Hansford and Bonnie the next day for dinner at Hansford's house.

After eating, the room grew tense. Jake and Hans went to the living room and the women went to a separate room to talk.

"I've been thinking about that man," said Jake, sitting in his chair, watching the fire without emotion, his voice monotonous. He drank whiskey from a glass. "He's out there."

"You think so? I thought he'd be dead," said Hans. He looked outside, as the wind picked up and carried leaves that scraped against the windows.

Jake watched him. "Oh, I have no doubt he's alive."

"Why are you so sure?"

"I just know it. He's smart, much smarter than I thought."

"Maybe you should let it go, Jake." Hans leaned back in the chair, relaxed but attentive still.

"Why? I could find him still. Anything's possible. Why should I stop now?"

Hans shook his head and leaned his elbow on the chair. "Some things just aren't worth remembering. Like bad memories, you learn from them and forget the memory. No reason to keep bringing up the past."

"Wise advice for your age," said Jake. His eyes went back to the fire. He nodded slowly, like Li Min used to do when in agreement.

"You think that's true—what I said?"

"Yes, I think you're right about that. But some things can never be forgotten."

"Like what?" asked Hans.

Jake turned his head and listened. He heard the women upstairs. Then he looked back at Hans. "Like my brother turning me in to the law or the look of Agatha's face when I found her out in the wild. You can't move on from those memories. They are vivid."

"You can look at the memory differently though," said Hans.

"How?"

"You give some reason why it happened and make sure it doesn't happen again."

"You'd still remember," Jake said.

"Sure, but only every now and then. But this time you'll look at the memory differently. You'll know it was only once, and it won't happen again."

Jake sat there and thought about what he said.

After a while, Jake and Agatha said goodbye to Hans and Bonnie and left. On the way home Agatha said, "Did you confront him?"

"No."

"Why wouldn't you?" she said. She

stopped and glanced back from where they came.

"It wasn't the right time. I was figuring him out still."

"Wouldn't you want to know?"

"I'll ask him," he said.

"When?"

"Tomorrow."

CONFRONTATION

A day later Jake invited Hans to go fishing. Fishing was a hobby of Jake's. He would fish in many places across the surrounding beaches.

"I haven't fished in a long time," said Hans after being asked if he wanted to fish.

"That's all right. I can help you out," said Jake. "It's not hard at all. The only problem will be the birds. I saw them get real feisty and steal someone's fish before." He shook his head and smiled. "They're nasty thieves."

The place they fished was on a beach. Behind them was a hill. It was a secluded place. No one could be seen.

"Why didn't you want to fish closer to the city?" said Hans.

"You can catch more out here," Jake said to

him. "Why don't you start? I'll show you a spot I like."

He walked around boulders that prevented the beach from being eroded too much. Then he showed him the spot and let him fish there while he went back for his fishing pole. It was cold that day, and the wind blew their hair every which way. It smelled of salt in the air, and high above were seagulls calling. Hans climbed one boulder and sat on it. Then he waited for a bite, but he was aloof, watching the whitecaps in the ocean, and not very interested in fishing. Then Hans heard Jake behind him, which surprised him. He thought he was farther down the beach, behind another boulder.

Then Hans turned and saw Jake holding a Colt in his hand that was pointed down to the sand.

"I knew it was you, Hans," said Jake.

Hans reeled in and looked back at the ocean. "Then why didn't you confront me before?"

"I've been doing that this entire time," he said. "Mostly I've been waiting for you to say something. When I first saw you at the warehouse months back, I thought you looked familiar. I just couldn't accept it until now."

"You going to kill me? I thought we were friends."

"I don't know what we are now," said Jake. "You were stringing me along without telling me the truth."

"Hell, Jake, I thought you'd kill me." He put the fishing pole down. "I'm not armed."

"It doesn't matter either way."

"I had nothing to do with your brother's death. I just wanted the horses. Donavan Nealey is the man who killed your brother, and I already killed Donavan. His brother, Walden, took the fall for him."

"Why'd you help that girl, Delilah?"

"Who?"

"The girl you stole from Elisha. Elisha McAlister. You let her go. Why?" Jake spoke quickly. He felt his heart quicken, though he knew his aim would be dead-on no matter how sweaty his palms were, just like how it used to be.

"I told you. I just wanted the horses."

"Were the Nealey's friends of yours?"

"They were nothing to me."

"You could say that about anyone," said Jake. He walked closer to Hans and brought his chin up a little. "You could say that about me."

"That's not true. I would always call you a friend."

Jake squinted at him. He felt his boots getting sucked in the wet sand and felt his hands getting numb from the cold. He put the gun back in the holster and sighed. Then Hans turned and saw two men come from behind a big boulder. It was Ray Philips and another man, both holding pistols.

"Why didn't you do it?" Ray Philips yelled to Jake. He had to yell over the waves crashing against the beach.

Jake backed up. "If anything'll happen, it will be with the law. This would be murder."

"You turning me in?" said Hans, facing the men that appeared suddenly. He looked at the two men, one older with a black and grey beard, the other young, clean shaven with black curly hair. The man with the black hair said nothing and only pointed the pistol at Hans. His eyes went to Jake, unsure of him.

"You said there was one," said the curly-haired man.

"It is," said Ray, pointing to Hans.

"What the hell is this?" yelled Hans to the two strangers that were about forty to fifty feet away. "You going to kill me? Who are you?"

"You killed my brother, Enor Philips," said Ray. His lips trembled. "You slaughtered him!"

The man with the curly hair turned to Ray,

his eyes going to so many places at once, confused.

Jake said to Ray, "You need to—"

But a shot had gone off from Ray's pistol, striking the boulder beside Hans. Jake and Hans got behind two separate boulders. Jake poked his head up and saw the curly haired man aim his pistol at Jake and shoot.

"They're shooting at me too," said Jake.

Hans took out his Remington Revolver and shot at Ray's shoulder peeking out from behind the boulder. He could hear yelling and panting.

"You said you were unarmed," said Jake.

"Sorry, Jake. I lied." He smiled and shot again, missing the curly haired man but not by much. He leaned his back against the boulder and breathed heavily. "Who is that black haired man?"

"Someone Ray hired to help him kill you."

"Were you planning to tell me that?"

"In the next minute I was," said Jake. "But you saw how we got interrupted."

"Are you turning me into the law?" Hans gripped the revolver and listened for any footsteps.

Jake looked down at his own revolver and shook his head. "No, I won't. I just wanted to talk."

Another shot went off, right above their

heads. Jake peeked to the side of the boulder and shot Ray. There was no yelling this time. Then Hans shot the black-haired man that had shot just as Jake had shot.

Jake and Hans went to see the men. They were dead. It was silent again except for the wind and the waves. The waves clapped against the boulders behind their backs. They approached the two bodies and took the guns away.

"That's that," said Hans.

"You strung me along like a fool. You know that?" Jake said to Hans. "How many months have we known each other?"

Hans put his gun away and faced him.

"All you had to do was tell me what happened," said Jake.

"Go ahead and kill me if that's what you want. Go ahead." He put his arms out to his sides, waiting. Then, as Jake looked away to the ocean, Hans lowered his arms and waited.

Jake sat down on a boulder and looked to see if anyone was about. His hands went limp, as if they were heavy. "What did you want out of all this? What was the goal?"

"I just wanted to know you," said Hans, speaking almost in excitement. "Hell, you're Jake McAlister. You robbed banks and trains for years. No one could catch you. I read about you in the papers as a boy. When I saw you walk into my office, all angry and tough-looking, I figured you'd kill me right then if I told you what happened with me and your brother. Jake, I wasn't fooling with you."

"You should have told me," he said. "I wasted all this time searching for the bastard that was right ahead of me." Jake looked up at Hans. "You know what this means?"

"What?"

"It means the two men that killed my brother, the Nealey brothers, are dead. It means my brother is avenged."

Hans sat down on another boulder and relaxed his shoulders. "You don't hate me, do you?"

"If I hated you, I wouldn't be wasting my time talking to you."

"You know," said Hans, "your brother wasn't a bad man for turning you in. Maybe he thought you'd get shot one day. You had a bounty on your head, didn't you?"

Jake nodded.

"Maybe he thought you'd get shot robbing a bank or train. And he didn't want that to happen."

"Maybe so," said Jake.

"Maybe he was looking out for you, like a big brother does. Did you think of that?"

"He turned me in to save my life?" he asked. "Is that what you're saying?"

"I think so."

"I had a lot of close calls in my life," said Jake. "I don't know how I'm still alive. Well, Ron always said I should work like every man does. Now I do. I suppose he turned me away from all that mess I was in when I was young."

"You're still young. You have time."

Jake smiled and stood up. "How about you? You a rustler or are you a better man?"

"I'm the same as you. I got tired of all that. I live a clean life now."

"Then we better head home." He glanced back at the setting sun and grabbed the fishing poles. "Our wives will be angry we didn't catch any fish."

The Arctic Oil Works, San Francisco.
MONOLITHIC CONSTRUCTION.
RANSOME & SMITH CO.   –   –   101 SANSOME STREET, SAN FRANCISCO.

BOOKS BY LUCAS SCHMIDT

Jack Flynn and the Pony Kid

The Wanted

Bear Creek Massacre

Courage Stands Alone

Flight From Chains (Jeremiah Jameson Book 1)

Dust of the Run (Jeremiah Jameson Book 2)

Son of Law (Jeremiah Jameson Book 3)

Bandit